THE COMPLETE TALES OF HENRY JAMES
VOLUME ONE: 1864–1868

THE COMPLETE TALES OF

HENRY JAMES

EDITED WITH AN

INTRODUCTION BY

LEON EDEL

1

1864–1868

J. B. LIPPINCOTT COMPANY

PHILADELPHIA AND NEW YORK

PRINTED IN THE UNITED STATES OF AMERICA
LIBRARY OF CONGRESS CATALOG CARD NUMBER 62-11335

CONTENTS

GENERAL INTRODUCTION

In 1888, when James was forty-five and had produced the equivalent of a lifetime of fiction—some ten novels and half a hundred short stories—he explained to Robert Louis Stevenson that he wanted "to leave a multitude of pictures of my time, projecting my small circular frame upon as many different spots as possible." He was planning, he said, to go in both for quantity and quality, so that the stories would "constitute a total having a certain value as observation and testimony." This was an ambitious programme; but James had a way of keeping his promises. Between the year of his letter to Stevenson and the end of the first decade of the new century, he more than doubled the number of his tales as well as of his novels. He wrote one hundred and twelve tales in all. In this and the ensuing volumes they are assembled in their totality for the first time.

He had from the first worked in the shorter form. Ten years of story-telling—in various lengths—preceded his first significant novel. And it was with a slender tale, about a spirited little American girl in Rome, that he made his enduring reputation. "Daisy Miller" was of the 1870's, and there was at least one masterpiece of the short form for each decade. "The Aspern Papers" was of the 1880's; "The Turn of the Screw" of the 1890's and "The Beast in the Jungle" came early in this century. From time to time he would collect a group of tales to form a volume; during some years he issued two or three, and on occasion he almost glutted his own market. But he never exhausted the back-log he had created in the magazines. His first collection, *A Passionate Pilgrim and Other Tales* of 1875, contained but six of the twenty-seven tales he had written by that time. He did not care to

7

revive all of his tales: some he disowned as mere apprentice-work. Others did not fit the scheme or tone of the given volume. As he advanced in life, his earlier volumes went out of print and were superseded by later collections. The largest group of his tales ever assembled by him were the fifty-two included in the New York Edition of his selected fictional writings—less than half of his short story total.

Since his death some thirty or forty of his tales have been shuffled and reshuffled in various editions. His stories are unusually long and editors have tended to choose the shortest. As a result, many fine tales—such as "Lady Barberina"—have remained unavailable to the general reader. In placing all of these within covers, and in chronological order, this edition makes it possible at last for James's tales to be read in the order in which he produced them and to demonstrate his development and growth in a form which he found a constant challenge and in which he achieved a singular mastery.

II

James defined his personal art of the novel in his late prefaces to the New York Edition; and in these he also defined, with great clarity, his theory of the short story. He preferred to speak of short narratives as "tales," and to use the French word *nouvelle*, which so many of his editors obstinately insist on translating as "short novel." The French *nouvelle* has always been a much more elastic form than the English or American "short story." It has had many great masters; and its appeal to James resided in its being of unprescribed length. It possessed always *a length proper to itself.* For this reason, he spoke of it as "the beautiful and blest *nouvelle.*" He deplored the general tendency of magazines to disregard questions of "organic" form, and to consider short stories in terms of their shortness—that is to make them conform to some arbitrary word-count. This does not mean that he favoured an undisciplined prolixity. What he believed in was "masterly brevity," as he put it, and even more—"the idea beautifully developed." This was possible only in the tale, as consecrated long ago in prose by Boccaccio and in poetry by Chaucer. The closest James was to come to the magazine requirements of his day was in two tales of five thousand words each. His average tale runs from ten to twenty thousand words. And there is one which exceeds fifty thousand. This explains why, as he advanced in his career, he found it increasingly difficult to place his stories in the magazines.

By modern standards, fifty thousand words would be considered a short novel. James however, called the 53,000-word "Turn of the Screw" a tale, and the 58,000 *Reverberator* a short novel: and he explained with great clarity where the difference lay. There were, for him, two kinds of short narratives—the "anecdote" and the "picture." The anecdote, he said, was an account of "something that has oddly happened to someone." To remain an anecdote, it had to point directly to that person, and to keep him at the very centre of the story. On occasion, an anecdote tended to acquire "a surface really much larger than the mere offered face of the work." By becoming a dramatic action, in which the "something that has oddly happened" to the hero or the heroine happens to other characters as well, the anecdote ceases to be itself. It has evolved into a short novel.* This is why *The Reverberator* was counted among the novels, and the ghost story among the tales.

* The short novels of James are *Watch and Ward, The Europeans, Confidence, Washington Square, The Reverberator, The Spoils of Poynton, What Maisie Knew, The Sacred Fount* and the two plays converted into novels, *The Other House* and *The Outcry.* By James's definition, all the "short novels" in Mr Philip Rahv's collection *The Great Short Novels of Henry James* must be called tales.

The story which was a "picture" differed from the "anecdote" in that it was not susceptible of becoming a dramatic
action. It was usually a composition in a small frame—a
foreground, a background, a centre of composition. "I
rejoice in the anecdote," James said, "but I revel in the
picture." He asked above all for recognition of "shades and
differences, varieties and styles" instead of the "blank
misery" in the Anglo-Saxon world of the measured and undefined tale, the rule of the word-count.

III

It is not easy to offer a general description of a landscape as
highly individualised as that of Henry James's tales. He spoke
of them as a family "quite organised as such, with its proper
representatives, its 'heads', its subdivisions and its branches,
its poor relations perhaps not least." The world of his tales
is visual, plastic, analytical; as in his novels, it is large and
leisurely and peopled by the civilised and the self-aware.
It is a world of manners and problems of behaviour; there is
no violence; the emphasis is rather on intensities of feeling.
The medium is often verbal irony, satire, paradox. He is
constantly experimental, that is willing to search for new
ways of telling his story. We can best divide his tales into
"early, middle, and late," and to attempt a broad characterisa-
tion of each, while recognising there are bound to be exceptions and overlappings in the different periods.

The early tales contain a good deal of apprentice-work.
James had been a student of method long before he began
to write and in his first tale, published anonymously, he
revealed a considerable awareness of the art of manipula-
ting the reader, making him look in certain directions and

listen to certain talk. He had a strong flair for dramatic dialogue. His apprentice tales told of failure in love, renunciation, the reticence of young men, the unfathomableness of
young women, the general fickleness of the female sex. They
are rather melancholy and romantic, as young tales can be,
and rather devoid of the later wit: they have a lugubrious
atmosphere, for all their skill. The settings were generally
American—salt-boxes, and frame houses, the abundant
greenery of the landscape, certain New York streets and
mansions, the aspect of Newport. From the first James painted
minutely; and he was subtle and reflective. He was concerned
not so much with plot, as with personal relations.

The tales of his middle period mark his emergence as a
brilliant and witty observer of life on both sides of the
Atlantic. They represent his discovery of his European-
American subject and his ability to render it in a high, dry,
humorous light. There is an extraordinary play of intellectual
humour as he shows Americans looking at Europe and
Europeans at America. And his amused and aloof observation of Anglo-American society seems to be a source of end-
less fascination to him. He studies its manners, its idiosyn-
crasies, its codes, its decencies, its shabbinesses, its pathos. In
his strictly "international" stories he is a chiding critic of
American egalitarianism and "newspaperism"; he describes
the spittoons carefully arranged—as in parade formation—in
the Capitol rotunda and the noisy aspect of American hotels,
where the children roller-skate in the corridors or lie fast
asleep late in the evening in the big lobby armchairs, wholly
unparented. On the subject of maternal laxity, the glorifica-
tion of the child in America, he is as eloquent as any child-
psychologist of to-day. And when he discovers that the
British enjoy to excess these observations of his homeland,
he promptly demonstrates his impartiality by describing
British society: particularly the rudeness and arrogance of
certain members of the British upper classes—"an aristocracy

is bad manners organised" was one of his pointed aphorisms. James was a creator of maxims, and his epigrammatic style did him constant service in evoking the human picturesque. When it came to painting scenes he was unmatched in his precision and his genius for essential detail: Washington Street in Boston, snow-piled and jammed with horse-cars, lives for us again in his tales, as do the people within the large-windowed houses in Beacon Street; or in his unforgettable picture of "rotten row" in Hyde Park, which provides a perfect setting for the drama of Lady Barberina. His minute notations of English life surprised the English; he saw so much that they took for granted. In all his writings he kept a certain "distance" from his material, which his contemporary critics often remarked. If this faculty for holding himself aloof, for transferring his vision to an analytical observer, made at times for coldness, it gave James also a clarity undisturbed by irrelevant emotion.

A great part of the "natural history" of the American woman is written into the tales of the middle period. James studied her with a mixture of affection, awe, and profound mistrust. Whether he is describing the flattened-out mother of Daisy Miller, or the irrelevant parents of the self-made Pandora Day, or the powerful "managerial" woman, he is concerned with the American male's tendency to idealise womanhood, glorify children and abdicate all human and civilised responsibility to the wife.

"An American woman who respects herself," said Mrs Westgate, turning to Beaumont with her bright expository air, "must buy something every day of her life. If she cannot do it herself, she must send out some member of her family for the purpose."

By this simple economy the husband is made aware that his dollars are put to constant use. His job in American life was simply to provide the dollars. James understood the power-driven matron—American or British—to the very tips of her manicured fingers. There is a simple little story seldom reprinted about a widow named Mrs Temperly—the name is artfully suggestive—in which the hero, wishing to marry one of her daughters, watches her in full control of family, servants, and her Paris salon. He admires her; he wonders how she can accomplish so much, and with such ease. "And does she do it so well without a man?" he asks himself. "There must be so many details a woman can't tackle." For even when he counts the governess and the intimate friends, all he sees is a "multiplication of petticoats." Then it comes over him: "She *was* a man as well as a woman—the masculine element was included in her nature. He was sure that she bought her horses without being cheated, and very few men could do that."

IV

The tales of the late period, at first glance, might have been written by someone else, so great a change has occurred. The story-teller's mood is profoundly altered—but not his temperament. With middle-age his tales cease to be minutely descriptive. The discussion of manners and the behaviour of American girls gradually disappear: the preoccupation with problems of conduct gives way to a study of states of feeling and of dilemmas of existence. He begins to probe the "unlived" life of his characters and to portray "poor sensitive gentlemen" who discover too late the price they have paid for their sensitivity and their insulation against the shock of experience. We might speak of these tales to-day as being in the "existential" mode. They partake of that "tragic vision" which so many critics have found in James, the essence of which is contained in the poignant exclamation of Prince

Amerigo in *The Golden Bowl*—"Everything's terrible, *cara* —in the heart of man."

In the late years everything *was* terrible in the heart of man for Henry James; and yet for the elderly artist, the fascination of this terror and the need to explore it, remained. At the same time his tragic insight did not supersede his sense of high comedy. His study of nightmare and terror was carried on in such tales as "The Altar of the Dead" and "The Beast in the Jungle," rejected by the magazines but celebrated to-day, in which James presented the consequences of extreme egotism and failures in spiritual sharing and showed men who have sealed their eyes to the world and the love around them. The late tales are studies of "predicaments"—this explains the titles of such volumes as *Embarrassments*, *Terminations* or *The Soft Side*—of individuals frustrated and defeated who arrive at the ultimate tragedy—that of helplessly knowing the emptiness of their past. These are the writings of a psychologist who no longer worried about external realism, because he knew the reality and power of inner experience. During the years of the late 1890's he wrote his "tales of the quasi-supernatural and the gruesome," adding new dimensions to the ghostly tale, as the popularity of "The Turn of the Screw" attests. And at the same time, in a brilliant vein of satire, he brought into being a series of tales which displayed his unexhausted wit. These are his "tales of the literary life." They chide the public for its Philistinism toward art; they mock the blindness of critics; and they laugh at literary journalists and lion-hunters in the drawing-rooms. The literary tales make no pretence of reality: James kills off all his *personae* in "The Figure in the Carpet," and leaves the puzzled literary journalist still seeking the secret of Vereker's work. Or he creates a novelist who wants to be a best-seller, but who always succeeds in writing a "distinguished" book which does not sell; and describes how a lady novelist, who sells in the tens of thousands, dreams of being a distinguished failure.

These are artificial comedies, or fables for critics, drawn with high good humour from Henry James's own rueful experiences. They are studies of stupidity and ignorance in public places; in them an old anger has been transmuted into urbane laughter, and a lesson in gentle and suave "criticism of life."

V

One value of having James's tales "complete" resides in our being able to see chronologically the historian of manners, the psychologist, the civilised mind and the profound moralist, turning his "small circular frame" upon experience and doing this in a developing style. At the beginning there is a camera-like sharpness, all focus and clear image; at the end it becomes "impressionistic;" no hard lines are tolerated, and the great phrases and images reverberate like a tolling bell. "To me," said William Dean Howells long ago, "there is a perpetual delight in his way of saying things." Many readers have testified to this; James is one of the few modern writers who can be reread with pleasure. A single reading never exhausts the richness of his prose or the detail of his observation.

The world of his stories is peopled largely by the upper classes, the leisured of *The Better Sort*, or *The Soft Side*. But his tales are not as limited as this statement would suggest. We find also in them school-teachers and grocery clerks; artists' models and penny-a-liners; impoverished bohemians and dowdy dowagers, and families who jump their hotel-bills from one resort to another. James was concerned not with classes of people, or their "station in life," so much as with their hopelessness and uncertainty, with individuals who—poor or rich—nourish illusions and suffer the frustrations and indignities of life. His most popular ghost story is about a poor governess who has taken a position in a rich home and is nervously trying to please her employer. No writer has given us a more compassionate picture of people lost in great cities; or evoked with more power "the bench of desolation"—the drama of human loneliness.

His tales belong to an age of greater leisure than ours. He develops them unhurriedly; he takes his reader step by step into his given situation. There is a fascination in watching him go about his business: he is always precise, always master of his material, always ready to clear the way and confront his audience. Then he brushes in the detail and his anecdote is told, his picture painted. He has a way of making us hear a number of voices, including his own, and of seeing the world through many eyes. And whether he wears the mask of comedy or of tragedy, we are aware that he is summarising life, capturing some fragment of it, seeking its essence. And he achieved his intention: his tales "constitute a total having a certain value as observation and testimony." To which we might add that the most memorable of his tales do much more: they have become a part of human experience, they have entered into the fabric of our language and our literature, and conveyed to us a sense of how genius can find an undiminished fascination in the episodic, the anecdotal and the pictorial of the human scene.

LEON EDEL

New York 1961

INTRODUCTION: 1864–1868

THE earliest tales of Henry James—those written between 1864 and 1868—were set down in the actuality and the aftermath of the American Civil War. As might be expected, they are pervaded by the national gloom; and they reflect a personal melancholy as well. Three deal directly with the effects of the war; three foreshadow James's exploration of private lives and personal relations; three belong to the ghostly or "gruesome-fantastic" category. Of the remaining two, one is James's earliest apprentice tale, an adolescent venture into melodrama and murder out of Balzac or Merimée; the other is the first of a long line of tales he will write about painters and their paintings.

These tales, then, form a casual and unplanned overture to an extraordinary career in story-telling; and as in overtures small phrases offer hints of greater themes. The tales possess a rather precocious baggage of "technique." The writer is a prodigy of the "picture" and the "scene." Certain of his remarks disclose the care with which he has been reading the French story-tellers; and the substance of some of the tales shows him to be in the direct line of Hawthorne, who was but lately dead when James began to write. Of his other American predecessor, Edgar Allan Poe, who helped to perfect the short story on the western side of the Atlantic, there seems to be no suggestion. The French models predominate; but, in the texture of the tales, one feels the presence of Henry James's saturation with the great world of English fiction. He has consorted with all the novelists. Thus his first heroine reads *Scottish Chiefs* and is wooed by a young man named Robert Bruce. James reminds his American readers that civil wars and border strife are by no means new to history.

The sadness of the early tales must be understood in the light of James's weight of suffering during these "untried years," the strange fate of a youth seeking to launch his literary self in the midst of a national blood-bath. Confined by ill-health to the home front, he was conscious of mourning mothers and weeping widows. He watched his friends and brothers march off—singing and confident—and saw them brought home, straight from the neighbouring battlefields, to linger over their wounds or die. Soldiers or correspondents might describe some little corner of the war; Brady's camera might endlessly multiply various scenes and personalities; but Henry James could look at the narrower home front— in Newport, in Boston, or New York—and experience the full force of the young Republic's tragedy. He was to speak of it years later in one of his reverberating phrases as a "vast visitation."

His three war tales give us varying aspects of life behind the lines. In "The Story of a Year" he tells us clearly he has "no intention of following Lieutenant Ford to the seat of the war. The exploits of his campaign are recorded in the public journals of the day where the curious may still pursue them." And he adds, speaking out of the preface to the *Comédie Humaine*, "My own taste has always been with the reverse of the picture." He will chronicle not public events but private lives: *l'envers de l'histoire contemporaine.*

For others, then, the thunder of the battlefields. Stendhal had described in vivid pictures the moments of Waterloo. But Thackeray had shown Becky Sharp leading her life on the margin of history, even as in our own time holiday swimmers and sunbathers, on the lesser Normandy beaches, waved cheerfully to the procession of war as it passed along the highways. In his second tale Henry James looked at the images of battle suggested by the cloud-scenery of the brilliant American skies, and recorded the history of those who wait and suffer, the mother and the intended, counting the daily hours for the fate of the son and the lover. In "Poor Richard," another of his Civil War tales, James produced a rather loutish hero, full of bombast of love, but ill-at-ease in the presence of military uniforms. Richard is a sad case indeed; and yet he is capable of moments of genuine dramatic power, as when, in the presence of one suitor, he tells another a lie, to turn him away from a farewell call on the heroine. "That was brilliantly done," says the Major to Richard, who squirms inwardly over his failure to speak the truth. We agree; both the character (and his author) have brought off a rather good scene.

It is in the third of his war tales that James conveys most deeply the sense of the story-teller who feels his material while still awkwardly trying to melt it into his form. We watch the melancholy Colonel Mason, in his untidy hotel room in New York, war-weary, ill of his wounds, responding to the unexpected visit of an aunt, who will take him to her country home. He listens to the rustle of her dress as she leaves; and the way in which she gently closes the door; and the sound of her retreating footsteps—and begins to weep. Suddenly he has been reminded, after the blood, and the agony, of "the exquisite side of life."

The writer who at twenty-five could tell a tale with such consummate touches of feeling had, in reality, no reason for despair. And the other tales in this volume are concerned with states of bewilderment and with the unfathomable Dianas of the American scene. Women are a puzzle to James's heroes: to be sure they were something of a puzzle to the Victorians before they put on short skirts and went out into the world to obtain equality with men. The Victorian heroes, nevertheless, managed a marriage, and children, sooner or later. Some even lived happily, more or less, ever after. The Jamesian heroes seldom did—if they survived. A young man in love, looking at the painting of his bride, sees a side of her he does not wish to know. The landscape painter falls in love, but he is not certain of his bride. In the fantasy of "De Grey," there is a family curse which dispatches brides (once they have provided the family with an heir). Marriage, in other words, is an extreme hazard in the early James. Husbands sometimes prey on wives; wives prey on husbands. Ego clashes with ego. In his earliest tale, published anonymously in an Abolitionist magazine in New York, the wife plots to have her lame husband drowned. And yet there is exuberant boyish art in the way James makes her go about her gruesome—and operatic—business: the brutal boatman seizing the jug of milk intended for the child; the woman bargaining with the boatman to do the murder; her maid spying on the heroine through a keyhole, as she swallows brandy by the glassful and scans the sea with her glass. Later Jamesian "observers" will do their keyhole-peeping much less openly.

And already the writer has a sense of the ghostly. One of the most successful stories in this volume is "The Romance of Certain Old Clothes," in which James, coming closest to Hawthorne, depicts a strong rivalry between two sisters; he places the real before us, squarely and objectively, and then skilfully mingles it with the unusual and the eerie, after the fashion of his predecessor.

By the time James had published his seventh tale, "The Story of a Masterpiece," a critic in the *Nation* was saying that "within the somewhat narrow limits to which he confines himself, Mr James is the best writer of short stories in America." This was praise indeed for a writer in his mid-twenties. What were the narrow limits? The young James could characterise persons, but he was more a writer of mood than of "plot." His personages are "cold," and described from a distance; they avoid coming into close quarters with one another; instead they talk—they veritably "spout"—at each other. Heroes often abdicate from the start; they are ready for death when the world offers them life. Even in so

shaded a piece of story-telling as "A Day of Days," in which
James describes a chance encounter in the country, the author's
predilection for separating his people, instead of bringing
them together, resembles that of the Russians, whom he had
not yet read. A promising meeting ends in a shy farewell.
These tales, stepchildren of the romantic movement, are
nevertheless anti-romantic in their treatment of love. If the
young Jamesian imagination was to gild Europe and art,
literature and the contemplative life, the realist was already
at work looking at love and marriage as a practical and
calculated affair—not in cynicism so much as in the belief
that it represented a perpetual threat to a sovereign existence.

The tales of James's fledgling years have more than an
antiquarian interest. Their deepest interest, for those who
hold the short story in affection, resides in their constant
effort to capture for literature some small image of life.
This was the challenge the artist, writing his tales in Ash-
burton Place in Boston, and later in Quincy Street in Cam-
bridge, felt. "In every novel," he wrote (in his first long
critical article when he was twenty-three), "the work is
divided between the writer and the reader." And he went on
to say that the writer, in reality, had to create the reader very
much as he created his characters: by working on what was
plastic in the reader, that is on what the reader offered of his
own experience and awareness. Proust was to say this elo-
quently in the twentieth century: to describe how the reader,
in the act of participating in a novel, actually becomes that
novel. James's understanding was precocious. The great
point, he argued, was to obtain the reader's help: "I hold that
there is a way. It is perhaps a secret; but until it is found out, I
think that the art of story-telling cannot be said to have
approached perfection."

Here then was the double dedication of the young story-
teller. To discover this secret—and to "approach perfection." What his earliest tales show, is his gentle probing of

the narrative form and an awkward artistry which is no less art for all its awkwardness. They display the literary gift, all the power of dedication, that will lead James to ultimate triumph.

L.E.

A TRAGEDY OF ERROR

I

A LOW English phaeton was drawn up before the door of the post office of a French seaport town. In it was seated a lady, with her veil down and her parasol held closely over her face. My story begins with a gentleman coming out of the office and handing her a letter.

He stood beside the carriage a moment before getting in. She gave him her parasol to hold, and then lifted her veil, showing a very pretty face. This couple seemed to be full of interest for the passers by, most of whom stared hard and exchanged significant glances. Such persons as were looking on at the moment saw the lady turn very pale as her eyes fell on the direction of the letter. Her companion saw it too, and instantly stepping into the place beside her, took up the reins, and drove rapidly along the main street of the town, past the harbor, to an open road skirting the sea. Here he slackened pace. The lady was leaning back, with her veil down again, and the letter lying open in her lap. Her attitude was almost that of unconsciousness, and he could see that her eyes were closed. Having satisfied himself of this, he hastily possessed himself of the letter, and read as follows:

SOUTHAMPTON, *July 16th*, 18—.

MY DEAR HORTENSE: You will see by my postmark that I am a thousand leagues nearer home than when I last wrote, but I have hardly time to explain the change. M. P—— has given me a most unlooked-for *congé*. After so many months of separation, we shall be able to spend a few weeks together. God be praised! We got in here from New York this morning, and I have had the good luck to find a vessel, the *Armorique*, which sails straight for H——. The mail leaves directly, but we shall probably be detained a few hours by the tide; so this will reach you a day before I arrive: the master calculates we shall get in early Thursday morning. Ah, Hortense! how the time drags! Three whole days! If I did not write from New York, it is because I was unwilling to torment you with an expectancy which, as it is, I venture to hope, you will find long enough. Farewell. To a warmer greeting!

Your devoted

C.B.

When the gentleman replaced the paper on his companion's lap, his face was almost as pale as hers. For a moment he gazed fixedly and vacantly before him, and a half-suppressed curse escaped his lips. Then his eyes reverted to his neighbor. After some hesitation, during which he allowed the reins to hang so loose that the horse lapsed into a walk, he touched her gently on the shoulder.

"Well, Hortense," said he, in a very pleasant tone, "what's the matter; have you fallen asleep?"

Hortense slowly opened her eyes, and, seeing that they had left the town behind them, raised her veil. Her features were stiffened with horror.

"Read that," said she, holding out the open letter.

The gentleman took it, and pretended to read it again.

"Ah! M. Bernier returns. Delightful!" he exclaimed.

"How, delightful?" asked Hortense; "we mustn't jest at so serious a crisis, my friend."

"True," said the other, "it will be a solemn meeting. Two years of absence is a great deal."

"O Heaven! I shall never dare to face him," cried Hortense, bursting into tears.

Covering her face with one hand, she put out the other toward that of her friend. But he was plunged in so deep a reverie, that he did not perceive the movement. Suddenly he came to, aroused by her sobs.

"Come, come," said he, in the tone of one who wishes to coax another into mistrust of a danger before which he does not himself feel so secure but that the sight of a companion's indifference will give him relief. "What if he does come? He need learn nothing. He will stay but a short time, and sail away again as unsuspecting as he came."

"Learn nothing! You surprise me. Every tongue that greets him, if only to say *bon jour*, will wag to the tune of a certain person's misconduct."

"Bah! People don't think about us quite as much as you fancy. You and I, *n'est-ce-pas?* we have little time to concern ourselves about our neighbors' failings. Very well, other people are in the same box, better or worse. When a ship goes to pieces on those rocks out at sea, the poor devils who are pushing their way to land on a floating spar, don't bestow many glances on those who are battling with the waves beside them. Their eyes are fastened to the shore, and all their care is for their own safety. In life we are all afloat on a tumultuous sea; we are all struggling toward some *terra firma* of wealth or love or leisure. The roaring of the waves we kick up about us and the spray we dash into our eyes deafen and blind us to the sayings and doings of our fellows. Provided we climb high and dry, what do we care for them?"

"Ay, but if we don't? When we've lost hope ourselves, we want to make others sink. We hang weights about their necks, and dive down into the dirtiest pools for stones to cast at them. My friend, you don't feel the shots which are not aimed at you. It isn't of you the town talks, but of me: a poor woman throws herself off the pier yonder, and drowns before a kind hand has time to restrain her, and her corpse floats over the water for all the world to look at. When her husband comes up to see what the crowd means, is there any lack of kind friends to give him the good news of his wife's death?"

"As long as a woman is light enough to float, Hortense, she is not counted drowned. It's only when she sinks out of sight that they give her up."

Hortense was silent a moment, looking at the sea with swollen eyes.

"Louis," she said at last, "we were speaking metaphorically: I have half a mind to drown myself literally."

"Nonsense!" replied Louis, "an accused pleads *not guilty*, and hangs himself in prison. What do the papers say? People talk, do they? Can't you talk as well as they? A woman is in the wrong from the moment she holds her tongue and refuses battle. And that you do too often. That pocket handkerchief is always more or less of a flag of truce."

"I'm sure I don't know," said Hortense indifferently; "perhaps it is."

There are moments of grief in which certain aspects of the subject of our distress seem as irrelevant as matters entirely foreign to it. Her eyes were still fastened on the sea. There was another silence. "O my poor Charles!" she murmured, at length, "to what a hearth do you return!"

"Hortense," said the gentleman, as if he had not heard her, although, to a third person, it would have appeared that it was because he had done so that he spoke: "I do not need to tell you that it will never happen to me to betray our secret. But I will answer for it that so long as M. Bernier is at home no mortal shall breathe a syllable of it."

"What of that?" sighed Hortense. "He will not be with me ten minutes without guessing it."

"Oh, as for that," said her companion, dryly, "that's your own affair."

"Monsieur de Meyrau!" cried the lady.

"It seems to me," continued the other, "that in making such a guarantee, I have done my part of the business."

"Your part of the business!" sobbed Hortense.

M. de Meyrau made no reply, but with a great cut of the

whip sent the horse bounding along the road. Nothing more was said. Hortense lay back in the carriage with her face buried in her handkerchief, moaning. Her companion sat upright, with contracted brows and firmly set teeth, looking straight before him, and by an occasional heavy lash keeping the horse at a furious pace. A wayfarer might have taken him for a ravisher escaping with a victim worn out with resistance. Travellers to whom they were known would perhaps have seen a deep meaning in this accidental analogy. So, by a *détour*, they returned to the town.

When Hortense reached home, she went straight up to a little boudoir on the second floor, and shut herself in. This room was at the back of the house, and her maid, who was at that moment walking in the long garden which stretched down to the water, where there was a landing place for small boats, saw her draw in the window blind and darken the room, still in her bonnet and cloak. She remained alone for a couple of hours. At five o'clock, some time after the hour at which she was usually summoned to dress her mistress for the evening, the maid knocked at Hortense's door, and offered her services. Madame called out, from within, that she had a *migraine*, and would not be dressed.

"Can I get anything for madame?" asked Josephine; "a *tisane*, a warm drink, something?"

"Nothing, nothing."

"Will madame dine?"

"No."

"Madame had better not go wholly without eating."

"Bring me a bottle of wine—of brandy."

Josephine obeyed. When she returned, Hortense was standing in the doorway, and as one of the shutters had meanwhile been thrown open, the woman could see that, although her mistress's hat had been tossed upon the sofa, her cloak had not been removed, and that her face was very pale. Josephine felt that she might not offer sympathy nor ask questions.

"Will madame have nothing more?" she ventured to say, as she handed her the tray.

Madame shook her head, and closed and locked the door.

Josephine stood a moment vexed, irresolute, listening. She heard no sound. At last she deliberately stooped down and applied her eye to the keyhole.

This is what she saw:

Her mistress had gone to the open window, and stood with her back to the door, looking out at the sea. She held the bottle by the neck in one hand, which hung listlessly by her side; the other was resting on a glass half filled with water, standing, together with an open letter, on a table beside her. She kept this position until Josephine began to grow tired of waiting. But just as she was about to arise in despair of gratifying her curiosity, madame raised the bottle and glass, and filled the latter full. Josephine looked more eagerly. Hortense held it a moment against the light, and then drained it down.

Josephine could not restrain an involuntary whistle. But her surprise became amazement when she saw her mistress prepare to take a second glass. Hortense put it down, however, before its contents were half gone, as if struck by a sudden thought, and hurried across the room. She stooped down before a cabinet, and took out a small opera glass. With this she returned to the window, put it to her eyes, and again spent some moments in looking seaward. The purpose of this proceeding Josephine could not make out. The only result visible to her was that her mistress suddenly dropped the lorgnette on the table, and sank down on an armchair, covering her face with her hands.

Josephine could contain her wonderment no longer. She hurried down to the kitchen.

"Valentine," said she to the cook, "what on earth can be the matter with Madame? She will have no dinner, she is drinking brandy by the glassful, a moment ago she was looking out to sea with a lorgnette, and now she is crying dreadfully with an open letter in her lap."

The cook looked up from her potato-peeling with a significant wink.

"What can it be," said she, "but that monsieur returns?"

II

AT six o'clock, Josephine and Valentine were still sitting together, discussing the probable causes and consequences of the event hinted at by the latter. Suddenly Madame Bernier's bell rang. Josephine was only too glad to answer it. She met her mistress descending the stairs, combed, cloaked, and veiled, with no traces of agitation, but a very pale face.

"I am going out," said Madame Bernier; "if M. le Vicomte comes, tell him I am at my mother-in-law's, and wish him to wait till I return."

Josephine opened the door, and let her mistress pass; then stood watching her as she crossed the court.

"Her mother-in-law's," muttered the maid; "she has the face!"

When Hortense reached the street, she took her way, not through the town, to the ancient quarter where that ancient lady, her husband's mother, lived, but in a very different direction. She followed the course of the quay, beside the harbor, till she entered a crowded region, chiefly the residence of fishermen and boatmen. Here she raised her veil. Dusk was beginning to fall. She walked as if desirous to attract as little observation as possible, and yet to examine narrowly the population in the midst of which she found herself. Her dress was so plain that there was nothing in her appearance to solicit attention; yet, if for any reason a passer by had happened to notice her, he could not have helped being struck by the contained intensity with which she scrutinized every figure she met. Her manner was that of a person seeking to recognize a long-lost friend, or perhaps, rather, a long-lost enemy, in a crowd. At last she stopped before a flight of steps, at the foot of which was a landing place for half a dozen little boats, employed to carry passengers between the two sides of the port, at times when the drawbridge above was closed for the passage of vessels. While she stood she was witness of the following scene:

A man, in a red woollen fisherman's cap, was sitting on the top of the steps, smoking the short stump of a pipe, with his face to the water. Happening to turn about, his eye fell on a little child, hurrying along the quay toward a dingy tenement close at hand, with a jug in its arms.

"Hullo, youngster!" cried the man; "what have you got there? Come here."

The little child looked back, but, instead of obeying, only quickened its walk.

"The devil take you, come here!" repeated the man angrily, "or I'll wring your beggarly neck. You won't obey your own uncle, eh?"

The child stopped, and ruefully made its way to its relative, looking around several times toward the house, as if to appeal to some counter authority.

"Come, make haste!" pursued the man, "or I shall go and fetch you. Move!"

The child advanced to within half a dozen paces of the steps, and then stood still, eyeing the man cautiously, and hugging the jug tight.

"Come on, you little beggar, come up close."

The youngster kept a stolid silence, however, and did not budge. Suddenly its self-styled uncle leaned forward, swept out his arm, clutched hold of its little sunburned wrist, and dragged it toward him.

"Why didn't you come when you were called?" he asked, running his disengaged hand into the infant's frowsy mop of hair, and shaking its head until it staggered. "Why didn't you come, you unmannerly little brute, eh?—eh?—eh?" accompanying every interrogation with a renewed shake.

The child made no answer. It simply and vainly endeavored to twist its neck around under the man's gripe, and transmit some call for succor to the house.

"Come, keep your head straight. Look at me, and answer me. What's in that jug? Don't lie."

"Milk."

"Who for?"

"Granny."

"Granny be hanged."

The man disengaged his hands, lifted the jug from the child's feeble grasp, tilted it toward the light, surveyed its contents, put it to his lips, and exhausted them. The child, although liberated, did not retreat. It stood watching its uncle drink until he lowered the jug. Then, as he met its eyes, it said:

"It was for the baby."

For a moment the man was irresolute. But the child seemed to have a foresight of the parental resentment, for it had hardly spoken when it darted backward and scampered off, just in time to elude a blow from the jug, which the man sent clattering at its heels. When it was out of sight, he faced about to the water again, and replaced the pipe between his teeth with a heavy scowl and a murmur that sounded to Madame Bernier very like—"I wish the baby'd choke."

Hortense was a mute spectator of this little drama. When it was over, she turned around, and retraced her steps twenty yards with her hand to her head. Then she walked straight back, and addressed the man.

"My good man," she said, in a very pleasant voice, "are you the master of one of these boats?"

He looked up at her. In a moment the pipe was out of his mouth, and a broad grin in its place. He rose, with his hand to his cap.

"I am, madame, at your service."

"Will you take me to the other side?"

"You don't need a boat; the bridge is closed," said one of his comrades at the foot of the steps, looking that way.

"I know it," said Madame Bernier; "but I wish to go to the cemetery, and a boat will save me half a mile walking."

"The cemetery is shut at this hour."

"*Allons*, leave madame alone," said the man first spoken to. "This way, my lady."

Hortense seated herself in the stern of the boat. The man took the sculls.

"Straight across?" he asked.

Hortense looked around her. "It's a fine evening," said she; "suppose you row me out to the lighthouse, and leave me at the point nearest the cemetery on our way back."

"Very well," rejoined the boatman; "fifteen sous," and began to pull lustily.

"*Allez*, I'll pay you well," said Madame.

"Fifteen sous is the fare," insisted the man.

"Give me a pleasant row, and I'll give you a hundred," said Hortense.

Her companion said nothing. He evidently wished to appear not to have heard her remark. Silence was probably the most dignified manner of receiving a promise too munificent to be anything but a jest.

For some time this silence was maintained, broken only by the trickling of the oars and the sounds from the neighboring shores and vessels. Madame Bernier was plunged in a sidelong scrutiny of her ferryman's countenance. He was a man of about thirty-five. His face was dogged, brutal, and sullen. These indications were perhaps exaggerated by the dull monotony of his exercise. The eyes lacked a certain rascally gleam which had appeared in them when he was so *empressé* with the offer of his services. The face was better then—that is, if vice is better than ignorance. We say a countenance is "lit up" by a smile; and indeed that momentary flicker does the office of a candle in a dark room. It sheds a ray upon the dim upholstery of our souls. The visages of poor men, generally, know few alternations. There is a large class of human beings whom fortune restricts to a single change of expression, or, perhaps, rather to a single expression. Ah me! the faces which wear either nakedness or rags; whose repose is stagnation, whose activity vice; ignorant at their worst, infamous at their best!

"Don't pull too hard," said Hortense at last. "Hadn't you better take breath a moment?"

"Madame is very good," said the man, leaning upon his oars. "But if you had taken me by the hour," he added, with a return of the vicious grin, "you wouldn't catch me loitering."

"I suppose you work very hard," said Madame Bernier.

The man gave a little toss of his head, as if to intimate the inadequacy of any supposition to grasp the extent of his labors.

"I've been up since four o'clock this morning, wheeling bales and boxes on the quay, and plying my little boat. Sweating without five minutes' intermission. *C'est comme ça.* Sometimes I tell my mate I think I'll take a plunge in the basin to dry myself. Ha! ha! ha!"

"And of course you gain little," said Madame Bernier.

"Worse than nothing. Just what will keep me fat enough for starvation to feed on."

"How? you go without your necessary food?"

"Necessary is a very elastic word, madame. You can narrow it down, so that in the degree above nothing it means luxury. My necessary food is sometimes thin air. If I don't deprive myself of that, it's because I can't."

"Is it possible to be so unfortunate?"

"Shall I tell you what I have eaten to-day?"

"Do," said Madame Bernier.

"A piece of black bread and a salt herring are all that have passed my lips for twelve hours."

"Why don't you get some better work?"

"If I should die to-night," pursued the boatman, heedless of the question, in the manner of a man whose impetus on the track of self-pity drives him past the signal flags of relief, "what would there be left to bury me? These clothes I have on might buy me a long box. For the cost of this shabby old suit, that hasn't lasted me a twelve-month, I could get one that I wouldn't wear out in a thousand years. *La bonne idée!*"

"Why don't you get some work that pays better?" repeated Hortense.

The man dipped his oars again.

"Work that pays better? I must work for work. I must earn that too. Work is wages. I count the promise of the next week's employment the best part of my Saturday night's pocketings. Fifty casks rolled from the ship to the storehouse mean two things: thirty sous and fifty more to roll the next day. Just so a crushed hand, or a dislocated shoulder, mean twenty francs to the apothecary and *bon jour* to my business."

"Are you married?" asked Hortense.

"No, I thank you. I'm not cursed with that blessing. But I've an old mother, a sister, and three nephews, who look to me for support. The old woman's too old to work; the lass is too lazy, and the little ones are too young. But they're none of them too old or young to be hungry, *allez*. I'll be hanged if I'm not a father to them all."

There was a pause. The man had resumed rowing. Madame Bernier sat motionless, still examining her neighbor's physiognomy. The sinking sun, striking full upon his face, covered it with an almost lurid glare. Her own features being darkened against the western sky, the direction of them was quite indistinguishable to her companion.

"Why don't you leave the place?" she said at last.

"Leave it! how?" he replied, looking up with the rough avidity with which people of his class receive proposals touching their interests, extending to the most philanthropic suggestions

that mistrustful eagerness with which experience has taught
them to defend their own side of a bargain—the only form of
proposal that she has made them acquainted with.

"Go somewhere else," said Hortense.

"Where, for instance!"

"To some new country—America."

The man burst into a loud laugh. Madame Bernier's face
bore more evidence of interest in the play of his features than
of that discomfiture which generally accompanies the consciousness of ridicule.

"There's a lady's scheme for you! If you'll write for furnished apartments, *là-bas*, I don't desire anything better. But
no leaps in the dark for me. America and Algeria are very fine
words to cram into an empty stomach when you're lounging
in the sun, out of work, just as you stuff tobacco into your pipe
and let the smoke curl around your head. But they fade away
before a cutlet and a bottle of wine. When the earth grows so
smooth and the air so pure that you can see the American coast
from the pier yonder, then I'll make up my bundle. Not before."

"You're afraid, then, to risk anything?"

"I'm afraid of nothing, *moi*. But I am not a fool either. I
don't want to kick away my *sabots* till I am certain of a pair of
shoes. I can go barefoot here. I don't want to find water where
I counted on land. As for America, I've been there already."

"Ah! you've been there?"

"I've been to Brazil and Mexico and California and the West
Indies."

"Ah!"

"I've been to Asia, too."

"Ah!"

"*Pardio*, to China and India. Oh, I've seen the world! I've
been three times around the Cape."

"You've been a seaman then?"

"Yes, ma'am; fourteen years."

"On what ship?"

"Bless your heart, on fifty ships."

"French?"

"French and English and Spanish; mostly Spanish."

"Ah?"

"Yes, and the more fool I was."

"How so?"

"Oh, it was a dog's life. I'd drown any dog that would play half the mean tricks I used to see."

"And you never had a hand in any yourself?"

"*Pardon*, I gave what I got. I was as good a Spaniard and as great a devil as any. I carried my knife with the best of them, and drew it as quickly, and plunged it as deep. I've got scars, if you weren't a lady. But I'd warrant to find you their mates on a dozen Spanish hides!"

He seemed to pull with renewed vigor at the recollection. There was a short silence.

"Do you suppose," said Madame Bernier, in a few moments —"do you remember—that is, can you form any idea whether you ever killed a man?"

There was a momentary slackening of the boatman's oars. He gave a sharp glance at his passenger's countenance, which was still so shaded by her position, however, as to be indistinguishable. The tone of her interrogation had betrayed a simple, idle curiosity. He hesitated a moment, and then gave one of those conscious, cautious, dubious smiles, which may cover either a criminal assumption of more than the truth or a guilty repudiation of it.

"*Mon Dieu!*" said he, with a great shrug, "there's a question! . . . . . I never killed one without a reason."

"Of course not," said Hortense.

"Though a reason in South America, *ma foi!*" added the boatman, "wouldn't be a reason here."

"I suppose not. What would be a reason there?"

"Well, if I killed a man in Valparaiso—I don't say I did,

mind—it's because my knife went in farther than I intended."

"But why did you use it at all?"

"I didn't. If I had, it would have been because he drew his against me."

"And why should he have done so?"

"*Ventrebleu!* for as many reasons as there are craft in the harbor."

"For example?"

"Well, that I should have got a place in a ship's company that he was trying for."

"Such things as that? is it possible?"

"Oh, for smaller things. That a lass should have given me a dozen oranges she had promised him."

"How odd!" said Madame Bernier, with a shrill kind of laugh. "A man who owed you a grudge of this kind would just come up and stab you, I suppose, and think nothing of it?"

"Precisely. Drive a knife up to the hilt into your back, with an oath, and slice open a melon with it, with a song, five minutes afterward."

"And when a person is afraid, or ashamed, or in some way unable to take revenge himself, does he—or it may be a woman —does she, get some one else to do it for her?"

"*Parbleu!* Poor devils on the lookout for such work are as plentiful all along the South American coast as *commissionaires* on the street corners here." The ferryman was evidently surprised at the fascination possessed by this infamous topic for so lady-like a person; but having, as you see, a very ready tongue, it is probable that his delight in being able to give her information and hear himself talk were still greater. "And then down there," he went on, "they'll never forget a grudge. If a fellow doesn't serve you one day, he'll do it another. A Spaniard's hatred is like lost sleep—you can put it off for a time, but it will gripe you in the end. The rascals always keep their promises to themselves. . . . . An enemy on shipboard is jolly fun. It's like bulls tethered in the same field. You can't stand still half a minute except against a wall. Even when he makes friends with you, his favors never taste right. Messing with him is like drinking out of a pewter mug. And so it is everywhere. Let your shadow once flit across a Spaniard's path, and he'll always see it there. If you've never lived in any but these damned clockworky European towns, you can't imagine the state of things in a South American seaport—one half the population waiting round the corner for the other half. But I don't see that it's so much better here, where every man's a spy on every other. There you meet an assassin at every turn, here a *sergent de ville*. . . . . At all events, the life *là bas* used to remind me, more than anything else, of sailing in a shallow channel, where you don't know what infernal rock you may ground on. Every man has a standing account with his neighbor, just as madame has at her *fournisseur's*; and, *ma foi*, those are the only accounts they settle. The master of the *Santiago* may pay me one of these days for the pretty names I heaved after him when we parted company, but he'll never pay me my wages."

A short pause followed this exposition of the virtues of the Spaniard.

"You yourself never put a man out of the world, then?" resumed Hortense.

"Oh, *que si!* . . . . Are you horrified?"

"Not at all. I know that the thing is often justifiable."

The man was silent a moment, perhaps with surprise, for the next thing he said was:

"Madame is Spanish?"

"In that, perhaps, I am," replied Hortense.

Again her companion was silent. The pause was prolonged. Madame Bernier broke it by a question which showed that she had been following the same train of thought.

"What is sufficient ground in this country for killing a man?"

The boatman sent a loud laugh over the water. Hortense drew her cloak closer about her.

"I'm afraid there is none."

"Isn't there a right of self-defence?"

"To be sure there is—it's one I ought to know something about. But it's one that *ces messieurs* at the Palais make short work with."

"In South America and those countries, when a man makes life insupportable to you, what do you do?"

"*Mon Dieu!* I suppose you kill him."

"And in France?"

"I suppose you kill yourself. Ha! ha! ha!"

By this time they had reached the end of the great breakwater, terminating in a lighthouse, the limit, on one side, of the inner harbor. The sun had set.

"Here we are at the lighthouse," said the man; "it's growing dark. Shall we turn?"

Hortense rose in her place a few moments, and stood looking out to sea. "Yes," she said at last, "you may go back—slowly." When the boat had headed round she resumed her old position, and put one of her hands over the side, drawing it through the water as they moved, and gazing into the long ripples.

At last she looked up at her companion. Now that her face caught some of the lingering light of the west, he could see that it was deathly pale.

"You find it hard to get along in the world," said she: "I shall be very glad to help you."

The man started, and stared a moment. Was it because this remark jarred upon the expression which he was able faintly to discern in her eyes? The next, he put his hand to his cap.

"Madame is very kind. What will you do?"

Madame Bernier returned his gaze.

"I will trust you."

"Ah!"

"And reward you."

"Ah? Madame has a piece of work for me?"

"A piece of work," Hortense nodded.

The man said nothing, waiting apparently for an explanation. His face wore the look of lowering irritation which low natures feel at being puzzled.

"Are you a bold man?"

Light seemed to come in this question. The quick expansion of his features answered it. You cannot touch upon certain subjects with an inferior but by the sacrifice of the barrier which separates you from him. There are thoughts and feelings and glimpses and foreshadowings of thoughts which level all inequalities of station.

"I'm bold enough," said the boatman, "for anything *you* want me to do."

"Are you bold enough to commit a crime?"

"Not for nothing."

"If I ask you to endanger your peace of mind, to risk your personal safety for me, it is certainly not as a favor. I will give you ten times the weight in gold of every grain by which your conscience grows heavier in my service."

The man gave her a long, hard look through the dim light.

"I know what you want me to do," he said at last.

"Very well," said Hortense; "will you do it?"

He continued to gaze. She met his eyes like a woman who has nothing more to conceal.

"State your case."

"Do you know a vessel named the *Armorique*, a steamer?"

"Yes, it runs from Southampton."

"It will arrive to-morrow morning early. Will it be able to cross the bar?"

"No; not till noon."

"I thought so. I expect a person by it—a man."

Madame Bernier appeared unable to continue, as if her voice had given way.

"Well, well?" said her companion.

"He's the person"—she stopped again.

"The person who—?"

"The person whom I wish to get rid of."

For some moments nothing was said. The boatman was the first to speak again.

"Have you formed a plan?"

Hortense nodded.

"Let's hear it."

"The person in question," said Madame Bernier, "will be impatient to land before noon. The house to which he returns will be in view of the vessel if, as you say, she lies at anchor. If he can get a boat, he will be sure to come ashore. *Eh bien!*— but you understand me."

"Aha! you mean my boat—*this* boat?"

"O God!"

Madame Bernier sprang up in her seat, threw out her arms, and sank down again, burying her face in her knees. Her companion hastily shipped his oars, and laid his hands on her shoulders.

"*Allons donc*, in the devil's name, don't break down," said he; "we'll come to an understanding."

Kneeling in the bottom of the boat, and supporting her by his grasp, he succeeded in making her raise herself, though her head still drooped.

"You want me to finish him in the boat?"

No answer.

"Is he an old man?"

Hortense shook her head faintly.

"My age?"

She nodded.

"*Sapristi!* it isn't so easy."

"He can't swim," said Hortense, without looking up; "he— he is lame."

"*Nom de Dieu!*" The boatman dropped his hands. Hortense looked up quickly. Do you read the pantomime?

"Never mind," added the man at last, "it will serve as a sign."

"*Mais oui*. And besides that, he will ask to be taken to the Maison Bernier, the house with its back to the water, on the extension of the great quay. *Tenez*, you can almost see it from here."

"I know the place," said the boatman, and was silent, as if asking and answering himself a question.

Hortense was about to interrupt the train of thought which she apprehended he was following, when he forestalled her.

"How am I to be sure of my affair?" asked he.

"Of your reward? I've thought of that. This watch is a pledge of what I shall be able and glad to give you afterward. There are two thousand francs' worth of pearls in the case."

"*Il faut fixer la somme*," said the man, leaving the watch untouched.

"That lies with you."

"Good. You know that I have the right to ask a high price."

"Certainly. Name it."

"It's only on the supposition of a large sum that I will so much as consider your proposal. *Songez donc*, that it's a MUR-DER you ask of me."

"The price—the price?"

"*Tenez*," continued the man, "poached game is always high. The pearls in that watch are costly because it's worth a man's life to get at them. You want me to be your pearl diver. Be it so. You must guarantee me a safe descent—it's a descent, you know—ha!—you must furnish me the armor of safety; a little gap to breathe through while I'm at my work—the thought of a capful of Napoleons!"

"My good man, I don't wish to talk to you or to listen to your sallies. I wish simply to know your price. I'm not bargaining for a pair of chickens. Propose a sum."

The boatman had by this time resumed his seat and his oars. He stretched out for a long, slow pull, which brought him closely face to face with his temptress. This position, his body bent forward, his eyes fixed on Madame Bernier's face, he kept for some seconds. It was perhaps fortunate for Hortense's purpose at that moment—it had often aided her purposes before —that she was a pretty woman.* A plain face might have emphasised the utterly repulsive nature of the negotiation. Suddenly, with a quick, convulsive movement, the man completed the stroke.

"*Pas si bête!* propose one yourself."

"Very well," said Hortense, "if you wish it. *Voyons:* I'll give you what I can. I have fifteen thousand francs' worth of jewels. I'll give you them, or, if they will get you into trouble, their value. At home, in a box I have a thousand francs in gold. You shall have those. I'll pay your passage and outfit to America. I have friends in New York. I'll write to them to get you work."

"And you'll give your washing to my mother and sister *hein?* Ha! ha! Jewels, fifteen thousand francs; one thousand more makes sixteen; passage to America—first class—five hundred francs; outfit—what does Madame understand by that?"

"Everything needful for your success *là-bas.*"

"A written denial that I am an assassin? *Ma foi,* it were better not to remove the impression. It's served me a good turn, on this side of the water at least. Call it twenty-five thousand francs."

"Very well; but not a sous more."

"Shall I trust you?"

"Am I not trusting you? It is well for you that I do not allow myself to think of the venture I am making."

"Perhaps we're even there. We neither of us can afford to make account of certain possibilities. Still, I'll trust you, too...."

---

* I am told that there was no resisting her smile; and that she had at her command, in moments of grief, a certain look of despair which filled even the roughest hearts with sympathy, and won over the kindest to the cruel cause.

Tiens!" added the boatman, "here we are near the quay." Then
with a mock-solemn touch of his cap, "Will Madame still visit
the cemetery?"

"Come, quick, let me land," said Madame Bernier, impatiently.

"We *have* been among the dead, after a fashion," persisted
the boatman, as he gave her his hand.

III

I T was more than eight o'clock when Madame Bernier reached
her own house.

"Has M. de Meyrau been here?" she asked of Josephine.

"Yes, ma'am; and on learning that Madame was out, he left
a note, *chez monsieur.*"

Hortense found a sealed letter on the table in her husband's
old study. It ran as follows:

"I was desolated at finding you out. I had a word to tell you.
I have accepted an invitation to sup and pass the night at
C——, thinking it would look well. For the same reason I
have resolved to take the bull by the horns, and go aboard the
steamer on my return, to welcome M. Berñier home—the
privilege of an old friend. I am told the *Armorique* will anchor
off the bar by daybreak. What do you think? But it's too late
to let me know. Applaud my *savoir faire*—you will, at all
events, in the end. You will see how it will smoothe matters."

"Baffled! baffled!" hissed Madame, when she had read the
note; "God deliver me from my friends!" She paced up and
down the room several times, and at last began to mutter to
herself, as people often do in moments of strong emotion:
"Bah! but he'll never get up by daybreak. He'll oversleep himself, especially after to-night's supper. The other will be before

him. . . . . Oh, my poor head, you've suffered too much to fail in the end!"

Josephine reappeared to offer to remove her mistress's things. The latter, in her desire to reassure herself, asked the first question that occurred to her.

"Was M. le Vicomte alone?"

"No madame; another gentleman was with him—M. de Saulges, I think. They came in a hack, with two portmanteaus."

Though I have judged best, hitherto, often from an exaggerated fear of trenching on the ground of fiction, to tell you what this poor lady did and said, rather than what she thought, I may disclose what passed in her mind now:

"Is he a coward? is he going to leave me? or is he simply going to pass these last hours in play and drink? He might have stayed with me. Ah! my friend, you do little for me, who do so much for you; who commit murder, and—Heaven help me! —suicide for you! . . . . But I suppose he knows best. At all events, he will make a night of it."

When the cook came in late that evening, Josephine, who had sat up for her, said:

"You've no idea how Madame is looking. She's ten years older since this morning. Holy mother! what a day this has been for her!"

"Wait till to-morrow," said the oracular Valentine.

Later, when the women went up to bed in the attic, they saw a light under Hortense's door, and during the night Josephine, whose chamber was above Madame's, and who couldn't sleep (for sympathy, let us say), heard movements beneath her, which told that her mistress was even more wakeful than she.

IV

THERE was considerable bustle around the *Armorique* as she anchored outside the harbor of H——, in the early dawn of the following day. A gentleman, with an overcoat, walking stick, and small valise, came alongside in a little fishing boat, and got leave to go aboard.

"Is M. Bernier here?" he asked of one of the officers, the first man he met.

"I fancy he's gone ashore, sir. There was a boatman inquiring for him a few minutes ago, and I think he carried him off."

M. de Meyrau reflected a moment. Then he crossed over to the other side of the vessel, looking landward. Leaning over the bulwarks he saw an empty boat moored to the ladder which ran up the vessel's side.

"That's a town boat, isn't it?" he said to one of the hands standing by.

"Yes, sir."

"Where's the master?"

"I suppose he'll be here in a moment. I saw him speaking to one of the officers just now."

De Meyrau descended the ladder, and seated himself at the stern of the boat. As the sailor he had just addressed was handing down his bag, a face with a red cap looked over the bulwarks.

"Hullo, my man!" cried De Meyrau, "is this your boat?"

"Yes, sir, at your service," answered the red cap, coming to the top of the ladder, and looking hard at the gentleman's stick and portmanteau.

"Can you take me to town, to Madame Bernier's, at the end of the new quay?"

"Certainly, sir," said the boatman, scuttling down the ladder, "you're just the gentleman I want."

An hour later Hortense Bernier came out of the house, and began to walk slowly through the garden toward the terrace which overlooked the water. The servants, when they came down at an early hour, had found her up and dressed, or rather, apparently, not undressed, for she wore the same clothes as the evening before.

"*Tiens!*" exclaimed Josephine, after seeing her, "Madame gained ten years yesterday; she has gained ten more during the night."

When Madame Bernier reached the middle of the garden she halted, and stood for a moment motionless, listening. The next, she uttered a great cry. For she saw a figure emerge from below the terrace, and come limping toward her with out-outstretched arms.

THE STORY OF A YEAR

I

My story begins as a great many stories have begun within the last three years, and indeed as a great many have ended; for, when the hero is despatched, does not the romance come to a stop?

In early May, two years ago, a young couple I wot of strolled homeward from an evening walk, a long ramble among the peaceful hills which inclosed their rustic home. Into these peaceful hills the young man had brought, not the rumor, (which was an old inhabitant,) but some of the reality of war, —a little whiff of gunpowder, the clanking of a sword; for, although Mr John Ford had his campaign still before him, he wore a certain comely air of camp-life which stamped him a very Hector to the steady-going villagers, and a very pretty fellow to Miss Elizabeth Crowe, his companion in this sentimental stroll. And was he not attired in the great brightness of blue and gold which befits a freshly made lieutenant? This was a strange sight for these happy Northern glades; for, although the first Revolution had boomed awhile in their midst, the honest yeomen who defended them were clad in sober homespun, and it is well known that His Majesty's troops wore red.

These young people, I say, had been roaming. It was plain that they had wandered into spots where the brambles were thick and the dews heavy,—nay, into swamps and puddles where the April rains were still undried. Ford's boots and trousers had imbibed a deep foretaste of the Virginia mud; his companion's skirts were fearfully bedraggled. What great

49

enthusiasm had made our friends so unmindful of their steps?
What blinding ardor had kindled these strange phenomena:
a young lieutenant scornful of his first uniform, a well-bred
young lady reckless of her stockings?

Good reader, this narrative is averse to retrospect.

Elizabeth (as I shall not scruple to call her outright) was
leaning upon her companion's arm, half moving in concert
with him, and half allowing herself to be led, with that instinc-
tive acknowledgment of dependence natural to a young girl
who has just received the assurance of lifelong protection.
Ford was lounging along with that calm, swinging stride which
often bespeaks, when you can read it aright, the answering con-
ciousness of a sudden rush of manhood. A spectator might
have thought him at this moment profoundly conceited. The
young girl's blue veil was dangling from his pocket; he had
shouldered her sun-umbrella after the fashion of a musket on
a march: he might carry these trifles. Was there not a vague
longing expressed in the strong expansion of his stalwart shoulders, in the fond accommodation of his pace to hers,—her pace
so submissive and slow, that, when he tried to match it, they
almost came to a delightful standstill,—a silent desire for the
whole fair burden?

They made their way up a long swelling mound, whose top
commanded the sunset. The dim landscape which had been
brightening all day to the green of spring was now darkening
to the gray of evening. The lesser hills, the farms, the brooks,
the fields, orchards, and woods, made a dusky gulf before the
great splendor of the west. As Ford looked at the clouds, it
seemed to him that their imagery was all of war, their great
uneven masses were marshalled into the semblance of a battle.
There were columns charging and columns flying and standards floating,—tatters of the reflected purple; and great cap-
tains on colossal horses, and a rolling canopy of cannon-smoke
and fire and blood. The background of the clouds, indeed, was
like a land on fire, or a battle-ground illumined by another

sunset, a country of blackened villages and crimsoned pastures. The tumult of the clouds increased; it was hard to believe them inanimate. You might have fancied them an army of gigantic souls playing at football with the sun. They seemed to sway in confused splendor; the opposing squadrons bore each other down; and then suddenly they scattered, bowling with equal velocity towards north and south, and gradually fading into the pale evening sky. The purple pennons sailed away and sank out of sight, caught, doubtless, upon the brambles of the intervening plain. Day contracted itself into a fiery ball and vanished.

Ford and Elizabeth had quietly watched this great mystery of the heavens.

"That is an allegory," said the young man, as the sun went under, looking into his companion's face, where a pink flush seemed still to linger: "it means the end of the war. The forces on both sides are withdrawn. The blood that has been shed gathers itself into a vast globule and drops into the ocean."

"I'm afraid it means a shabby compromise," said Elizabeth, "Light disappears, too, and the land is in darkness."

"Only for a season," answered the other. "We mourn our dead. Then light comes again, stronger and brighter than ever. Perhaps you'll be crying for me, Lizzie, at that distant day."

"Oh, Jack, didn't you promise not to talk about that?" says Lizzie, threatening to anticipate the performance in question.

Jack took this rebuke in silence, gazing soberly at the empty sky. Soon the young girl's eyes stole up to his face. If he had been looking at anything in particular, I think she would have followed the direction of his glance; but as it seemed to be a very vacant one, she let her eyes rest.

"Jack," said she, after a pause, "I wonder how you'll look when you get back."

Ford's soberness gave way to a laugh.

"Uglier than ever. I shall be all incrusted with mud and gore. And then I shall be magnificently sunburnt, and I shall have a beard."

"Oh, you dreadful!" and Lizzie gave a little shout. "Really, Jack, if you have a beard, you'll not look like a gentleman."

"Shall I look like a lady, pray?" says Jack.

"Are you serious?" asked Lizzie.

"To be sure. I mean to alter my face as you do your misfitting garments,—take in on one side and let out on the other. Isn't that the process? I shall crop my head and cultivate my chin."

"You've a very nice chin, my dear, and I think it's a shame to hide it."

"Yes, I know my chin's handsome; but wait till you see my beard."

"Oh, the vanity!" cried Lizzie, "the vanity of men in their faces! Talk of women!" and the silly creature looked up at her lover with most inconsistent satisfaction.

"Oh, the pride of women in their husbands!" said Jack, who of course knew what she was about.

"You're not my husband, Sir. There's many a slip"——
But the young girl stopped short.

"Twixt the cup and the lip," said Jack. "Go on. I can match your proverb with another. 'There's many a true word,' and so forth. No, my darling: I'm not your husband. Perhaps I never shall be. But if anything happens to me, you'll take comfort, won't you?"

"Never!' said Lizzie, tremulously.

"Oh, but you must; otherwise, Lizzie, I should think our engagement inexcusable. Stuff! who am I that you should cry for me?"

"You are the best and wisest of men. I don't care; you *are*."

"Thank you for your great love, my dear. That's a delightful illusion. But I hope Time will kill it, in his own good way, before it hurts any one. I know so many men who are worth infinitely more than I—men wise, generous, and brave—that I shall not feel as if I were leaving you in an empty world."

"Oh, my dear friend!" said Lizzie, after a pause, "I wish you could advise me all my life."

"Take care, take care," laughed Jack; "you don't know what you are bargaining for. But will you let me say a word now? If by chance I'm taken out of the world, I want you to beware of that tawdry sentiment which enjoins you to be 'constant to my memory.' My memory be hanged! Remember me at my best,—that is, fullest of the desire of humility. Don't inflict me on people. There are some widows and bereaved sweethearts who remind me of the peddler in that horrible murder-story, who carried a corpse in his pack. Really, it's their stock in trade. The only justification of a man's personality is his rights. What rights has a dead man?—Let's go down."

They turned southward and went jolting down the hill.

"Do you mind this talk, Lizzie?" asked Ford.

"No," said Lizzie, swallowing a sob, unnoticed by her companion in the sublime egotism of protection; "I like it."

"Very well," said the young man, "I want my memory to help you. When I am down in Virginia, I expect to get a vast deal of good from thinking of you,—to do my work better, and to keep straighter altogether. Like all lovers, I'm horribly selfish. I expect to see a vast deal of shabbiness and baseness and turmoil, and in the midst of it all I'm sure the inspiration of patriotism will sometimes fail. Then I'll think of you. I love you a thousand times better than my country, Liz.—Wicked? So much the worse. It's the truth. But if I find your memory makes a milksop of me, I shall thrust you out of the way, without ceremony,—I shall clap you into my box or between the leaves of my Bible, and only look at you on Sunday."

"I shall be very glad, Sir, if that makes you open your Bible frequently," says Elizabeth, rather demurely.

"I shall put one of your photographs against every page,"

cried Ford; "and then I think I shall not lack a text for my meditations. Don't you know how Catholics keep little pictures of their adored Lady in their prayer-books?"

"Yes, indeed," said Lizzie; "I should think it would be a very soul-stirring picture, when you are marching to the front, the night before a battle,—a poor, stupid girl, knitting stupid socks, in a stupid Yankee village."

Oh, the craft of artless tongues! Jack strode along in silence a few moments, splashing straight through a puddle; then, ere he was quite clear of it, he stretched out his arm and gave his companion a long embrace.

"And pray what am I to do," resumed Lizzie, wondering, rather proudly perhaps, at Jack's averted face, "while you are marching and countermarching in Virginia?"

"Your duty, of course," said Jack, in a steady voice, which belied a certain little conjecture of Lizzie's. "I think you will find the sun will rise in the east, my dear, just as it did before you were engaged."

"I'm sure I didn't suppose it wouldn't," says Lizzie.

'By duty I don't mean anything disagreeable, Liz," pursued the young man. "I hope you'll take your pleasure, too. I wish you might go to Boston, or even to Leatherborough, for a month or two."

"What for, pray?"

"What for? Why, for the fun of it: to 'go out', as they say."

"Jack, do you think me capable of going to parties while you are in danger?"

"Why not? Why should I have all the fun?"

"Fun? I'm sure you're welcome to it all. As for me, I mean to make a new beginning."

"Of what?"

"Oh, of everything. In the first place, I shall begin to improve my mind. But don't you think it's horrid for women to be reasonable?"

"Hard, say you?"

"Horrid,—yes, and hard too. But I mean to become so. Oh, girls are such fools, Jack! I mean to learn to like boiled mutton and history and plain sewing, and all that. Yet, when a girl's engaged, she's not expected to do anything in particular."

Jack laughed, and said nothing; and Lizzie went on.

"I wonder what your mother will say to the news. I think I know."

"What?"

"She'll say you've been very unwise. No, she won't: she never speaks so to you. She'll say I've been very dishonest or indelicate, or something of that kind. No, she won't either: she doesn't say such things, though I'm sure she thinks them. I don't know what she'll say."

"No, I think not, Lizzie, if you indulge in such conjectures. My mother never speaks without thinking. Let us hope that she may think favorably of our plan. Even if she doesn't"——

Jack did not finish his sentence, nor did Lizzie urge him. She had a great respect for his hesitations. But in a moment he began again.

"I was going to say this, Lizzie: I think for the present our engagement had better be kept quiet."

Lizzie's heart sank with a sudden disappointment. Imagine the feelings of the damsel in the fairy-tale, whom the disguised enchantress had just empowered to utter diamonds and pearls, should the old beldame have straightway added that for the present mademoiselle had better hold her tongue. Yet the disappointment was brief. I think this enviable young lady would have tripped home talking very hard to herself, and have been not ill pleased to find her little mouth turning into a tightly clasped jewel-casket. Nay, would she not on this occasion have been thankful for a large mouth,—a mouth huge and un-natural,—stretching from ear to ear? Who wish to cast their pearls before swine? The young lady of the pearls was, after all, but a barnyard miss. Lizzie was too proud of Jack to be vain. It's well enough to wear our own hearts upon our sleeves; but for those of others, when intrusted to our keeping, I think we had better find a more secluded lodging.

"You see, I think secrecy would leave us much freer," said Jack,—"leave *you* much freer."

"Oh, Jack, how can you?" cried Lizzie. "Yes, of course; I shall be falling in love with someone else. Freer! Thank you, Sir!"

"Nay, Lizzie, what I'm saying is really kinder than it sounds. Perhaps you *will* thank me one of these days."

"Doubtless! I've already taken a great fancy to George Mackenzie."

"Will you let me enlarge on my suggestion?"

"Oh, certainly! You seem to have your mind quite made up."

"I confess I like to take account of possibilities. Don't you know mathematics are my hobby? Did you ever study algebra? I always have an eye on the unknown quantity."

"No, I never studied algebra. I agree with you, that we had better not speak of our engagement."

"That's right, my dear. You're always right. But mind, I don't want to bind you to secrecy. Hang it, do as you please! Do what comes easiest to you, and you'll do the best thing. What made me speak is my dread of the horrible publicity which clings to all this business. Nowadays, when a girl's engaged, it's no longer, 'Ask mamma,' simply; but, 'Ask Mrs Brown, and Mrs Jones, and my large circle of acquaintance,— Mrs Grundy, in short.' I say nowadays, but I suppose it's always been so."

"Very well, we'll keep it all nice and quiet," said Lizzie, who would have been ready to celebrate her nuptials according to the rites of the Esquimaux, had Jack seen fit to suggest it.

"I know it doesn't look well for a lover to be so cautious," pursued Jack; "but you understand me, Lizzie, don't you?"

"I don't entirely understand you, but I quite trust you."

"God bless you! My prudence, you see, is my best strength.

Now, if ever, I need my strength. When a man's a-wooing,
Lizzie, he is all feeling, or he ought to be; when he's accepted,
then he begins to think."

"And to repent, I suppose you mean."

"Nay, to devise means to keep his sweetheart from repent-
ing. Let me be frank. Is it the greatest fools only that are the
best lovers? There's no telling what may happen, Lizzie. I want
you to marry me with your eyes open. I don't want you to feel
tied down or taken in. You're very young, you know. You're
responsible to yourself of a year hence. You're at an age when
no girl can count safely from year's end to year's end."

"And you, Sir!" cries Lizzie; "one would think you were a
grandfather."

"Well, I'm on the way to it. I'm a pretty old boy. I mean
what I say. I may not be entirely frank, but I think I'm sincere.
It seems to me as if I'd been fibbing all my life before I told
you that your affection was necessary to my happiness. I mean
it out and out. I never loved anyone before, and I never will
again. If you had refused me half an hour ago, I should have
died a bachelor. I have no fear for myself. But I have for you.
You said a few minutes ago that you wanted me to be your
adviser. Now you know the function of an adviser is to perfect
his victim in the art of walking with his eyes shut. I sha'n't be
so cruel."

Lizzie saw fit to view these remarks in a humorous light.
"How disinterested!" quoth she: "how very self-sacrificing!
Bachelor indeed! For my part, I think I shall become a Mor-
mon!"—I verily believe the poor misinformed creature fancied that in Utah it is the ladies who are guilty of polygamy.

Before many minutes they drew near home. There stood
Mrs Ford at the garden gate, looking up and down the road,
with a letter in her hand.

"Something for you, John," said his mother, as they approached. "It looks as if it came from camp.—Why, Elizabeth,
look at your skirts!"

"I know it," says Lizzie, giving the articles in question a shake. "What is it, Jack?"

"Marching orders!" cried the young man. "The regiment leaves day after to-morrow. I must leave by the early train in the morning. Hurray!" And he diverted a sudden gleeful kiss into a filial salute.

They went in. The two women were silent, after the manner of women who suffer. But Jack did little else than laugh and talk and circumnavigate the parlor, sitting first here and then there,—close beside Lizzie and on the opposite side of the room. After a while Miss Crowe joined in his laughter, but I think her mirth might have been resolved into articulate heart-beats. After tea she went to bed, to give Jack opportunity for his last filial *épanchements*. How generous a man's intervention makes women! But Lizzie promised to see her lover off in the morning.

"Nonsense!" said Mrs Ford. "You'll not be up. John will want to breakfast quietly."

"I shall see you off, Jack," repeated the young lady, from the threshold.

Elizabeth went upstairs buoyant with her young love. It had dawned upon her like a new life,—a life positively worth the living. Hereby she would subsist and cost nobody anything. In it she was boundlessly rich. She would make it the hidden spring of a hundred praiseworthy deeds. She would begin the career of duty: she would enjoy boundless equanimity: she would raise her whole being to the level of her sublime passion. She would practise charity, humility, piety,—in fine, all the virtues: together with certain *morceaux* of Beethoven and Chopin. She would walk the earth like one glorified. She would do homage to the best of men by inviolate secrecy. Here, by I know not what gentle transition, as she lay in the quiet dark-ness, Elizabeth covered her pillow with a flood of tears.

Meanwhile Ford, downstairs, began in this fashion. He was lounging at his manly length on the sofa, in his slippers.

"May I light a pipe, mother?"

"Yes, my love. But please be careful of your ashes. There's a newspaper."

"Pipes don't make ashes.—Mother, what do you think?" he continued between the puffs of his smoking; "I've got a piece of news."

"Ah?" said Mrs Ford, fumbling for her scissors; "I hope it's good news."

"I hope you'll think it so. I've been engaging myself"— puff,—puff—"to Lizzie Crowe." A cloud of puffs between his mother's face and his own. When they had cleared away, Jack felt his mother's eyes. Her work was in her lap. "To be married, you know," he added.

In Mrs Ford's view, like the king in that of the British Constitution, her only son could do no wrong. Prejudice is a stout bulwark against surprise. Moreover, Mrs Ford's motherly instinct had not been entirely at fault. Still, it had by no means kept pace with fact. She had been silent, partly from doubt, partly out of respect for her son. As long as John did not doubt of himself, he was right. Should he come to do so, she was sure he would speak. And now, when he told her the matter was settled, she persuaded herself that he was asking her advice.

"I've been expecting it," she said, at last.

"You have? Why didn't you speak?"

"Well, John, I can't say I've been hoping it."

"Why not?"

"I am not sure of Lizzie's heart," said Mrs Ford, who, it may be well to add, was very sure of her own.

Jack began to laugh. "What's the matter with her heart?"

"I think Lizzie's shallow," said Mrs Ford; and there was that in her tone which betokened some satisfaction with this adjective.

"Hang it! she is shallow," said Jack. "But when a thing's shallow, you can see to the bottom. Lizzie doesn't pretend **to** be deep. I want a wife, mother, that I can understand. That's the only wife I can love. Lizzie's the only girl I ever understood, and the first I ever loved. I love her very much,—more than I can explain to you."

"Yes, I confess it's inexplicable. It seems to me," she added, with a bad smile, "like infatuation."

Jack did not like the smile; he liked it even less than the remark. He smoked steadily for a few moments, and then he said,—

"Well, mother, love is notoriously obstinate, you know. We shall not be able to take the same view of this subject: suppose we drop it."

"Remember that this is your last evening at home, my son," said Mrs Ford.

"I do remember. Therefore I wish to avoid disagreement."

There was a pause. The young man smoked, and his mother sewed, in silence.

"I think my position, as Lizzie's guardian," resumed Mrs Ford, "entitles me to an interest in the matter."

"Certainly, I acknowledged your interest by telling you of our engagement."

Further pause.

"Will you allow me to say," said Mrs Ford, after a while, "that I think this a little selfish?"

"Allow you? Certainly, if you particularly desire it. Though I confess it isn't very pleasant for a man to sit and hear his future wife pitched into,—by his own mother, too."

"John, I am surprised at your language."

"I beg your pardon," and John spoke more gently. "You mustn't be surprised at anything from an accepted lover.—I'm sure you misconceive her. In fact, mother, I don't believe you know her."

Mrs Ford nodded, with an infinite depth of meaning; and from the grimness with which she bit off the end of her thread it might have seemed that she fancied herself to be executing a human vengeance.

"Ah, I know her only too well!"

"And you don't like her?"

Mrs Ford performed another decapitation of her thread.

"Well, I'm glad Lizzie has one friend in the world," said Jack.

"Her best friend," said Mrs Ford, "is the one who flatters her least. I see it all, John. Her pretty face has done the business."

The young man flushed impatiently.

"Mother," said he, "you are very much mistaken. I'm not a boy nor a fool. You trust me in a great many things; why not trust me in this?"

"My dear son, you are throwing yourself away. You deserve for your companion in life a higher character than that girl."

I think Mrs Ford, who had been an excellent mother, would have liked to give her son a wife fashioned on her own model.

"Oh, come, mother," said he, "that's twaddle. I should be thankful if I were half as good as Lizzie."

"It's the truth, John, and your conduct—not only the step you've taken, but your talk about it—is a great disappointment to me. If I have cherished any wish of late, it is that my darling boy should get a wife worthy of him. The household governed by Elizabeth Crowe is not the home I should desire for anyone I love."

"It's one to which you should always be welcome, Ma'am," said Jack.

"It's not a place I should feel at home in," replied his mother.

"I'm sorry," said Jack. And he got up and began to walk about the room. "Well, well, mother," he said at last, stopping in front of Mrs Ford, "we don't understand each other. One of these days we shall. For the present let us have done with discussion. I'm half sorry I told you."

"I'm glad of such a proof of your confidence. But if you hadn't, of course Elizabeth would have done so."

"No, Ma'am, I think not."

"Then she is even more reckless of her obligations than I thought her."

"I advised her to say nothing about it."

Mrs Ford made no answer. She began slowly to fold up her work.

"I think we had better let the matter stand," continued her son. "I'm not afraid of time. But I wish to make a request of you: you won't mention this conversation to Lizzie, will you? or allow her to suppose that you know of our engagement? I have a particular reason."

Mrs Ford went on smoothing out her work. Then she suddenly looked up.

"No, my dear, I'll keep your secret. Give me a kiss."

II

I HAVE no intention of following Lieutenant Ford to the seat of war. The exploits of his campaign are recorded in the public journals of the day, where the curious may still peruse them. My own taste has always been for unwritten history, and my present business is with the reverse of the picture.

After Jack went off, the two ladies resumed their old homely life. But the homeliest life had now ceased to be repulsive to Elizabeth. Her common duties were no longer wearisome: for the first time, she experienced the delicious companionship of thought. Her chief task was still to sit by the window knitting soldiers' socks; but even Mrs Ford could not help owning that she worked with a much greater diligence, yawned, rubbed her eyes, gazed up and down the road less, and indeed produced a much more comely article. Ah, me! if half the lovesome fancies that flitted through Lizzie's spirit in those busy hours could have found their way into the texture of the dingy yarn, as it was slowly wrought into shape, the eventual wearer of the socks would have been as light-footed as Mercury. I am afraid I should make the reader sneer, were I to rehearse some of this little fool's diversions. She passed several hours daily in Jack's old chamber: it was in this sanctuary, indeed, at the sunny south window, overlooking the long road, the wood-crowned heights, the gleaming river, that she worked with most pleasure and profit. Here she was removed from the untiring glance of the elder lady, from her jarring questions and commonplaces; here she was alone with her love,—that greatest commonplace in life. Lizzie felt in Jack's room a certain impress of his personality. The idle fancies of her mood were bodied forth in a dozen sacred relics. Some of these articles Elizabeth carefully cherished. It was rather late in the day for her to assert a literary taste,—her reading having begun and ended (naturally enough) with the ancient fiction of the "Scottish Chiefs." So she could hardly help smiling, herself, sometimes, at her interest in Jack's old college tomes. She carried several of them to her own apartment, and placed them at the foot of her little bed, on a book-shelf adorned, besides, with a pot of spring violets, a portrait of General McClellan, and a likeness of Lieutenant Ford. She had a vague belief that a loving study of their well-thumbed verses would remedy, in some degree, her sad intellectual deficiencies. She was sorry she knew so little: as sorry, that is, as she might be, for we know that she was shallow. Jack's omniscience was one of his most awful attributes. And yet she comforted herself with the thought that, as he had forgiven her ignorance, she herself might surely forget it. Happy Lizzie, I envy you this easy path to knowledge! The volume she most frequently consulted was an old German "Faust," over which she used to fumble with a battered lexicon. The secret of this preference was in certain marginal notes in pencil, signed "J." I hope they were really of Jack's making.

Lizzie was always a small walker. Until she knew Jack, this had been quite an unsuspected pleasure. She was afraid, too, of the cows, geese, and sheep,—all the agricultural *spectra* of the feminine imagination. But now her terrors were over. Might she not play the soldier, too, in her own humble way? Often with a beating heart, I fear, but still with resolute, elastic steps, she revisited Jack's old haunts; she tried to love Nature as he had seemed to love it; she gazed at his old sunsets; she fathomed his old pools with bright plummet glances, as if seeking some lingering trace of his features in their brown depths, stamped there as on a fond human heart; she sought out his dear name, scratched on the rocks and trees,—and when night came on, she studied, in her simple way, the great starlit canopy, under which, perhaps, her warrior lay sleeping; she wandered through the green glades, singing snatches of his old ballads in a clear voice, made tuneful with love,—and as she sang, there mingled with the everlasting murmur of the trees the faint sound of a muffled bass, borne upon the south wind like a distant drum-beat, responsive to a bugle. So she led for some months a very pleasant idyllic life, face to face with a strong, vivid memory, which gave everything and asked nothing. These were doubtless to be (and she half knew it) the happiest days of her life. Has life any bliss so great as this pensive ecstasy? To know that the golden sands are dropping one by one makes servitude freedom, and poverty riches.

In spite of a certain sense of loss, Lizzie passed a very blissful summer. She enjoyed the deep repose which, it is to be hoped, sanctifies all honest betrothals. Possible calamity weighed lightly upon her. We know that when the columns of battle-smoke leave the field, they journey through the heavy air to a thousand quiet homes, and play about the crackling blaze of as many firesides. But Lizzie's vision was never clouded. Mrs Ford might gaze into the thickening summer dusk and wipe her spectacles; but her companion hummed her old ballad-ends with an unbroken voice. She no more ceased to smile under evil tidings than the brooklet ceases to ripple beneath the projected shadow of the roadside willow. The self-given promises of that tearful night of parting were forgotten. Vigilance had no place in Lizzie's scheme of heavenly idleness. The idea of moralizing in Elysium!

It must not be supposed that Mrs Ford was indifferent to Lizzie's mood. She studied it watchfully, and kept note of all its variations. And among the things she learned was, that her companion knew of her scrutiny, and was, on the whole, indifferent to it. Of the full extent of Mrs Ford's observation, however, I think Lizzie was hardly aware. She was like a reveller in a brilliantly lighted room, with a curtainless window, conscious, and yet heedless, of passers-by. And Mrs Ford may not inaptly be compared to the chilly spectator on the dark side of the pane. Very few words passed on the topic of their common thoughts. From the first, as we have seen, Lizzie guessed at her guardian's probable view of her engagement: an abasement incurred by John. Lizzie lacked what is called a sense of duty; and, unlike the majority of such temperaments, which contrive to be buoyant on the glistening bubble of Dignity, she had likewise a modest estimate of her dues. Alack, my poor heroine had no pride! Mrs Ford's silent censure awakened no resentment. It sounded in her ears like a dull, soporific hum. Lizzie was deeply enamoured of what a French book terms her *aises intellectuelles*. Her mental comfort lay in the ignoring of problems. She possessed a certain native insight which revealed many of the horrent inequalities of her pathway; but she found it so cruel and disenchanting a faculty, that blindness was infinitely preferable. She preferred repose to order, and mercy to justice. She was speculative, without being critical. She was continually wondering, but she never inquired. This world was the riddle; the next alone would be the answer.

So she never felt any desire to have an "understanding" with Mrs Ford. Did the old lady misconceive her? it was her own business. Mrs Ford apparently felt no desire to set herself right. You see, Lizzie was ignorant of her friend's promise. There were moments when Mrs Ford's tongue itched to speak. There were others, it is true, when she dreaded any explanation which would compel her to forfeit her displeasure. Lizzie's happy self-sufficiency was most irritating. She grudged the young girl the dignity of her secret; her own actual knowledge of it rather increased her jealousy, by showing her the import-ance of the scheme from which she was excluded. Lizzie, being in perfect good-humor with the world and with herself, abated no jot of her personal deference to Mrs Ford. Of Jack, as a good friend and her guardian's son, she spoke very freely. But Mrs Ford was mistrustful of this semi-confidence. She would not, she often said to herself, be wheedled against her principles. Her principles! Oh for some shining blade of pur-pose to hew down such stubborn stakes! Lizzie had no thought of flattering her companion. She never deceived anyone but herself. She could not bring herself to value Mrs Ford's good-will. She knew that Jack often suffered from his mother's obstinacy. So her unbroken humility shielded no unavowed purpose. She was patient and kindly from nature, from habit. Yet I think, that, if Mrs Ford could have measured her benign-ity, she would have preferred, on the whole, the most open defiance. "Of all things," she would sometimes mutter, "to be patronized by that little piece!" It was very disagreeable, for instance, to have to listen to *portions* of her own son's letters.

These letters came week by week, flying out of the South like white-winged carrier-doves. Many and many a time, for very pride, Lizzie would have liked a larger audience. Portions of them certainly deserved publicity. They were far too good for her. Were they not better than that stupid war-correspon-dence in the "Times," which she so often tried to read in vain?

They contained long details of movements, plans of campaigns, military opinions and conjectures, expressed with the emphasis habitual to young sub-lieutenants. I doubt whether General Halleck's despatches laid down the law more absolutely than Lieutenant Ford's. Lizzie answered in her own fashion. It must be owned that hers was a dull pen. She told her dearest, dearest Jack how much she loved and honored him, and how much she missed him, and how delightful his last letter was, (with those beautifully drawn diagrams,) and the village gossip, and how stout and strong his mother continued to be,—and again, how she loved, etc., etc., and that she remained his loving L. Jack read these effusions as became one so beloved. I should not wonder if he thought them very brilliant.

The summer waned to its close, and through myriad silent stages began to darken into autumn. Who can tell the story of those red months? I have to chronicle another silent transition. But as I can find no words delicate and fine enough to describe the multifold changes of Nature, so, too, I must be content to give you the spiritual facts in gross.

John Ford became a veteran down by the Potomac. And, to tell the truth, Lizzie became a veteran at home. That is, her love and hope grew to be an old story. She gave way, as the strongest must, as the wisest will, to time. The passion which in her simple, shallow way, she had confided to the woods and waters reflected their outward variations; she thought of her lover less, and with less positive pleasure. The golden sands had run out. Perfect rest was over. Mrs Ford's tacit protest began to be annoying. In a rather resentful spirit, Lizzie forbore to read any more letters aloud. These were as regular as ever. One of them contained a rough camp-photograph of Jack's newly bearded visage. Lizzie declared it was "too ugly for anything," and thrust it out of sight. She found herself skipping his military dissertations, which were still as long and written in as handsome a hand as ever. The "too good," which used to be uttered rather proudly, was now rather a wearisome

truth. When Lizzie in certain critical moods tried to qualify
Jack's temperament, she said to herself that he was too literal.
Once he gave her a little scolding for not writing oftener.
"Jack can make no allowances," murmured Lizzie. "He can
understand no feelings but his own. I remember he used to say
that moods were diseases. His mind is too healthy for such
things; his heart is too stout for ache or pain. The night before
he went off he told me that Reason, as he calls it, was the rule
of life. I suppose he thinks it the rule of love, too. But his heart
is younger than mine,—younger and better. He has lived
through awful scenes of danger and bloodshed and cruelty, yet
his heart is purer." Lizzie had a horrible feeling of being *blasée*
of this one affection. "Oh, God bless him!" she cried. She
felt much better for the tears in which this soliloquy ended. I
fear she had begun to doubt her ability to cry about Jack.

III

CHRISTMAS came. The Army of the Potomac had stacked its
muskets and gone into winter-quarters. Miss Crowe received
an invitation to pass the second fortnight in February at the
great manufacturing town of Leatherborough. Leatherborough
is on the railroad, two hours south of Glenham, at the mouth
of the great river Tan, where this noble stream expands into
its broadest smile, or gapes in too huge a fashion to be disguised by a bridge.

"Mrs Littlefield kindly invites you for the last of the
month," said Mrs Ford, reading a letter behind the tea-urn.

It suited Mrs Ford's purpose—a purpose which I have not
space to elaborate—that her young charge should now go forth
into society and pick up acquaintances.

Two sparks of pleasure gleamed in Elizabeth's eyes. But, as

she had taught herself to do of late with her protectress, she mused before answering.

"It is my desire that you should go," said Mrs Ford, taking silence for dissent.

The sparks went out.

"I intend to go," said Lizzie, rather grimly. "I am much obliged to Mrs Littlefield."

Her companion looked up.

"I intend you shall. You will please to write this morning."

For the rest of the week the two stitched together over muslins and silks, and were very good friends. Lizzie could scarcely help wondering at Mrs Ford's zeal on her behalf. Might she not have referred it to her guardian's principles? Her wardrobe, hitherto fashioned on the Glenham notion of elegance, was gradually raised to the Leatherborough standard of fitness. As she took up her bedroom candle the night before she left home, she said,—

"I thank you very much, Mrs Ford, for having worked so hard for me,—for having taken so much interest in my outfit. If they ask me at Leatherborough who made my things, I shall certainly say it was you."

Mrs Littlefield treated her young friend with great kindness. She was a good-natured, childless matron. She found Lizzie very ignorant and very pretty. She was glad to have so great a beauty and so many lions to show.

One evening Lizzie went to her room with one of the maids, carrying half a dozen candles between them. Heaven forbid that I should cross that virgin threshold—for the present! But we will wait. We will allow them two hours. At the end of that time, having gently knocked, we will enter the sanctuary. Glory of glories! The faithful attendant has done her work. Our lady is robed, crowned, ready for worshippers.

I trust I shall not be held to a minute description of our dear Lizzie's person and costume. Who is so great a recluse as never

to have beheld young ladyhood in full dress? Many of us have
sisters and daughters. Not a few of us, I hope, have female connections of another degree, yet no less dear. Others have
looking-glasses. I give you my word for it that Elizabeth made
as pretty a show as it is possible to see. She was of course well-
dressed. Her skirt was of voluminous white, puffed and trimmed in wondrous sort. Her hair was profusely ornamented
with curls and braids of its own rich substance. From her waist
depended a ribbon, broad and blue. White with coral ornaments, as she wrote to Jack in the course of the week. Coral
ornaments, forsooth! And pray, Miss, what of the other jewels
with which your person was decorated,—the rubies, pearls,
and sapphires? One by one Lizzie assumes her modest gimcracks: her bracelet, her gloves, her handkerchief, her fan, and
then—her smile. Ah, that strange crowning smile!

An hour later, in Mrs Littlefield's pretty drawing-room,
amid music, lights, and talk, Miss Crowe was sweeping a grand
curtsy before a tall, sallow man, whose name she caught from
her hostess's redundant murmur as Bruce. Five minutes later,
when the honest matron gave a glance at her newly started
enterprise from the other side of the room, she said to herself
that really, for a plain country-girl, Miss Crowe did this kind
of thing very well. Her next glimpse of the couple showed
them whirling round the room to the crashing thrum of the
piano. At eleven o'clock she beheld them linked by their finger-
tips in the dazzling mazes of the reel. At half-past eleven she
discerned them charging shoulder to shoulder in the serried
columns of the Lancers. At midnight she tapped her young
friend gently with her fan.

"Your sash is unpinned, my dear.—I think you have danced
often enough with Mr Bruce. If he asks you again, you had
better refuse. It's not quite the thing.—Yes, my dear, I know.
—Mr Simpson, will you be so good as to take Miss Crowe
down to supper?"

I'm afraid young Simpson had rather a snappish partner.

After the proper interval, Mr Bruce called to pay his respects to Mrs Littlefield. He found Miss Crowe also in the drawing-room. Lizzie and he met like old friends. Mrs Littlefield was a willing listener; but it seemed to her that she had come in at the second act of the play. Bruce went off with Miss Crowe's promise to drive with him in the afternoon. In the afternoon he swept up to the door in a prancing, tinkling sleigh. After some minutes of hoarse jesting and silvery laughter in the keen wintry air, he swept away again with Lizzie curled up in the buffalo-robe beside him, like a kitten in a rug. It was dark when they returned. When Lizzie came in to the sitting-room fire, she was congratulated by her hostess upon having made a "conquest."

"I think he's a most gentlemanly man," says Lizzie.

"So he is, my dear," said Mrs Littlefield; "Mr Bruce is a perfect gentleman. He's one of the finest young men I know. He's not so young either. He's a little too yellow for my taste; but he's beautifully educated. I wish you could hear his French accent. He has been abroad I don't know how many years. The firm of Bruce and Robertson does an immense business."

"And I'm so glad," cries Lizzie, "he's coming to Glenham in March! He's going to take his sister to the water-cure."

"Really?—poor thing! She has very good manners."

"What do you think of his looks?" asked Lizzie, smoothing her feather.

"I was speaking of Jane Bruce. I think Mr Bruce has fine eyes."

"I must say I like tall men," says Miss Crowe.

"Then Robert Bruce is your man," laughs Mr Littlefield. "He's as tall as a bell-tower. And he's got a bell-clapper in his head, too."

"I believe I will go and take off my things," remarks Miss Crowe, flinging up her curls.

Of course it behoved Mr Bruce to call next day and see how

Miss Crowe had stood her drive. He set a veto upon her intended departure, and presented an invitation from his sister for the following week. At Mrs Littlefield's instance, Lizzie accepted the invitation, despatched a laconic note to Mrs Ford, and stayed over for Miss Bruce's party. It was a grand affair. Miss Bruce was a very great lady: she treated Miss Crowe with every attention. Lizzie was thought by some persons to look prettier than ever. The vaporous gauze, the sunny hair, the coral, the sapphires, the smile, were displayed with renewed success. The master of the house was unable to dance; he was summoned to sterner duties. Nor could Miss Crowe be induced to perform, having hurt her foot on the ice. This was of course a disappointment; let us hope that her entertainers made it up to her.

On the second day after the party, Lizzie returned to Glenham. Good Mr Littlefield took her to the station, stealing a moment from his precious business-hours.

"There are your checks," said he; "be sure you don't lose them. Put them in your glove."

Lizzie gave a little scream of merriment.

"Mr Littlefield, how can you? I've a reticule, Sir. But I really don't want you to stay."

"Well, I confess," said her companion.—"Hullo! there's your Scottish chief! I'll get him to stay with you till the train leaves. He may be going. Bruce!"

"Oh, Mr Littlefield, don't!" cries Lizzie. "Perhaps Mr Bruce is engaged."

Bruce's tall figure came striding towards them. He was astounded to find that Miss Crowe was going by this train. Delightful! He had come to meet a friend who had not arrived.

"Littlefield," said he, "you can't be spared from your business. I will see Miss Crowe off."

When the elder gentleman had departed, Mr Bruce conducted his companion into the car, and found her a comfortable seat, equidistant from the torrid stove and the frigid door.

Then he stowed away her shawls, umbrella, and reticule. She would keep her muff? She did well. What a pretty fur!

"It's just like your collar," said Lizzie. "I wish I had a muff for my feet," she pursued, tapping the floor.

"Why not use some of those shawls?" said Bruce; "let's see what we can make of them."

And he stooped down and arranged them as a rug, very neatly and kindly. And then he called himself a fool for not having used the next seat, which was empty; and the wrapping was done over again.

"I'm so afraid you'll be carried off!" said Lizzie. "What would you do?"

"I think I should make the best of it. And you?"

"I would tell you to sit down *there*"; and she indicated the seat facing her. He took it. "Now you'll be sure to," said Elizabeth.

"I'm afraid I shall, unless I put the newspaper between us." And he took it out of his pocket. "Have you seen the news?"

"No," says Lizzie, elongating her bonnet-ribbons. "What is it? Just look at that party."

"There's not much news. There's been a scrimmage on the Rappahannock. Two of our regiments engaged,—the Fifteenth and the Twenty-Eighth. Didn't you tell me you had a cousin or something in the Fifteenth?"

"Not a cousin, no relation, but an intimate friend,—my guardian's son. What does the paper say, please?" inquires Lizzie, very pale.

Bruce cast his eye over the report. "It doesn't seem to have amounted to much; we drove back the enemy, and recrossed the river at our ease. Our loss only fifty. There are no names," he added, catching a glimpse of Lizzie's pallor,—"none in this paper at least."

In a few moments appeared a newsboy crying the New York journals.

"Do you think the New York papers would have any names?" asked Lizzie.

"We can try," said Bruce. And he bought a "Herald," and unfolded it. "Yes, there *is* a list," he continued, some time after he had opened out the sheet. "What's your friend's name?" he asked, from behind the paper.

"Ford,—John Ford, second lieutenant," said Lizzie.

There was a long pause.

At last Bruce lowered the sheet, and showed a face in which Lizzie's pallor seemed faintly reflected.

"There *is* such a name among the wounded," he said; and, folding the paper down, he held it out, and gently crossed to the seat beside her.

Lizzie took the paper, and held it close to her eyes. But Bruce could not help seeing that her temples had turned from white to crimson.

"Do you see it?" he asked; "I sincerely hope it's nothing very bad."

"*Severely*," whispered Lizzie.

"Yes, but that proves nothing. Those things are most unreliable. *Do* hope for the best."

Lizzie made no answer. Meanwhile passengers had been brushing in, and the car was full. The engine began to puff, and the conductor to shout. The train gave a jog.

"You'd better go, Sir, or you'll be carried off," said Lizzie, holding out her hand, with her face still hidden.

"May I go on to the next station with you?" said Bruce.

Lizzie gave him a rapid look, with a deepened flush. He had fancied that she was shedding tears. But those eyes were dry; they held fire rather than water.

"No, no, Sir; you must not. I insist. Good bye."

Bruce's offer had cost him a blush, too. He had been prepared to back it with the assurance that he had business ahead, and, indeed, to make a little business in order to satisfy his conscience. But Lizzie's answer was final.

"Very well," said he, "*good* bye. You have my real sympathy, Miss Crowe. Don't despair. We shall meet again."

The train rattled away. Lizzie caught a glimpse of a tall figure with lifted hat on the platform. But she sat motionless, with her head against the windowframe, her veil down, and her hands idle.

She had enough to do to think, or rather to feel. It is fortunate that the utmost shock of evil tidings often comes first. After that everything is for the better. Jack's name stood printed in that fatal column like a stern signal for despair. Lizzie felt conscious of a crisis which almost arrested her breath. Night had fallen at midday: what was the hour? A tragedy had stepped into her life: was she spectator or actor? She found herself face to face with death: was it not her own soul masquerading in a shroud? She sat in a half-stupor. She had been aroused from a dream into a waking nightmare. It was like hearing a murder-shriek while you turn the page of your novel. But I cannot describe these things. In time the crushing sense of calamity loosened its grasp. Feeling lashed her pinions. Thought struggled to rise. Passion was still, stunned, floored. She had recoiled like a receding wave for a stronger onset. A hundred ghastly fears and fancies strutted a moment, pecking at the young girl's naked heart, like sandpipers on the weltering beach. Then, as with a great murmurous rush, came the meaning of her grief. The flood-gates of emotion were opened.

At last passion exhausted itself, and Lizzie thought. Bruce's parting words rang in her ears. She did her best to hope. She reflected that wounds, even severe wounds, did not necessarily mean death. Death might easily be warded off. She would go to Jack; she would nurse him; she would watch by him; she would cure him. Even if Death had already beckoned, she would strike down his hand: if Life had already obeyed, she would issue the stronger mandate of Love. She would stanch his wounds; she would unseal his eyes with her kisses; she would call till he answered her.

Lizzie reached home and walked up the garden path. Mrs Ford stood in the parlor as she entered, upright, pale, and rigid. Each read the other's countenance. Lizzie went towards her slowly and giddily. She must of course kiss her patroness. She took her listless hand and bent towards her stern lips. Habitually Mrs Ford was the most undemonstrative of women. But as Lizzie looked closer into her face, she read signs of a grief infinitely more potent than her own. The formal kiss gave way: the young girl leaned her head on the old woman's shoulder and burst into sobs. Mrs Ford acknowledged those tears with a slow inclination of the head, full of a certain grim pathos: she put out her arms and pressed them closer to her heart.

At last Lizzie disengaged herself and sat down.

"I am going to him," said Mrs Ford.

Lizzie's dizziness returned. Mrs Ford was going,—and she, she?

"I am going to nurse him, and with God's help to save him."

"How did you hear?"

"I have a telegram from the surgeon of the regiment"; and Mrs Ford held out a paper.

Lizzie took it and read: "Lieutenant Ford dangerously wounded in the action of yesterday. You had better come on."

"I should like to go myself," said Lizzie: "I think Jack would like to have me."

"Nonsense! A pretty place for a young girl! I am not going for sentiment; I am going for use."

Lizzie leaned her head back in her chair, and closed her eyes. From the moment they had fallen upon Mrs Ford, she had felt a certain quiescence. And now it was a relief to have responsibility denied her. Like most weak persons, she was glad to step out of the current of life, now that it had begun to quicken into action. In emergencies, such persons are tacitly counted out; and they as tacitly consent to the arrangement. Even to the sensitive spirit there is a certain meditative rapture in standing on the quiet shore, (beside the ruminating cattle,) and watching the hurrying, eddying flood, which makes up for the loss of dignity. Lizzie's heart resumed its peaceful throbs. She sat, almost dreamily, with her eyes shut.

"I leave in an hour," said Mrs Ford. "I am going to get ready.—Do you hear?"

The young girl's silence was a deeper consent than her companion supposed.

IV

IT was a week before Lizzie heard from Mrs Ford. The letter, when it came, was very brief. Jack still lived. The wounds were three in number, and very serious; he was unconscious; he had not recognized her; but still the chances either way were thought equal. They would be much greater for his recovery nearer home; but it was impossible to move him. "I write from the midst of horrible scenes," said the poor lady. Subjoined was a list of necessary medicines, comforts, and delicacies, to be boxed up and sent.

For a while Lizzie found occupation in writing a letter to Jack, to be read in his first lucid moment, as she told Mrs Ford. This lady's man-of-business came up from the village to superintend the packing of the boxes. Her directions were strictly followed; and in no point were they found wanting. Mr Mackenzie bespoke Lizzie's admiration for their friend's wonderful clearness of memory and judgment. "I wish we had that woman at the head of affairs," said he. " 'Gad, I'd apply for a Brigadier-Generalship."—"I'd apply to be sent South," thought Lizzie. When the boxes and letters were despatched, she sat down to await more news. Sat down, say I? Sat down, and rose, and wondered, and sat down again. These were lonely, weary days. Very different are the idleness of love and the idleness of grief. Very different is it to be alone with your hope and alone with your despair. Lizzie failed to rally her musings. I do not mean to say that her sorrow was very poignant, although she fancied it was. Habit was a great force in her simple nature; and her chief trouble now was that habit refused to work. Lizzie had to grapple with the stern tribulation of a decision to make, a problem to solve. She felt that there was some spiritual barrier between herself and repose. So she began in her usual fashion to build up a false repose on the hither side of belief. She might as well have tried to float on the Dead Sea. Peace eluding her, she tried to resign herself to tumult. She drank deep at the well of self-pity, but found its waters brackish. People are apt to think that they may temper the penalties of misconduct by self-commiseration, just as they season the long aftertaste of beneficence by a little spice of self-applause. But the Power of Good is a more grateful master than the Devil. What bliss to gaze into the smooth gurgling wake of a good deed, while the comely bark sails on with floating pennon! What horror to look into the muddy sediment which floats round the piratic keel! Go, sinner, and dissolve it with your tears! And you, scoffing friend, there is a way out! Or would you prefer the window? I'm an honest man forevermore.

One night Lizzie had a dream,—a rather disagreeable one, —which haunted her during many waking hours. It seemed to her that she was walking in a lonely place, with a tall, dark-eyed man who called her wife. Suddenly, in the shadow of a tree, they came upon an unburied corpse. Lizzie proposed to dig him a grave. They dug a great hole and took hold the corpse to lift him in; when suddenly he opened his eyes. Then they saw that he was covered with wounds. He looked at them intently for some time, turning his eyes from one to the other. At last he solemnly said, "Amen!" and closed his eyes. Then she and her companion placed him in the grave, and shovelled the earth over him, and stamped it down with their feet.

He of the dark eyes and he of the wounds were the two constantly recurring figures of Lizzie's reveries. She could

never think of John without thinking of the courteous Leatherborough gentleman, too. These were the *data* of her problem.
These two figures stood like opposing knights, (the black and
the white,) foremost on the great chess-board of fate. Lizzie
was the wearied, puzzled player. She would idly finger the
other pieces, and shift them carelessly hither and thither; but
it was of no avail: the game lay between the two knights. She
would shut her eyes and long for some kind hand to come and
tamper with the board; she would open them and see the two
knights standing immovable, face to face. It was nothing new.
A fancy had come in and offered defiance to a fact; they must
fight it out. Lizzie generously inclined to the fancy, the unknown champion, with a reputation to make. Call her *blasée*,
if you like, this little girl, whose record told of a couple of
dances and a single lover, heartless, old before her time. Perhaps she deserves your scorn. I confess she thought herself ill-
used. By whom? by what? wherein? These were questions
Miss Crowe was not prepared to answer. Her intellect was unequal to the stern logic of human events. She expected two and
two to make five: as why should they not for the nonce? She
was like an actor who finds himself on the stage with a half-
learned part and without sufficient wit to extemporize. Pray,
where is the prompter? Alas, Elizabeth, that you had no
mother! Young girls are prone to fancy that when once they
have a lover, they have everything they need: a conclusion inconsistent with the belief entertained by many persons, that
life begins with love. Lizzie's fortunes became old stories to
her before she had half read them through. Jack's wounds and
danger were an old story. Do not suppose that she had exhausted the lessons, the suggestions of these awful events, their
inspirations, exhortations,—that she had wept as became the
horror of the tragedy. No: the curtain had not yet fallen, yet
our young lady had begun to yawn. To yawn? Aye, and to
long for the afterpiece. Since the tragedy dragged, might she
not divert herself with that well-bred man beside her?

Elizabeth was far from owning to herself that she had fallen away from her love. For my own part, I need no better proof of the fact than the dull persistency with which she denied it. What accusing voice broke out of the stillness? Jack's nobleness and magnanimity were the hourly theme of her clogged fancy. Again and again she declared to herself that she was unworthy of them, but that, if he would only recover and come home, she would be his eternal bond-slave. So she passed a very miserable month. Let us hope that her childish spirit was being tempered to some useful purpose. Let us hope so.

She roamed about the empty house with her footsteps tracked by an unlaid ghost. She cried aloud and said that she was very unhappy; she groaned and called herself wicked. Then, sometimes, appalled at her moral perplexities, she declared that she was neither wicked nor unhappy; she was contented, patient, and wise. Other girls had lost their lovers: it was the present way of life. Was she weaker than most women? Nay, but Jack was the best of men. If he would only come back directly, without delay, as he was, senseless, dying even, that she might look at him, touch him, speak to him! Then she would say that she could no longer answer for herself, and wonder (or pretend to wonder) whether she were not going mad. Suppose Mrs Ford should come back and find her in an unswept room, pallid and insane? or suppose she should die of her troubles? What if she should kill herself?—dismiss the servants, and close the house, and lock herself up with a knife? Then she would cut her arm to escape from dismay at what she had already done; and then her courage would ebb away with her blood, and, having so far pledged herself to despair, her life would ebb away with her courage: and then, alone, in darkness, with none to help her, she would vainly scream, and thrust the knife into her temple, and swoon to death. And Jack would come back, and burst into the house, and wander through the empty rooms, calling her name, and for all answer get a deathscent! These imaginings were the more creditable or discreditable to Lizzie, that she had never read "Romeo and Juliet." At any rate, they served to dissipate time,—heavy, weary time,—the more heavy and weary as it bore dark foreshadowings of some momentous event. If that event would only come, whatever it was, and sever this Gordian knot of doubt!

The days passed slowly: the leaden sands dropped one by one. The roads were too bad for walking; so Lizzie was obliged to confine her restlessness to the narrow bounds of the empty house, or to an occasional journey to the village, where people sickened her by their dull indifference to her spiritual agony. Still they could not fail to remark how poorly Miss Crowe was looking. This was true, and Lizzie knew it. I think she even took a certain comfort in her pallor and in her failing interest in her dress. There was some satisfaction in displaying her white roses amid the apple-cheeked prosperity of Main Street. At last Miss Cooper, the Doctor's sister, spoke to her:—

"How is it, Elizabeth, you look so pale, and thin, and worn out? What you been doing with yourself? Falling in love, eh? It isn't right to be so much alone. Come down and stay with us awhile,—till Mrs Ford and John come back," added Miss Cooper, who wished to put a cheerful face on the matter.

For Miss Cooper, indeed, any other face would have been difficult. Lizzie agreed to come. Her hostess was a busy, unbeautiful old maid, sister and housekeeper of the village physician. Her occupation here below was to perform the forgotten tasks of her fellowmen,—to pick up their dropped stitches, as she herself declared. She was never idle, for her general cleverness was commensurate with mortal needs. Her own story was, that she kept moving, so that folks couldn't see how ugly she was. And, in fact, her existence was manifest through her long train of good deeds,—just as the presence of a comet is shown by its tail. It was doubtless on the above principle that her visage was agitated by a perpetual laugh.

Meanwhile more news had been coming from Virginia. "What an absurdly long letter you sent John," wrote Mrs

Ford, in acknowledging the receipt of the boxes. "His first lucid moment would be very short, if he were to take upon himself to read your effusions. Pray keep your long stories till he gets well." For a fortnight the young soldier remained the same,—feverish, conscious only at intervals. Then came a change for the worse, which, for many weary days, however, resulted in nothing decisive. "If he could only be moved to Glenham, home, and old sights," said his mother, "I should have hope. But think of the journey!" By this time Lizzie had stayed out ten days of her visit.

One day Miss Cooper came in from a walk, radiant with tidings. Her face, as I have observed, wore a continual smile, being dimpled and punctured all over with merriment,—so that, when an unusual cheerfulness was super-diffused, it resembled a tempestuous little pool into which a great stone has been cast.

"Guess who's come," said she, going up to the piano, which Lizzie was carelessly fingering, and putting her hands on the young girl's shoulders. "Just guess!"

Lizzie looked up.

"Jack," she half gasped.

"Oh, dear, no, not that! How stupid of me! I mean Mr Bruce, your Leatherborough admirer."

"Mr Bruce! Mr Bruce!" said Lizzie. "Really?"

"True as I live. He's come to bring his sister to the Water-Cure. I met them at the post-office."

Lizzie felt a strange sensation of good news. Her finger-tips were on fire. She was deaf to her companion's rattling chronicle. She broke into the midst of it with a fragment of some triumphant, jubilant melody. The keys rang beneath her flashing hands. And then she suddenly stopped, and Miss Cooper, who was taking off her bonnet at the mirror, saw that her face was covered with a burning flush.

That evening, Mr Bruce presented himself at Doctor Cooper's, with whom he had a slight acquaintance. To Lizzie he was infinitely courteous and tender. He assured her, in very pretty terms, of his profound sympathy with her in her cousin's danger,—her cousin he still called him,—and it seemed to Lizzie that until that moment no one had begun to be kind. And then he began to rebuke her, playfully and in excellent taste, for her pale cheeks.

"Isn't it dreadful?" said Miss Cooper. "She looks like a ghost. I guess she's in love."

"He must be a good-for-nothing lover to make his mistress look so sad. If I were you, I'd give him up, Miss Crowe."

"I didn't know I looked sad," said Lizzie.

"You don't now," said Miss Cooper. "You're smiling and blushing. A'n't she blushing, Mr Bruce?"

"I think Miss Crowe has no more than her natural color," said Bruce, dropping his eye-glass. "What have you been doing all this while since we parted?"

"All this while? It's only six weeks. I don't know. Nothing. What have you?"

"I've been doing nothing, too. It's hard work."

"Have you been to any more parties?"

"Not one."

"Any more sleigh-rides?"

"Yes. I took one more dreary drive all alone,—over that same road, you know. And I stopped at the farm-house again, and saw the old woman we had the talk with. She remembered us, and asked me what had become of the young lady who was with me before. I told her you were gone home, but that I hoped soon to go and see you. So she sent you her love"——

"Oh, how nice!" exclaimed Lizzie.

"Wasn't it? And then she made a certain little speech; I won't repeat it, or we shall have Miss Cooper talking about your blushes again."

"I know," cried the lady in question: "she said she was very"——

"Very what?" said Lizzie.

"Very h-a-n-d——what everyone says."

"Very handy?" asked Lizzie. "I'm sure no one ever said that."

"Of course," said Bruce; "and I answered what everyone answers."

"Have you seen Mrs Littlefield lately?"

"Several times. I called on her the day before I left town, to see if she had any message for you."

"Oh, thank you! I hope she's well."

"Oh, she's as jolly as ever. She sent you her love, and hoped you would come back to Leatherborough very soon again. I told her, that, however it might be with the first message, the second should be a joint one from both of us."

"You're very kind. I should like very much to go again.— Do you like Mrs Littlefield?"

"Like her? Yes. Don't you? She's thought a very pleasing woman."

"Oh, she's very nice.—I don't think she has much conversation."

"Ah, I'm afraid you mean she doesn't backbite. We've always found plenty to talk about."

"That's a very significant tone. What, for instance?"

"Well, we *have* talked about Miss Crowe."

"Oh, you have? Do you call that having plenty to talk about?"

"We *have* talked about Mr Bruce,—haven't we, Elizabeth?" said Miss Cooper, who had her own notion of being agreeable.

It was not an altogether bad notion, perhaps; but Bruce found her interruptions rather annoying, and insensibly allowed them to shorten his visit. Yet, as it was, he sat till eleven o'clock,—a stay quite unprecedented at Glenham.

When he left the house, he went splashing down the road with a very elastic tread, springing over the starlit puddles, and trolling out some sentimental ditty. He reached the inn, and went up to his sister's sitting-room.

"Why, Robert, where have you been all this while?" said Miss Bruce.

"At Dr Cooper's."

"Dr Cooper's? I should think you had! Who's Dr Cooper?"

"Where Miss Crowe's staying."

"Miss Crowe? Ah, Mrs Littlefield's friend! Is she as pretty as ever?"

"Prettier,—prettier,—prettier. *Ta-ra-ta! tara-ta!*"

"Oh, Robert, do stop that singing! You'll rouse the whole house."

V

LATE one afternoon, at dusk, about three weeks after Mr Bruce's arrival, Lizzie was sitting alone by the fire, in Miss Cooper's parlor, musing, as became the place and hour. The Doctor and his sister came in, dressed for a lecture.

"I'm sorry you won't go, my dear," said Miss Cooper. "It's a most interesting subject: 'A Year of the War.' All the battles and things described, you know."

"I'm tired of war," said Lizzie.

"Well, well, if you're tired of the war, we'll leave you in peace. Kiss me good-bye. What's the matter? You look sick. You are homesick, a'n't you?"

"No, no,—I'm very well."

"Would you like me to stay at home with you?"

"Oh, no! pray, don't!"

"Well, we'll tell you all about it. Will they have programmes, James? I'll bring her a programme.—But you really feel as if you were going to be ill. Feel of her skin, James."

"No, you needn't, Sir," said Lizzie. "How queer of you, Miss Cooper! I'm perfectly well."

And at last her friends departed. Before long the servant came with the lamp, ushering Mr Mackenzie.

"Good evening, Miss," said he. "Bad news from Mrs Ford."

"Bad news?"

"Yes, Miss. I've just got a letter stating that Mr John is growing worse and worse, and that they look for his death from hour to hour.—It's very sad," he added, as Elizabeth was silent.

"Yes, it's very sad," said Lizzie.

"I thought you'd like to hear it."

"Thank you."

"He was a very noble young fellow," pursued Mr Mackenzie.

Lizzie made no response.

"There's the letter," said Mr Mackenzie, handing it over to her.

Lizzie opened it.

"How long she is reading it!" thought her visitor. "You can't see so far from the light, can you, Miss?"

"Yes," said Lizzie.—"His poor mother! Poor woman!"

"Aye, indeed, Miss,—she's the one to be pitied."

"Yes, she's the one to be pitied," said Lizzie. "Well!" and she gave him back the letter.

"I thought you'd like to see it," said Mackenzie, drawing on his gloves; and then, after a pause,—"I'll call again, Miss, if I hear anything more. Good night!"

Lizzie got up and lowered the light, and then went back to her sofa by the fire.

Half an hour passed; it went slowly; but it passed. Still lying there in the dark room on the sofa, Lizzie heard a ring at the door-bell, a man's voice and a man's tread in the hall. She rose and went to the lamp. As she turned it up, the parlor door opened. Bruce came in.

"I was sitting in the dark," said Lizzie; "but when I heard you coming, I raised the light."

"Are you afraid of me?" said Bruce.

"Oh, no! I'll put it down again. Sit down."

"I saw your friends going out," pursued Bruce; "so I knew I should find you alone.—What are you doing here in the dark?"

"I've just received very bad news from Mrs Ford about her son. He's much worse, and will probably not live.

"Is it possible?"

"I was thinking about that."

"Dear me! Well, that's a sad subject. I'm told he was a very fine young man."

"He was,—very," said Lizzie.

Bruce was silent awhile. He was a stranger to the young officer, and felt that he had nothing to offer beyond the commonplace expressions of sympathy and surprise. Nor had he exactly the measure of his companion's interest in him.

"If he dies," said Lizzie, "it will be under great injustice."

"Ah! what do you mean?"

"There wasn't a braver man in the army."

"I suppose not."

"And, oh, Mr Bruce," continued Lizzie, "he was so clever and good and generous! I wish you had known him."

"I wish I had. But what do you mean by injustice? Were these qualities denied him?"

"No indeed! Everyone that looked at him could see that he was perfect."

"Where's the injustice, then? It ought to be enough for him that you should think so highly of him."

"Oh, he knew that," said Lizzie.

Bruce was a little puzzled by his companion's manner. He watched her, as she sat with her cheek on her hand, looking at the fire. There was a long pause. Either they were too friendly or too thoughtful for the silence to be embarrassing. Bruce broke it at last.

"Miss Crowe," said he, "on a certain occasion, some time ago, when you first heard of Mr Ford's wounds, I offered you my company, with the wish to console you as far as I might for what seemed a considerable shock. It was, perhaps, a bold offer for so new a friend; but, nevertheless, in it even then my heart spoke. You turned me off. Will you let me repeat it? Now, with a better right, will you let me speak out all my heart?"

Lizzie heard this speech, which was delivered in a slow and hesitating tone, without looking up or moving her head, except, perhaps, at the words "turned me off". After Bruce had ceased, she still kept her position.

"You'll not turn me off now?" added her companion.

She dropped her hand, raised her head, and looked at him a moment: he thought he saw the glow of tears in her eyes. Then she sank back upon the sofa with her face in the shadow of the mantelpiece.

"I don't understand you, Mr Bruce," said she.

"Ah, Elizabeth! am I such a poor speaker. How shall I make it plain? When I saw your friends leave home half an hour ago, and reflected that you would probably be alone, I determined to go right in and have a talk with you that I've long been wanting to have. But first I walked half a mile up the road, thinking hard,—thinking how I should say what I had to say. I made up my mind to nothing, but that somehow or other I should say it. I would trust,—I *do* trust your frankness, kindness, and sympathy, to a feeling corresponding to my own. Do you understand that feeling? Do you know that I love you? I do, I do, I do! You *must* know it. If you don't, I solemnly swear it. I solemnly ask you, Elizabeth, to take me for your husband."

While Bruce said these words, he rose, with their rising passion, and came and stood before Lizzie. Again she was motionless.

"Does it take you so long to think?" said he, trying to read her indistinct features; and he sat down on the sofa beside her and took her hand.

At last Lizzie spoke.

"Are you sure," said she, "that you love me?"

"As sure as that I breathe. Now, Elizabeth, make me as sure that I am loved in return."

"It seems very strange, Mr Bruce," said Lizzie.

"What seems strange? Why should it? For a month I've been trying, in a hundred dumb ways, to make it plain: and now, when I swear it, it only seems strange!"

"What do you love me for?"

"For? For yourself, Elizabeth."

"Myself? I am nothing."

"I love you for what you are,—for your deep, kind heart, —for being so perfectly a woman."

Lizzie drew away her hand, and her lover rose and stood before her again. But now she looked up into his face, questioning when she should have answered, drinking strength from his entreaties for her replies. There he stood before her, in the glow of the firelight, in all his gentlemanhood, for her to accept or reject. She slowly rose and gave him the hand she had withdrawn.

"Mr Bruce, I shall be very proud to love you," she said.

And then, as if this effort was beyond her strength, she half staggered back to the sofa again. And still holding her hand, he sat down beside her. And there they were still sitting when they heard the Doctor and his sister come in.

For three days Elizabeth saw nothing of Mr Mackenzie. At last, on the fourth day, passing his office in the village, she went in and asked for him. He came out of his little back parlour with his mouth full and a beaming face.

"Good-day, Miss Crowe, and good news!"

"*Good* news?" cried Lizzie.

"Capital!" said he, looking hard at her, while he put on his spectacles. "She writes that Mr John—won't you take a seat?

—has taken a sudden and unexpected turn for the better. Now's the moment to save him; it's an equal risk. They were to start for the North the second day after date. The surgeon comes with them. So they'll be home—of course they'll travel slowly—in four or five days. Yes, Miss, it's a remarkable Providence. And that noble young man will be spared to the country, and to those who love him, as I do."

"I had better go back to the house and have it got ready," said Lizzie, for an answer.

"Yes, Miss, I think you had. In fact, Mrs Ford made that request."

The request was obeyed. That same day Lizzie went home. For two days she found it her interest to overlook, assiduously, a general sweeping, scrubbing, and provisioning. She allowed herself no idle moment until bed-time. Then——But I would rather not be the chamberlain of her agony. It was the easier to work, as Mr Bruce had gone to Leatherborough on business.

On the fourth evening, at twilight, John Ford was borne up to the door on his stretcher, with his mother stalking beside him in rigid grief, and kind, silent friends pressing about with helping hands.

> "Home they brought her warrior dead,
>   She nor swooned nor uttered cry."

It was, indeed, almost a question, whether Jack was not dead. Death is not thinner, paler, stiller. Lizzie moved about like one in a dream. Of course, when there are so many sympathetic friends, a man's family has nothing to do,—except exercise a little self-control. The women huddled Mrs Ford to bed; rest was imperative; she was killing herself. And it was significant of her weakness that she did not resent this advice. In greeting her, Lizzie felt as if she were embracing the stone image on the top of a sepulchre. She, too, had her cares anticipated. Good Doctor Cooper and his sister stationed themselves at the young man's couch.

The Doctor prophesied wondrous things of the change of climate; he was certain of a recovery. Lizzie found herself very shortly dealt with as an obstacle to this consummation. Access to John was prohibited. "Perfect stillness, you know, my dear," whispered Miss Cooper, opening his chamber door on a crack, in a pair of very creaking shoes. So for the first evening that her old friend was at home Lizzie caught but a glimpse of his pale, senseless face, as she hovered outside the long train of his attendants. If we may suppose any of these kind people to have had eyes for aught but the sufferer, we may be sure that they saw another visage equally sad and white. The sufferer? It was hardly Jack, after all.

When Lizzie was turned from Jack's door, she took a covering from a heap of draperies that had been hurriedly tossed down in the hall: it was an old army blanket. She wrapped it round her, and went out on the verandah. It was nine o'clock; but the darkness was filled with light. A great wanton wind— the ghost of the raw blast which travels by day—had arisen, bearing long, soft gusts of inland spring. Scattered clouds were hurrying across the white sky. The bright moon, careering in their midst, seemed to have wandered forth in frantic quest of the hidden stars.

Lizzie nestled her head in the blanket, and sat down on the steps. A strange earthy smell lingered in that faded old rug, and with it a faint perfume of tobacco. Instantly the young girl's senses were transported as they had never been before to those far-off Southern battlefields. She saw men lying in swamps, puffing their kindly pipes, drawing their blankets closer, canopied with the same luminous dusk that shone down upon her comfortable weakness. Her mind wandered amid these scenes till recalled to the present by the swinging of the garden gate. She heard a firm, well-known tread crunching the gravel. Mr Bruce came up the path. As he drew near the steps, Lizzie arose. The blanket fell back from her head, and Bruce started at recognizing her.

"Hullo! You, Elizabeth? What's the matter?"

Lizzie made no answer.

"Are you one of Mr Ford's watchers?" he continued, coming up the steps; "how is he?"

Still she was silent. Bruce put out his hands to take hers, and bent forward as if to kiss her. She half shook him off, and retreated toward the door.

"Good heavens!" cried Bruce; "what's the matter? Are you moonstruck? Can't you speak?"

"No,—no,—not to-night," said Lizzie, in a choking voice. "Go away,—go away!"

She stood holding the door-handle, and motioning him off. He hesitated a moment, and then advanced. She opened the door rapidly, and went in. He heard her lock it. He stood looking at it stupidly for some time, and then slowly turned round and walked down the steps.

The next morning Lizzie arose with the early dawn, and came downstairs. She went to the room where Jack lay, and gently opened the door. Miss Cooper was dozing in her chair. Lizzie crossed the threshold, and stole up to the bed. Poor Ford lay peacefully sleeping. There was his old face, after all, —his strong, honest features refined, but not weakened, by pain. Lizzie softly drew up a low chair, and sat down beside him. She gazed into his face,—the dear honored face into which she had so often gazed in health. It was strangely handsomer: body stood for less. It seemed to Lizzie, that, as the fabric of her lover's soul was more clearly revealed,—the veil of the temple rent wellnigh in twain,—she could read the justification of all her old worship. One of Jack's hands lay outside the sheets,—those strong, supple fingers, once so cunning in workmanship, so frank in friendship, now thinner and whiter than her own. After looking at it for some time, Lizzie gently grasped it. Jack slowly opened his eyes. Lizzie's heart began to throb; it was as if the stillness of the sanctuary had given a sign. At first there was no recognition in the young man's gaze.

Then the dull pupils began visibly to brighten. There came to his lips the commencement of that strange moribund smile which seems so ineffably satirical of the things of this world. O imposing spectacle of death! O blessed soul, marked for promotion! What earthly favor is like thine? Lizzie sank down on her knees, and, still clasping John's hand, bent closer over him.

"Jack,—dear, dear Jack," she whispered, "do you know me?"

The smile grew more intense. The poor fellow drew out his other hand, and slowly, feebly placed it on Lizzie's head, stroking down her hair with his fingers.

"Yes, yes," she murmured; "you know me, don't you? I am Lizzie, Jack. Don't you remember Lizzie?"

Ford moved his lips inaudibly, and went on patting her head.

"This is home, you know," said Lizzie; "this is Glenham. You haven't forgotten Glenham? You are with your mother and me and your friends. Dear, darling Jack!"

Still he went on, stroking her head; and his feeble lips tried to emit some sound. Lizzie laid her head down on the pillow beside his own, and still his hand lingered caressingly on her hair.

"Yes, you know me," she pursued; "you are with your friends now forever,—with those who will love and take care of you, oh, forever!"

"I'm very badly wounded," murmured Jack, close to her ear.

"Yes, yes, my dear boy, but your wounds are healing. I will love you and nurse you forever."

"Yes, Lizzie, our old promise," said Jack: and his hand fell upon her neck, and with its feeble pressure he drew her closer, and she wet his face with her tears.

Then Miss Cooper, awakening, rose and drew Lizzie away.

"I am sure you excite him, my dear. It is best he should have none of his family near him,—persons with whom he has associations, you know."

Here the Doctor was heard gently tapping on the window, and Lizzie went round to the door to admit him.

She did not see Jack again all day. Two or three times she ventured into the room, but she was banished by a frown, or a finger raised to the lips. She waylaid the Doctor frequently. He was blithe and cheerful, certain of Jack's recovery. This good man used to exhibit as much moral elation at the prospect of a cure as an orthodox believer at that of a new convert: it was one more body gained from the Devil. He assured Lizzie that the change of scene and climate had already begun to tell: the fever was lessening, the worst symptoms disappearing. He answered Lizzie's reiterated desire to do something by directions to keep the house quiet and the sick-room empty.

Soon after breakfast, Miss Dawes, a neighbor, came in to relieve Miss Cooper, and this indefatigable lady transferred her attention to Mrs Ford. Action was forbidden her. Miss Cooper was delighted for once to be able to lay down the law to her vigorous neighbor, of whose fine judgment she had always stood in awe. Having bullied Mrs Ford into taking her breakfast in the little sitting-room, she closed the doors, and prepared for "a good long talk." Lizzie was careful not to break in upon this interview. She had bidden her patroness good morning, asked after her health, and received one of her temperate osculations. As she passed the invalid's door, Doctor Cooper came out and asked her to go and look for a certain roll of bandages, in Mr John's trunk, which had been carried into another room. Lizzie hastened to perform this task. In fumbling through the contents of the trunk, she came across a packet of letters in a well-known feminine hand-writing. She pocketed it, and, after disposing of the bandages, went to her own room, locked the door, and sat down to examine the letters. Between reading and thinking and sighing and (in spite of herself) smiling, this process took the whole morning. As she came down to dinner, she encountered Mrs Ford and Miss

Cooper, emerging from the sitting-room, the good long talk being only just concluded.

"How do you feel, Ma'am?" she asked of the elder lady,— "rested?"

For all answer Mrs Ford gave a look—I had almost said a scowl—so hard, so cold, so reproachful, that Lizzie was transfixed. But suddenly its sickening meaning was revealed to her. She turned to Miss Cooper, who stood pale and fluttering beside the mistress, her everlasting smile glazed over with a piteous, deprecating glance; and I fear her eyes flashed out the same message of angry scorn they had just received. These telegraphic operations are very rapid. The ladies hardly halted: the next moment found them seated at the dinner-table with Miss Cooper scrutinising her napkin-mark and Mrs Ford saying grace.

Dinner was eaten in silence. When it was over, Lizzie returned to her own room. Miss Cooper went home, and Mrs Ford went to her son. Lizzie heard the firm low click of the lock as she closed the door. Why did she lock it? There was something fatal in the silence that followed. The plot of her little tragedy thickened. Be it so: she would act her part with the rest. For the second time in her experience, her mind was lightened by the intervention of Mrs Ford. Before the scorn of her own conscience, (which never came), before Jack's deepest reproach, she was ready to bow down,—but not before that long-faced Nemesis in black silk. The leaven of resentment began to work. She leaned back in her chair, and folded her arms, brave to await results. But before long she fell asleep. She was aroused by a knock at her chamber-door. The afternoon was far gone. Miss Dawes stood without.

"Elizabeth, Mr John wants very much to see you, with his love. Come down very gently: his mother is lying down. Will you sit with him while I take my dinner?—Better? Yes, ever so much."

Lizzie betook herself with trembling haste to Jack's bedside.

He was propped up with pillows. His pale cheeks were slightly flushed. His eyes were bright. He raised himself, and, for such feeble arms, gave Lizzie a long, strong embrace.

"I've not seen you all day, Lizzie," said he. "Where have you been?"

"Dear Jack, they wouldn't let me come near you. I begged and prayed. And I wanted so to go to you in the army; but I couldn't. I wish, I wish I had!"

"You wouldn't have liked it, Lizzie. I'm glad you didn't. It's a bad, bad place."

He lay quietly, holding her hands and gazing at her.

"Can I do anything for you, dear?" asked the young girl. "I would work my life out. I'm so glad you're better!"

It was some time before Jack answered,—

"Lizzie," said he, at last, "I sent for you to look at you.— You are more wondrously beautiful than ever. Your hair is brown,—like—like nothing; your eyes are blue; your neck is white. Well, well!"

He lay perfectly motionless, but for his eyes. They wandered over her with a kind of peaceful glee, like sunbeams playing on a statue. Poor Ford lay, indeed, not unlike an old wounded Greek, who at falling dusk has crawled into a temple to die, steeping the last dull interval in idle admiration of sculptured Artemis.

"Ah, Lizzie, this is already heaven!" he murmured.

"It will be heaven when you get well," whispered Lizzie.

He smiled into her eyes:—

"You say more than you mean. There should be perfect truth between us. Dear Lizzie, I am not going to get well. They are all very much mistaken. I am going to die. I've done my work. Death makes up for everything. My great pain is in leaving you. But you, too, will die one of these days; remember that. In all pain and sorrow, remember that."

Lizzie was able to reply only by the tightening grasp of her hands.

"But there is something more," pursued Jack. "Life *is* as good as death. Your heart has found its true keeper; so we shall all three be happy. Tell him I bless him and honor him. Tell him God, too, blesses him. Shake hands with him for me," said Jack, feebly moving his pale fingers. "My mother," he went on—"be very kind to her. She will have great grief, but she will not die of it. She'll live to great age. Now, Lizzie, I can't talk any more; I wanted to say farewell. You'll keep me farewell,—you'll stay with me awhile,—won't you? I'll look at you till the last. For a little while you'll be mine, holding my hands—so—until death parts us."

Jack kept his promise. His eyes were fixed in a firm gaze long after the sense had left them.

In the early dawn of the next day, Elizabeth left her sleepless bed, opened the window, and looked out on the wide prospect, still cool and dim with departing night. It offered freshness and peace to her hot head and restless heart. She dressed herself hastily, crept downstairs, passed the death-chamber, and stole out of the quiet house. She turned away from the still sleeping village and walked towards the open country. She went a long way without knowing it. The sun had risen high when she bethought herself to turn. As she came back along the brightening highway, and drew near home, she saw a tall figure standing beneath the budding trees of the garden, hesitating, apparently, whether to open the gate. Lizzie came upon him almost before he had seen her. Bruce's first movement was to put out his hands, as any lover might; but as Lizzie raised her veil, he dropped them.

"Yes, Mr Bruce," said Lizzie, "I'll give you my hand once more,—in farewell."

"Elizabeth!" cried Bruce, half stupefied, "in God's name, what do you mean by these crazy speeches?"

"I mean well. I mean kindly and humanely to you. And I mean justice to my old—old love."

She went to him, took his listless hand, without looking

into his wild, smitten face, shook it passionately, and then, wrenching her own from his grasp, opened the gate and let it swing behind her.

"No! no! no!" she almost shrieked, turning about in the path. "I forbid you to follow me!"

But for all that, he went in.

A LANDSCAPE-PAINTER

Do you remember how, a dozen years ago, a number of our friends were startled by the report of the rupture of young Locksley's engagement with Miss Leary? This event made some noise in its day. Both parties possessed certain claims to distinction: Locksley in his wealth, which was believed to be enormous, and the young lady in her beauty, which was in truth very great. I used to hear that her lover was fond of comparing her to the Venus of Milo; and, indeed, if you can imagine the mutilated goddess with her full complement of limbs, dressed out by Madame de Crinoline, and engaged in small-talk beneath the drawing-room chandelier, you may obtain a vague notion of Miss Josephine Leary. Locksley, you remember, was rather a short man, dark, and not particularly good-looking; and when he walked about with his betrothed it was half a matter of surprise that he should have ventured to propose to a young lady of such heroic proportions. Miss Leary had the gray eyes and auburn hair which I have always attributed to the famous statue. The one defect in her face, in spite of an expression of great candour and sweetness, was a certain lack of animation. What it was besides her beauty that attracted Locksley I never discovered; perhaps, since his attachment was so short-lived, it was her beauty alone. I say that his attachment was of brief duration, because the break was understood to have come from him. Both he and Miss Leary very wisely held their tongues on the matter; but among their friends and enemies it of course received a hundred explanations. That most popular with Locksley's well-wishers was, that he had backed out (these events are discussed, you know, in fashionable circles very much as an expected prize-fight which has miscarried is canvassed in reunions of another kind) only on flagrant evidence of the lady's—what, faithlessness?—on overwhelming proof of the most *mercenary* spirit on the part of Miss Leary. You see, our friend was held capable of doing battle for an "idea." It must be owned that this was a novel charge; but, for myself, having long known Mrs Leary, the mother, who was a widow with four daughters, to be an inveterate old screw, it was not impossible for me to believe that her first-born had also shown the cloven foot. I suppose that the young lady's family had, on their own side, a very plausible version of their disappointment. It was, however, soon made up to them by Josephine's marriage with a gentleman of expectations very nearly as brilliant as those of her old suitor. And what was *his* compensation? That is precisely my story.

Locksley disappeared, as you will remember, from public view. The events above alluded to happened in March. On calling at his lodgings in April I was told he had gone to the country. But toward the last of May I met him. He told me that he was on the look-out for a quiet, unfrequented place at the seaside, where he might rusticate and sketch. He was looking very poorly. I suggested Newport, and I remember he hardly had the energy to smile at the simple joke. We parted without my having been able to satisfy him, and for a very long time I quite lost sight of him. He died seven years ago, at the age of thirty-five. For five years, accordingly, he managed to shield his life from the eyes of men. Through circumstances which I need not go into, a good many of his personal belongings have become mine. You will remember that he was a man of what are called cultivated tastes; that is, he was fond of reading, wrote a little, and painted a good deal. He wrote some rather amateurish verse, but he produced a number of remarkable paintings. He left a mass of papers, on many subjects, few of which are calculated to be generally interesting. A few of them, however, I highly prize—that portion which constitutes his private diary. It extends from his twenty-fifth to his thirtieth year, at which period it breaks off suddenly. If you will come to my house I will show you such of his pictures and sketches as I possess, and, I trust, convert you to my opinion that he had in him the stuff of a charming artist. Meanwhile I will place before you the last hundred pages of his diary, as an answer to your inquiry regarding the ultimate view taken by the great Nemesis of his treatment of Miss Leary—his scorn of the magnificent Venus Victrix. The recent passing away of the one person who had a voice paramount to mine in the disposal of Locksley's effects enables me to act without reserve.

Chowderville, June 9th.—I have been sitting some minutes, pen in hand, wondering whether on this new earth, beneath this new sky, I had better resume this occasional history of nothing at all. I think I will at all events make the experiment. If we fail, as Lady Macbeth remarks, we fail. I find my entries have been longest when I have had least to say. I doubt not, therefore, that, once I have had a sufficient dose of dulness, I shall sit scribbling from morning till night. If nothing happens—— But my prophetic soul tells me that something *will* happen. I am determined that something shall—if it be nothing else than that I paint a picture.

When I came up to bed half-an-hour ago I was deadly sleepy. Now, after looking out of the window a little, my brain is immensely refreshed, and I feel as if I could write till morning. But, unfortunately, I have nothing to write about. And then, if I expect to rise early, I must turn in betimes. The whole village is asleep, godless metropolitan that I am! The lamps on the square, outside, flicker in the wind; there is nothing abroad but the blue darkness and the smell of the rising tide. I have spent the whole day on my legs, trudging from one side of the peninsula to the other. What a trump is old Mrs Monkhouse, to have thought of this place! I must write her a letter of passionate thanks. Never before have I seen such a pretty little coast—never before have I been so taken with wave and rock and cloud. I am filled with ecstasy at the life, light, and transparency of the air. I am enamoured of all the moods and tenses of the ocean; and as yet, I suppose, I have not seen half of them. I came in to supper hungry, weary, footsore, sunburnt, dirty—happier, in short, than I have been for a twelvemonth. And now, if you please, for the prodigies of the brush!

June 11th.—Another day afoot, and also afloat. I resolved this morning to leave this abominable little tavern; I can't stand my feather-bed another night. I determined to find some other prospect than the town-pump and the "drug-store." I questioned my host, after breakfast, as to the possibility of getting lodgings in any of the outlying farms and cottages. But my host either did not or would not know anything about the matter. So I resolved to wander forth and seek my fortune —to roam inquisitive through the neighbourhood and appeal to the indigenous sentiment of hospitality. But never have I seen a folk so devoid of this amiable quality. By dinner-time I had given up in despair. After dinner I strolled down to the harbour, which is close at hand. The brightness and breeziness of the water tempted me to hire a boat and resume my explorations. I procured an old tub, with a short stump of a mast, which, being planted quite in the centre, gave the craft much the appearance of an inverted mushroom. I made for what I took to be, and what is, an island, lying long and low, some four or five miles over against the town. I sailed for half-an-hour directly before the wind, and at last found myself aground on the shelving beach of a quiet little cove. Such a dear little cove—so bright, so still, so warm, so remote from Chowderville, which lay in the distance, white and semi-circular! I leaped ashore, and dropped my anchor. Before me rose a steep cliff, crowned with an old ruined fort or tower. I made my way up, and round to the landward entrance. The fort is a hollow old shell; looking upwards, from the beach, you see the harmless blue sky through the gaping loopholes. Its interior is choked with rocks and brambles and masses of fallen masonry. I scrambled up to the parapet, and obtained a noble sea-view. Beyond the broad bay I saw the miniature town and country mapped out before me; and on the other hand, I saw the infinite Atlantic—over which, by the by, all the pretty things are brought from Paris. I spent the whole afternoon in wandering hither and thither on the hills that encircle the little cove in which I had landed, heedless of the minutes and the miles, watching the sailing clouds and the flitting, gleaming sails, listening to the musical attrition of the tidal pebbles, passing the time anyhow. The only particular sensation I remember was that of being ten years old again, together with a general impression of Saturday afternoon, of the liberty to go in wading or even swimming, and of the prospect of limping home in the dusk with a wondrous story of having almost caught a turtle. When I returned I found—but I know very well what I found, and I need hardly repeat it here for my mortification. Heaven knows I never was a practical character. What thought I about the tide? There lay the old tub, high and dry, with the rusty anchor protruding from the flat green stones and the shallow puddles left by the receding wave. Moving the boat an inch, much more a dozen yards, was quite beyond my strength. I slowly reascended the cliff, to see if from its summit any help was discernible. None was within sight, and I was about to go down again, in profound dejection, when I saw a trim little sail-boat shoot out from behind a neighbouring bluff, and advance along the shore. I quickened pace. On reaching the beach I found the newcomer standing out about a hundred yards. The man at the helm appeared to regard me with some interest. With a mute prayer that his disposition might not be hostile—he didn't look like a wild islander—I invited him by voice and gesture to make for a little point of rocks a short distance above us, where I proceeded to join him. I told him my story, and he readily took me aboard. He was a civil old gentleman, of the seafaring sort, who appeared to be cruising about in the evening-breeze for his pleasure. On landing I visited the proprietor of my old tub, related my misadventure, and offered to pay damages if the boat shall turn out in the morning to have sustained any. Meanwhile, I suppose, it is held secure against the next tidal revolution, however violent.

But for my old gentleman. I have decidedly picked up an acquaintance, if not made a friend. I gave him a very good cigar, and before we reached home we had become thoroughly intimate. In exchange for my cigar he gave me his name; and there was that in his tone which seemed to imply that I had by no means the worst of the exchange. His name is Richard Quarterman, "though most people," he added, "call me Cap'n, for respect." He then proceeded to inquire my own titles and pretensions. I told him no lies, but I told him only half the truth; and if he chooses to indulge mentally in any romantic understatements, why, he is welcome, and bless his simple heart! The fact is, I have simply broken with the past. I have decided, coolly and calmly, as I believe, that it is necessary to my success, or, at any rate, to my happiness, to abjure for a while my conventional self, and to assume a simple, natural character. How can a man be simple and natural who is known to have a large income? That is the supreme curse. It's bad enough to have it; to be known to have it, to be known only because you have it, is most damnable. I suppose I am too proud to be successfully rich. Let me see how poverty will serve my turn. I have taken a fresh start—I have determined to stand upon my merits. If they fail me I shall fall back upon my dollars, but with God's help I will test them, and see what kind of stuff I am made of. To be young, strong and poor— such in this blessed nineteenth century, is the great basis of solid success. I have resolved to take at least one brief draught from the founts of inspiration of my time. I replied to Captain Quarterman with such reservations as a brief survey of these principles dictated. What a luxury to pass in a poor man's mind for his brother! I begin to respect myself. Thus much the Captain knows: that I am an educated man, with a taste for painting; that I have come hither for the purpose of studying and sketching coast-scenery; toning myself up with the sea air. I have reason to believe, moreover, that he suspects me of limited means and of being of a very frugal mind. Amen! *Vogue la galère!* But the point of my story is in his very hospitable offer of lodgings—I had been telling him of my want of success in the morning in the pursuit of the same. He is a queer mixture of the gentleman of the old school and the hot-headed merchant-captain.

"Young man," said he, after taking several meditative puffs of his cigar, "I don't see the point of your living in a tavern when there are folks about you with more house-room than they know what to do with. A tavern is only half a house, just as one of these new-fashioned screw-propellers is only half a ship. Suppose you walk round and take a look at my place. I own quite a respectable tenement over yonder to the left of the town. Do you see that old wharf with the tumble-down warehouses, and the long row of elms behind it? I live right in the midst of the elms. We have the sweetest little garden in the world, stretching down to the water's edge. It's all as quiet as anything can be, short of a churchyard. The back windows, you know, overlook the harbour; and you can see twenty miles up the bay, and fifty miles out to sea. You can paint to yourself there the livelong day, with no more fear of intrusion than if you were out yonder at the light-ship. There's no one but myself and my daughter, who's a perfect lady, sir. She teaches music in a young ladies' school. You see, money's an object, as they say. We have never taken boarders yet, because none ever came in our track; but I guess we can learn the ways. I suppose you've boarded before; you can put us up to a thing or two."

There was something so kindly and honest in the old man's weather-beaten face, something so friendly in his address, that

I forthwith struck a bargain with him, subject to his daughter's approval. I am to have her answer to-morrow. This same daughter strikes me as rather a dark spot in the picture. Teacher in a young ladies' school—probably the establishment of which Mrs Monkhouse spoke to me. I suppose she's over thirty. I think I know the species.

June 12*th*, A.M.—I have really nothing to do but to scribble. "Barkis is willing." Captain Quarterman brought me word this morning that his daughter makes no objection. I am to report this evening; but I shall send my slender baggage in an hour or two.

P.M.—Here I am, domiciled, almost domesticated. The house is less than a mile from the inn, and reached by a very pleasant road, which skirts the harbour. At about six o'clock I presented myself; Captain Quarterman had described the place. A very civil old negress admitted me, and ushered me into the garden, where I found my friends watering their flowers. The old man was in his house-coat and slippers—he gave me a cordial welcome. There is something delightfully easy in his manners—and in Miss Quarterman's, too for that matter. She received me very nicely. The late Mrs Quarterman was probably a superior being. As for the young lady's being thirty, she is about twenty-four. She wore a fresh white dress, with a blue ribbon on her neck, and a rosebud in her button-hole—or whatever corresponds to the button-hole on the feminine bosom. I thought I discerned in this costume, a vague intention of courtesy, of gaiety, of celebrating my arrival. I don't believe Miss Quarterman wears white muslin every day. She shook hands with me, and made me a pleasing little speech about their taking me in. "We have never had any inmates before," said she; "and we are consequently new to the business. I don't know what you expect. I hope you don't expect a great deal. You must ask for anything you want. If we can give it, we shall be very glad to do so; if we can't, I give you warning that we shall simply tell you so." Brava, Miss Quarterman!

The best of it is, that she is decidedly beautiful—and in the grand manner; tall, and with roundness in her lines. What is the orthodox description of a pretty girl?—white and red? Miss Quarterman is not a pretty girl, she is a handsome woman. She leaves an impression of black and red; that is, she is a brunette with colour. She has a great deal of wavy black hair, which encircles her head like a dusky glory, a smoky halo. Her eyebrows, too, are black, but her eyes themselves are of a rich blue gray, the colour of those slate-cliffs which I saw yesterday, weltering under the tide. She has perfect teeth, and her smile is almost unnaturally brilliant. Her chin is surpassingly round. She has a capital movement, too, and looked uncommonly well as she strolled in the garden-path with a big spray of geranium lifted to her nose. She has very little to say, apparently; but when she speaks, it is to the point, and if the point suggests it, she doesn't hesitate to laugh very musically. Indeed, if she is not talkative, it is not from timidity. Is it from indifference? Time will elucidate this, as well as other mysteries. I cling to the hypothesis that she is amiable. She is, moreover, intelligent; she is probably fond of keeping herself *to* herself, as the phrase is, and is even, possibly, very proud. She is, in short, a woman of character. There you are, Miss Quarterman, at as full length as I can paint you. After tea she gave us some music in the parlour. I confess that I was more taken with the picture of the dusky little room, lighted by the single candle on the piano, and by her stately way of sitting at the instrument, than by the quality of her playing, though that is evidently high.

June 18th.—I have now been here almost a week. I occupy two very pleasant rooms. My painting-room is a large and rather bare apartment, with a very good north-light. I have decked it out with a few old prints and sketches, and have already grown very fond of it. When I had disposed my artistic odds and ends so as to make it look as much like a studio as possible, I called in my hosts. The Captain snuffed about, silently, for some moments, and then inquired hopefully if I had ever tried my hand at a ship. On learning that I had not yet got to ships, he relapsed into a prudent reserve. His daughter smiled and questioned, very graciously, and called everything beautiful and delightful; which rather disappointed me, as I had taken her to be a woman of some originality. She is rather a puzzle. Or is she, indeed, a very commonplace person, and the fault in me, who am for ever taking women to mean a great deal more than their Maker intended? Regarding Miss Quarterman I have collected a few facts. She is not twenty-four, but twenty-seven years old. She has taught music ever since she was twenty, in a large boarding-school just out of the town, where she originally obtained her education. Her salary in this establishment, which is, I believe, a tolerably flourishing one, and the proceeds of a few additional lessons, constitute the chief revenues of the household. But the Captain fortunately owns his house, and his needs and habits are of the simplest kind. What does he or his daughter know of the great worldly theory of necessities, the great worldly scale of pleasures? The young lady's only luxuries are a subscription to the circulating library, and an occasional walk on the beach, which, like one of Miss Brontë's heroines, she paces in company with an old Newfoundland dog. I am afraid she is sadly ignorant. She reads nothing but novels. I am bound to believe, however, that she has derived from the perusal of these works a certain second-hand acquaintance with life. "I read all the novels I can get," she said yesterday; "but I only like the good ones. I do so like *The Missing Bride,* which I have just finished." I must set her to work at some of the masters. I should like some of those fretful daughters of gold, in New York, to see how this woman lives. I wish, too, that half a dozen of *ces messieurs* of the clubs might take a peep at the present way of life of their humble servant. We breakfast at eight o'clock. Immediately afterwards Miss Quarterman, in a shabby old bonnet and shawl, starts off to school. If the weather is fine the Captain goes a-fishing, and I am left quite to my own devices. Twice I have accompanied the old man. The second time I was lucky enough to catch a big blue-fish, which we had for dinner. The Captain is an excellent specimen of the pure navigator, with his loose blue clothes, his ultra-divergent legs, his crisp white hair, his jolly thick-skinned visage. He comes of a sea-faring English race. There is more or less of the ship's cabin in the general aspect of this antiquated house. I have heard the wind whistle about its walls, on two or three occasions, in true mid-ocean style. And then the illusion is heightened, somehow or other, by the extraordinary intensity of the light. My painting-room is a grand observatory of the clouds. I sit by the half-hour watching them sail past my high uncurtained windows. At the back part of the room something tells you that they belong to an ocean-sky; and there, in truth, as you draw nearer, you behold the vast gray complement of sea. This quarter of the town is perfectly quiet. Human activity seems to have passed over it, never again to return, and to have left a deposit of melancholy resignation. The streets are clean, bright and airy; but this fact only deepens the impression of vanished uses. It seems to say that the protecting heavens look down on their decline and can't help them. There is something ghostly in the perpetual stillness. We frequently hear the rattling of the yards and the issuing of orders on the barks and schooners anchored out in the harbour.

June 28th.—My experiment works far better than I had hoped. I am thoroughly at my ease; my peace of mind quite passeth understanding. I work diligently; I have none but pleasant thoughts. The past has almost lost its bitterness. For a week, now, I have been out sketching daily. The Captain carries me to a certain point on the shore of the bay, I disembark and strike across the uplands to a spot where I have taken a kind of tryst with a particular effect of rock and shadow, which has been tolerably faithful to its appointment. Here I set up my easel, and paint till sunset. Then I retrace my steps and meet the boat. I am in every way much encouraged; the horizon of my work grows perceptibly wider. And then I am inexpressibly happy in the conviction that I am not wholly unfit for a life of (moderate) industry and (comparative) privation. I am quite in love with my poverty, if I may call it so. And why should I not? At this rate I don't spend eight hundred a year.

July 12th.—We have been having a week of bad weather: constant rain, night and day. This is certainly at once the brightest and the blackest spot in New England. The skies can smile, assuredly, but they have also lachrymal moods. I have been painting rather languidly, and at a great disadvantage, at my window. . . . . . Through all this pouring and pattering Miss Miriam—her name is Miriam, and it exactly fits her—sallies forth to her pupils. She envelops her beautiful head in a great woollen hood, her beautiful figure in a kind of feminine mackintosh; her feet she puts into heavy clogs, and over the whole she balances a cotton umbrella. When she comes home, with the rain-drops glistening on her rich cheeks and her dark lashes, her cloak bespattered with mud and her hands red with the cool damp, she is a very honourable figure. I never fail to make her a very low bow, for which she repays me with a familiar, but not a vulgar, nod. The working-day side of her character is what especially pleases me in Miss Quarterman. This holy working-dress sits upon her with the fine effect of an antique drapery. Little use has she for whale-bones and furbelows. What a poetry there is, after all, in red hands! I kiss yours, Mademoiselle. I do so because you are self-helpful; because you earn your living; because you are honest, simple, and ignorant (for a sensible woman, that is); because you speak and act to the point; because, in short, you are so unlike—certain of your sisters.

July 16th.—On Monday it cleared up generously. When I went to my window, on rising, I found sky and sea looking, for their brightness and freshness, like a clever English water-colour. The ocean is of a deep purple blue; above it, the pure,

bright sky looks pale, though it hangs over the island horizon
a canopy of denser tissue. Here and there on the dark, breezy
water gleams the white cap of a wave, or flaps the white cloak
of a fishing-boat. I have been sketching sedulously; I have discovered, within a couple of miles' walk, a large, lonely pond,
set in a really grand landscape of barren rocks and grassy
slopes. At one extremity is a broad outlook on the open sea;
at the other, buried in the foliage of an apple-orchard, stands
an old haunted-looking farm-house. To the west of the pond
is a wide expanse of rock and grass, of sand and marsh. The
sheep browse over it—poorly—as they might upon a High-
land moor. Except a few stunted firs and cedars, there is not a
tree in sight. When I want shade I have to look for it in the
shelter of one of the large stones which hold up to the sun a
shoulder coated with delicate gray, figured over with fine,
pale, sea-green moss, or else in one of the long, shallow dells
where a tangle of blackberry-bushes hedges about a pool that
reflects the sky. I am giving my best attention to a plain brown
hillside, and trying to make it look like something in nature;
and as we have now had the same clear sky for several days,
I have almost finished quite a satisfactory little study. I go
forth immediately after breakfast. Miss Quarterman supplies
me with a little parcel of bread and cold meat, which at the
noonday hour, in my sunny solitude, within sight of the
slumbering ocean, I voraciously convey to my lips with my
discoloured fingers. At seven o'clock I return to tea, at which
repast we each tell the story of our day's work. For poor Miss
Quarterman it is always the same story: a wearisome round of
visits to the school, and to the houses of the mayor, the parson,
the butcher, the baker, whose young ladies, of course, all
receive instruction on the piano. But she doesn't complain, nor,
indeed, does she look very weary. When she has put on a fresh
light dress for tea, and arranged her hair anew, and with these
improvements flits about with the quiet hither and thither of
her gentle footstep, preparing our evening meal peeping into

the teapot, cutting the solid loaf—or when, sitting down on
the low door-step, she reads out select scraps from the evening-
paper—or else, when tea being over, she folds her arms (an
attitude which becomes her mightily) and, still sitting on the
door-step, gossips away the evening in comfortable idleness,
while her father and I indulge in the fragrant pipe and watch
the lights shining out, one by one, in different quarters of the
darkening bay: at these moments she is as pretty, as cheerful, as
careless as it becomes a sensible woman to be. What a pride the
Captain takes in his daughter, and she, in return, how perfect
is her devotion to the old man! He is proud of her grace, of
her tact, of her good sense, of her wit, such as it is. He believes
her to be the most accomplished of women. He waits upon her
as if, instead of his old familiar Miriam, she were some new
arrival—say a daughter-in-law lately brought home. And à
propos of daughters-in-law, if I were his own son he could not
be kinder to me. They are certainly—nay, why should I not
say it?—we are certainly a very happy little household. Will
it last for ever? I say we, because both father and daughter have
given me a hundred assurances—he direct, and she, if I don't
flatter myself, after the manner of her sex, indirect—that I am
already a valued friend. It is natural enough that they should
like me, because I have tried to please them. The way to the
old man's heart is through a studied consideration of his
daughter. He knows, I imagine, that I admire Miss Quarterman, but if I should at any time fall below the mark of ceremony, I should have an account to settle with him. All this is
as it should be. When people have to economise with the
dollars and cents, they have a right to be splendid in their
feelings. I have done my best to be nice to the stately Miriam
without making love to her. That I haven't done *that*, however, is a fact which I do not, in any degree, set down here to
my credit; for I would defy the most impertinent of men (who-
ever he is) to forget himself with this young lady. Those animated eyes have a power to keep people in their place. I

mention the circumstance simply because in future years, when my charming friend shall have become a distant shadow, it will be pleasant, in turning over these pages, to find written testimony to a number of points which I shall be apt to charge solely upon my imagination. I wonder whether Miss Quarterman, in days to come, referring to the tables of her memory for some trivial matter-of-fact, some prosaic date or half-buried landmark, will also encounter this little secret of ours, as I may call it—will decipher an old faint note to this effect, overlaid with the memoranda of intervening years. Of course she will. Sentiment aside, she is a woman of a retentive faculty. Whether she forgives or not I know not; but she certainly doesn't forget. Doubtless, virtue is its own reward; but there is a double satisfaction in being polite to a person on whom it tells!

Another reason for my pleasant relations with the Captain is, that I afford him a chance to rub up his rusty worldly lore and trot out his little scraps of old-fashioned reading, some of which are very curious. It is a great treat for him to spin his threadbare yarns over again to a submissive listener. These warm July evenings, in the sweet-smelling garden, are just the proper setting for his traveller's tales. An odd enough understanding subsists between us on this point. Like many gentlemen of his calling, the Captain is harassed by an irresistible desire to romance, even on the least promising themes; and it is vastly amusing to observe how he will auscultate, as it were, his auditor's inmost mood, to ascertain whether it is in condition to be practised upon. Sometimes his artless fables don't "take" at all: they are very pretty, I conceive, in the deep and briny well of the Captain's fancy, but they won't bear being transplanted into the dry climate of my land-bred mind. At other times, the auditor being in a dreamy, sentimental, and altogether unprincipled mood, he will drink the old man's salt-water by the bucketful and feel none the worse for it. Which is the worse, wilfully to tell, or wilfully to believe, a pretty little falsehood which will not hurt any one? I suppose you can't believe wilfully; you only pretend to believe. My part of the game, therefore, is certainly as bad as the Captain's. Perhaps I take kindly to his beautiful perversions of fact because I am myself engaged in one, because I am sailing under false colours of the deepest dye. I wonder whether my friends have any suspicion of the real state of the case. How should they? I take for granted that I play my little part pretty well. I am delighted to find it comes so easy. I do not mean that I find little difficulty in foregoing my old luxuries and pleasures—for to these, thank heaven, I was not so indissolubly wedded that one wholesome shock could not loosen my bonds—but that I manage more cleverly than I expected to stifle those innumerable tacit allusions which might serve effectually to belie my character.

Sunday, July 20th.—This has been a very pleasant day for me; although in it, of course, I have done no manner of work. I had this morning a delightful *tête-à-tête* with my hostess. She had sprained her ankle coming down stairs, and so, instead of going forth to Sunday-school and to meeting, she was obliged to remain at home on the sofa. The Captain, who is of a very punctilious piety, went off alone. When I came into the parlour, as the church-bells were ringing, Miss Quarterman asked me if I never went to a place of worship.

"Never when there is anything better to do at home," said I.

"What is better than going to church?" she asked, with charming simplicity.

She was reclining on the sofa, with her foot on a pillow and her Bible in her lap. She looked by no means afflicted at having to be absent from divine service; and, instead of answering her question, I took the liberty of telling her so.

"I *am* sorry to be absent," said she. "You know it's my only festival in the week."

"So you look upon it as a festival."

"Isn't it a pleasure to meet one's acquaintance? I confess I am never deeply interested in the sermon, and I very much dislike teaching the children; but I like wearing my best bonnet, and singing in the choir, and walking part of the way home with——"

"With whom?"

"With anyone who offers to walk with me."

"With Mr Prendergast, for instance," said I.

Mr Prendergast is a young lawyer in the village, who calls here once a week, and whose attentions to Miss Quarterman have been remarked.

"Yes," she answered, "Mr Prendergast will do as an instance."

"How he will miss you!"

"I suppose he will. We sing off the same book. What are you laughing at? He kindly permits me to hold the book, while he stands with his hands in his pockets. Last Sunday I quite lost patience. 'Mr Prendergast,' said I, 'do hold the book! Where are your manners?' He burst out laughing in the midst of the reading. He will certainly have to hold the book to-day."

"What a masterful soul he is! I suppose he will call after meeting."

"Perhaps he will. I hope so."

"I hope he won't," said I, frankly. "I am going to sit down here and talk to you, and I wish our conversation not to be interrupted."

"Have you anything particular to say?"

"Nothing so particular as Mr Prendergast, perhaps."

Miss Quarterman has a very pretty affectation of being more matter-of-fact than she really is.

"His rights, then," she remarked, "are paramount to yours."

"Ah, you admit that he has rights?"

"Not at all. I simply assert that you have none."

"I beg your pardon. I have claims which I mean to enforce.

I have a claim upon your undivided attention when I pay you a morning-call."

"You have had all the attention I am capable of. Have I been so very rude?"

"Not so very rude, perhaps, but rather inconsiderate. You have been sighing for the company of a third person, whom you can't expect me to care much about."

"Why not, pray? If I, a lady, can put up with Mr Prendergast's society, why shouldn't you, one of his own sex?"

"Because he is so outrageously conceited. You, as a lady, or at any rate as a woman, like conceited men."

"Ah, yes; I have no doubt that I, as a woman, have all kinds of weak tastes. That's a very old story."

"Admit, at any rate, that our friend is conceited."

"Admit it! Why, I have said so a hundred times. I have told him so."

"Indeed, it has come to that, then?"

"To what, pray?"

"To that critical point in the friendship of a lady and gentleman when they bring against each other all kinds of delightful accusations and rebukes. Take care, Miss Quarterman! A couple of intelligent New-Englanders, of opposite sexes, young, unmarried, are pretty far gone, when they begin to scan each other's faults. So you told Mr Prendergast that he is conceited? And I suppose you added that he was also dreadfully satirical and sceptical? What was his rejoinder? Let me see. Did he ever tell you that you were a wee bit affected?"

"No; he left that for you to say, in this very ingenious manner. Thank you, sir."

"He left it for me to deny, which is a great deal prettier. Do you think the manner ingenious?"

"I think the matter, considering the day and hour, very profane, Mr Locksley. Suppose you go away and let me peruse my Bible."

"Meanwhile what shall I do?"

"Go and read yours, if you have one."

"My Bible," I said, "is the female mind."

I was nevertheless compelled to retire, with the promise of a second audience in half-an-hour. Poor Miss Quarterman owes it to her conscience to read a certain number of chapters. In what a terrible tradition she has been reared, and what an edifying spectacle is the piety of women! Women find a place for everything in their commodious little minds, just as they do in their wonderfully sub-divided trunks when they go on a journey. I have no doubt that this young lady stows away her religion in a corner, just as she does her Sunday-bonnet—and, when the proper moment comes, draws it forth, and reflects, while she puts it on before the glass and blows away the strictly imaginary dust (for what worldly impurity can penetrate through half a dozen layers of cambric and tissue-paper?): "Dear me, what a comfort it is to have a nice, fresh holiday-creed!"—When I returned to the parlour Miriam was still sitting with her Bible in her lap. Somehow or other I no longer felt in the mood for jesting; so I asked her, without chaffing, what she had been reading, and she answered me in the same tone. She inquired how I had spent my half-hour.

"In thinking good Sabbath thoughts," I said. "I have been walking in the garden." And then I spoke my mind. "I have been thanking heaven that it has led me, a poor friendless wanderer, into so peaceful an anchorage."

"Are you so very poor and friendless?"

"Did you ever hear of an art-student who was not poor? Upon my word, I have yet to sell my first picture. Then, as for being friendless, there are not five people in the world who really care for me."

"*Really* care? I am afraid you look too close. And then I think five good friends is a very large number. I think myself very well-off with half-a-one. But if you are friendless, it's probably your own fault."

"Perhaps it is," said I, sitting down in the rocking-chair;

"and also, perhaps it isn't. Have you found me so very difficult to live with? Haven't you, on the contrary, found me rather sociable?"

She folded her arms, and quietly looked at me for a moment, before answering. I shouldn't wonder if I blushed a little.

"You want a lump of sugar, Mr Locksley; that's the long and short of it. I haven't given you one since you have been here. How you must have suffered! But it's a pity you couldn't have waited a little longer, instead of beginning to put out your paws and bark. For an artist, you are very slap-dash. Men never know how to wait. 'Have I found you very difficult to live with? haven't I found you sociable?' Perhaps, after all, considering what I have in my mind, it is as well that you asked for your lump of sugar. I have found you very indulgent. You let us off easily, but you wouldn't like us a bit if you didn't pity us. Don't I go deep? Sociable? ah, well, no—decidedly not! You are entirely too particular. You are considerate of me, because you know that I know that you are so. There's the rub, you see: I know that you know that I know it! Don't interrupt me; I am going to be striking. I want you to under-stand why I don't consider you sociable. You call poor Mr Prendergast conceited; but, really, I believe he has more humility than you. He envies my father and me—thinks us so cultivated. You don't envy any one, and yet I don't think you're a saint. You treat us kindly because you think virtue in a lowly station ought to be encouraged. Would you take the same amount of pains for a person you thought your equal, a person equally averse with yourself to being under an obligation? There are differences. Of course it's very delightful to fascinate people. Who wouldn't? There is no harm in it, as long as the fascinator doesn't set up for a public benefactor. If I were a man, a clever man like yourself, who had seen the world, who was not to be dazzled and encouraged, but to be listened to, counted with, would you be equally amiable? It will perhaps seem absurd to you, and it will certainly seem egotistical, but I consider myself sociable, for all that I have only a couple of friends—my father and Miss Blankenberg. That is, I mingle with people without any *arrière-pensée*. Of course the people I see are mainly women. Not that I wish you to do so: on the contrary, if the contrary is agreeable to you. But I don't believe you mingle in the same way with men. You may ask me what I know about it! Of course I know nothing; I simply guess. When I have done, indeed, I mean to beg your pardon for all I have said; but until then, give me a chance. You are incapable of exposing yourself to be bored, whereas I take it as my waterproof takes the rain. You have no idea what heroism I show in the exercise of my profession! Every day I have occasion to pocket my pride and to stifle my sense of the ridiculous—of which of course you think I haven't a bit. It is for instance a constant vexation to me to be poor. It makes me frequently hate rich women; it makes me despise poor ones. I don't know whether you suffer acutely from the smallness of your own means; but if you do, I dare say you shun rich men. I don't, I like to bleed; to go into rich people's houses, and to be very polite to the ladies, especially if they are very much dressed, very ignorant and vulgar. All women are like me in this respect, and all men more or less like you. That is, after all, the text of my sermon. Compared with us it has always seemed to me that you are arrant cowards—that we alone are brave. To be sociable you must have a great deal of patience. You are too fine a gentleman. Go and teach school, or open a corner-grocery, or sit in a law-office all day, waiting for clients: then you will be sociable. As yet you are only selfish. It *is* your own fault if people don't care for you; you don't care for them. That you should be indifferent to their good opinion is all very well; but you don't care for their indifference. You are amiable, you are very kind, and you are also very lazy. You consider that you are working now, don't you? Many persons would not call it work."

It was now certainly my turn to fold my arms.

"And now," added my companion, as I did so, "be so good as to excuse me."

"This was certainly worth waiting for," said I. "I don't know what answer to make. My head swims. Sugar, did you say? I don't know whether you have been giving me sugar or vitriol. So you advise me to open a corner-grocery, do you?"

"I advise you to do something that will make you a little less satirical. You had better marry, for instance."

"*Je ne demande pas mieux.* Will you have me? I can't afford it."

"Marry a rich woman."

I shook my head.

"Why not?" asked Miss Quarterman. "Because people would accuse you of being mercenary? What of that? I mean to marry the first rich man who offers. Do you know that I am tired of living alone in this weary old way, teaching little girls their scales, and turning and patching my dresses? I mean to marry the first man who offers."

"Even if he is poor?"

"Even if he is poor and has a hump."

"I am your man, then. Would you take me if I were to offer?"

"Try and see."

"Must I get upon my knees?"

"No, you needn't even do that. Am I not on mine? It would be too fine an irony. Remain as you are, lounging back in your chair, with your thumbs in your waistcoat."

If I were writing a romance now, instead of transcribing facts, I would say that I knew not what might have happened at this juncture had not the door opened and admitted the Captain and Mr Prendergast. The latter was in the highest spirits.

"How are you, Miss Miriam? So you have been breaking

your leg, eh? How are you, Mr Locksley? I wish I were a doctor now. Which is it, right or left?"

In this simple fashion he made himself agreeable to Miss Miriam. He stopped to dinner and talked without ceasing. Whether our hostess had talked herself out in her very animated address to myself an hour before, or whether she preferred to oppose no obstacle to Mr Prendergast's fluency, or whether she was indifferent to him, I know not; but she held her tongue with that easy grace, that charming tacit intimation of "We could if we would," of which she is so perfect a mistress. This very interesting woman has a number of pretty traits in common with her town-bred sisters; only, whereas in these they are laboriously acquired, in her they are richly natural. I am sure that, if I were to plant her in Madison Square to-morrow, she would, after one quick, all-compassing glance, assume the *nil admirari* in a manner to drive the finest lady of them all to despair. Prendergast is a man of excellent intentions but no taste. Two or three times I looked at Miss Quarterman to see what impression his sallies were making upon her. They seemed to produce none whatever. But I know better, *moi*. Not one of them escaped her. But I suppose she said to herself that her impressions on this point were no business of mine. Perhaps she was right. It is a disagreeable word to use of a woman you admire; but I can't help fancying that she has been a little soured. By what? Who shall say? By some old love-affair, perhaps.

July 24th.—This evening the Captain and I took a half-hour's turn about the port. I asked him frankly, as a friend, whether Prendergast wants to marry his daughter.

"I guess he does," said the old man, "and yet I hope he don't. You know what he is: he's smart, promising, and already sufficiently well-off. But somehow he isn't for a man what my Miriam is for a female."

"That he isn't!" said I; "and honestly, Captain Quarterman, I don't know who is——"

"Unless it be yourself," said the Captain.

"Thank you. I know a great many ways in which Mr Prendergast is more worthy of her than I."

"And I know one in which you are more worthy of her than he—that is in being what we used to call one of the old sort."

"Miss Quarterman made him sufficiently welcome in her quiet way on Sunday," I rejoined.

"Oh, she respects him," said Quarterman. "As she's situated, she might marry him on that. You see, she's weary of hearing little girls drum on the piano. With her ear for music," added the Captain, "I wonder she has borne it so long."

"She is certainly meant for better things," said I.

"Well," answered the Captain, who has an honest habit of deprecating your agreement when it occurs to him that he has obtained it for sentiments which fall somewhat short of the stoical—"well," said he, with a very dry, edifying expression, "she's born to do her duty. We are all of us born for that."

"Sometimes our duty is rather dismal," said I.

"So it be; but what's the help for it? I don't want to die without seeing my daughter provided for. What she makes by teaching is a pretty slim subsistence. There was a time when I thought she was going to be fixed for life, but it all blew over. There was a young fellow here, from down Boston way, who came about as near to it as you can come when you actually don't. He and Miriam were excellent friends. One day Miriam came up to me, and looked me in the face, and told me she had passed her word.

"'Who to?' says I, though of course I knew, and Miriam told me as much. 'When do you expect to marry?' I asked.

"'When Alfred'—his name was Alfred—'grows rich enough,' says she.

"'When will that be?'

"'It may not be for years,' said poor Miriam.

"A whole year passed, and, so far as I could see, the young man hadn't accumulated very much. He was for ever running to and fro between this place and Boston. I asked no questions, because I knew that my poor girl wished it so. But at last, one day, I began to think it was time to take an observation, and see whereabouts we stood.

"'Has Alfred made his little pile yet?' I asked.

"'I don't know, father,' said Miriam.

"'When are you to be married?'

"'Never!' said my poor little girl, and burst into tears. 'Please ask me no questions,' said she. 'Our engagement is over. Ask me no questions.'

"'Tell me one thing,' said I: 'Where is that d—d scoundrel who has broken my daughter's heart?'

"You should have seen the look she gave me.

"'Broken my heart, sir? You are very much mistaken. I don't know who you mean.'

"'I mean Alfred Bannister,' said I. That was his name.

"'I believe Mr Bannister is in China,' says Miriam, as grand as the Queen of Sheba. And there was an end of it. I never learnt the ins and outs of it. I have been told that Bannister is amassing considerable wealth in the China-trade."

August 7th.—I have made no entry for more than a fortnight. They tell me I have been very ill; and I find no difficulty in believing them. I suppose I took cold, sitting out so late, sketching. At all events, I have had a mild intermittent fever. I have slept so much, however, that the time has seemed rather short. I have been tenderly nursed by this kind old mariner, his daughter, and his black domestic. God bless them, one and all! I say his daughter, because old Cynthia informs me that for half-an-hour one morning, at dawn, after a night during which I had been very feeble, Miss Quarterman relieved guard at my bedside, while I lay sleeping like a log. It is very jolly to see sky and ocean once again. I have got myself into my easy-chair, by the best window, with my shutters closed and the lattice open; and here I sit with my book on my knee, scratching away feebly enough. Now and then I peep from my cool, dark sick-chamber out into the world of light. High noon at midsummer—what a spectacle! There are no clouds in the sky, no waves on the ocean, the sun has it all to himself. To look long at the garden makes the eyes water. And we—"Hobbs, Nobbs, Stokes and Nokes"—propose to paint that luminosity. *Allons donc!*

The handsomest of women has just tapped, and come in with a plate of early peaches. The peaches are of a gorgeous colour and plumpness; but Miss Quarterman looks pale and thin. The hot weather doesn't agree with her, and besides she is over-worked. Damn her drudgery! Of course I thanked her warmly for her attentions during my illness. She disclaims all gratitude, and refers me to her father and the dusky Cynthia.

"I allude more especially," I said, "to that little hour at the end of a weary night when you stole in, like a kind of moral Aurora, and drove away the shadows from my brain. That morning, you know, I began to get better."

"It was indeed a very little hour," said Miss Quarterman, colouring. "It was about ten minutes." And then she began to scold me for presuming to touch a pen during my convalescence. She laughs at me, indeed, for keeping a diary at all. "Of all things, a sentimental man is the most despicable!" she exclaimed.

I confess I was somewhat nettled—the thrust seemed gratuitous.

"Of all things a woman without sentiment is the most wanting in sweetness."

"Sentiment and sweetness are all very well when you have time for them," said Miss Quarterman. "I haven't. I am not rich enough. Good morning!"

Speaking of another woman, I would say that she flounced out of the room. But such was the gait of Juno when she moved stiffly over the grass from where Paris stood with Venus holding the apple, gathering up her divine vestment and leaving the others to guess at her face.

Juno has just come back to say that she forgot what she came for half-an-hour ago. What will I be pleased to like for dinner?

"I have just been writing in my diary that you flounced out of the room," said I.

"Have you, indeed? Now you can write that I have bounced in. There's a nice cold chicken downstairs," etc. etc.

August 14th.—This afternoon I sent for a light vehicle, and treated Miss Quarterman to a drive. We went successively over the three beaches. What a spin we had coming home! I shall never forget that breezy trot over Weston's Beach. The tide was very low, and we had the whole glittering, weltering strand to ourselves. There was a heavy blow last night, which has not yet subsided, and the waves have been lashed into a magnificent fury. Trot, trot, trot, trot, we trundled over the hard sand. The sound of the horse's hoofs rang out sharp against the monotone of the thunderous surf, as we drew nearer and nearer to the long line of the cliffs. At our left, almost from the zenith of the pale evening-sky to the high western horizon of the tumultuous dark-green sea, was suspended, so to speak, one of those gorgeous vertical sunsets that Turner sometimes painted. It was a splendid confusion of purple and green and gold—the clouds flying and floating in the wind like the folds of a mighty banner borne by some triumphal fleet which had rounded the curve of the globe. As we reached the point where the cliffs begin I pulled up, and we remained for some time looking at their long, diminishing, crooked perspective, blue and dun as it receded, with the white surge playing at their feet.

August 17th.—This evening, as I lighted my bedroom-candle, I saw that the Captain had something to say to me. So I waited below until my host and his daughter had performed their usual osculation, and the latter had given me that confiding hand-shake which I never fail to extract.

"Prendergast has got his discharge," said the old man, when he heard his daughter's door close.

"What do you mean?"

He pointed with his thumb to the room above, where we heard, through the thin partition, the movement of Miss Quarterman's light step.

"You mean that he has proposed to Miss Miriam?"

The Captain nodded.

"And has been refused?"

"Flat."

"Poor fellow!" said I, very honestly. "Did he tell you himself?"

"Yes, with tears in his eyes. He wanted me to speak for him. I told him it was no use. Then he began to say hard things of my poor girl."

"What kind of things?"

"A pack of falsehoods. He says she has no heart. She has promised always to regard him as a friend; it's more than I will, hang him!"

"Poor fellow!" said I; and now, as I write, I can only repeat considering what a hope was here disappointed, Poor fellow!

August 23*rd.*—I have been lounging about all day, thinking of it, dreaming of it, spooning over it, as they say. This is a decided waste of time. I think, accordingly, the best thing for me to do is to sit down and lay the ghost by writing out my little story.

On Thursday evening, Miss Quarterman happened to intimate that she had a holiday on the morrow, it being the birthday of the lady in whose establishment she teaches.

"There is to be a tea-party at four o'clock in the afternoon for the resident pupils and teachers," Miriam said. "Tea at four! what do you think of that? And then there is to be a speech-making by the smartest young lady. As my services are not required I propose to be absent. Suppose, father, you take us out in your boat. Will you come, Mr Locksley? We shall have a neat little picnic. Let us go over to old Fort Plunkett, across the bay. We will take our dinner with us, and send Cynthia to spend the day with her sister, and put the house-key in our pocket, and not come home till we please."

I entered into the project with passion, and it was accord-ingly carried into execution the next morning, when—about ten o'clock—we pushed off from our little wharf at the garden-foot. It was a perfect summer's day; I can say no more for it; and we made a quiet run over to the point of our destination. I shall never forget the wondrous stillness which brooded over earth and water as we weighed anchor in the lee of my old friend—or old enemy—the ruined fort. The deep, translucent water reposed at the base of the warm sunlit cliff like a great basin of glass, which I half expected to hear shiver and crack as our keel ploughed through it. And how colour and sound stood out in the transparent air! How audibly the little ripples on the beach whispered to the open sky. How our irreverent voices seemed to jar upon the privacy of the little cove! The delicate rocks doubled themselves without a flaw in the clear, dark water. The gleaming white beach lay fringed with its deep deposits of odorous sea-weed, which looked like masses of black lace. The steep, straggling sides of the cliffs lifted their rugged angles against the burning blue of the sky. I remember, when Miss Quarterman stepped ashore and stood upon the beach, relieved against the cool darkness of a recess in the cliff, while her father and I busied ourselves with gathering up our baskets and fastening the anchor—I remember, I say, what a picture she made. There is a certain purity in the air of this place which I have never seen surpassed—a lightness, a brilli-ancy, a crudity, which allows perfect liberty of self-assertion to each individual object in the landscape. The prospect is ever more or less like a picture which lacks its final process, its reduction to unity. Miss Quarterman's figure, as she stood there on the beach, was almost *criarde;* but how it animated the whole scene! Her light muslin dress, gathered up over her white petticoat, her little black mantilla, the blue veil which she had knotted about her neck, the little silken dome which she poised over her head in one gloved hand, while the other retained her crisp draperies, and which cast down upon her face a sharp circle of shade, where her cheerful eyes shone darkly and her parted lips said things I lost—these are some of the points I hastily noted.

"Young woman," I cried out, over the water, "I do wish you might know how pretty you look!"

"How do you know I don't?" she answered. "I should think I might. You don't look so badly yourself. But it's not I; it's the aerial perspective."

"Hang it—I am going to become profane!" I called out again.

"Swear ahead," said the Captain.

"I am going to say you are infernally handsome."

"Dear me! is that all?" cried Miss Quarterman, with a little light laugh which must have made the tutelar sirens of the cove ready to die with jealousy down in their submarine bowers.

By the time the Captain and I had landed our effects our companion had tripped lightly up the forehead of the cliff—in one place it is very retreating—and disappeared over its crown. She soon returned, with an intensely white pocket-handkerchief added to her other provocations, which she waved to us, as we trudged upward, carrying our baskets. When we stopped to take breath on the summit and wipe our foreheads, we of course rebuked her for roaming about idly with her parasol and gloves.

"Do you think I am going to take any trouble or do any work?" cried Miss Miriam, in the greatest good-humour. "Is not this my holiday? I am not going to raise a finger, nor soil these beautiful gloves, for which I paid so much at Mr Dawson's at Chowderville. After you have found a shady place for your provisions, I should like you to look for a spring. I am very thirsty."

"Find the spring yourself, miss," said her father. "Mr Locksley and I have a spring in this basket. Take a pull, sir."

And the Captain drew forth a stout black bottle.

"Give me a cup, and I will look for some water," said Miriam. "Only I'm so afraid of the snakes! If you hear a scream you may know it's a snake."

"Screaming snakes!" said I; "that's a new species."

What cheap fun it all sounds now! As we looked about us shade seemed scarce, as it generally is in this region. But Miss Quarterman, like the very adroit and practical young person she is, for all that she would have me believe the contrary, immediately discovered flowing water in the shelter of a pleasant little dell, beneath a clump of firs. Hither, as one of the young gentlemen who imitate Tennyson would say, we brought our basket, he and I; while Miriam dipped the cup, and held it dripping to our thirsty lips, and laid the cloth, and on the grass disposed the platters round. I should have to be a poet, indeed, to describe half the happiness and the silly sweetness and artless revelry of this interminable summer's day. We ate and drank and talked; we ate occasionally with our fingers, we drank out of the necks of our bottles, and we talked with our mouths full, as befits (and excuses) those who talk perfect nonsense. We told stories without the least point. The Captain and I made atrocious puns. I believe, indeed, that Miss Quarterman herself made one little punkin, as I called it. If there had been any superfluous representative of humanity present to notice the fact, I should say that we made fools of ourselves. But as there was no one to criticise us we were brilliant enough. I am conscious myself of having said several witty things, which Miss Quarterman understood: *in vino veritas*. The dear old Captain twanged the long bow indefatigably. The bright high sun dawdled above us, in the same place, and drowned the prospect with light and warmth. One of these days I mean to paint a picture which, in future ages, when my dear native land shall boast a national school of art, will hang in the Salon Carré of the great central museum (located, let us say, in Chicago) and recall to folks—or rather make them forget—Giorgione, Bordone, and Veronese: A Rural Festival; three persons feasting under some trees; scene, nowhere in particular; time and hour, problematical. Female figure, a rich *brune*; young man reclining on his elbow; old man drinking. An empty sky, with no end of expression. The whole stupendous in colour, drawing, feeling. Artist uncertain; supposed to be Robinson, 1900.

After dinner the Captain began to look out across the bay, and, noticing the uprising of a little breeze, expressed a wish to cruise about for an hour or two. He proposed to us to walk along the shore to a point a couple of miles northward, and there meet the boat. His daughter having agreed to this proposition, he set off with the lightened hamper, and in less than half-an-hour we saw him standing out from shore. Miss Quarterman and I did not begin our walk for a long, long time. We sat and talked beneath the trees. At our feet a wide cleft in the hills—almost a glen—stretched down to the silent beach; beyond lay the familiar ocean-line. But, as many philosophers have observed, there is an end to all things. At last we got up. My companion remarked that, as the air was freshening, she supposed she ought to put on her shawl. I helped her to fold it into the proper shape, and then I placed it on her shoulders; it being an old shawl of faded red (Canton crape, I believe they call it), which I have seen very often. And then she tied her veil once more about her neck, and gave me her hat to hold, while she effected a partial redistribution of her hair-pins. By way of being humorous, I spun her hat round on my stick; at which she was kind enough to smile, as with downcast face and uplifted elbows she fumbled among her braids. And then she shook out the creases of her dress and drew on her gloves; and finally she said "Well!"—that inevitable tribute to time and morality which follows upon even the mildest forms of dissipation. Very slowly it was that we wandered down the little glen. Slowly, too, we followed the course of the narrow and sinuous beach, as it keeps to the foot of the low cliffs. We encountered no sign of human life. Our conversation I need hardly repeat. I think I may trust it to the keeping of my memory; it was the sort of thing that comes back to one—after. If something ever happens which I think *may*, that apparently idle hour will seem, as one looks back, very symptomatic, and what we didn't say be perceived to have been more significant than what we did. There was something between us—there *is* something between us—and we listened to its impalpable presence—I liken it to the hum (very faint) of an unseen insect —in the golden stillness of the afternoon. I must add that if she expects, foresees, if she waits, she does so with a supreme serenity. If she is my fate (and she has the air of it), she is conscious that it's *her* fate to be so.

September 1st.—I have been working steadily for a week. This is the first day of autumn. Read aloud to Miss Quarterman a little Wordsworth.

September 10th. Midnight.—Worked without interruption —until yesterday, inclusive, that is. But with the day now closing—or opening—begins a new era. My poor vapid old diary, at last you shall hold a *fact*.

For three days past we have been having damp, autumnal weather; dusk has gathered early. This evening, after tea, the Captain went into town—on business, as he said: I believe, to attend some Poorhouse or Hospital Board. Miriam and I went into the parlour. The place seemed cold; she brought in the lamp from the dining-room, and proposed we should have a little fire. I went into the kitchen, procured half-a-dozen logs, and, while she drew the curtains and wheeled up the table, I kindled a lively, crackling blaze. A fortnight ago she would not have allowed me to do this without a protest. She would not have offered to do it herself—not she!—but she would have said that I was not here to serve, but to be served, and would at least have made a show of calling the negress. I should have had my own way, but we have changed all that. Miriam went to her piano, and I sat down to a book. I read not a word, but sat considering my fate and watching it come nearer and nearer. For the first time since I have known her (my fate) she had put on a dark, warm dress; I think it was of the material called alpaca. The first time I saw her (I remember such things) she wore a white dress with a blue neck-ribbon; now she wore a black dress with the same ribbon. That is, I remember wondering, as I sat there eyeing her, whether it *was* the same ribbon, or merely another like it. My heart was in my throat; and yet I thought of a number of trivialities of the same kind. At last I spoke.

"Miss Quarterman," I said, "do you remember the first evening I passed beneath your roof, last June?"

"Perfectly," she replied, without stopping.

"You played that same piece."

"Yes; I played it very badly, too. I only half knew it. But it is a showy piece, and I wished to produce an effect. I didn't know then how indifferent you are to music."

"I paid no particular attention to the piece. I was intent upon the performer."

"So the performer supposed."

"What reason had you to suppose so?"

"I am sure I don't know. Did you ever know a woman to be able to give a reason when she has guessed aright?"

"I think they generally contrive to make up a reason afterwards. Come, what was yours?"

"Well, you stared so hard."

"Fie! I don't believe it. That's unkind."

"You said you wished me to invent a reason. If I really had one, I don't remember it."

"You told me you remembered the occasion in question perfectly."

"I meant the circumstances. I remember what we had for

tea; I remember what dress I wore. But I don't remember my feelings. They were naturally not very memorable."

"What did you say when your father proposed that I should come here?"

"I asked how much you would be willing to pay?"

"And then?"

"And then, if you looked respectable."

"And then?"

"That was all. I told my father to do as he pleased."

She continued to play, and leaning back in my chair I continued to look at her. There was a considerable pause.

"Miss Quarterman," said I, at last.

"Well, sir?"

"Excuse me for interrupting you so often. But"—and I got up and went to the piano—"but, you know, I thank heaven that it has brought you and me together."

She looked up at me and bowed her head with a little smile, as her hands still wandered over the keys.

"Heaven has certainly been very good to us," said she.

"How much longer are you going to play?" I asked.

"I'm sure I don't know. As long as you like."

"If you want to do as I like, you will stop immediately."

She let her hands rest on the keys a moment, and gave me a rapid, questioning look. Whether she found a sufficient answer in my face I know not; but she slowly rose, and, with a very pretty affectation of obedience, began to close the instrument. I helped her to do so.

"Perhaps you would like to be quite alone," she said. "I suppose your own room is too cold."

"Yes," I answered, "you have hit it exactly. I wish to be alone. I wish to monopolise this cheerful blaze. Hadn't you better go into the kitchen and sit with the cook? It takes you women to make such cruel speeches."

"When we women are cruel, Mr Locksley, it is the merest accident. We are not wilfully so. When we learn that we have been unkind we very humbly ask pardon, without even knowing what our crime has been." And she made me a very low curtsey.

"I will tell you what your crime has been," said I. "Come and sit by the fire. It's rather a long story."

"A long story? Then let me get my work."

"Confound your work! Excuse me, but you exasperate me. I want you to listen to me. Believe me, you will need all your attention."

She looked at me steadily a moment, and I returned her glance. During that moment I was reflecting whether I might put my arm round her waist and kiss her; but I decided that I might do nothing of the sort. She walked over and quietly seated herself in a low chair by the fire. Here she patiently folded her arms. I sat down before her.

"With you, Miss Quarterman," said I, "one must be very explicit. You are not in the habit of taking things for granted. You have a great deal of imagination, but you rarely exercise it on behalf of other people."

"Is that my crime?" asked my companion.

"It's not so much a crime as a vice, and perhaps not so much a vice as a virtue. Your crime is, that you are so stone-cold to a poor devil who loves you."

She burst into a rather shrill laugh. I wonder whether she thought I meant Prendergast.

"Who are you speaking for, Mr Locksley?" she asked.

"Are there so many? For myself."

"Honestly?"

"Do you think me capable of deceiving you?"

"What is that French phrase that you are for ever using? I think I may say '*Allons donc!*'"

"Let us speak plain English, Miss Quarterman."

"'Stone-cold' is certainly very plain English. I don't see the relative importance of the two branches of your proposition. Which is the principal, and which the subordinate clause—

that I am stone-cold, as you call it, or that you love me, as you call it?"

"As I call it? What would you have me call it? For pity's sake, Miss Quarterman, be serious, or I shall call it something else. Yes, I love you. Don't you believe it?"

"How can I help believing what you tell me?"

"Dearest, bravest of women," said I.

And I attempted to take her hand.

"No, no, Mr Locksley," said she—"not just yet, if you please."

"Actions speak louder than words," said I.

"There is no need of speaking loud. I hear you perfectly."

"I certainly shall not whisper," said I; "although it is the custom, I believe, for lovers to do so. Will you be my wife?"

I don't know whether *she* whispered or not, but before I left her she consented.

September 12th.—We are to be married in about three weeks.

September 19th.—I have been in New York a week, transacting business. I got back yesterday. I find everyone here talking about our engagement. Miriam tells me that it was talked about a month ago, and that there is a very general feeling of disappointment that I am so very poor.

"Really, if you don't mind it," I remarked, "I don't see why others should."

"I don't know whether you are poor or not," says Miriam, "but I know that I am rich."

"Indeed! I was not aware that you had a private fortune," etc. etc.

This little farce is repeated in some shape every day. I am very idle. I smoke a great deal, and lounge about all day, with my hands in my pockets. I am free from that ineffable weariness of ceaseless *buying* which I suffered from six months ago. That intercourse was conducted by means of little parcels, and I have resolved that this engagement, at all events, shall have no connection with the shops. I was cheated of my poetry once;

I shan't be a second time. Fortunately there is not much danger of this, for my mistress is positively lyrical. She takes an enthusiastic interest in her simple outfit—showing me triumphantly certain of her purchases, and making a great mystery about others, which she is pleased to denominate table-cloths and napkins. Last evening I found her sewing buttons on a table-cloth. I had heard a great deal of a certain pink silk dress, and this morning, accordingly, she marched up to me, arrayed in this garment, upon which all the art and taste and eyesight, and all the velvet and lace, of Chowderville have been lavished.

"There is only one objection to it," said Miriam, parading before the glass in my painting-room: "I am afraid it is above our station."

"By Jove! I will paint your portrait in it and make our fortune," said I. "All the other men who have handsome wives will bring them to be painted."

"You mean all the women who have handsome dresses," Miriam replied, with great humility.

Our wedding is fixed for next Thursday. I tell Miriam that it will be as little of a wedding, and as much of a marriage, as possible. Her father and her good friend Miss Blankenberg (the schoolmistress) alone are to be present. My secret oppresses me considerably; but I have resolved to keep it for the honeymoon, when it may leak out as occasion helps it. I am harassed with a dismal apprehension that if Miriam were to discover it now, the whole thing would have to be done over again. I have taken rooms at a romantic little watering-place called Cragthorpe, ten miles off. The hotel is already quite purged of cockneys, and we shall be almost alone.

September 28th.—We have been here two days. The little transaction in the church went off smoothly. I am truly sorry for the Captain. We drove directly over here, and reached the place at dusk. It was a raw, black day. We have a couple of good rooms, close to the savage sea. I am nevertheless afraid I have made a mistake. It would perhaps have been wiser to go to New York. These things are not immaterial; we make our own heaven, but we scarcely make our own earth. I am writing at a little table by the window, looking out on the rocks, the gathering dusk, the rising fog. My wife has wandered down to the rocky platform in front of the house. I can see her from here, bareheaded, in that old crimson shawl, talking to one of the landlord's little boys. She has just given the infant a kiss, bless her tender heart! I remember her telling me once that she was very fond of little boys; and, indeed, I have noticed that they are seldom too dirty for her to take on her knee. I have been reading over these pages for the first time in—I don't know when. They are filled with *her*—even more in thought than in word. I believe I will show them to her when she comes in. I will give her the book to read, and sit by her, watching her face—watching the great secret dawn upon her.

Later.—Somehow or other, I can write this quietly enough; but I hardly think I shall ever write any more. When Miriam came in I handed her this book.

"I want you to read it," said I.

She turned very pale, and laid it on the table, shaking her head.

"I know it," she said.

"What do you know?"

"That you have ever so much money. But believe me, Mr Locksley, I am none the worse for the knowledge. You intimated in one place in your book that I am fitted by nature for wealth and splendour. I verily believe I am. You pretend to hate your money; but you would not have had me without it. If you really love me—and I think you do—you will not let this make any difference. I am not such a fool as to attempt to talk now about what passed through me when you asked me to—to do *this*. But I remember what I said."

"What do you expect me to do?" I asked. "Shall I call you some horrible name and cast you off?"

"I expect you to show the same courage that I am showing.

I never said I loved you. I never deceived you in that. I said I would be your wife. So I will, faithfully. I haven't so much heart as you think; and yet, too, I have a great deal more. I am incapable of more than one deception.—Mercy! didn't you see it? didn't you know it? see that I saw it? know that I knew it? It was diamond cut diamond. You cheated me and I mystified you. Now that you tell me your secret I can tell you mine. *Now* we are free, with the fortune that you know. Excuse me, but it sometimes comes over me! *Now* we can be good and honest and true. It was all a make-believe virtue before."

"So you read that thing?" I asked: actually—strange as it may seem—for something to say.

"Yes, while you were ill. It was lying with your pen in it, on the table. I read it because I suspected. Otherwise I wouldn't have done so."

"It was the act of a false woman," said I.

"A false woman? No, it was the act of any woman—placed as I was placed. You don't believe it?" And she began to smile. "Come, you may abuse me in your diary if you like—I shall never peep into it again!"

A DAY OF DAYS

Mr HERBERT MOORE, a gentleman of the highest note in
the scientific world, and a childless widower, finding himself
at last unable to reconcile his sedentary habits with the manage-
ment of a household, had invited his only sister to come and
superintend his domestic affairs. Miss Adela Moore had assented the more willingly to his proposal as by her mother's
death she had recently been left without a formal protector.
She was twenty-five years of age, and was a very active member
of what she and her friends called society. She was almost
equally at home in the best company of three great cities, and
she had encountered most of the adventures which await a
young girl on the threshold of life. She had become rather
hastily and imprudently engaged, but she had eventually succeeded in disengaging herself. She had spent a summer or two
in Europe, and she had made a voyage to Cuba with a dear
friend in the last stage of consumption, who had died at the
hotel in the Havana. Although by no means perfectly beautiful
in person she was yet thoroughly pleasing, rejoicing in what
young ladies are fond of calling an *air*; that is, she was tall and
slender, with a long neck, a low forehead, and a handsome
nose. Even after six years of the best company, too, she still
had excellent manners. She was, moreover, mistress of a very
pretty little fortune, and was accounted clever without detriment to her amiability and amiable without detriment to her
wit. These facts, as the reader will allow, might have ensured
her the very best prospects; but he has seen that she had found
herself willing to forfeit her prospects and bury herself in the
country. It seemed to her that she had seen enough of the world

and of human nature, and that a period of seclusion might yield
a fine refreshment. She had begun to suspect that for a girl of
her age she was unduly old and wise—and, what is more, to
suspect that others suspected as much. A great observer of life
and manners, so far as her opportunities went, she conceived
that it behoved her to organise the results of her observation
into principles of conduct and belief. She was becoming—so
she argued—too impersonal, too critical, too intelligent, too
contemplative, too just. A woman had no business to be so
just. The society of nature, of the great expansive skies and the
primeval woods, would check the morbid development of her
brain-power. She would spend her time in the fields and merely
vegetate; walk and ride, and read the old-fashioned books in
Herbert's library.

She found her brother established in a very pretty house, at
about a mile's distance from the nearest town, and at about six
miles' distance from another town, the seat of a small but
ancient college, before which he delivered a weekly lecture.
She had seen so little of him of late years that his acquaintance
was almost to make; but there were no barriers to break down.
Herbert Moore was one of the simplest and least aggressive of
men, and one of the most patient and conscientious of students.
He had had a vague notion that Adela was a young woman of
extravagant pleasures, and that, somehow, on her arrival, his
house would be overrun with the train of her attendant revel-
lers. It was not until after they had been six months together
that he became aware that his sister led almost an ascetic life.
By the time six more months had passed Adela had recovered a
delightful sense of youth and *naïveté*. She learned, under her
brother's tuition, to walk—nay, to climb, for there were great
hills in the neighbourhood—to ride and to botanise. At the end
of a year, in the month of August, she received a visit from an
old friend, a girl of her own age, who had been spending July
at a watering-place, and who was now about to be married.
Adela had begun to fear that she had declined into an almost

irreclaimable rusticity and had rubbed off the social facility, the "knowledge of the world" for which she was formerly distinguished; but a week spent in intimate conversation with her friend convinced her not only that she had not forgotten much that she had feared, but had also not forgotten much that she had hoped. For this, and other reasons, her friend's departure left her slightly depressed. She felt lonely and even a little elderly—she had lost another illusion. Laura Benton, for whom a year ago she had entertained a serious regard, now impressed her as a very flimsy little person, who talked about her lover with almost indecent flippancy.

Meanwhile, September was slowly running its course. One morning Mr Moore took a hasty breakfast and started to catch the train for Slowfield, whither a scientific conference called him, which might, he said, release him that afternoon in time for dinner at home, or might, on the other hand, detain him till the night. It was almost the first time during the term of Adela's rustication that she had been left alone for several hours. Her brother's quiet presence was inappreciable enough; yet now that he was at a distance she felt a singular sense of freedom: a return of that condition of early childhood when, through some domestic catastrophe, she had for an infinite morning been left to her own devices. What should she do? she asked herself, with the smile that she reserved for her maidenly monologues. It was a good day for work, but it was a still better one for play. Should she drive into town and call on a lot of tiresome local people? Should she go into the kitchen and try her hand at a pudding for dinner? She felt a delectable longing to do something illicit, to play with fire, to discover some Bluebeard's closet. But poor Herbert was no Bluebeard; if she were to burn down his house he would exact no amends. Adela went out to the verandah, and, sitting down on the steps, gazed across the country. It was apparently the last day of summer. The sky was faintly blue; the woody hills were putting on the morbid colours of autumn; the great pine-grove behind the house seemed to have caught and imprisoned the protesting breezes. Looking down the road toward the village, it occurred to Adela that she might have a visit, and so human was her mood that if any of the local people were to come to her she felt it was in her to humour them. As the sun rose higher she went in and established herself with a piece of embroidery in a deep bow-window, in the second story, which, betwixt its muslin curtains and its external framework of high-creeping plants, commanded most insidiously the principal approach to the house. While she drew her threads she surveyed the road with a deepening conviction that she was destined to have a caller. The air was warm, yet not hot; the dust had been laid during the night by a gentle rain. It had been from the first a source of complaint among Adela's new friends that she was equally gracious to all men, and, what was more remarkable, to all women. Not only had she dedicated herself to no friendships, but she had committed herself to no preferences. Nevertheless, it was with an imagination by no means severely impartial that she sat communing with her open casement. She had very soon made up her mind that, to answer the requirements of the hour, her visitor must be of a sex as different as possible from her own; and as, thanks to the few differences in favour of any individual she had been able to discover among the young males of the country-side, her roll-call in this her hour of need was limited to a single name, so her thoughts were now centred upon the bearer of that name, Mr Weatherby Pynsent, the Unitarian minister. If instead of being Miss Moore's story this were Mr Pynsent's, it might easily be condensed into the simple statement that he was very far gone indeed. Although affiliated to a richer ceremonial than his own she had been so well pleased with one of his sermons, to which she had allowed herself to lend a tolerant ear, that, meeting him some time afterward, she had received him with what she considered a rather knotty doctrinal question; whereupon, gracefully waiving the question, he had asked permission to call upon her and talk over her "difficulties." This short interview had enshrined her in the young minister's heart; and the half a dozen occasions on which he had subsequently contrived to see her had each contributed another candle to her altar. It is but fair to add, however, that, although a captive, Mr Pynsent was as yet no captor. He was simply an honourable young parson, who happened at this moment to be the most sympathetic companion within reach. Adela, at twenty-five years of age, had both a past and a future. Mr Pynsent reminded her of the one and gave her a foretaste of the other.

So, at last, when, as the morning waned toward noon, Adela descried in the distance a man's figure treading the grassy margin of the road, and swinging his stick as he came, she smiled to herself with some complacency. But even while she smiled she became conscious that her heart was beating quite idiotically. She rose, and, resenting her gratuitous emotion, stood for a moment half resolved to see no one at all. As she did so she glanced along the road again. Her friend had drawn nearer, and as the distance lessened she began to perceive that he was not her friend. Before many moments her doubts were removed; the gentleman was a stranger. In front of the house three roads went their different ways, and a spreading elm, tall and slim, like the feathery sheaf of a gleaner, with an ancient bench beneath it, made an informal *rond-point*. The stranger came along the opposite side of the highway, and when he reached the elm stopped and looked about him, as if to verify some direction that had been given him. Then he deliberately crossed over. Adela had time to see, unseen, that he was a robust young man, with a bearded chin and a soft white hat. After the due interval Becky the maid came up with a card somewhat rudely superscribed in pencil:

THOMAS LUDLOW,
New York.

Turning it over in her fingers, Adela saw the gentleman had

made use of the reverse of a pasteboard abstracted from the basket on her own drawing-room table. The printed name on the other side was dashed out; it ran: *Mr Weatherby Pynsent.*

"He asked me to give you this, ma'am," said Becky. "He helped himself to it out of the tray."

"Did he ask for me by name?"

"No, ma'am; he asked for Mr Moore. When I told him Mr Moore was away, he asked for some of the family. I told him you was all the family, ma'am."

"Very well," said Adela, "I will go down." But, begging her pardon, we will precede her by a few steps.

Tom Ludlow, as his friends called him, was a young man of twenty-eight, concerning whom you might have heard the most various opinions; for, as far as he was known (which, indeed, was not very far), he was at once one of the best liked and one of the best hated of men. Born in one of the lower walks of New York life, he still seemed always to move in his native element. A certain crudity of manner and aspect proved him to belong to the great vulgar, muscular, popular majority. On this basis, however, he was a sufficiently good-looking fellow: a middle-sized, agile figure, a head so well shaped as to be handsome, a pair of inquisitive, responsive eyes, and a large, manly mouth, constituting the most expressive part of his equipment. Turned upon the world at an early age, he had, in the pursuit of a subsistence, tried his head at everything in succession, and had generally found it to be quite as hard as the opposing substance; and his person may have been thought to reflect this experience in an air of taking success too much for granted. He was a man of strong faculties and a strong will, but it is doubtful whether his feelings were stronger than he. People liked him for his directness, his good-humour, his general soundness and serviceableness, and disliked him for the same qualities under different names; that is, for his impudence, his offensive optimism, his inhuman avidity for facts. When his friends insisted upon his noble disinterestedness, his enemies were wont to reply it was all very well to ignore, to suppress, one's own sensibilities in the pursuit of knowledge, but to trample on the rest of mankind at the same time betrayed an excess of zeal. Fortunately for Ludlow, on the whole, he was no great listener, and even if he had been, a certain plebeian thick-skinnedness would always have saved his tenderer parts; although it must be added that, if, like a genuine democrat, he was very insensitive, like a genuine democrat, too, he was unexpectedly proud. His tastes, which had always been for the natural sciences, had recently led him to the study of fossil remains, the branch cultivated by Herbert Moore; and it was upon business connected with this pursuit that, after a short correspondence, he had now come to see him.

As Adela went to him he came out from the window, where he had been looking at the lawn. She acknowledged the friendly nod which he apparently intended for a greeting.

"Miss Moore, I believe," said Ludlow.

"Miss Moore," said Adela.

"I beg your pardon for this intrusion, but as I have come from a distance to see Mr Moore, on business, I thought I might venture either to ask at headquarters how he may most easily be reached, or even to give you a message for him." These words were accompanied with a smile under the influence of which it had been written on the scroll of Adela's fate that she was to descend from her pedestal.

"Pray make no apologies," she said. "We hardly recognise such a thing as intrusion in this simple little place. Won't you sit down? My brother went away only this morning, and I expect him back this afternoon."

"This afternoon? indeed. In that case I believe I'll wait. It was very stupid of me not to have dropped a word beforehand. But I have been in the city all summer long, and I shall not be sorry to squeeze a little vacation out of this business. I'm tremendously fond of the country, and I have been working for many months in a musty museum."

"It's possible that my brother may not come home until the evening," Adela said. "He was uncertain. You might go to him at Slowfield."

Ludlow reflected a moment, with his eyes on his hostess. "If he does return in the afternoon, at what hour will he arrive?"

"Well, about three."

"And my own train leaves at four. Allow him a quarter of an hour to come from town and myself a quarter of an hour to get there (if he would give me his vehicle back). In that case I should have about half an hour to see him. We couldn't do much talk, but I could ask him the essential questions. I wish chiefly to ask him for some letters—letters of recommendation to some foreign scientists. He is the only man in this country who knows how much I know. It seems a pity to take two superfluous—that is, possibly superfluous—railway-journeys of an hour apiece; for I should probably come back with him, Don't you think so?" he asked, very frankly.

"You know best," said Adela. "I am not particularly fond of the journey to Slowfield, even when it's absolutely necessary."

"Yes; and then this is such a lovely day for a good long ramble in the fields. That's a thing I haven't had since I don't know when. I guess I'll remain." And he placed his hat on the floor beside him.

"I am afraid, now that I think of it," said Adela, "that there is no train until so late an hour that you would have very little time left on your arrival to talk with my brother, before the hour at which he himself might have determined to start for home. It's true that you might induce him to stop over till the evening."

"Dear me! I shouldn't want to do that. It might be very inconvenient for Mr Moore, don't you see? Besides, I shouldn't have time. And then I always like to see a man in his home— or at some place of my own; a man, that is, whom I have any regard for—and I have a very great regard for your brother,

Miss Moore. When men meet at a half way house neither feels
at his ease. And then this is such an attractive country residence
of yours," pursued Ludlow, looking about him.

"Yes, it's a very pretty place," said Adela.

Ludlow got up and walked to the window. "I want to look
at your view," he remarked. "A lovely little spot. You are a
happy woman, Miss Moore, to have the beauties of nature
always before your eyes."

"Yes, if pretty scenery can make one happy, I ought to be
happy." And Adela was glad to regain her feet and stand on
the other side of the table, before the window.

"Don't you think it can?" asked Ludlow, turning round.
"I don't know, though; perhaps it can't. Ugly sights can't
make you unhappy, necessarily. I have been working for a year
in one of the narrowest, darkest, dirtiest, busiest streets in New
York, with rusty bricks and muddy gutters for scenery. But I
think I can hardly set up to be miserable. I wish I could! It
might be a claim on your benevolence." As he said these words
he stood leaning against the window-shutter, outside the curtain, with folded arms. The morning light covered his face,
and, mingled with that of his radiant laugh, showed Adela that
his was a nature very much alive.

"Whatever else he may be," she said to herself, as she stood
within the shade of the other curtain, playing with the paper-
knife, which she had plucked from the table, "I think he is
honest. I am afraid he isn't a gentleman—but he isn't a bore."
She met his eye, freely, for a moment. "What do you want of
my benevolence?" she asked, with an abruptness of which she
was perfectly conscious. "Does he wish to make friends," she
pursued, tacitly, "or does he merely wish to pay me a vulgar
compliment? There is bad taste, perhaps, in either case, but
especially in the latter." Meanwhile her visitor had already
answered her.

"What do I want of your benevolence? Why, what does
one want of any pleasant thing in life?"

"Dear me, if you never have anything pleasanter than that!" our heroine exclaimed.

"It will do very well for the present occasion," said the young man, blushing, in a large masculine way, at his own quickness of repartee.

Adela glanced toward the clock on the chimney-piece. She was curious to measure the duration of her acquaintance with this breezy invader of her privacy, with whom she so suddenly found herself bandying jokes so personal. She had known him some eight minutes.

Ludlow observed her movement. "I am interrupting you and detaining you from your own affairs," he said; and he moved toward his hat. "I suppose I must bid you good-morning." And he picked it up.

Adela stood at the table and watched him cross the room. To express a very delicate feeling in terms comparatively crude, she was loth to see him depart. She divined, too, that he was very sorry to go. The knowledge of this feeling on his side, however, affected her composure but slightly. The truth is—we say it with all respect—Adela was an old hand. She was modest, honest and wise; but, as we have said, she had a past —a past of which importunate swains in the guise of morning-callers had been no inconsiderable part; and a great dexterity in what may be called outflanking these gentlemen was one of her registered accomplishments. Her liveliest emotion at present, therefore, was less one of annoyance at her companion than of surprise at her own mansuetude, which was yet undeniable. "Am I dreaming?" she asked herself. She looked out of the window, and then back at Ludlow, who stood grasping his hat and stick, contemplating her face. Should she give him leave to remain? "He is honest," she repeated; "why should I not be honest for once? I am sorry you are in a hurry," she said, aloud.

"I am in no hurry," he answered.

Adela turned her face to the window again, and toward the opposite hills. There was a moment's pause.

"I thought *you* were in a hurry," said Ludlow.

Adela shifted her eyes back to where they could see him. "My brother would be very glad that you should stay as long as you like. He would expect me to offer you what little hospitality is in my power."

"Pray, offer it then."

"That is very easily done. This is the parlour, and there, beyond the hall, is my brother's study. Perhaps you would like to look at his books and collections. I know nothing about them, and I should be a very poor guide. But you are welcome to go in and use your discretion in examining what may interest you."

"This, I take it, would be but another way of separating from you."

"For the present, yes."

"But I hesitate to take such liberties with your brother's things as you recommend."

"Recommend? I recommend nothing."

"But if I decline to penetrate into Mr Moore's sanctum, what alternative remains?"

"Really—you must make your own alternative."

"I think you mentioned the parlour. Suppose I choose that."

"Just as you please. Here are some books, and if you like I will bring you some periodicals. There are ever so many scientific papers. Can I serve you in any other way? Are you tired by your walk? Would you like a glass of wine?"

"Tired by my walk?—not exactly. You are very kind, but I feel no immediate desire for a glass of wine. I think you needn't trouble yourself about scientific periodicals either. I am not exactly in the mood to read." And Ludlow pulled out his watch and compared it with the clock. "I am afraid your clock is fast."

"Yes," said Adela; "very likely."

"Some ten minutes. Well, I suppose I had better be walking." And, coming toward Adela, he extended his hand.

She gave him hers. "It is a day of days for a long, slow ramble," she said.

Ludlow's only rejoinder was his hand-shake. He moved slowly toward the door, half accompanied by Adela. "Poor fellow!" she said to herself. There was a summer-door, composed of lattices painted green, like a shutter; it admitted into the hall a cool, dusky light, in which Adela looked pale. Ludlow pushed its wings apart with his stick, and disclosed a landscape, long, deep, and bright, framed by the pillars of the porch. He stopped on the threshold, swinging his cane. "I hope I shall not lose my way," he said.

"I hope not. My brother will not forgive me if you do."

Ludlow's brows were slightly contracted by a frown, but he contrived to smile with his lips. "When shall I come back?" he asked, abruptly.

Adela found but a low tone—almost a whisper—at her command to answer—"Whenever you please."

The young man turned round, with his back to the bright doorway, and looked into Adela's face, which was now covered with light. "Miss Moore," said he, "it's very much against my will that I leave you at all!"

Adela stood debating within herself. After all, what if her companion should stay with her? It would, under the circumstances, be an adventure; but was an adventure necessarily a criminal thing? It lay wholly with herself to decide. She was her own mistress, and she had hitherto been a just mistress. Might she not for once be a generous one? The reader will observe in Adela's meditation the recurrence of this saving clause "for once." It was produced by the simple fact that she had begun the day in a romantic mood. She was prepared to be interested; and now that an interesting phenomenon had presented itself, that it stood before her in vivid human—nay, manly—shape, instinct with reciprocity, was she to close her hand to the liberality of fate? To do so would be only to expose herself the more, for it would imply a gratuitous insult to human nature. Was not the man before her redolent of good intentions, and was that not enough? He was not what Adela had been used to call a gentleman; at this conviction she had arrived by a rapid diagonal, and now it served as a fresh starting-point. "I have seen all the gentlemen can show me" (this was her syllogism): "let us try something new! I see no reason why you should run away so fast, Mr Ludlow," she said, aloud.

"I think it would be the greatest piece of folly I ever committed!" cried the young man.

"I think it would be rather a pity," Adela remarked.

"And you invite me into your parlour again? I come as *your* visitor, you know. I was your brother's before. It's a simple enough matter. We are old friends. We have a solid common ground in your brother. Isn't that about it?"

"You may adopt whatever theory you please. To my mind it is indeed a very simple matter."

"Oh, but I wouldn't have it too simple," said Ludlow, with a genial smile.

"Have it as you please!"

Ludlow leaned back against the doorway. "Look here, Miss Moore; your kindness makes me as gentle as a little child. I am passive; I am in your hands; do with me what you please. I can't help contrasting my fate with what it might have been but for you. A quarter of an hour ago I was ignorant of your existence; you were not in my programme. I had no idea your brother had a sister. When your servant spoke of 'Miss Moore,' upon my word I expected something rather elderly—something venerable—some rigid old lady, who would say, 'exactly,' and 'very well, sir,' and leave me to spend the rest of the morning tilting back in a chair on the piazza of the hotel. It shows what fools we are to attempt to forecast the future."

"We must not let our imagination run away with us in any direction," said Adela, sententiously.

"Imagination? I don't believe I have any. No, madam"—

and Ludlow straightened himself up—"I live in the present. I write my programme from hour to hour—or, at any rate, I will in the future."

"I think you are very wise," said Adela. "Suppose you write a programme for the present hour. What shall we do? It seems to me a pity to spend so lovely a morning indoors. There is something in the air—I can't imagine what—which seems to say it is the last day of summer. We ought to commemorate it. How should you like to take a walk?" Adela had decided that, to reconcile her aforesaid benevolence with the proper maintenance of her dignity, her only course was to be the perfect hostess. This decision made, very naturally and gracefully she played her part. It was the one possible part; and yet it did not preclude those delicate sensations with which so rare an episode seem charged: it simply legitimated them. A romantic adventure on so conventional a basis would assuredly hurt no one.

"I should like a walk very much," said Ludlow; "a walk with a halt at the end of it."

"Well, if you will consent to a short halt at the beginning of it," Adela rejoined, "I will be with you in a very few minutes." When she returned, in her little hat and jacket, she found her friend seated on the steps of the verandah. He arose and gave her a card.

"I have been requested, in your absence, to hand you this." Adela read with some compunction the name of Mr Weatherby Pynsent.

"Has he been here?" she asked. "Why didn't he come in?"

"I told him you were not at home. If it wasn't true then, it was going to be true so soon that the interval was hardly worth taking account of. He addressed himself to me, as I seemed from my position to be quite in possession; that is, I put myself in his way, as it were, so that he had to speak to me: but I confess he looked at me as if he doubted my word. He hesitated as to whether he should confide his name to me, or whether he should ring for the servant. I think he wished to show me that he suspected my veracity, for he was making rather grimly for the doorbell when I, fearing that once inside the house he might encounter the living truth, informed him in the most good-humoured tone possible that I would take charge of his little tribute, if he would trust me with it."

"It seems to me, Mr Ludlow, that you are a strangely un-scrupulous man. How did you know that Mr Pynsent's business was not urgent?"

"I didn't know it! But I knew it could be no more urgent than mine. Depend upon it, Miss Moore, you have no case against me. I only pretend to be a man; to have admitted that sweet little cleric—isn't he a cleric, eh?—would have been the act of an angel."

Adela was familiar with a sequestered spot, in the very heart of the fields, as it seemed to her, to which she now proposed to conduct her friend. The point was to select a goal neither too distant nor too near, and to adopt a pace neither too rapid nor too slow. But although Adela's happy valley was at least two miles away, and they had dawdled immensely over the interval, yet their arrival at a certain little rustic gate, beyond which the country grew vague and gently wild, struck Adela as sudden. Once on the road she felt a precipitate conviction that there could be no evil in an excursion so purely pastoral and no guile in a spirit so deeply sensitive to the influences of nature, and to the melancholy aspect of incipient autumn, as that of her companion. A man with an unaffected relish for small children is a man to inspire young women with a con-fidence; and so, in a less degree, a man with a genuine feeling for the unsophisticated beauties of a casual New England land-scape may not unreasonably be regarded by the daughters of the scene as a person whose motives are pure. Adela was a great observer of the clouds, the trees, and the streams, the sounds and colours, the transparent airs and blue horizons of her adop-ted home; and she was reassured by Ludlow's appreciation of these modest phenomena. His enjoyment of them, deep as it was, however, had to struggle against the sensuous depression natural to a man who has spent the summer looking over dry specimens in a laboratory, and against an impediment of a less material order—the feeling that Adela was a remarkably attractive woman. Still, naturally a great talker, he uttered his various satisfactions with abundant humour and point. Adela felt that he was decidedly a companion for the open air—he was a man to make use even to abuse, of the wide horizon and the high ceiling of nature. The freedom of his gestures, the sonority of his voice, the keenness of his vision, the general vivacity of his manners, seemed to necessitate and to justify a universal absence of resisting surfaces. They passed through the little gate and wandered over empty pastures, until the ground began to rise, and stony surfaces to crop through the turf; when, after a short ascent, they reached a broad plateau, covered with boulders and shrubs, which lost itself on one side in a short, steep cliff, whence fields and marshes stretched down to the opposite river, and on the other, in scattered clumps of cedar and maple, which gradually thickened and multiplied, until the horizon in that quarter was purple with mild masses of forest. Here was both sun and shade—the unobstructed sky, or the whispering dome of a circle of trees which had always reminded Adela of the stone-pipes of the Villa Borghese. Adela led the way to a sunny seat among the rocks which commanded the course of the river, where the murmuring cedars would give them a kind of human company.

"It has always seemed to me that the wind in the trees is always the voice of coming changes," Ludlow said.

"Perhaps it is," Adela replied. "The trees are for ever talking in this melancholy way, and men are for ever changing."

"Yes, but they can only be said to express the foreboding of coming events—that is what I mean—when there is someone there to hear them; and more especially someone in whose life a change is, to his knowledge, about to take place. Then they are quite prophetic. Don't you know Longfellow says so?"

"Yes, I know Longfellow says so. But you seem to speak from your own inspiration."

"Well, I rather think I do."

"Is there some great change hanging over you?"

"Yes, rather an important one."

"I believe that's what men say when they are going to be married," said Adela.

"I am going to be divorced, rather. I am going to Europe."

"Indeed! soon?"

"To-morrow," said Ludlow, after an instant's pause.

"Oh!" exclaimed Adela. "How I envy you!"

Ludlow, who sat looking over the cliff and tossing stones down into the plain, observed a certain inequality in the tone of his companion's two exclamations. The first was nature, the second art. He turned his eyes upon her, but she had directed hers away into the distance. Then, for a moment, he retreated within himself and thought. He rapidly surveyed his position. Here was he, Tom Ludlow, a hard-headed son of toil; without fortune, without credit, without antecedents, whose lot was cast exclusively with vulgar males, and who had never had a mother, a sister, nor a well-bred sweetheart, to pitch his voice for the feminine tympanum, who had seldom come nearer an indubitable lady than, in a favouring crowd, to receive a mechanical "thank you" (as if he were a policeman) for some accidental assistance: here he found himself up to his neck in a sudden pastoral with a young woman who was evidently altogether superior. That it was in him to enjoy the society of such a person (provided, of course, she were not a chit) he very well knew; but he had never happened to suppose that he should find it open to him. Was he now to infer that this brilliant gift was his—the gift of what is called in the relation between the sexes success? The inference was at least logical. He had made a good impression. Why else should an eminently discriminating girl have fraternised with him at such a rate? It was with a little thrill of satisfaction that Ludlow reflected upon the directness of his course. "It all comes back to my old theory that a process can't be too simple. I used no arts. In such an enterprise I shouldn't have known where to begin. It was my ignorance of the regular way that saved me. Women like a gentleman, of course; but they like a man better." It was the little touch of nature he had detected in Adela's tone that set him thinking; but as compared with the frankness of his own attitude it betrayed after all no undue emotion. Ludlow had accepted the fact of his adaptability to the idle mood of a cultivated woman in a thoroughly rational spirit, and he was not now tempted to exaggerate its bearings. He was not the man to be intoxicated by a triumph after all possibly superficial. "If Miss Moore is so wise—or so foolish—as to like me half an hour for what I am, she is welcome," he said to himself. "Assuredly," he added, as he glanced at her intelligent profile, "she will not like me for what I am not." It needs a woman, however, far more intelligent than (thank heaven!) most women are—more intelligent, certainly, than Adela was—to guard her happiness against a clever man's consistent assumption of her intelligence; and doubtless it was from a sense of this general truth that, as Ludlow continued to observe his companion, he felt an emotion of manly tenderness. "I wouldn't offend her for the world," he thought. Just then Adela, conscious of his contemplation, looked about; and before he knew it, Ludlow had repeated aloud, "Miss Moore, I wouldn't offend you for the world."

Adela eyed him for a moment with a little flush that subsided into a smile. "To what dreadful impertinence is that the prelude?" she inquired.

"It's a prelude to nothing. It refers to the past—to any possible displeasure I may have caused you."

"Your scruples are unnecessary, Mr Ludlow. If you had given me offence, I should not have left you to apologise for it. I should not have left the matter to occur to you as you sat dreaming charitably in the sun."

"What would you have done?"

"Done? nothing. You don't imagine I would have scolded you—or snubbed you—or answered you back, I take it. I would have left undone—what, I can't tell you. Ask yourself what I *have* done. I am sure I hardly know myself," said Adela, with some intensity. "At all events, here I am sitting with you in the fields, as if you were a friend of many years. Why do you speak of offence?" And Adela (an uncommon accident with her) lost command of her voice, which trembled ever so slightly. "What an odd thought! why should you offend me? Do I seem so open to that sort of thing?" Her colour had deepened again, and her eyes had brightened. She had forgotten herself, and before speaking had not, as was her wont, sought counsel of that staunch conservative, her taste. She had spoken from a full heart—a heart which had been filling rapidly, since the outset of their walk, with a feeling almost passionate in its quality, and which that little puff of the actual conveyed in Mr Ludlow's announcement of his departure had caused to overflow. The reader may give this feeling whatever name he chooses. We will content ourselves with saying that Adela had played with fire so effectually that she had been scorched. The slight violence of the speech just quoted may represent her sensation of pain.

"You pull one up rather short, Miss Moore," said Ludlow. "A man says the best he can."

Adela made no reply—for a moment she hung her head. Was she to cry out because she was hurt? Was she to thrust her injured heart into a company in which there was, as yet at least, no question of hearts? No! here our reserved and contemplative heroine is herself again. Her part was still to be the youthful woman of the world, the perfect young lady. For our own part, we can imagine no figure more engaging than this civilised and disciplined personage under such circumstances; and if Adela had been the most accomplished of coquettes she could not have assumed a more becoming expression than the air of judicious consideration which now covered her features. But having paid this generous homage to propriety, she felt free to suffer in secret. Raising her eyes from the ground, she abruptly addressed her companion.

"By the way, Mr Ludlow, tell me something about yourself."

Ludlow burst into a laugh. "What shall I tell you?"

"Everything."

"Everything? Excuse me, I'm not such a fool. But do you know that's a very tempting request you make? I suppose I ought to blush and hesitate; but I never yet blushed or hesitated in the right place."

"Very good. There is one fact. Continue. Begin at the beginning."

"Well, let me see. My name you know. I am twenty-eight years old."

"That's the end," said Adela.

"But you don't want the history of my babyhood, I take it. I imagine that I was a very big, noisy, ugly baby—what's called a 'splendid infant.' My parents were poor, and, of course, honest. They belonged to a very different set—or 'sphere,' I suppose you call it—from any you probably know. They were working people. My father was a chemist, in a small way of business, and I suspect my mother was not above using her hands to turn a penny. But although I don't remember her, I am sure she was a good, sound woman; I feel her occasionally in my own sinews. I myself have been at work all my life, and a very good worker I am, let me tell you. I am not patient, as I imagine your brother to be—although I have more patience than you might suppose—but I don't let go easily. If I strike you as very egotistical, remember 'twas you began it. I don't know whether I am clever, and I don't much care; that's a kind of metaphysical, sentimental, vapid word. But I know what I want to know, and I generally manage to find it out. I don't know much about my moral nature; I have no doubt I am beastly selfish. Still, I don't like to hurt peoples' feelings, and I am rather fond of poetry and flowers. I don't believe I am very 'high-toned,' all the same. I should not be at all surprised to discover I was prodigiously conceited; but I am afraid the discovery wouldn't cut me down much. I am remarkably hard to keep down, I know. Oh, you would think me a great brute if you knew me. I shouldn't recommend anyone to count too much on my being of an amiable disposition. I am often very much bored with people who are fond of me—because some of them are, really; so I am afraid I am ungrateful. Of course, as a man speaking to a woman, there's nothing for it but to say I am very low; but I hate to talk about things you can't prove. I have got very little 'general culture,' you know, but first and last I have read a great many books—and, thank heaven, I remember things. And I have some tastes, too. I am very fond of music. I have a good young voice of my own; *that* I can't help knowing; and I am not one to be bullied about pictures. I know how to sit on a horse, and how to row a boat. Is that enough? I am conscious of a great inability to say anything to the point. To put myself in a nutshell, I am a greedy specialist —and not a bad fellow. Still, I am only what I am—a very common creature."

"Do you call yourself a very common creature because you really believe yourself to be one, or because you are weakly tempted to disfigure your rather flattering catalogue with a great final blot?"

"I am sure I don't know. You show more subtlety in that one question than I have shown in a whole string of affirmations. You women are strong on asking embarrassing questions. Seriously, I believe I *am* second-rate. I wouldn't make such an admission to every one though. But to you, Miss Moore, who sit there under your parasol as impartial as the muse of history, to you I owe the truth. I am no man of genius. There is something I miss; some final distinction I lack; you may call it what you please. Perhaps it's humility. Perhaps you can find it in Ruskin, somewhere. Perhaps it's delicacy—perhaps it's imagination. I am very vulgar, Miss Moore. I am the vulgar son of vulgar people. I use the word, of course, in its literal sense. So much I grant you at the outset, but it's my last concession!"

"Your concessions are smaller than they sound. Have you any sisters?"

"Not a sister; and no brothers, nor cousins, nor uncles, nor aunts."

"And you sail for Europe to-morrow?"

"To-morrow, at ten o'clock."

"To be away how long?"

"As long as I can. Five years, if possible."

"What do you expect to do in those five years?"

"Well, study."

"Nothing but study?"

"It will all come back to that, I guess. I hope to enjoy myself considerably, and to look at the world as I go. But I must not waste time; I am growing old."

"Where are you going?"

"To Berlin. I wanted to get some letters of introduction from your brother."

"Have you money? Are you well off?"

"Well off? Not I, heaven forgive me! I am very poor. I have in hand a little money that has just come to me from an unexpected quarter: an old debt owing my father. It will take me to Germany and keep me for six months. After that I shall work my way."

"Are you happy? Are you contented?"

"Just now I am pretty comfortable, thank you."

"But shall you be so when you get to Berlin?"

"I don't promise to be contented; but I am pretty sure to be happy."

"Well," said Adela, "I sincerely hope you will succeed in everything."

"Thank you, awfully," said Ludlow.

Of what more was said at this moment no record may be given here. The reader has been put into possession of the key of our friends' conversation; it is only needful to say that in this key it was prolonged for half an hour more. As the minutes elapsed Adela found herself drifting further and further away from her anchorage. When at last she compelled herself to consult her watch and remind her companion that there remained but just time enough for them to reach home in anticipation of her brother's arrival, she knew that she was rapidly floating seaward. As she descended the hill at her companion's side she felt herself suddenly thrilled by an acute temptation. Her first instinct was to close her eyes upon it, in the trust that when she should open them again it would have vanished; but she found that it was not to be so uncompromisingly dismissed. It pressed her so hard that before she walked a mile homeward she had succumbed to it, or had at least given it the pledge of that quickening of the heart which accompanies a bold resolution. This little sacrifice allowed her no breath for idle words, and she accordingly advanced with a bent and listening head. Ludlow marched along, with no apparent diminution of his habitual buoyancy of mien, talking as fast and loud as at the outset. He risked a prophecy that Mr Moore would not have returned, and charged Adela with a comical message of regrets. Adela had begun by wondering whether the approach of their separation had wrought within him any sentimental depression at all commensurate with her own, with that which sealed her lips and weighed upon her heart; and now she was debating as to whether his express declaration that he felt "awfully blue" ought necessarily to remove her doubts. Ludlow followed up this declaration with a very pretty review of the morning, and a leave-taking speech which, whether intensely sincere or not, struck Adela as at least in very good taste. He might be a common creature—but he was certainly a very uncommon one. When they reached the

garden-gate it was with a fluttering heart that Adela scanned
the premises for some accidental sign of her brother's presence.
She felt that there would be an especial fitness in his not having
returned. She led the way in. The hall table was bare of his
usual hat and overcoat, his silver-headed stick was not in the
corner. The only object that struck her was Mr Pynsent's card,
which she had deposited there on her exit. All that was represented by that little white ticket seemed a thousand miles away.
She looked for Mr Moore in his study, but it was empty.

As Adela went back from her quest into the drawing-room
she simply shook her head at Ludlow, who was standing before
the fire-place; and as she did so she caught her reflection in the
mantel-glass. "Verily," she said to herself, "I have travelled
far." She had pretty well unlearned her old dignities and forms,
but she was to break with them still more completely. It was
with a singular hardihood that she prepared to redeem the little
pledge which had been extorted from her on her way home.
She felt that there was no trial to which her generosity might
now be called which she would not hail with enthusiasm. Unfortunately, her generosity was not likely to be challenged;
although she nevertheless had the satisfaction of assuring herself at this moment that, like the mercy of the Lord, it was
infinite. Should she satisfy herself of her friend's? or should she
leave it delightfully uncertain? These had been the terms of
what has been called her temptation, at the foot of the hill.

"Well, I have very little time," said Ludlow; "I must get
my dinner and pay my bill and drive to the train." And he put
out his hand.

Adela gave him her own, without meeting his eyes. "You
are in a great hurry," she said, rather casually.

"It's not I who am in a hurry. It's my confounded destiny.
It's the train and the steamer."

"If you really wished to stay you wouldn't be bullied by the
train and the steamer."

"Very true—very true. But *do* I really wish to stay?"

"That's the question. That's exactly what I want to know."

"You ask difficult questions, Miss Moore."

"Difficult for me—yes."

"Then, of course, you are prepared to answer easy ones."

"Let me hear what you call easy."

"Well then, do you wish me to stay? All I have to do is to throw down my hat, sit down, and fold my arms for twenty minutes. I lose my train and my ship. I remain in America, instead of going to Europe."

"I have thought of all that."

"I don't mean to say it's a great deal. There are attractions on both sides."

"Yes, and especially on one. It *is* a great deal."

"And you request me to give it up—to renounce Berlin?"

"No; I ought not to do that. What I ask of you is whether, if I *should* so request you, you would say 'yes.'"

"That *does* make the matter easy for you, Miss Moore. What attractions do you hold out?"

"I hold out nothing whatever, sir."

"I suppose that means a great deal."

"A great deal of absurdity."

"Well, you are certainly a most interesting woman, Miss Moore—a charming woman."

"Why don't you call me irresistible at once, and bid me good morning?"

"I don't know but that I shall have to come to that. But I will give you no answer that leaves you at an advantage. Ask me to stay—order me to stay, if that suits you better—and I will see how it sounds. Come, you must not trifle with a man." He still held Adela's hand, and now they were looking watchfully into each other's eyes. He paused, waiting for an answer.

"Goodbye, Mr Ludlow," said Adela. "God bless you!" And she was about to withdraw her hand; but he held it.

"Are we friends?" said he.

Adela gave a little shrug of her shoulders. "Friends of three hours!"

Ludlow looked at her with some sternness. "Our parting could at best hardly have been sweet," said he; "but why should you make it bitter, Miss Moore?"

"If it's bitter, why should you try to change it?"

"Because I don't like bitter things."

Ludlow had caught a glimpse of the truth—that truth of which the reader has had a glimpse—and he stood there at once thrilled and annoyed. He had both a heart and a conscience. "It's not my fault," he murmured to the latter; but he was unable to add, in all consistency, that it was his misfortune. It would be very heroic, very poetic, very chivalric, to lose his steamer, and he felt that he could do so for sufficient cause—at the suggestion of a fact. But the motive here was less than a fact—an idea; less than an idea—a mere guess. "It's a very pretty little romance as it is," he said to himself. "Why spoil it? She's a different sort from any I have met, and just to have seen her like this—that is enough for me!" He raised her hand to his lips, pressed them to it, dropped it, reached the door, and bounded out of the garden gate.

MY FRIEND BINGHAM

Conscious as I am of a deep aversion to stories of a painful nature, I have often asked myself whether, in the events here set forth, the element of pain is stronger than that of joy. An affirmative answer to this question would have stood as a veto upon the publication of my story, for it is my opinion that the literature of horrors needs no extension. Such an answer, however, I am unwilling to pronounce; while, on the other hand, I hesitate to assume the responsibility of a decided negative. I have therefore determined to leave the solution to the reader. I may add, that I am very sensible of the superficial manner in which I have handled my facts. I bore no other part in the accomplishment of these facts than that of a cordial observer; and it was impossible that, even with the best will in the world, I should fathom the emotions of the actors. Yet, as the very faintest reflection of human passions, under the pressure of fate, possesses an immortal interest, I am content to appeal to the reader's sympathy, and to assure him of my own fidelity.

Towards the close of summer, in my twenty-eighth year, I went down to the seaside to rest from a long term of work, and to enjoy, after several years of separation, a *tête-à-tête* with an intimate friend. My friend had just arrived from Europe, and we had agreed to spend my vacation together by the side of the sounding sea, and within easy reach of the city. On taking possession of our lodgings, we found that we should have no fellow-idlers, and we hailed joyously the prospect of the great marine solitudes which each of us declared that he found so abundantly peopled by the other. I hasten to impart to the reader the following facts in regard to the man whom I found so good a companion.

George Bingham had been born and bred among people for whom, as he grew to manhood, he learned to entertain a most generous contempt,—people in whom the hereditary possession of a large property—for he assured me that the facts stood in the relation of cause and effect—had extinguished all intelligent purpose and principle. I trust that I do not speak rhetorically when I describe in these terms the combined ignorance and vanity of my friend's progenitors. It was their fortune to make a splendid figure while they lived, and I feel little compunction in hinting at their poverty in certain human essentials. Bingham was no declaimer, and indeed no great talker; and it was only now and then, in an allusion to the past as the field of a wasted youth, that he expressed his profound resentment. I read this for the most part in the severe humility with which he regarded the future, and under cover of which he seemed to salute it as void at least (whatever other ills it might contain) of those domestic embarrassments which had been the bane of his first manhood. I have no doubt that much may be said, within limits, for the graces of that society against which my friend embodied so violent a reaction, and especially for its good-humor,—that home-keeping benevolence which accompanies a sense of material repletion. It is equally probable that to persons of a simple constitution these graces may wear a look of delightful and enduring mystery; but poor Bingham was no simpleton. He was a man of opinions numerous, delicate, and profound. When, with the lapse of his youth, he awoke to a presentiment of these opinions, and cast his first interrogative glance upon the world, he found that in his own little section of it he and his opinions were a piece of melancholy impertinence. Left, at twenty-three years of age, by his father's death, in possession of a handsome property, and absolute master of his actions, he had thrown himself blindly into the world. But, as he afterwards assured me, so superficial was his knowledge of the real world,—the world of labor and inquiry,—that he had found himself quite incapable of intelligent action. In this manner he had wasted a great deal of time. He had travelled much, however; and, being a keen observer of men and women, he had acquired a certain practical knowledge of human nature. Nevertheless, it was not till he was nearly thirty years old that he had begun to live for himself. "By myself," he explained, "I mean something else than this monstrous hereditary faculty for doing nothing and thinking nothing." And he led me to believe, or I should rather say he allowed me to believe, that at this moment he had made a serious attempt to study. But upon this point he was not very explicit; for if he blushed for the manner in which he had slighted his opportunities, he blushed equally for the manner in which he had used them. It is my belief that he had but a limited capacity for study, and I am certain that to the end of his days there subsisted in his mind a very friendly relation between fancies and facts.

Bingham was *par excellence* a moralist, a man of sentiment. I know—he knew himself—that, in this busy Western world, this character represents no recognized avocation; but in the absence of such avocation, its exercise was nevertheless very dear to him. I protest that it was very dear to me, and that, at the end of a long morning devoted to my office-desk, I have often felt as if I had contributed less to the common cause than I have felt after moralizing—or, if you please, sentimentalizing —half an hour with my friend. He was an idler, assuredly; but his candor, his sagacity, his good taste, and, above all, a certain diffident enthusiasm which followed its objects with the exquisite trepidation of an unconfessed and despairing lover, —these things, and a hundred more, redeemed him from vulgarity. For three years before we came together, as I have intimated, my impressions of my friend had rested on his letters; and yet, from the first hour which we spent together, I felt that they had done him no wrong. We were genuine friends. I don't know that I can offer better proof of this than

by saying that, as our old personal relations resumed their
force, and the time-shrunken outlines of character filled themselves out, I greeted the reappearance of each familiar foible on
Bingham's part quite as warmly as I did that of the less punc-
tual virtue. Compared, indeed, with the comrade of earlier
years, my actual companion was a well-seasoned man of the
world; but with all his acquired humility and his disciplined
bonhomie, he had failed to divest himself of a certain fastidious-
ness of mind, a certain formalism of manner, which are the
token and the prerogative of one who has not been obliged to
address himself to practical questions. The charm bestowed by
these facts upon Bingham's conversation—a charm often
vainly invoked in their absence—is explained by his honest indifference to their action, and his indisposition to turn them to
account in the interest of the picturesque,—an advantage but
too easy of conquest for a young man, rich, accomplished, and
endowed with good looks and a good name. I may say, perhaps, that to a critical mind my friend's prime distinction would
have been his very positive refusal to drape himself, after the
current taste, with those brilliant stuffs which fortune had
strewn at his feet.

Of course, a great deal of our talk bore upon Bingham's
recent travels, adventures, and sensations. One of these last he
handled very frankly, and treated me to a bit of genuine
romance. He had been in love, and had been cruelly jilted, but
had now grown able to view the matter with much of the impartial spirit of those French critics whose works were his
favorite reading. His account of the young lady's character
and motives would indeed have done credit to many a clever
feuilleton. I was the less surprised, however, at his severely dispassionate tone, when, in retracing the process of his opinions,
I discerned the traces—the ravages, I may almost say—of a
solemn act of renunciation. Bingham had forsworn marriage.
I made haste to assure him that I considered him quite too
young for so austere a resolve.

"I can't help it," said he; "I feel a foreboding that I shall live and die alone."

"A foreboding?" said I. "What's a foreboding worth?"

"Well, then, rationally considered, my marriage is improbable."

"But it's not to be rationally considered," I objected. "It belongs to the province of sentiment."

"But you deny me sentiment. I fall back upon my foreboding."

"That's not sentiment,—it's superstition," I answered. "Your marrying will depend upon your falling in love; and your falling in love will certainly not depend upon yourself."

"Upon whom, then?"

"Upon some unknown fair one,—Miss A, B, or C."

"Well," said Bingham, submissively, "I wish she would make haste and reveal herself."

These remarks had been exchanged in the hollow of a cliff which sloped seaward, and where we had lazily stretched ourselves at length on the grass. The grass had grown very long and brown; and as we lay with our heads quite on a level with it, the view of the immediate beach and the gentle breakers was so completely obstructed by the rank, coarse herbage, that our prospect was reduced to a long, narrow band of deep blue ocean traversing its black fibres, and to the great vault of the sky. We had strolled out a couple of hours before, bearing each a borrowed shot-gun and accompanied by a friendly water-dog, somewhat languidly disposed towards the slaughter of wild ducks. We were neither of us genuine sportsmen, and it is certain that, on the whole, we meant very kindly to the ducks. It was at all events fated that on that day they should suffer but lightly at our hands. For the half-hour previous to the exchange of the remarks just cited, we had quite forgotten our real business; and, with our pieces lost in the grass beside us, and our dog, weary of inaction, wandering far beyond call, we looked like any straw-picking truants. At last Bingham rose to his feet, with the asseveration that it would never do for us to return empty-handed. "But, behold," he exclaimed, as he looked down across the breadth of the beach, "there is our friend of the cottage, with the sick little boy."

I brought myself into a sitting posture, and glanced over the cliff. Down near the edge of the water sat a young woman, tossing stones into it for the amusement of a child, who stood lustily crowing and clapping his hands. Her title to be called our friend lay in the fact, that on our way to the beach we had observed her issuing from a cottage hard by the hotel, leading by the hand a pale-faced little boy, muffled like an invalid. The hotel, as I have said, was all but deserted, and this young woman had been the first person to engage our idle observation. We had seen that, although plainly dressed, she was young, pretty, and modest; and, in the absence of heavier cares, these facts had sufficed to make her interesting. The question had arisen between us, whether she was a native of the shore, or a visitor like ourselves. Bingham inclined to the former view of the case, and I to the latter. There was, indeed, a certain lowliness in her aspect; but I had contended that it was by no means a rustic lowliness. Her dress was simple, but it was well made and well worn; and I noticed that, as she strolled along, leading her little boy, she cast upon sky and sea the lingering glance of one to whom, in their integrity, these were unfamiliar objects. She was the wife of some small trades- man, I argued, who had brought her child to the seaside by the physician's decree. But Bingham declared that it was utterly illogical to suppose her to be a mother of five years' mother- hood; and that, for his part, he saw nothing in her appearance inconsistent with rural influences. The child was her nephew, the son of a married sister, and she a sentimental maiden aunt. Obviously the volume she had in her hand was Tennyson. In the absence on both sides of authentic data, of course the debate was not prolonged; and the subject of it had passed from our memories some time before we again met her on the beach.

She soon became aware of our presence, however; and, with a natural sense of intrusion, we immediately resumed our walk. The last that I saw of her, as we rounded a turn in the cliff which concealed the backward prospect, was a sudden grasp of the child's arm, as if to withdraw him from the reach of a hastily advancing wave.

Half an hour's further walk led us to a point which we were not tempted to exceed. We shot between us some half a dozen birds; but as our dog, whose talents had been sadly misrepresented, proved very shy of the deep water, and succeeded in bringing no more than a couple of our victims to shore, we resolved to abstain from further destruction, and to return home quietly along the beach, upon which we had now descended.

"If we meet our young lady," said Bingham, "we can gallantly offer her our booty."

Some five minutes after he had uttered these words, a couple of great sea-gulls came flying landward over our heads, and, after a long gyration in mid-air, boldly settled themselves on the slope of the cliff at some three hundred yards in front of us, a point at which it projected almost into the waves. After a momentary halt, one of them rose again on his long pinions and soared away seaward; the other remained. He sat perched on a jutting boulder some fifteen feet high, sunning his fishy breast.

"I wonder if I could put a shot into him," said Bingham.

"Try," I answered; and, as he rapidly charged and levelled his piece, I remember idly repeating, while I looked at the great bird,

> "God save thee, ancient mariner,
>   From the fiends that plague thee thus!
>   Why look'st thou so? 'With my cross-bow
>   I shot the albatross.' "

"He's going to rise," I added.

But Bingham had fired. The creature rose, indeed, half slug-
gishly, and yet with too hideous celerity. His movement drew
from us a cry which was almost simultaneous with the report
of Bingham's gun. I cannot express our relation to what followed it better than by saying that it exposed to our sight,
beyond the space suddenly left vacant, the happy figure of the
child from whom we had parted but an hour before. He stood
with his little hands extended, and his face raised toward the
retreating bird. Of the sickening sensation which assailed our
common vision as we saw him throw back his hands to his
head, and reel downwards out of sight, I can give no verbal
account, nor of the rapidity with which we crossed the smooth
interval of sand, and rounded the bluff.

The child's companion had scrambled up the rocky bank
towards the low ledge from which he had fallen, and to which
access was of course all too easy. She had sunk down upon the
stones, and was wildly clasping the boy's body. I turned from
this spectacle to my friend, as to an image of equal woe. Bingham, pale as death, bounded over the stones, and fell on his
knees. The woman let him take the child out of her arms, and
bent over, with her forehead on a rock, moaning. I have never
seen helplessness so vividly embodied as in this momentary
group.

"Did it strike his head?" cried Bingham. "What the devil
was he doing up there?"

"I told him he'd get hurt," said the young woman, with
harrowing simplicity. "To shoot straight at him!—He's
killed!"

"Great heavens! Do you mean to say that I saw him?"
roared Bingham. "How did I know he was there? Did you
see us?"

The young woman woman shook her head. "Of course I
didn't see you. I saw you with your guns before. Oh, he's
killed!"

"He's not killed. It was mere duck shot. Don't talk such

stuff.—My own poor little man!" cried George. "Charles, where *were* our eyes?"

"He wanted to catch the bird," moaned our companion. "Baby, my boy! open your eyes. Speak to your mother. For God's sake, get some help!"

She had put out her hands to take the child from Bingham, who had half angrily lifted him out of her reach. The senseless movement with which, as she disengaged him from Bingham's grasp, he sank into her arms, was clearly the senselessness of death. She burst into sobs. I went and examined the child.

"He *may* not be killed," I said, turning to Bingham; "keep your senses. It's not your fault. We *couldn't* see each other."

Bingham rose stupidly to his feet.

"She must be got home," I said.

"We must get a carriage. Will you go or stay?"

I saw that he had seen the truth. He looked about him with an expression of miserable impotence. "Poor little devil!" he said, hoarsely.

"Will you go for a carriage?" I repeated, taking his hand, "or will you stay?"

Our companion's sobs redoubled their violence.

"I'll stay," said he. "Bring some woman."

I started at a hard run. I left the beach behind me, passed the white cottage at whose garden gate two women were gossiping, and reached the hotel stable, where I had the good fortune to find a vehicle at my disposal. I drove straight back to the white cottage. One of the women had disappeared, and the other was lingering among her flowers,—a middle-aged, keen-eyed person. As I descended and hastily addressed her, I read in her rapid glance an anticipation of evil tidings.

"The young woman who stays with you—" I began.

"Yes," she said, "my second-cousin. Well?"

"She's in trouble. She wants you to come to her. Her little boy has hurt himself." I had time to see that I need fear no hysterics.

"Where did you leave her?" asked my companion.

"On the beach."

"What's the matter with the child?"

"He fell from a rock. There's no time to be lost." There was a certain antique rigidity about the woman which was at once irritating and reassuring. I was impelled both to quicken her apprehensions and to confide in her self-control. "For all I know, ma'am," said I, "the child is killed."

She gave me an angry stare. "For all you know!" she exclaimed. "Where were your wits? Were you afraid to look at him?"

"Yes, half afraid."

She glanced over the paling at my vehicle. "Am I to get into that?" she asked.

"If you will be so good."

She turned short about, and re-entered the house, where, as I stood out among the dahlias and the pinks, I heard a rapid opening and shutting of drawers. She shortly reappeared, equipped for driving; and, having locked the house door, and pocketed the key, came and faced me, where I stood ready to help her into the wagon.

"We'll stop for the doctor," she began.

"The doctor," said I, "is of no use."

A few moments of hard driving brought us to my starting-point. The tide had fallen perceptibly in my absence; and I remember receiving a strange impression of the irretrievable nature of the recent event from the sight of poor Bingham, standing down at the low-watermark, and looking seaward with his hands in his pockets. The mother of his little victim still sat on the heap of stones where she had fallen, pressing her child to her breast. I helped my companion to descend, which she did with great deliberation. It is my belief that, as we drove along the beach, she derived from the expression of Bingham's figure, and from the patient aversion of his face, a suspicion of his relation to the opposite group. It was not till the elder woman had come within a few steps of her, that the younger became aware of her approach. I merely had time to catch the agonized appeal of her upward glance, and the broad compassion of the other's stooping movement, before I turned my back upon their encounter, and walked down towards my friend. The monotonous murmur of the waves had covered the sound of our wagonwheels, and Bingham stood all unconscious of the coming of relief,—distilling I know not what divine relief from the simple beauty of sea and sky. I had laid my hand on his shoulder before he turned about. He looked towards the base of the cliff. I knew that a great effusion of feeling would occur in its natural order; but how should I help him across the interval?

"That's her cousin," I said at random. "She seems a very capable woman."

"The child is quite dead," said Bingham, for all answer. I was struck by the plainness of his statement. In the comparative freedom of my own thoughts I had failed to make allowance for the embarrassed movement of my friend's. It was not, therefore, until afterwards that I acknowledged he had thought to better purpose than I; inasmuch as the very simplicity of his tone implied a positive acceptance (for the moment) of the dreadful fact which he uttered.

"The sooner they get home, the better," I said. It was evident that the elder of our companions had already embraced this conviction. She had lifted the child and placed him in the carriage, and she was now turning towards his mother and inviting her to ascend. Even at the distance at which I stood, the mingled firmness and tenderness of her gestures were clearly apparent. They seemed, moreover, to express a certain indifference to our movements, an independence of our further interference, which—fanciful as the assertion may look—was not untinged with irony. It was plain that, by whatever rapid process she had obtained it, she was already in possession of our story. "Thank God for strongminded women!" I exclaimed;—and yet I could not repress a feeling that it behooved me, on behalf of my friend, to treat as an equal with the vulgar movement of antipathy which he was destined to encounter, and of which, in the irresistible sequence of events, the attitude of this good woman was an index.

We walked towards the carriage together. "I shall not come home directly," said Bingham; "but don't be alarmed about me."

I looked at my watch. "I give you two hours," I said, with all the authority of my affection.

The new-comer had placed herself on the back seat of the vehicle beside the sufferer, who on entering had again possessed herself of her child. As I went about to mount in front, Bingham came and stood by the wheel. I read his purpose in his face,—the desire to obtain from the woman he had wronged some recognition of his *human* character, some confession that she dimly distinguished him from a wild beast or a thunderbolt. One of her hands lay exposed, pressing together on her knee the lifeless little hands of her boy. Bingham removed his hat, and placed his right hand on that of the young woman. I saw that she started at his touch, and that he vehemently tightened his grasp.

"It's too soon to talk of forgiveness," said he, "for it's too soon for me to think intelligently of the wrong I have done you. God has brought us together in a very strange fashion."

The young woman raised her bowed head, and gave my friend, if not just the look he coveted, at least the most liberal glance at her command,—a look which, I fancy, helped him to face the immediate future. But these are matters too delicate to be put into words.

I spent the hours that elapsed before Bingham's return to the inn in gathering information about the occupants of the cottage. Impelled by that lively intuition of calamity which is natural to women, the housekeeper of the hotel, a person of evident kindliness and discretion, lost no time in winning my confidence. I was not unwilling that the tragic incident which had thus arrested our idleness should derive its earliest publicity from my own lips; and I was forcibly struck with the exquisite impartiality with which this homely creature bestowed her pity. Miss Horner, I learned, the mistress of the cottage, was the last representative of a most respectable family, native to the neighboring town. It had been for some years her practice to let lodgings during the summer. At the close of the present season she had invited her kinswoman, Mrs Hicks, to spend the autumn with her. That this lady was the widow of a Baptist minister; that her husband had died some three years before; that she was very poor; that her child had been sickly, and that the care of his health had so impeded her exertions for a livelihood, that she had been intending to leave him with Miss Horner for the winter, and obtain a "situation" in town;— these facts were the salient points of the housekeeper's somewhat prolix recital.

The early autumn dusk had fallen when Bingham returned. He looked very tired. He had been walking for several hours, and, as I fancied, had grown in some degree familiar with his new responsibilities. He was very hungry, and made a vigorous attack upon his supper. I had been indisposed to eat, but the sight of his healthy appetite restored my own. I had grown weary of my thoughts, and I found something salutary in the apparent simplicity and rectitude of Bingham's state of mind.

"I find myself taking it very quietly," he said, in the course of his repast. "There is something so absolute in the nature of the calamity, that one is compelled to accept it. I don't see how I could endure to have mutilated the poor little mortal. To kill a human being is, after all, the least injury you can do him." He spoke these words deliberately, with his eyes on mine, and with an expression of perfect candor. But as he paused, and in spite of my perfect assent to their meaning, I could not help

mentally reverting to the really tragic phase of the affair; and
I suppose my features revealed to Bingham's scrutiny the
process of my thoughts. His pale face flushed a burning crimson, his lips trembled. "Yes, my boy!" he cried; "that's where
it's damnable." He buried his head in his hands, and burst into
tears.

We had a long talk. At the end of it, we lit our cigars, and
came out upon the deserted piazza. There was a lovely starlight, and, after a few turns in silence, Bingham left my side
and strolled off towards a bend in the road, in the direction of
the sea. I saw him stand motionless for a long time, and then I
heard him call me. When I reached his side, I saw that he had
been watching a light in the window of the white cottage. We
heard the village bell in the distance striking nine.

"Charles," said Bingham, "suppose you go down there and
make some offer of your services. God knows whom the poor
creatures have to look to. She has had a couple of men thrust
into her life. She must take the good with the bad."

I lingered a moment. "It's a difficult task," I said. "What
shall I say?"

Bingham silently puffed his cigar. He stood with his arms
folded, and his head thrown back, slowly measuring the starry
sky. "I wish she could come out here and look at that sky," he
said at last. "It's a sight for bereaved mothers. Somehow, my
dear boy," he pursued, "I never felt less depressed in my life.
It's none of my doing."

"It would hardly do for me to tell her that," said I.

"I don't know," said Bingham. "This isn't an occasion for
the exchange of compliments. I'll tell you what you may tell
her. I suppose they will have some funeral services within a
day or two. Tell her that I should like very much to be present."

I set off for the cottage. Its mistress in person introduced
me into the little parlor.

"Well, sir?" she said, in hard, dry accents.

"I've come," I answered, "to ask whether I can be of any assistance to Mrs Hicks."

Miss Horner shook her head in a manner which deprived her negation of half its dignity. "What assistance is possible?" she asked.

"A man," said I, "may relieve a woman of certain cares—"

"O, men are a blessed set! You had better leave Mrs Hicks to me."

"But will you at least tell me how she is,—if she has in any degree recovered herself?"

At this moment the door of the adjoining room was opened, and Mrs Hicks stood on the threshold, bearing a lamp,—a graceful and pathetic figure. I now had occasion to observe that she was a woman of decided beauty. Her fair hair was drawn back into a single knot behind her head, and the lamp-light deepened the pallor of her face and the darkness of her eyes. She wore a calico dressing-gown and a shawl.

"What do you wish?" she asked, in a voice clarified, if I may so express it, by long weeping.

"He wants to know whether he can be of any assistance," said the elder lady.

Mrs Hicks glanced over her shoulder into the room she had left. "Would you like to look at the child?" she asked, in a whisper.

"Lucy!" cried Miss Horner.

I walked straight over to Mrs Hicks, who turned and led the way to a little bed. My conductress raised her lamp aloft, and let the light fall gently on the little white-draped figure. Even the bandage about the child's head had not dispelled his short-lived prettiness. Heaven knows that to remain silent was easy enough; but Heaven knows, too, that to break the silence—and to break it as I broke it—was equally easy. "He must have been a very pretty child," I said.

"Yes, he was very pretty. He had black eyes. I don't know whether you noticed."

"No, I didn't notice," said I. "When is he to be buried?"

"The day after to-morrow. I am told that I shall be able to avoid an inquest."

"Mr Bingham has attended to that," I said. And then I paused, revolving his petition.

But Mrs Hicks anticipated it. "If you would like to be present at the funeral," she said, "you are welcome to come. —And so is your friend."

"Mr Bingham bade me ask leave. There is a great deal that I should like to say to you for him," I added, "but I won't spoil it by trying. It's his own business."

The young woman looked at me with her deep, dark eyes. "I pity him from my heart," she said, pressing her hands to her breast. "I had rather have my sorrow than his."

"They are pretty much one sorrow," I answered. "I don't see that you can divide it. You are two to bear it. Bingham is a wise, good fellow," I went on. "I have shared a great many joys with him. In Heaven's name," I cried, "don't bear hard on him!"

"How can I bear hard?" she asked, opening her arms and letting them drop. The movement was so deeply expressive of weakness and loneliness, that, feeling all power to reply stifled in a rush of compassion, I silently made my exit.

On the following day, Bingham and I went up to town, and on the third day returned in time for the funeral. Besides the two ladies, there was no one present but ourselves and the village minister, who of course spoke as briefly as decency allowed. He had accompanied the ladies in a carriage to the graveyard, while Bingham and I had come on foot. As we turned away from the grave, I saw my friend approach Mrs Hicks. They stood talking beside the freshly-turned earth, while the minister and I attended Miss Horner to the carriage. After she had seated herself, I lingered at the door, exchanging sober commonplaces with the reverend gentleman. At last Mrs Hicks followed us, leaning on Bingham's arm.

"Margaret," she said, "Mr Bingham and I are going to stay here awhile. Mr Bingham will walk home with me. I'm *very* much obliged to you, Mr Bland," she added, turning to the minister and extending her hand.

I bestowed upon my friend a glance which I felt to be half interrogative and half sympathetic. He gave me his hand, and answered the benediction by its pressure, while he answered the inquiry by his words. "If you are still disposed to go back to town this afternoon," he said, "you had better not wait for me. I may not have time to catch the boat."

I of course made no scruple of returning immediately to the city. Some ten days elapsed before I again saw Bingham; but I found my attention so deeply engrossed with work, that I scarcely measured the interval. At last, one morning, he came into my office.

"I take for granted," I said, "that you have not been all this time at B——."

"No; I've been on my travels. I came to town the day after you came. I found at my rooms a letter from a lawyer in Baltimore, proposing the sale of some of my property there, and I seized upon it as an excuse for making a journey to that city. I felt the need of movement, of action of some kind. But when I reached Baltimore, I didn't even go to see my correspondent. I pushed on to Washington, walked about for thirty-six hours, and came home."

He had placed his arm on my desk, and stood supporting his head on his hand, with a look of great physical exhaustion.

"You look very tired," said I.

"I haven't slept," said he. "I had such a talk with that woman!"

"I'm sorry that you should have felt the worse for it."

"I feel both the worse and the better. She talked about the child."

"It's well for her," said I, "that she was able to do it."

"She wasn't able, strictly speaking. She began calmly enough, but she very soon broke down."

"Did you see her again?"

"I called upon her the next day, to tell her that I was going to town, and to ask if I could be useful to her. But she seems to stand in perfect isolation. She assured me that she was in want of nothing."

"What sort of a woman does she seem to be, taking her in herself?"

"Bless your soul! I can't take her in herself!" cried Bingham, with some vehemence. "And yet, stay," he added; "she's a very pleasing woman."

"She's very pretty."

"Yes; she's very pretty. In years, she's little more than a young girl. In her ideas, she's one of 'the people.'"

"It seems to me," said I, "that the frankness of her conduct toward you is very much to her credit."

"It doesn't offend you, then?"

"Offend me? It gratifies me beyond measure."

"I think that, if you had seen her as I have seen her, it would interest you deeply. I'm at a loss to determine whether it's the result of great simplicity or great sagacity. Of course, it's absurd to suppose that, ten days ago, it could have been the result of anything but a beautiful impulse. I think that to-morrow I shall again go down to B——."

I allowed Bingham time to have made his visit and to have brought me an account of his further impressions; but as three days went by without his reappearance, I called at his lodgings. He was still out of town. The fifth day, however, brought him again to my office.

"I've been at B—— constantly," he said, "and I've had several interviews with our friend."

"Well; how fares it?"

"It fares well. I'm forcibly struck with her good sense. In matters of mind—in matters of soul, I may say—she has the touch of an angel, or rather the touch of a woman. That's quite sufficient."

"Does she keep her composure?"

"Perfectly. You can imagine nothing simpler and less senti-mental than her manner. She makes me forget myself most divinely. The child's death colors our talk; but it doesn't con-fine or obstruct it. You see she has her religion: she can afford to be natural."

Weary as my friend looked, and shaken by his sudden sub-jection to care, it yet seemed to me, as he pronounced these words, that his eye had borrowed a purer light and his voice a fresher tone. In short, where I discerned it, how I detected it, I know not; but I felt that he carried a secret. He sat poking with his walking-stick at a nail in the carpet, with his eyes dropped. I saw about his mouth the faint promise of a distant smile,—a smile which six months would bring to maturity.

"George," said I, "I have a fancy."

He looked up. "What is it?"

"You've lost your heart."

He stared a moment, with a sudden frown. "To whom?" he asked.

"To Mrs Hicks."

With a frown, I say, but a frown that was as a smile to the effect of my rejoinder. He rose to his feet; all his color deserted his face and rushed to his eyes.

"I beg your pardon if I'm wrong," I said.

Bingham had turned again from pale to crimson. "Don't beg *my* pardon," he cried. "You may say what you please. Beg *hers!*" he added, bitterly.

I resented the charge of injustice. "I've done *her* no wrong!" I answered. "I haven't said," I went on with a certain gleeful sense that I was dealing with massive truths,—"I haven't said that she had lost her heart to you!"

"Good God, Charles!" cried Bingham, "what a horrid imagination you have!"

"I am not responsible for my imagination."

"Upon my soul, I hope *I'*m not!" cried Bingham, passionately. "I have enough without that."

"George," I said, after a moment's reflection, "if I thought I had insulted you, I would make amends. But I have said nothing to be ashamed of. I believe that I have hit the truth. Your emotion proves it. I spoke hastily; but you must admit that, having caught a glimpse of the truth, I couldn't stand indifferent to it."

"The truth! the truth! What truth?"

"Aren't you in love with Mrs Hicks? Admit it like a man."

"Like a man! Like a brute. Haven't I done the woman wrong enough?"

"Quite enough, I hope."

"Haven't I turned her simple joys to bitterness?"

"I grant it."

"And now you want me to insult her by telling her that I love her?"

"I want you to tell her nothing. What you tell her is your own affair. Remember that, George. It's as little mine as it is the rest of the world's."

Bingham stood listening, with a contracted brow and his hand grasping his stick. He walked to the dusty office-window and halted a moment, watching the great human throng in the street. Then he turned and came towards me. Suddenly he stopped short. "God forgive me!" he cried; "I believe I do love her."

The fountains of my soul were stirred. "Combining my own hasty impressions of Mrs Hicks with yours, George," I said, "the consummation seems to me exquisitely natural."

It was in these simple words that we celebrated the sacred fact. It seemed as if, by tacit agreement, the evolution of this fact was result enough for a single interview.

A few days after this interview, in the evening, I called at Bingham's lodgings. His servant informed me that my friend

was out of town, although he was unable to indicate his whereabouts. But as I turned away from the door a hack drew up,
and the object of my quest descended, equipped with a
travelling-bag. I went down and greeted him under the gas-
lamp.

"Shall I go in with you?" I asked; "or shall I go my way?"

"You had better come in," said Bingham. "I have something to say.—I have been down to B——," he resumed,
when the servant had left us alone in his sitting-room. His tone
bore the least possible tinge of a confession; but of course it
was not as a confessor that I listened.

"Well," said I, "how is our friend?"

"Our friend—" answered Bingham. "Will you have a
cigar?"

"No, I thank you."

"Our friend— Ah, Charles, it's a long story."

"I sha'n't mind that, if it's an interesting one."

"To a certain extent it's a painful one. It's painful to come
into collision with incurable vulgarity of feeling."

I was puzzled. "Has that been your fortune?" I asked.

"It has been my fortune to bring Mrs Hicks into a great deal
of trouble. The case, in three words, is this. Miss Horner has
seen fit to resent, in no moderate terms, what she calls the
'extraordinary intimacy' existing between Mrs Hicks and myself. Mrs Hicks, as was perfectly natural, has resented her
cousin's pretension to regulate her conduct. Her expression
of this feeling has led to her expulsion from Miss Horner's
house."

"Has she any other friend to turn to?"

"No one, except some relatives of her husband, who are
very poor people, and of whom she wishes to ask no favors."

"Where has she placed herself?"

"She is in town. We came up together this afternoon. I
went with her to some lodgings which she had formerly
occupied, and which were fortunately vacant."

"I suppose it's not to be regretted that she has left B——. She breaks with sad associations."

"Yes; but she renews them too, on coming to town."

"How so?"

"Why, damn it," said Bingham, with a tremor in his voice, "the woman is utterly poor."

"Has she no resources whatever?"

"A hundred dollars a year, I believe,—worse than nothing."

"Has she any marketable talents or accomplishments?"

"I believe she is up to some pitiful needlework or other. Such a woman! O horrible world!"

"Does *she* say so?" I asked.

"She? No indeed. She thinks it's all for the best. I suppose it is. But it seems but a bad best."

"I wonder," said I, after a pause, "whether I might see Mrs Hicks. Do you think she would receive me?"

Bingham looked at me an instant keenly. "I suppose so," said he. "You can try."

"I shall go, not out of curiosity," I resumed, "but out of—"

"Out of what?"

"Well, in fine, I should like to see her again."

Bingham gave me Mrs Hicks's address, and in the course of a few evenings I called upon her. I had abstained from bestowing a fine name upon the impulse which dictated this act; but I am nevertheless free to declare that kindliness and courtesy had a large part in it. Mrs Hicks had taken up her residence in a plain, small house, in a decent by-street, where, upon presenting myself, I was ushered into a homely sitting-room (apparently her own), and left to await her coming. Her greeting was simple and cordial, and not untinged with a certain implication of gratitude. She had taken for granted, on my part, all possible sympathy and good-will; but as she had regarded me besides as a man of many cares, she had thought it improbable that we should meet again. It was no long time before I became conscious of that generous charm which Bingham had rigorously denominated her good-sense. Good-sense assuredly was there, but good-sense mated and prolific. Never had I seen, it seemed to me, as the moments elapsed, so exquisitely modest a use of such charming faculties,—an intelligence so sensible of its obligations and so indifferent to its privileges. It was obvious that she had been a woman of plain associations: her allusions were to homely facts, and her manner direct and unstudied; and yet, in spite of these limitations, it was equally obvious that she was a person to be neither patronized, dazzled, nor deluded. O the satisfaction which, in the course of that quiet dialogue, I took in this sweet infallibility! How it effaced her loneliness and poverty, and added dignity to her youth and beauty! It made her, potentially at least, a woman of the world. It was an anticipation of the self-possession, the wisdom, and perhaps even in some degree of the wit, which comes through the experience of society,—the result, on Mrs Hicks's part, of I know not what hours of suffering, despondency, and self-dependence. With whatever intentions, therefore, I might have come before her, I should have found it impossible to address her as any other than an equal, and to regard her affliction as anything less than an absolute mystery. In fact, we hardly touched upon it; and it was only covertly that we alluded to Bingham's melancholy position. I will not deny that in a certain sense I regretted Mrs Hicks's reserve. It is true that I had a very informal claim upon her confidence; but I had gone to her with a half-defined hope that this claim would be liberally interpreted. It was not even recognized; my vague intentions of counsel and assistance had lain undivined; and I departed with the impression that my social horizon had been considerably enlarged, but that my charity had by no means secured a pensioner.

Mrs Hicks had given me permission to repeat my visit, and after the lapse of a fortnight I determined to do so. I had seen Bingham several times in the interval. He was of course much interested in my impressions of our friend; and I fancied that my admiration gave him even more pleasure than he allowed himself to express. On entering Mrs Hicks's parlor a second time, I found him in person standing before the fireplace, and talking apparently with some vehemence to Mrs Hicks, who sat listening on the sofa. Bingham turned impatiently to the door as I crossed the threshold, and Mrs Hicks rose to welcome me with all due composure. I was nevertheless sensible that my entrance was ill-timed; yet a retreat was impossible. Bingham kept his place on the hearth-rug, and mechanically gave me his hand,—standing irresolute, as I thought, between annoyance and elation. The fact that I had interrupted a somewhat passionate interview was somehow so obvious, that, at the prompting of a very delicate feeling, Mrs Hicks hastened to anticipate my apologies.

"Mr Bingham was giving me a lecture," she said; and there was perhaps in her accent a faint suspicion of bitterness. "He will doubtless be glad of another auditor."

"No," said Bingham, "Charles is a better talker than listener. You shall have two lectures instead of one." He uttered this sally without even an attempt to smile.

"What is your subject?" said I. "Until I know that, I shall promise neither to talk nor to listen."

Bingham laid his hand on my arm. "He represents the world," he said, addressing our hostess. "You're afraid of the world. There, make your appeal."

Mrs Hicks stood silent a moment, with a contracted brow and a look of pain on her face. Then she turned to me with a half-smile. "I don't believe you represent the world," she said; "you are too good."

"She flatters you," said Bingham. "You wish to corrupt him, Mrs Hicks."

Mrs Hicks glanced for an instant from my friend to myself. There burned in her eyes a far-searching light, which consecrated the faint irony of the smile which played about her lips.

"O you men!" she said,—"you are so wise, so deep!" It was on Bingham that her eyes rested last; but after a pause, extending her hand, she transferred them to me. "Mr Bingham," she pursued, "seems to wish you to be admitted to our counsels. There is every reason why his friends should be my friends. You will be interested to know that he has asked me to be his wife."

"Have you given him an answer?" I asked.

"He was pressing me for an answer when you came in. He conceives me to have a great fear of the judgments of men, and he was saying very hard things about them. But they have very little, after all, to do with the matter. The world may heed it, that Mr Bingham should marry Mrs Hicks, but it will care very little whether or no Mrs Hicks marries Mr Bingham. You are the world, for me," she cried with beautiful inconsequence, turning to her suitor; "I know no other." She put out her hands, and he took them.

I am at a loss to express the condensed force of these rapid words,—the amount of passion, of reflection, of experience, which they seemed to embody. They were the simple utterance of a solemn and intelligent choice; and, as such, the whole phalanx of the Best Society assembled in judgment could not have done less than salute them. What honest George Bingham said, what I said, is of little account. The proper conclusion of my story lies in the highly dramatic fact that out of the depths of her bereavement—out of her loneliness and her pity—this richly gifted woman had emerged, responsive to the passion of him who had wronged her all but as deeply as he loved her. The reader will decide, I think, that this catastrophe offers as little occasion for smiles as for tears. My narrative is a piece of genuine prose.

It was not until six months had elapsed that Bingham's marriage took place. It has been a truly happy one. Mrs Bingham is now, in the fulness of her bloom, with a single exception, the most charming woman I know. I have often assured her—

once too often, possibly—that, thanks to that invaluable good-sense of hers, she is also the happiest. She has made a devoted wife; but—and in occasional moments of insight it has seemed to me that this portion of her fate is a delicate tribute to a fantastic principle of equity—she has never again become a mother. In saying that she has made a devoted wife, it may seem that I have written Bingham's own later history. Yet as the friend of his younger days, the comrade of his *belle jeunesse*, the partaker of his dreams, I would fain give him a sentence apart. What shall it be? He is a truly incorruptible soul; he is a confirmed philosopher; he has grown quite stout.

POOR RICHARD

I

MISS WHITTAKER'S garden covered a couple of acres, behind and beside her house, and at its further extremity was bounded by a large pasture, which in turn was bordered by the old disused towing-path beside the river, at this point a slow and shallow stream. Its low, flat banks were unadorned with rocks or trees, and a towing-path is not in itself a romantic promenade. Nevertheless, here sauntered bareheaded, on a certain spring evening, the mistress of the acres just mentioned and many more beside, in sentimental converse with an impassioned and beautiful youth.

She herself would have been positively plain, but for the frequent recurrence of a magnificent smile—which imparted a charm to her somewhat undistinguished features—and (in another degree) for the elegance of her dress, which expressed one of the later stages of mourning, and was of that voluminous abundance proper to women who are both robust and rich. The good looks of her companion, for very good they were, in spite of several defects, were set off by a shabby suit, as carelessly worn as it was inartistically made. His manner, as he walked and talked, was that of a nervous, headstrong man, wrought almost to desperation; while she had the air of a person a good deal bored but determined to be patient. A brief silence, however, had at last fallen upon them. Miss Whittaker strolled along quietly, looking at the slow-mounting moon, and the young man gazed on the ground, swinging his stick. Finally, with a heavy blow, he brought it to earth.

"Oh, Gertrude!" he cried, "I despise myself."

"That's very horrid," said Gertrude.

"And, Gertrude, I adore you."

"That's more horrid still," said Gertrude, with her eyes still on the moon. And then, suddenly and somewhat impatiently transferring them to her companion's face—"Richard," she asked, "what do you mean when you say you adore me?"

"Mean? I mean that I love you."

"Then why don't you say what you mean?"

The young man looked at her a moment. "Will you give me leave to say *all* I mean?"

"Oh dear!" Then, as he remained silent, "I wait for your words," Gertrude added.

Yet he still said nothing, but went striking vehemently at the weeds by the water's edge, like a young fellow who sees that he is wrong whatever line he takes.

"Gertrude!" he suddenly exclaimed, "what more do you want than the assurance that I love you?"

"I want nothing more. I am quite satisfied with that. You yourself seemed to wish to pile it up."

"Either you won't understand me," cried Richard, "or"— darting a vicious glance at her—"you can't!"

Miss Whittaker stopped and looked thoughtfully into his face. "In our position if it becomes you to sacrifice reflection to feeling, it becomes me to do the reverse. Listen to me, Richard. I *do* understand you, and better, I believe, than you understand yourself."

"Oh, you think me a baby, I know!"

But she continued, heedless of his interruption. "I thought that, by leaving you to yourself awhile, your feelings might become clearer to you. But they seem to be growing only more confused. I have been so fortunate, or so unfortunate, I hardly know which,"—and she smiled faintly,—"as to make you like me. That's all very well, but you must not make too much of it. Nothing could make me happier than to be liked by you, or by any one else. But here it must stop with you, as it stops with others."

"It does not stop here with others."

"I beg your pardon. You have no right to say that. It is partly out of justice to others that I speak to you as I am doing. I shall always be one of your best friends, but I shall never be more. It is best I should tell you this at once. I might trifle with you awhile and make you happy (since upon such a poor thing you seem to set your happiness) by allowing you to suppose that I care for you in another way; but the end would soon come, and then where should we be? You may, in your disappointment, call me heartless now—I freely give you leave to call me anything that will ease your mind—but what would you call me then? Friendship, Richard, is an excellent cure for love. Here is mine." And she held out her hand.

"No, I thank you," said Richard, gloomily folding his arms. "I know my own feelings," and he raised his voice. "Haven't I lived with them night and day for weeks and weeks? Great heaven, Gertrude Whittaker, this is no fancy! I'm not one of that sort. My whole life has gone into my love. God has let me idle it away hitherto only that I might begin it with you. Dear Gertrude, hear me! I have some, at least, of the faculties of a man. I know I'm not respectable, but I honestly believe I should repay anyone who would bear with me. It's true I have neither worked, nor persisted, nor studied, nor earned a cent. But, on the other hand, I have never cared for any woman before. I have waited for you. And now—now, after all, I am to sit down to simple liking—to friendship! The devil! Be friends with men whom you don't make mad! You do me!"

An honest flush rose to Gertrude's cheek. "So much the worse for you!" she cried, with a bitter laugh. "So much the worse for both of us! But what is your contention? Do you wish to marry me?"

Richard flinched a moment under this tacit proposition suddenly ringing in the air, but not from want of heart. "You have named it," he said.

"Well, then, I only pity you the more for your consistency. I can only entreat you again to rest content with what I have offered you. It's not such a bad substitute, Richard, as I understand it. What my love might be I don't know—I couldn't answer for that; but of the kind of interest I take in you I am very sure. We both have our duties in this matter, and I have resolved to take a liberal view of mine. I might lose patience with you, you know, and turn away from you altogether—leave you alone with your dreams, and let you break your heart. But it's rather by seeing more of me than by seeing less that your feelings will change."

"You don't mean it! And yours?"

"I have no doubt they will change, too; not in kind, but in degree. The better I know you, I am sure, the better I shall like you. The better too you will like me. Don't turn your back upon me—I speak the truth. You will get to entertain a serious opinion of me—which I'm sure you haven't now, or you wouldn't talk of my making you mad. But you must be patient. It's a singular fact that it takes longer to learn to live on rational terms with a woman than to fancy one adores her. A sense of madness is a very poor feeling to marry upon. You wish, of course, to leave off your idle life and your bad habits—you see I am so thoroughly your friend that I am not afraid of touching upon disagreeable facts, as I should be if I were your 'adored.' But you are so indolent, so irresolute, so undisciplined, so uneducated"—Gertrude spoke deliberately and watched the effect of her words—"that you find a change of life very difficult. I propose, with your consent, to appoint myself your care-taker. Henceforth my house will be open to you as to my dearest friend. Come as often and stay as long as you please. Not in a few weeks, perhaps, nor even in a few months, but in God's good time, you will be a capable young man, in working order—which I don't consider you now, and which I know you don't consider yourself. But I have a great opinion of your talents" (this was very shrewd of Gertrude), "and even of your nature. If I turn out to have done you a service, you will not want to marry me then."

Richard had silently listened, with a deepening frown. "That's all very pretty," he said; "but it's humbug—humbug from beginning to end. What's the meaning of all that rigmarole about the inconsistency of friendship and love? Such talk is enough to make one curse. Refuse me outright, and send me to the devil, if you must; but don't bemuddle your own brains at the same time. Ah, one little word knocks it all to pieces: I want you for my *wife!* You make an awful mistake in treating me as a boy—a deadly mistake. I *am* in working order—I began to live properly when I began to love you. I have sworn off drinking as effectually as if I hadn't touched a drop for twenty years. I hate it, I loathe it—I have drunk my last. No, Gertrude, I am no longer a boy—you have cured me of that. Hang it, that's why I love you! Don't you see? Ah, Gertrude,"—and his voice fell—"you are a great enchantress! You have no arts, you have none of the airs and graces of the girls that are called pretty; but you are an enchantress without them. It's your nature. You are so divinely, damnably honest! Those clever things you just said were meant for a dash of cold water, but you can't drown me by holding me under a spout. You will say it's nothing but common sense. Very likely; but that is the point. Your common sense captivates me—it's for that I love you."

There was something now so calmly resolute in his tone that Gertrude was sickened. She found herself weaker than he, while the happiness of both of them demanded that she should be stronger.

"Richard Maule," she said, "you are unkind!" There was a tremor in her voice as she spoke, and as she ceased speaking she burst into tears. A selfish sense of victory took possession of the young man. He threw his arm about her; but she shook it off. "You are a coward, sir!" she cried.

"Oh, softly!" said Richard, flushing angrily.

"You go too far; you persist beyond decency."

"You hate me now, I suppose," said Richard, brutally, like one at bay.

Gertrude brushed away her tears. "No, indeed," she answered, sending him a dry, clear glance. "To hate you I should have to have loved you. I pity you still."

Richard looked at her a moment. "I don't feel tempted to return the feeling, Gertrude," said he. "A woman with so much diplomacy as you needs no pity."

"I have not diplomacy enough to read your sarcasm, sir; but I have good-nature enough to excuse it, and I mean to keep my good-nature to the end. I mean to keep my temper, I mean to be just, I mean to be conclusive, and not to have to return to this matter. It's not for my pleasure, I would have you know, that I go into all this; I have nerves as well as you. Therefore listen to me once again. If I don't love you, Richard, in your way, I don't; and if I can't, I can't. We can't love by will. But with friendship, when it is once established, I believe the will and the reason may have a great deal to do. I will, therefore, put the whole of my mind into my friendship for you, and in that way we shall perhaps be even. Such a feeling—as I shall naturally show it—will, after all, not be very different from that other feeling you ask—as I should naturally show it. Bravely to reconcile himself to such difference as there is is no more than a man of honour ought to do. Do you understand me?"

"You have an admirable way of putting things. 'After all,' and 'such difference as there is'! The difference is the difference of marriage and no-marriage. I suppose you don't mean that you are willing to live with me without that ceremony?"

"You suppose correctly."

"Then why do you falsify matters? A woman is either a man's wife, or she isn't."

"Yes; and a woman is either a man's friend, or she isn't."

"And you are mine, and I am an ungrateful brute not to rest

satisfied! That's what you mean! Heaven knows you are right"
—and he paused a moment, with his eyes on the ground.
"Don't despise me, Gertrude," he went on—"I am not so ungrateful as I seem. I am very much obliged to you for the pains
you have taken. Of course I understand your not loving me.
You would be a grand fool if you did; and you are no fool,
Gertrude."

"No, I am no fool, Richard. It's a great responsibility—it's
dreadfully vulgar; but, on the whole, I am rather glad."

"So am I. I could hate you for it; but there is no doubt it's
why I love you. If you were a fool you might love me; but I
shouldn't love you, and if I must choose, I prefer that."

"Heaven has chosen for us. Ah, Richard," pursued Gertrude, with admirable simplicity, "let us be good and obey
heaven, and we shall be sure to be happy." And she held out
her hand once more.

Richard took it and raised it to his lips. She felt their pressure and withdrew it.

"Now you must leave me," she said. "Did you ride?"

"My horse is at the village."

"You can go by the river, then. Good-night."

"Good-night."

The young man moved away in the gathering dusk, and
Miss Whittaker stood for a moment looking after him.

II

To appreciate the importance of this conversation the reader
must know that Miss Gertrude Whittaker was a young woman
of four-and-twenty, whose father, recently deceased, had left
her alone in the world, with a large fortune, accumulated by
various enterprises in that part of the State. He had appointed
a distant and elderly kinswoman, by name Miss Pendexter, as

his daughter's household companion; and an old friend of his own, known to combine shrewdness with integrity, as her financial adviser. Motherless, country-bred, with rather thick features, Gertrude on reaching her majority had neither the tastes nor the manners of a fine lady. Of a vigorous, active constitution, with a warm heart, a cool head, and a very pretty talent for affairs, she was, in virtue both of her wealth and of her tact, one of the principal persons of the country-side. These facts had forced her into a prominence which she made no attempt to elude, and in which she now felt thoroughly at home. She knew herself to be a power in the land; she knew that, present and absent, she was continually talked about as the rich Miss Whittaker; and although as modest as a woman need be, she was neither so timid nor so nervous as to wish to shirk her implied obligations. Her feelings were indeed, throughout, strong, rather than delicate; and yet there was in her whole nature, as the world had learned to look at it, a kind of genial discretion which attracted universal respect. She was impulsive, yet circumspect; thrifty, yet open-handed; literal, yet addicted to joking; keenly observant of human distinctions, yet almost indiscriminately hospitable; with an immense fund of common sense beneath all; and yet beyond this—like the priest behind the king—and despite her preponderantly prosaic and, as it were, secular tone, a certain latent suggestion of heroic possibilities which he who had once become sensible of them (supposing him to be young and enthusiastic) would linger about her hoping to elicit, as you might stand and inhale a florid and vigorous dahlia which, for an instant, in your passage, should have proved delightfully fragrant. It is upon the actual existence, in more minds than one, of a mystifying sense of this desultory aroma that our story is based.

Richard Maule and Gertrude Whittaker were old friends. They had, in the first place, gone democratically to the town-school together, as children; and then their divergent growth, as boy and girl, had been conscious of an elastic bond in a

continued intimacy between Gertrude and Fanny Maule,
Richard's sister, who, however, in the fulness of time had
married and followed her husband to California. With her departure the old relations of habit between her brother and her
friend had slackened and gradually ceased. Richard had grown
up a rebellious and troublesome boy, with a disposition combining stolid apathy and hot-headed eagerness in equal, con-
tradictory proportions. Losing both of his parents before he
was well out of jackets, he had found himself at the age of sixteen in possession actual, and as he supposed uncontested, of
the paternal acres. It was not long, however, before those
turned up who were disposed to question his immediate ability
to manage them; the result of which was, that the property was
leased for five years, and that Richard was taken bodily possession of by a maternal uncle, living on a farm of his own
some three hundred miles away. Here our young man spent
the remainder of his minority, ostensibly learning agriculture
with his cousins, but actually learning nothing. He had very
soon established, and had subsequently enjoyed without a day's
interval, the reputation of an ill-natured fool. He was dull, dis-
obliging, brooding, lowering. Reading and shooting he liked
a little, because they were solitary pastimes; but he was very
slow in acquiring the arts which help a man to live happily with
others. It was possible to get on with him only because he was
at once too selfish and too simple for mischief. As soon as he
came of age he entered upon the enjoyment of the old place on
which his boyhood had been passed, and to which he appeared
to cling the more perversely as it was known to be very thin
land. He avoided his neighbours, his father's former associates;
he seemed to take pleasure in braving their disapproval of his
queer proceedings; he informed them that he wanted no help
but what he paid for, and that he expected to work his farm for
himself and by himself. In short, he proved himself to their
satisfaction egregiously ungrateful and conceited. They were
not slow to discover that his incapacity was as great as his

vanity. In two years he had more than undone the work of the late lessee, who had tried some clever experiments on the thankless soil. At the end of three years people spoke of him as cracked; it seemed to those who observed him that there was something so wanton in his errors as really to impugn his sanity. He appeared to have accepted this view of his condition, and to have given up all pretence of work. He went about silent and sullen, like a man who feels that he has a quarrel with fate. About this time it became generally known that he was often the worse for liquor; and he hereupon acquired the deplorable reputation of a man worse than unsociable—a man who boozes alone—although it was still doubtful whether this practice was the cause or the effect of his poor crops. About this time, too, he began again to see something of Gertrude Whittaker. For many months after his return he had been held at his distance, together with most of the local swains, by the knowledge of her father's extreme hostility to all suitors and fortune-hunters, and then, subsequently, by the illness preceding the old man's death. When, however, at last, on the expiration of her term of mourning, Miss Whittaker opened to society her long-blockaded ports, Richard had, to all the world's amazement, been among the first to profit by this extension of the general privilege and to cast anchor in the wide and peaceful waters of her friendship. He found himself at this moment, considerably to his surprise, in his twenty-fourth year; that is, a few months younger than the heiress.

It was impossible that she should not have gathered from mere juxtaposition an impression of the poor figure he cut in the world, and of his peculiar relation to his neighbours and his own affairs. Thanks to this impression, Richard found a very warm welcome—the welcome of easy compassion. Gertrude gave him all the back-news of his sister Fanny, with whom he had dropped correspondence, and, impelled by Fanny's complaints of his long silence, ventured upon a friendly recommendation that he should go straight home and write a letter

to California. Richard sat before her, gazing at her out of his
dark eyes, and not only attempting no defence of his conduct,
but rejoicing dumbly in the utter absence of any possible
defence—his exposure seemed so delightful. He wished he
could be scolded like that every day or two; nothing had ever
touched him so softly. He carried away an extraordinary sense
of general alleviation; and forthwith began a series of visits
which, in the space of some ten weeks, culminated in the interview I have set before the reader. Painfully diffident in the
company of most women, Richard had not from the first
known what it was to be shy with Gertrude. As a man of the
world finds it useful to refresh his social energies by an occasional *tête-à-tête* of an hour with himself, so Richard, with
whom solitude was the rule, derived a certain austere satisfaction from an hour's contact with this young lady's quick wits
and good-humour, her liberal way of life and active charity.
Gradually, however, from a salutory process, this became a
regular luxury. It was now pleasant to go to Gertrude because
he enjoyed the contagion of her own success—because he witnessed her happiness without a sensation of envy—because he
forgot his entanglements and bad habits—because, finally, his
soul slept away its troubles beneath her kind, clear eye, very
much as his body had often slept away its weariness in the
shade of a murmuring apple-tree. But the soul, like the body,
will not sleep long without dreaming; and it will not dream
often without wishing at last to tell its dreams. Richard had
one day ventured to impart his visions to Gertrude, and the
revelation apparently had not been at all to her taste.

The fact that this blundering youth had somehow worked
himself into an intimacy with Miss Whittaker very soon became public property among their neighbours; and in the
hands of these good people, naturally enough, received an
important addition in the inference that—strange as it might
seem—she was going to change her name for his. He was, of
course, regarded as a very lucky fellow, and the prevalence of

this impression was doubtless not without its effect on the forbearance of certain long-suffering creditors. And even if she
was not to marry him, it was further argued, she might yet lend
him money; for it was assumed without question that the
necessity of raising money was the mainspring of Richard's
suit. It must be declared without delay that this assumption
was precipitate and unfair. Our hero had faults enough, but a
mercenary habit was not one of them; nor was an excessive
concern on the subject of his debts one of his virtues. As for
Gertrude, wherever else her perception of her friend's feelings
may have been at fault, it was not at fault on this point. That
he loved her as desperately as he tried to make her believe she
indeed doubted; but it never occurred to her to question his
disinterestedness. And so, on the other hand, it was strictly because she was not in love with him that she resisted him, and
not on account of the disparity of their fortunes. In accepting
his very simple and natural overtures to friendship, in calling
him "Richard" in remembrance of old days, and in submitting
generally to the terms of their old acquaintance, she had fore-
seen no dangerous complications. She had regarded him as one
more helpless human being to "look after." She had espoused
his interests (like all good women, Gertrude was ever more or
less of a partisan) because she loved his sister and because she
pitied himself. She would stand to him *in loco sororis*. The
reader has seen that she had given herself a long day's work.

It is not to be supposed that Richard's comparatively pacific
retreat at the close of the walk by the river implied any instinct
of resignation to the prospects which Gertrude had opened to
him. It is explained rather by an intensity of purpose so deep
as to believe it could take its time. This was not the end of his
suit, but the beginning. He would not give in until he was
positively beaten. It was all very well, he reflected, that Gertrude should reject him. Such a woman as she ought properly
to be striven for, and there was something ridiculous in the
idea that she should be easily won, whether by himself or by

another. Richard was a slow thinker, but he thought more
wisely then he talked; and he now took back all his angry
boasts of accomplished self-mastery and humbly surveyed the
facts of the case. He was on the way to recovery, but he was
by no means cured, and yet his very humility assured him that
he was curable. He was no hero, certainly, but he was better
than his life; he was no scholar, but, in his own view at least,
he was not an ass. He was good enough to be better; he was
good enough not to sit by the hour soaking his limited understanding in whiskey. And at the very least, if he was not worthy
to possess Gertrude, he was yet worthy to strive to obtain her,
and to live for evermore upon the glory of there having been
such a question between himself and the great Miss Whittaker.
He would raise himself then to that level from which he could
address her as an equal, from which he would have a right to
insist on something. How he would do this he was at a loss to
determine. He was conscious of a great deal of crude intention,
but he cursed the ignorance which was such an obstacle to his
doing anything in particular. He longed vaguely for some con-
tinuous muscular effort, at the end of which he should find
himself face to face with his mistress. But as, instead of being a
Pagan hero, with an enticing task-list of impossibilities, he was
a plain New England cultivator, with a bad conscience, and
nature with him and not against him—as, after slaying his
dragon, after renouncing liquor, his work was a simple operation in common sense—in view of these facts he found but
little inspiration in his prospect. Nevertheless he fronted it
bravely. He was not to obtain Gertrude by making a fortune,
but by making himself a man, by learning to live. But as to
learn to live is to learn to work, he would find some use for his
valour. He would keep sober and clear-headed; he would re-
trieve his land and pay his debts. Then let her refuse him if she
could—or if she dared!

Meanwhile Gertrude, on her side, sat quietly at home, turning over in her own fashion a dozen little plans for her friend's

redemption and for making the stream of his passion turn some other mill. Not but that she meant rigorously to fulfil her part of the engagement to which she had invited him in that painful scene by the river. Yet, with however much of the same firmness and mildness she might still meet him, she could not feel secure against repeated intrusion without the knowledge of a partial change, at least, in Richard's own attitude. Such a change could only be effected through some preparatory change in his life; and a change in his life could be brought only about by the introduction of some new influence. This influence, unfortunately, was hard to find. However positively Gertrude had dwelt upon the practical virtue of her friendship, she was, on further reflection, led to ask herself whether it mightn't be helped in its work. He was welcome enough to that, but he needed something more. It suddenly occurred to her, one morning, after Richard's image had been crossing and recrossing her mental vision for a couple of hours with wearisome pertinacity, that a world of good might accrue to him through the acquaintance of a person so clever, so superior as Captain Severn. There was no one who would not be better for knowing such a man. She would recommend Richard to his kindness, and him she would recommend to Richard's— what? Here was the rub! Where was there common ground between Richard and such a one as he? To beg him to try to like Richard was easy; to ask Richard to care for *him* was absurd. If Richard could only know him the matter would take care of itself—he would take a fancy to him in spite of every prejudice. But to begin to praise any object to her young friend was just the way to make him hate it. He himself was such a subject for pity that it had never occurred to her to recommend anyone to his benevolence. All the world seemed above him, and he was therefore out of sorts with all the world. If she could put her hand on some creature less favoured of nature and of fortune than himself, he might feel some sympathy for such a being. Captain Severn had, to her knowledge, not been a darling of destiny, but he was apparently quite contented with his lot, and thus he was raised several degrees above Richard, who would be certain to find a tacit rebuke in his resignation. Still, for all this, Gertrude would bring them together. She had a high opinion of the Captain's generosity, and if Richard should wantonly throw away such a chance the loss would be his own. It may be thought that in this enterprise Captain Severn was somewhat inconsiderately handled. But women have been known to show their affection for a man by sending him as a missionary to the cannibals. These words suggest the propriety of a short description of the person to whom they refer.

III

EDMUND SEVERN was a man of eight-and-twenty, who, having for some time combated fortune and his own inclinations as a mathematical tutor in a country-college, had, on the opening of the war, transferred his abilities to a more heroic field. The regiment of volunteers to which he belonged, and which was now a part of the army of the Potomac, had been raised in Miss Whittaker's district, and she had given almost every man in it—as a rich woman could do—some sign that her thoughts were with him. His soldiership, like his scholarship, was solid rather than brilliant. He was not destined to be heard of at home, nor to be lifted out of regimental work; but on many an important occasion in Virginia he had proved himself in a modest way a very useful officer. Coming up, early in the war, with a severe wound, to be nursed by a married sister who was domiciled in Gertrude's neighbourhood, he was, like all his fellow-sufferers within a wide circuit, very soon honoured with a visit of anxious inquiry from Miss Whittaker, who was as yet known to him only by report, and who transmitted to him the warmest assurance of sympathy and interest, together with the liveliest offers of assistance; and incidentally, as it were, to these, a copious collection of specimens from her hot-house and her store-room. Severn had taken the air for the first time in Gertrude's own cushioned barouche, which she had sent to his door at an early stage of his convalescence, and which of course he had immediately made use of to pay his respects to his benefactress. He was taken aback by the humility with which, on this occasion, betwixt smiles and tears, she protested that to be of service to the suffering brave was a sacred privilege. The Captain liked her on the spot, and thought of nothing else as he drove home. Half-a-dozen visits, during the ensuing month, more than sufficed to convert him into what is called an admirer; but as the weeks passed by he perceived there were great obstacles to his ripening into a real aspirant. Captain Severn was a serious man; he was conscientious, discreet, deliberate, unused to act without a definite purpose. He liked to see where he was going, and never went far simply because the country was pretty; he wanted to know where he should arrive. In pursuance of this tradition he had asked himself whether he was prepared to face the consequences of falling in love with our young lady. Since he had taken a vow, a twelvemonth before, not to marry until, by some means or another, he should have an income to point to, no great change had come to pass in his fortunes. He was still a poor man and an unsettled one; he was still awaiting his real vocation. Moreover, while subject to the chances of war, he thought it wrong to draw a woman on; he shrank in horror from the thought of converting some fresh girl into a figure of mourning. Miss Whittaker pleased him as he had never been pleased, but that seemed to him no reason for recanting his principles. He could no more afford to marry a rich woman than a poor one. When he should have earned enough money for two to live upon, then he would be free to marry whomsoever he might fancy—a beggar or an heiress. The truth is that the Captain was a great deal too proud. It was his fault that he

could not bring himself to forget the difference between his
poverty and Gertrude's wealth. He would of course have resented the insinuation that the superior fortune of the woman
he loved could seem to him a reason for not declaring his love;
but there is no doubt that in the case before us the sentiment
in question didn't dare—or hadn't as yet dared—to lift its
head. Severn had a deep aversion to being in debt. It is probable that, after all, he would have accepted obligations gracefully enough from a person with certain rights; but while a
woman was as yet neither his mistress nor his wife, the idea of
being beholden to her was odious to him. It would have been
a question with one who knew him whether at this juncture
these logical ice-blocks were destined to resist the warmth of
Gertrude's charms, or gradually to evaporate and flood the
position. There would have been no question, however, but
that he could keep up his consistency only at the cost of a considerable moral strain. At this moment, then, Severn had made
up his mind that Gertrude was not for him, and that it behoved
him to walk very straight. That Miss Whittaker, with a hundred rational cares, was anything less than supremely oblivious
of him individually, it never occurred to him to suspect. The
truth is that Gertrude's private and personal emotions were
entertained in a chamber of her heart so remote from the por-
tals of speech that no sound of their revelry found its way into
the world. She thought of her modest, soldierly, scholarly
friend as a gentleman who would perhaps some day take to
wife some woman, who, however nice she might be, couldn't
be as nice as he. But what was *she* to him? A local roadside
figure—at the very most a sort of millionaire Maud Müller—
with whom it was pleasant for a lonely wayfarer to exchange
a friendly good-morning. Her duty was to fold her arms resignedly, to sit quietly on the sofa and watch a great happiness
sink below the horizon. With this impression on Gertrude's
part it is not surprising that Severn was not wrenched out of
himself. The prodigy was apparently to be wrought—if

wrought at all—by her taking her loss for granted. This left nothing between them but her casual hospitality, and the effect of that method, as yet, upon Severn had been none other than its effect upon all the world. It kept him in his best form. They talked and fraternised, and moreover they watched each other, but they breathed not a word of what each was thinking about most. It was with perfect honesty, therefore, that she had rebutted Richard's insinuation that the Captain enjoyed any especial favour. He was only another of her social pensioners.

The result of Gertrude's meditations was that she despatched a note to each of her two friends, requesting them to take tea with her on the following day. A couple of hours before tea-time she received a visit from one Major Luttrel, who was recruiting for a United States regiment at a large town, some ten miles away, and who had ridden over in the afternoon, in accordance with a general invitation conveyed to him through an old lady who had bespoken Miss Whittaker's consideration for him as a man of delightful manners and wonderful talents. Gertrude had replied to her venerable friend, with her wonted alacrity, that she would be very glad to see Major Luttrel should he ever come that way, and then had thought no more about him until his card was brought to her as she was dressing for the evening. He found so much to say to her that the interval passed very rapidly for both of them, before the simultaneous entrance of Miss Pendexter and of Gertrude's guests. The two officers were already slightly known to each other, and Richard was introduced to each of them. They eyed the distracted-looking young farmer with some curiosity. Richard's was at all times a figure to attract attention; but now he was really dramatic (so Severn thought at least) with his careless garments, his pale, handsome face, his dark mistrustful eyes, his nervous movements. Major Luttrel, who struck Gertrude as at once very agreeable and the least bit in the world insufferable, was, of course, invited to remain—which he straightway consented to do; and it soon became evident to Miss Whittaker that her little plan would have no fruit. Richard practised a certain defiant, conscious silence, which, as she feared, gave him eventually a very pretentious air. His companions displayed that half-confessed effort to shine and to outshine natural to clever men who find themselves concurring to the entertainment of a young and agreeable woman. Richard sat by, wondering in splenetic amazement whether he were an ignorant boor or they were only a pair of grimacing comedians. He decided, correctly enough, in substance, for the former hypothesis; for it seemed to him that Gertrude's extreme accommodation (for as such he viewed it) of her tone and her manner to theirs was only another proof of her tremendous cleverness. How magnanimous an impulse on Richard's part was this submission for the sake of the woman he loved to a fact damning to his own vanity, could have been determined only by one who knew the proportions of that vanity. He writhed and chafed under the polish of tone and the variety of allusion by which the two officers consigned him to insignificance; but he was soon lost in wonder at the richness of resource of their hostess. For a moment it seemed to him that she ought to spare him an exhibition by which he could only be mortified—for didn't she know his thoughts, she who was the cause of them all? But the next instant he asked himself, with a great revulsion of feeling, whether he was afraid to see the proof of how superior she was to himself. As he gulped down the sickening fact of his comparative, nay, absolute ignorance of the great world represented by his rivals, he felt like anticipating its consequences by a desperate sally into the very field of their conversation. To some such movement Gertrude was continually inviting him by her glances, her smiles, her questions, by certain little calculated silences. But poor Richard knew that if he should attempt to talk he would choke; and this assurance he imparted to his friend in a look piteously eloquent. He was conscious of a sensation under which his heart was fast turning into a fiery furnace, destined to consume all his good resolutions. He could not answer for the future now. Suddenly, as tea was drawing to a close, he became aware that Captain Severn had sunk into a silence very nearly as helpless as his own, and that he was covertly watching the progress of a lively dialogue between Miss Whittaker and Major Luttrel. He had the singular experience of seeing his own feelings reflected in the Captain's face; that is, he discovered there an incipient jealousy. Severn too was in love!

IV

On rising from table Gertrude proposed an adjournment to the garden, where she was very fond of entertaining her friends at this hour. The sun had sunk behind a long line of hills, far beyond the opposite bank of the river, a portion of which was discernible through a gap in the intervening wood. The high-piled roof and chimney-stacks, the picturesquely crowded surface, of the old patched and renovated farm-house which constituted Miss Whittaker's residence, were ruddy with the declining rays. Our friends' long shadows were thrown over the smooth grass. Gertrude, having graciously gone to meet the gentlemen's desire for their cigars, suggested a stroll toward the river. Before she knew it she had accepted Major Luttrel's arm; and, as Miss Pendexter preferred remaining at home, Severn and Richard found themselves lounging side by side at a short distance behind their hostess. Gertrude, who had noticed the taciturnity which had suddenly fallen upon Captain Severn, and in her simplicity had referred it to some unwitting failure of attention on her own part, hoped to make up for her neglect by having him at her own side. She was in some degree consoled, however, by the sight of his conjunction with Richard. As for Richard, now that he was on his feet and in the open air, he found it easier to speak.

"Who is that fellow?" he asked, nodding toward the Major.

"Major Luttrel, of the —th Artillery."

"I don't like his face much," said Richard.

"Don't you?" rejoined Severn, amused at his companion's bluntness. "He's not handsome, but he looks like a soldier."

"He looks like a scoundrel, I think," said Richard.

Severn laughed outright, so that Gertrude glanced back at him. "Dear me! I think you put it rather strongly. He seems to me a very pleasant member of society."

Richard was sorely perplexed. He had expected to find acceptance for his bitterest animadversions, and lo! here was the Captain fighting for his enemy. Such a man as that was no rival. So poor a reviler could be but a poor adorer. Nevertheless, a certain new-born scepticism in regard to his old fashion of measuring human motives prevented him from adopting this conclusion as final. He would try another question.

"Do you know Miss Whittaker well?"

"Tolerably well. She was very kind to me when I was ill. Since then I have seen her a good many times."

"That's a way she has, being kind to people who are in trouble," Richard remarked, with a shrewdness which he thought superior. But as the Captain merely puffed his cigar responsively, he pursued, "What do you think of her appearance?"

"I like it very much," said the Captain.

"She isn't beautiful," said Richard, with calculation.

Severn was silent a moment, and then, just as Richard was about to dismiss him from his thoughts, as neither formidable nor satisfactory, he replied, with some emphasis, "You mean she isn't pretty. She *is* beautiful, I think, in spite of the irregularity of her face. It's the sort of face you don't forget. She has no features, no colour, no lilies nor roses, no attitudes; but she has *looks*, expressions."

Severn spoke Richard's mind as well as his own. That "She

isn't beautiful" had been an extempore version of the young man's most cherished dogma, namely, She is beautiful. The reader will remember that he had so translated it on a former occasion. Now, all that he felt was a sense of gratitude to the Captain for having put it so much more finely than he, the above being his choicest public expression of it. But the Captain's eyes, somewhat brightened by his short but significant speech, were following Gertrude's slow steps. Richard saw that he could learn more from them than from any further oral declaration, for something in the lips beneath them seemed to indicate that *they* had judged themselves to have said enough, and they were obviously not the lips of a simpleton. As he thus deferred, with unwonted courtesy, to the Captain's silence, and transferred his gaze sympathetically to Gertrude's shapely shoulders and to her listening ear, he gave utterance to a tell-tale sigh—a sigh which there was no mistaking. Severn looked about; it was now his turn to probe a little. "Good heavens," he exclaimed, "that boy is in love with her!"

After the first shock of surprise he accepted this fact with rational calmness. Why shouldn't he be in love with her? "*Je le suis bien*," said the Captain; "or, rather, I'm not." Could it be, Severn pursued, that *he* was a favourite? He was an under-bred young farmer, but it was plain that he had a soul of his own. He almost wished indeed that Richard might turn out to be in Gertrude's good graces. "But if he is," he reflected, "why should he sigh like the wind in the chimney? It is true that there is no arguing for lovers. I, who am out in the cold, take my comfort in whistling most impertinently. It may be that my friend here groans for very bliss. I confess, however, that he scarcely looks like a gratified swain."

And forthwith this faint-hearted gentleman felt a twinge of pity for Richard's probable ill-luck; and as he compared it with the elaborately defensive condition of his own affections he felt a further pang of self-contempt. But it was easier to restore the equilibrium of his self-respect by an immediate cession of the field than by contesting it against this wofully wounded knight. "Whether he wins her or not, he'll fight for her," the Captain mused; and, as he glanced at Major Luttrel, he felt there was some comfort in that. He didn't fancy the Major so very much.

They had now reached the water's edge, where Gertrude, having made her companion pause, turned round to await her other guests. As they came up Severn saw, or thought he saw (which is a very different thing), that her first look was at Richard. The "admirer" in his breast rose fratricidal for a moment against the quiet observer; but the next it was pinioned again. "Amen," said the Captain; "it's none of my business."

At this moment Richard was soaring very high. The end of his bad feelings had been a sudden exaltation. He looked at the scene before him with all sorts of remarkable ideas. Why should he stand tongue-tied, sulking at opportunity, when all nature beckoned him into the field? There was the river-path where, a fortnight before, he had found an eloquence attested by Gertrude's tears. There was the admirable Gertrude herself, whose hand he had kissed and whose waist he had clasped. Surely, he was master here! Before he knew it he had begun to express himself—rapidly, nervously, almost defiantly. Major Luttrel having made an observation about the prettiness of the river, Richard entered upon a description of its general character and its superior beauty in that part of its course which traversed his own property, together with an enumeration of the fish which were to be found in it and a story about a great overflow ten years before. He spoke with sufficient volubility, but with a kind of angry shyness, his head thrown back and his eyes on the opposite bank. At last he stopped, feeling that he had given proof of his manhood, and looked towards Gertrude, whose eyes he had been afraid to meet until he had seen his adventure to a close. But she was looking at Captain Severn, under the impression that Richard had secured his auditor.

Severn was looking at Luttrel, and Luttrel at Miss Whittaker; and all were apparently so deep in observation that they had marked neither his speech nor his silence. "Truly," thought the young man, "I'm well out of the circle!" But he was determined to be patient still, which was assuredly, all things considered, a very enlightened resolution. Yet there was always something spasmodic and unnatural in Richard's magnanimity. A touch in the wrong place would cause it to collapse. It was Gertrude's evil fortune to administer this puncture. As the party turned about toward the house Richard stepped to her side and offered her his arm, hoping in his heart—so implicitly did he count upon her sympathy, so almost boyishly, filially, did he depend upon it—for some covert token that his heroism, such as it was, had not been lost upon her.

But Gertrude, intensely preoccupied by the desire to repair her fancied injustice to the Captain, shook her head at him without even meeting his eye. "Thank you," she said; "I want Captain Severn;" who forthwith approached.

Poor Richard felt his feet touch the ground again, and at that instant he could have flung the Captain into the stream. Major Luttrel placed himself at Gertrude's other elbow, and Richard stood behind them, almost livid with spite, and half resolved to turn upon his heel and make his way home by the river. But it occurred to him that a more elaborate vengeance would be to follow the trio before him back to the lawn, and then show them how well he could dispense with their company. Accordingly, when they reached the house, he stood aloof and bade Gertrude a grim good-night. He trembled with eagerness to see whether she would make an attempt to detain him. But Miss Whittaker, reading in his voice—it had grown too dark to see his face at the distance at which he stood—the story of some fancied affront, and unconsciously contrasting it, perhaps, with Severn's clear and unwarped accents, obeyed what she deemed a prompting of self-respect, and gave him, without her hand, a farewell as cold as his own. It is but fair to

add that, a couple of hours later, as she reviewed the incidents
of the evening, she repented very characteristically of this little
act of justice.

V

RICHARD hardly knew how he got through the following
week. He found occupation, to a much greater extent than he
suspected, in a sordid yet at the same time heroic struggle with
himself. For several months now he had been leading, under
Gertrude's inspiration, a very decent and sober life. So long
as he was at comparative peace with Gertrude and with himself,
such a life was more than easy; it was delightful. It produced a
moral buoyancy infinitely more delicate than the exhilaration
of liquor. There was a kind of fascination in keeping the score
of his abstinence. Having abjured excesses, he practised temperance after the fashion of a novice: nothing would suit him
but not to drink at all. He was like an unclean man who, having
washed himself clean, remains in the water to splash about. He
wished to be religiously, superstitiously pure. This was easy,
as I have said, so long as his goddess smiled, even though it
were as a goddess indeed—as a creature unattainable. But when
she frowned and the heavens grew dark, Richard's sole dependence was his own good intention—as flimsy a trust for an
upward scramble, one would have predicted, as a tuft of grass
on the face of a perpendicular cliff. Flimsy as it looked, however, it served him. It started and crumbled, but it held, if only
by a single fibre. When Richard had cantered fifty yards away
from Gertrude's gate in a fit of stupid rage, he suddenly pulled
up his horse and gulped down his passion, swearing an oath
that, suffer what torments of feeling he might, he would not at
least break the continuity of his reform. It was enough to be
drunk in mind; he would not be drunk in body. A singular,
almost comical feeling of antagonism to Gertrude lent force to

this resolution. "No, madam," he cried within himself, "I shall *not* fall back. Do your best! I shall keep straight." We recover from great offences and afflictions by the aid of the same egotism they were perhaps meant to chasten. Richard went to bed that night fasting as grimly as a Trappist monk; and his foremost impulse the next day was to stupefy himself with some drudgery. He found no task to his taste; but he spent the day so actively, in mechanically getting rid of the time, that Gertrude's image found no chance to be importunate. He was engaged in the work of self-preservation, the most serious and absorbing work possible to man. Compared to this question of his own manhood it sometimes seemed not very important, after all, that Gertrude should listen to him. He tried later to build up a virtue by the most ruthless experiments and tests. He took long rides over the country, passing within a stone's throw of as many of the scattered wayside taverns as could be combined in a single circuit. As he drew near them he sometimes slackened his pace, as if he were about to dismount, pulled up his horse, gazed a moment, then, thrusting in his spurs, galloped away again like one pursued. At other times, in the late evening, when the window-panes were aglow with the ruddy light within, he would walk slowly by, looking at the stars, and, after maintaining this stoical pace for a couple of miles, would hurry home to his own dim and lonely dwelling. Having successfully performed this feat a certain number of times, he found his desire for Gertrude coming back to him, but bereft in the interval of a jealousy which now seemed to him to have been fantastic. One morning, at any rate, he leaped upon his horse and cantered back to Miss Whittaker's.

He had made himself comparatively sure of his will; but he was yet to acquire the mastery of his impulses. As he gave up his horse, according to his wont, to one of the men at the stable, he saw another animal, which he recognised as Captain Severn's. "Steady, my boy," he murmured to himself, as he would have done to a frightened steed. On the steps of the house he

encountered the Captain, who had just taken his leave. Richard
gave him a nod which was intended to be very friendly, and
Severn nodded back, but didn't speak. Richard observed, however, that he was very pale, and that he was pulling a rosebud
to pieces, as he walked; whereupon our young man quickened
his step. Finding the parlour empty, he instinctively crossed
over to a small room adjoining it, which Gertrude had converted into a conservatory; and as he did so, hardly knowing
it, he lightened his heavy-shod tread. The glass door was open
and Richard looked in. There stood Gertrude, with her back
to him, bending apart with her hands a couple of tall flowering
plants, and looking through the glazed partition behind them.
Advancing a step, and glancing over the poor girl's shoulder,
Richard had just time to see Severn mounting his horse at the
stable-door, before Gertrude, startled by his approach, turned
hastily round. Her face was flushed hot, her eyes brimming
with tears.

"You!" she exclaimed, sharply.

Richard's head swam. That single word was so charged
with an invidious distinction that it seemed the death-knell of
all his hopes. He stepped inside the room and closed the door,
keeping his hand on the knob.

"Gertrude," he said, "you love that man!"

"Well, sir?"

"Do you confess it?" cried Richard.

"Confess it? Richard Maule, how dare you use such language? I am in no humour for a scene. Let me pass."

Gertrude was angry; but as for Richard, it may almost be
said that he was mad. "One scene a day is enough, I suppose,"
he cried. "What are these tears about? Wouldn't he have you?
Did he refuse you, as you refused me? Unfortunate creature!"

Gertrude looked at him a moment with concentrated scorn.
"You poor idiot!" she said, for all answer. She pushed his
hand from the latch, flung open the door, and moved rapidly
away.

Left alone, Richard sank down on a sofa and covered his face with his hands. It burned them, but he sat motionless, repeating to himself, mechanically, as if to avert thought, "You poor idiot! you poor idiot!" At last he got up and made his way out.

It seemed to Gertrude, for several hours after this incident, that she had a remarkably strong case against fortune. It is not necessary to repeat here the words she had exchanged with Captain Severn. They had come within an ace of a mutual understanding, and when a single movement of the hand of either would have jerked aside the curtain that hung between them, some malignant influence had paralysed them both. Had they too much pride?—too little imagination? We must content ourselves with supposing so. Severn had walked blindly across the yard, saying to himself, "She belongs to another," and adding, as he saw Richard, "and such another!" Gertrude had stood at her window, repeating, under her breath, "He belongs to himself, himself alone." And as if this were not enough, when misconceived, slighted, wounded, she had turned back to her old, passionless, dutiful past, on the path of retreat to this asylum Richard Maule had arisen to forewarn her that she should find no peace even at home. There was something in the impertinence of his appearance at this moment which gave her a feeling that fate was against her, and there even entered into her mind a certain element of dread of the man whose passion was so insistent. She felt that it was out of place any longer to pity him. He was the slave of his passion, but his passion was strong. In her reaction against Severn's exaggerated respect, it gratified her, after a little, to remember that Richard had been brutal. He, at least, had ventured to insult her—he had loved her enough to forget himself. He had dared to make himself odious in her eyes, because he had cast away conventional forms. What cared he for the impression he made? He cared only for the impression he received. The violence of this reaction, however, was the measure of its

duration. It was impossible that she should walk backward so
fast without stumbling. Brought to her senses by this accident,
she became aware that her judgment had deserted its post.
She smiled to herself as she reflected that it had been taking
holiday for a whole afternoon. "Richard was right," she said
to herself. "I am no fool, I can't be a fool if I try. I am too
thoroughly my father's daughter for that. I love that man, but
I love myself better. Of course, then, I don't deserve to have
him. If I loved him in a way to merit his love, I would sit
down at this moment and write him a note telling him that if
he does not come back to me I shall die. But I shall neither
write the note nor die. I shall live and grow stout, and look
after my chickens and my flowers and my colts, and thank the
Lord in my old age that I have never done anything immodest.
Well! I am as He made me. Whether I shall ever deceive
others, I know not; but I certainly shall never deceive myself.
I am quite as sharp as Gertrude Whittaker; and this it is that
has kept me from making a fool of myself and writing to poor
Richard the note that I wouldn't write to Captain Severn. I
needed to fancy myself wronged. I suffer so little—I needed a
sensation. So, shrewd Yankee that I am, I thought I would get
one cheaply by taking up that unhappy boy. Heaven preserve
me from the heroics, especially the economical heroics! The
one heroic course possible I decline. What, then, have I to
complain of? Must I tear my hair because a man of taste has
resisted my unspeakable charms? To be charming you must be
charmed yourself, or at least you must be able to be charmed;
and that apparently I am not. I didn't love him, or he would
have known it. If you won't risk anything how can you
demand of others that they shall?"

But at this point of her meditations Gertrude almost broke
down. She felt that she was assigning herself but a dreary
future. Never to be loved but by an intemperate, uneducated
boy, who would never grow older, was a cheerless prospect,
for it seemed to convert her into a kind of maiden-aunt. Yet

her conscience smote her for her meditated falsity to Richard, her momentary readiness to succumb to the temptation to revert to him out of pique. She recoiled from this thought as from an act cruel and immoral. Was he any better suited to her now than he had been a month before? Was she to apply for comfort where she would not apply for counsel? Was she to drown her vexation at losing Captain Severn in a passion got up for the occasion? Having done the young man so bitter a wrong in intention, nothing would appease her magnanimous remorse (as time went on) but to repair it in fact. She went so far as to regret the harsh words she had cast upon him in the conservatory. He had been insolent and unmannerly, but he had an excuse. Much should be forgiven him, for he loved much. Even now that Gertrude had imposed upon her feelings a sterner regimen than ever, she could not defend herself from a sweet and sentimental thrill—a thrill in which, as we have intimated, there was something of a tremor—at the recollection of his strident accents and his angry eyes. It was far from her to desire a renewal, however brief, of this exhibition. She wished simply to efface from the young man's morbid mind the impression that she really scorned him, for she knew that against such an impression he was capable of taking the most reckless and ruinous comfort.

Before many mornings had passed, accordingly, she had a horse saddled, and, dispensing with attendance, took her way to his straggling farm. The house-door and half the windows stood open; but no answer came to her repeated summons. She rode round to the rear of the house, to the barn-yard, thinly tenanted by a few common fowl, and across the yard to a road which skirted its lower extremity and was accessible by an open gate. No human figure was in sight; nothing was visible in the hot stillness but the scattered and ripening crops, over which, in spite of her nervous solicitude, Miss Whittaker cast the glance of a connoisseur. A great uneasiness filled her mind as she measured the wide fields, apparently abandoned by their young master, and reflected that she perhaps was the cause of his absence. Ah, where was Richard? As she looked and listened in vain, her heart rose to her throat, and she felt herself on the point of calling wistfully upon his name. But her voice was stayed by the sound of a heavy rumble of cart-wheels, beyond a turn in the road. She touched up her horse and cantered along until she reached the bend. A great four-wheeled cart, laden with masses of newly-broken stone and drawn by four oxen, was slowly advancing towards her. Beside it, patiently cracking his whip and shouting monotonously, walked a young man in a slouched hat and a red shirt, with his trousers thrust into his dusty boots. As he saw Gertrude he halted a moment, amazed, and then advanced, flicking the air with his whip. Gertrude's heart went out to him in a sigh of really tender relief. Her next reflection was that he had never looked so well. The truth is that, in this rough adjustment, the native barbarian appeared to his advantage. His face and neck were browned by a week in the fields, his eye was clear, his step seemed to have learned a certain manly dignity from its attendance on the heavy bestial tramp. Gertrude, as he reached her side, pulled up her horse and held out her gloved fingers to his brown, dusty hand. He took them, looked for a moment into her face, and for the second time raised them to his lips.

"Excuse my glove," she said, with a little smile.

"Excuse mine," he answered, exhibiting his sunburnt, work-stained hand.

"Richard," said Gertrude, "you never had less need of excuse in your life. You never looked half so well."

He fixed his eyes upon her a moment. "Why, you have forgiven me!" he exclaimed.

"Yes, I have forgiven you—both you and myself. We both of us behaved very absurdly, but we both of us had reason. I wish you had come back."

Richard looked about him, apparently at a loss for a rejoinder. "I have been very busy," he said, at last, with a simplicity of tone slightly studied. He was always wishing to produce an effect upon her, and it seemed to him just then that this was the way.

It was a certain instinct of calculation, too, that forbade Gertrude to express all the joy which this assurance gave her. Excessive joy would have implied undue surprise; and it was a part of her plan frankly to expect the best things of her companion. "If you have been busy I congratulate you. What have you been doing?

"Oh, a hundred things! I have been quarrying, and draining, and clearing, and doing a lot of chores. I thought the best thing was just to put my own hands to it. I am going to make a stone fence along the great lot on the hill there. Wallace is for ever grumbling about his boundaries. I mean to fix them once for all. What are you laughing at?"

"I am laughing at certain foolish apprehensions that I have been indulging for a week past. You are wiser than I, Richard. I have no imagination."

"Do you mean that *I* have? I haven't enough to guess what you do mean."

"Why, do you suppose, have I come over this morning?"

"Because you thought I was sulking on account of your having called me an idiot."

"Sulking, or worse. What do I deserve for the wrong I have done you?"

"You have done me no wrong. You reasoned fairly enough. You are not obliged to know me better than I know myself. It's just like you to be ready to take back that bad word, and try to make yourself believe that it was unjust. But it was perfectly just, and therefore I have managed to bear it. I *was* an idiot at that moment—a nasty, impudent idiot. I don't know whether that man had been saying sweet things to you. But if he had you wouldn't have objected—your face told that; I should have been less than a man, I should be unworthy of your—your affection, if I had failed to see it. I did see it—I saw it clearly as I see those oxen now; and yet I bounced in with my own ill-timed claims. To do so was to be an awful ass. To have been other than an ass would have been to have waited, to have backed out, to have bitten my tongue off before I spoke, to have done anything but what I did. I have no right to claim you Gertrude, until I can woo you better than that. It was the most fortunate thing in the world that you spoke as you did: it was even kind. It saved me all the misery of groping about for a starting-point. Not to have spoken as you did would have been to let me off far too easy; and then, probably, I should have sulked, or, as you very considerately say, done worse. I had made a false move in the game, and the only thing to do was to repair it. But you were not obliged to know that I would so readily admit my move to have been false. Whenever I have made a fool of myself, before, I have been for sticking it out, and trying to turn all mankind—that is, *you*—into a fool, too so that I shouldn't be an exception. But this time, I think, I had a kind of inspiration. I felt that my case was desperate. I felt that if I adopted my folly now I adopted it for ever. The other day I met a man who had just come home from Europe, and who spent last summer in Switzerland. He was telling me about the mountain-climbing over there—how they get over the glaciers, and all that. He said that you sometimes came upon great slippery, snow-covered slopes that end short off in a precipice, and that if you stumble or lose your footing as you cross them diagonally, why, you go shooting down, and you're gone; that is, but for one little dodge. You have a long walking-pole, with a sharp end, you know, and as you feel yourself sliding—it's as likely as not to be in a sitting posture—you just take this and ram it into the snow before you, and there you are, stopped. The thing is, of course, to drive it in far enough, so that it won't yield or break; and in any case it hurts infernally to come whizzing down upon this upright pole. But the interruption gives you time to pick yourself up. Well, so it was with me the other day. I stumbled and fell; I slipped, and was whizzing downward; but I just drove in my pole and pulled up short. It nearly tore me in two; but it saved my life." Richard made this speech with one hand leaning on the neck of Gertrude's horse, and the other on his own side, and with his head slightly thrown back and his eyes on hers. She had sat quietly in her saddle, looking down at him. He had spoken slowly and deliberately, but without hesitation and without heat. "This is not romance, it's reality," thought Gertrude. And this feeling it was that dictated her reply, divesting it of sentiment so effectually as almost to make it sound trivial.

"It was fortunate you had an alpenstock," she said.

"I shall never travel without one again."

"Never, at least, with a companion who has the bad habit of pushing you off the path."

"Oh, you may push all you like," said Richard. "I give you leave. But isn't this enough about myself?"

"That's as you think."

"Well, it's all I have to say for the present, except that I am tremendously glad to see you, and that of course you will stay awhile."

"But you have your work to do."

"Oh, I say, never you mind my work. I have earned my dinner this morning, if you have no objection; and I propose to share it with you. So we will go back to the house." He turned her horse's head about, started up his oxen with his voice, and walked along beside her on the grassy roadside, with one hand on the horse's mane and the other swinging his whip.

Before they reached the yard-gate Gertrude had thought over what he had just said to her. "Enough about himself," she said, silently echoing his words. "Yes, heaven be praised, it *is* about himself. I am but a means in this matter—he himself, his own character, his own happiness, is the end." Under this conviction it seemed to her that her part was appreciably simplified. Richard was learning wisdom and self-control, and to exercise his reason—such was the suit that he was destined to gain. Her duty was as far as possible to remain passive, and not to interfere with the working of the gods who had selected her as the instrument of their miracle. As they reached the gate Richard made a trumpet of his hands, and sent a ringing summons into the fields; whereupon a farm-boy approached, and, with an undisguised stare of amazement at Gertrude, took charge of his master's team. Gertrude rode up to the doorstep, where her host assisted her to dismount, and bade her go in and make herself at home, while he busied himself with the bestowal of her horse. She found that, in her absence, the old woman who administered her friend's household had reappeared, and had laid out the preparations for his mid-day meal. By the time he returned, with his face and head shining from a fresh ablution and his shirt-sleeves decently concealed by a coat, Gertrude had apparently won the complete confidence of Mrs Catching.

Gertrude doffed her hat, and tucked up her riding-skirt, and sat down, face to face with her entertainer, over his crumpled table-cloth. The young man played the host very tenderly and naturally; and Gertrude hardly knew whether to infer from his perfect self-possession that her star was already on the wane, or that it was higher in the heavens than ever. The solution of her doubts was not far to seek; Richard was absolutely at his ease in her presence. He had told her indeed that she intoxicated him; and truly, in those moments when she was compelled to oppose her quiet surfaces to his crude unrest, her whole presence seemed to him to have a kind of wine-like strength. He had told her that she was an enchantress, and this assertion, too, had its measure of truth. But her spell was a steady one; it sprang not from her beauty, her wit, her grace—it sprang from her character. In other words, Gertrude exercised the magnificent power of making her lover forget her face. Agreeably to this fact, his most frequent feeling when he was with her was a consciousness of the liberty to be still—a sensation not unlike that which in the early afternoon, as he lounged in his orchard with a pipe, he derived from the sight of the hot, vaporous hills. He was innocent of that delicious trouble which Gertrude's thoughts had touched upon as a not unnatural result of her visit, and which another woman's fancy would perhaps have demanded as an indispensable proof of its success. "Porphyro grew faint," the poet assures us, as he stood in Madeline's chamber on Saint Agnes's eve. But Richard did not in the least grow faint now that his mistress was actually filling his musty old room with her voice, her touch, her looks; that she was sitting in his unfrequented chairs, trailing her skirt over his faded carpet, casting her perverted image upon his cheap mirror, and breaking his daily bread. He was not fluttered when he sat at her well-served table and trod her muffled floors—why then should he be fluttered now? Miss Whittaker was herself in all places, and (once granted that she was not in trouble) to be at her side was to drink peace as fully in one place as in another.

Richard accordingly ate a great working-day dinner in Gertrude's despite, and she ate a small one for his sake. She asked questions, moreover, and offered counsel, with very sisterly freedom. She deplored the rents in his table-cloth and the dismemberments of his furniture; and although by no means absurdly fastidious in the matter of household elegance, she could not but think that Richard would be a happier and a better man if he were a little more comfortable. She forbore, however, to criticise the poverty of his domestic arrangements, for she felt that the obvious answer was that such a state of things was the penalty of his living alone; and it was desirable, under the circumstances, that this idea should remain inarticulate.

When at last Gertrude began to bethink herself of going, Richard broke a long silence by the following question: "Gertrude, *do* you love that man?"

"My dear sir," she said, "I refused to tell you before, because you asked the question as a right. Of course you do so

no longer. No—I don't love him. I have been near to it—but
I have missed it. And now good-bye."

For a week after her visit Richard worked with renewed
tenacity and felt like a hero. But one morning he woke up with
all his courage gone, and limpness and languor in its place. He
had been straining his faith in himself to an extreme tension,
and the cord had suddenly snapped. In the hope that Gertrude's tender fingers might repair it he rode over to her,
towards evening. On his way through the village he found
people gathered in knots, reading fresh copies of the Boston
newspapers over each other's shoulders, and learned that
tidings had just come of a great battle in Virginia, which was
also a great defeat. He procured a copy of the paper from a
man who had done with it, and made haste to Gertrude's
dwelling.

She received his story with all the passionate imprecations
and regrets that were then in fashion. Before long Major Luttrel presented himself, and for half-an-hour there was no talk
but about the battle. The talk, however, was chiefly between
Gertrude and the Major, who found considerable ground for
differing opinion, she being a rabid Republican, and he in cool
opposition. Richard sat by, listening apparently, but with the
detachment of one to whom the matter of the discourse was of
much less interest than the manner of those engaged in it. At
last, when tea was announced, Gertrude told her friends, very
frankly, that she would not invite them to remain—that her
heart was too heavy with her country's woes and with visions
of carnage and suffering, to allow her to play the hostess—and
that in short she was in the humour to be alone. Of course
there was nothing for the gentlemen but to obey: but Richard
went out cursing the law under which, in the hour of his mistress's sorrow, his company was a bore, not a cure. He watched
in vain, as he bade her farewell, for some little sign that she
would like him to stay but that as she wished to get rid of his
companion civility demanded she should dismiss them both.

No such sign was forthcoming, for the simple reason that Gertrude was sensible of no such undercurrent. The men mounted their horses in silence, and rode slowly along the lane which led from Miss Whittaker's stables to the highroad. As they approached the top of the lane they perceived in the twilight a mounted figure coming towards them. Richard's heart began to beat with an angry foreboding, which was confirmed as the rider drew near and disclosed the features of Captain Severn. Major Luttrel and he, being bound to exchange some greeting, pulled up their horses; and as an attempt to pass them in narrow quarters would have been a greater incivility than even Richard was prepared to commit, he halted likewise.

"This is ugly news, isn't it?" said Severn. "It has determined me to go back to-morrow."

"Go back where?" asked Richard.

"To my regiment."

"Are you quite on your feet?" asked Major Luttrel. "How is that hole in your side?"

"It's so much better that I believe it can finish getting well down there as easily as here. Goodbye, Major; perhaps we shall meet again." And he shook hands with Major Luttrel. "Goodbye, Mr Maule." And, somewhat to Richard's surprise, he stretched over and held out his hand to him.

Richard felt that it was tremulous, and, looking hard into his face, thought he saw there a kind of agitation, of choked emotion. Hereupon his fancy coursed back to Gertrude, sitting where he had left her, in the sentimental twilight, alone with her heavy heart. With a word, he reflected, a single little word, a look, a gesture, this happy man whose hand I hold can heal her distress. "Oh," he cried to himself, "that by this hand I might hold him fast for ever!"

It seemed to the Captain that Richard's grasp was needlessly protracted and severe. "What a fist the young horse-breaker has!" he thought. "Good-bye," he repeated aloud, disengaging himself.

"Good-bye," said Richard. And then he added, he hardly knew why, "Are you going to bid good-bye to Miss Whittaker?"

"Of course I am. Isn't she at home?"

Whether Richard really paused or not before he answered, he never knew. There suddenly arose such a tumult in his bosom that it seemed to him several moments before he became conscious of his reply. But it is probable that to Severn it came only too soon.

"No," said Richard; "she's not at home. She is out for the evening. We have just been calling." As he spoke he shot a glance at his companion, armed with a challenge of his impending denial. But the Major just met his glance and then dropped his eyes. This slight motion was a horrible revelation —he had served the Major too!

"Dear me, I'm so sorry," said Severn, slacking his rein— "I'm so very sorry!" And from his saddle he looked down toward the house more longingly and regretfully than he knew.

Richard felt himself turning from pale to consuming crimson. There was a simple sincerity in Severn's words which was almost irresistible. For a moment he was on the point of shouting out a loud denial of his falsehood. "She is there, she's alone and in tears, awaiting you! Go to her—and be damned!" But before he could gather his words into his throat they were arrested by Major Luttrel's cool, clear voice, which, in its urbanity, seemed to mock at retractation.

"My dear Captain," said the Major, "I shall be very glad to take charge of any message."

"Thank you, Major. Pray do. Say how extremely sorry I was. It was my last chance. Good-bye again." And Captain Severn hastily turned his horse about, gave him his spurs and galloped away, leaving his friends standing alone in the middle of the road. As the sound of his retreat expired, Richard, in spite of himself, drew a long breath. He sat motionless in the saddle, hanging his head.

"Mr Maule," the Major remarked at last, "that was very brilliantly done."

Richard looked up. "I never told a lie before—never!"

"Upon my soul, then, you did it uncommonly well. You did it so well I almost believed you. No wonder poor Severn did!"

Richard was silent; then suddenly he broke out, "In God's name, sir, why don't you call me a blackguard? I have done a beastly act!"

"Oh come," said the Major, "you needn't mind that with me. We will take everything that's proper in the way of remorse for granted—consider that said. I feel bound to let you know that I am really much obliged to you. If you hadn't stopped him off, how do you know but that I might have done so?"

"If you had, I would have given you the lie in your teeth."

"Would you, indeed? It's very fortunate, then, that I held my tongue. If you will have it so, I won't deny that your little invention sounded very ugly. I'm devilish glad I didn't have anything to do with it, if you come to that."

Richard felt his wit sharpened by his red-hot scorn—a scorn far greater for his companion than for himself. "I am glad to hear that it did sound ugly. To me it seemed beautiful, holy, just. For the space of a moment it seemed absolutely right that I should say what I did. But you saw my fault in its horrid nakedness, and yet you let it pass. You have no excuse."

"I beg your pardon. You are immensely ingenious, but you are remarkably wrong. Are you going to make out that I am the guilty party? Upon my word, you are a cool hand. I *have* an excuse. I have the excuse of being interested in Miss Whittaker's not having other people running after her."

"So I suppose. But you have no disinterested regard for her. Otherwise——"

Major Luttrel laid his hand on Richard's bridle. "Mr Maule," said he, "I have no wish to talk metaphysics over this matter. You had better say no more. I know that your feelings are not of an enviable kind, and I am therefore prepared to be good-natured with you. But you must be civil yourself. You have done a nasty thing, you are ashamed of it, and you wish to shift the responsibility upon me, which is more shabby still. My advice is that you behave like a man of spirit and swallow your little scruples. I trust you are not going to make a fool of yourself by any apology or any fancied reparation. As for its having seemed holy and just to do what you did, that is mere gammon. A fib is a fib, and as such is often excusable. As anything else—as a thing beautiful, holy, or just—it's quite inexcusable. Yours was a fib to you, and a fib to me. It serves me, and I accept it. I suppose you understand me. I adopt it. You don't suppose it was because I was frightened by those big black eyes of yours that I held my tongue. As for my having a disinterested regard for Miss Whittaker, I have no report to make to you about it. I will simply say that I intend, if possible, to marry her."

"She'll not have you. She'll never marry a cold-blooded cheat."

"I think she'll prefer him to a hot-blooded one. Do you want to pick a quarrel with me? Do you want to make me lose my temper? I shall refuse you that satisfaction. You have been a coward, and you want to frighten someone before you go to bed and make up for it. Touch me and I'll kill you, but I propose not to notice your animadversions. Have you anything to say? No? Well, then, good evening." And Major Luttrel started away.

It was with white rage that Richard was dumb. Had he been but a cat's-paw after all? Heaven forbid! He sat irresolute for an instant, and then turned suddenly and cantered back to Gertrude's gate. Here he stopped again; but after a short pause he went in over the gravel, with a fast-beating heart, wishing Luttrel had been there to see him. For a moment he fancied he heard the sound of the Major's returning steps. If he would only come and find him at confession—it would be so easy to confess before him! He went along beside the house to the front, and stopped beneath the open window of the drawing-room.

"Gertrude!" he cried softly, from his saddle.

Gertrude immediately appeared. "Mercy—*you!*" she exclaimed.

Her voice was neither harsh nor sweet; but her words and her intonation recalled vividly to Richard's mind the scene in the conservatory, and they seemed to him keenly expressive of disappointment. He was invaded by a mischievous conviction that she had been expecting Captain Severn, or that at the least she had mistaken his voice for the Captain's. The truth is she had half imagined it might be—Richard's call having been little more than a loud whisper. The young man sat looking up at her, silent.

"What do you want?" she asked. "Can I do anything for you?"

Richard was not destined to do his duty that evening. A certain indefinable dryness of tone on Gertrude's part was the inevitable result of her finding that this whispered invocation came from poor Richard. She had been following her own thoughts. Captain Severn had told her a fortnight before that, in case of news of a defeat, he should not await the expiration of his leave of absence to return. Such news had now come, and it was clear to her that her friend would immediately take his departure. Naturally he would come and bid her farewell, and still more naturally she had her vision of what might pass between them at such a crisis. To tell the whole truth, it was under the pressure of these reflections that, twenty minutes before, Gertrude had dismissed our two gentlemen. That this long story should be told in the dozen words with which she greeted Richard will seem strange to the disinterested reader. But in those words poor Richard, with a lover's clairvoyance, read it at a single glance. The same rush of resentment, the same sinking of the heart that he had felt in the conservatory took possession of him once more. To be witness of Severn's passion for Gertrude—that he could endure. To be witness of Gertrude's passion for Severn—against that obligation his reason rebelled.

"What is it you wish, Richard?" Gertrude repeated. "Have you forgotten anything?"

"Nothing—nothing!" cried the young man. "It's no matter."

He gave a great pull at his bridle, and almost brought his horse back on his haunches, and then, wheeling him about on himself, he thrust in his spurs and galloped out of the gate.

On the highway he came upon Major Luttrel, who stood looking down the lane.

"I'm going to the devil, sir!" cried Richard. "Give me your hand on it."

Luttrel held out his hand. "My poor young man," said he, "you are quite out of your mind. I'm sorry for you. You haven't been making a fool of yourself?"

"I haven't made it better—I have made it worse!"

Luttrel didn't quite understand, but he breathed more freely. "You had better go home and go to bed," he said. "You will make yourself ill by all these gyrations."

"I—I'm afraid to go home," said Richard, in a broken voice. "For God's sake, come with me!"—and the wretched fellow burst into tears. "I am too bad for any company but yours," he cried, in his sobs.

The Major winced, but he took pity. "Come, come," said he, "we shall wriggle through. I will go home with you."

They rode off together. That night Richard went to bed miserably drunk; although Major Luttrel had left him at ten o'clock, adjuring him to drink no more. He awoke next the morning in a violent fever; and before evening the doctor, whom one of his hired men had brought to his bedside, had come and looked grave and pronounced him very ill.

VI

In country districts, where life is quiet, small accidents loom large; and accordingly Captain Severn's sudden departure for his regiment became very rapidly known among Gertrude's neighbours. She herself heard it from her coachman, who had heard about it in the village, where the Captain had been seen to take the early train. She received the news calmly enough to outward appearance, but a great tumult rose and died in her breast. He had gone without a word of farewell! Perhaps in the hurry of sudden preparation he had not had time to call upon her. Still, bare civility would have dictated his dropping her a line of writing—he who must have read in her eyes the feeling which her lips refused to utter, and who had been indebted to her for considerable attentions. It was not often that Gertrude threw back into her friends' teeth their acceptance of the hospitality which it had been placed in her power to offer them; but if she now mutely reproached Captain Severn with ingratitude, it was because he had failed further than in appearing to forget what she had done for him—he had also lost all remembrance of the way she had done it. It is but natural to expect that our dearest friends will give us credit for our deepest feelings; and Gertrude had constituted Edmund Severn her dearest friend. She had not, indeed, asked his assent to this arrangement, but she had made it the occasion of all kinds of tacit vows; she had given him the flower of her womanly charity, and, when his moment came, he had turned from her without a look. Gertrude shed no tears. It seemed to her that she had given her friend tears enough, and that to expend her soul in weeping would be to waste something that was now too precious. She would think no more of Edmund Severn. He should be as little to her for the future as she was to him.

It was very easy to make this resolution: to keep it Gertrude found another matter. She could not think of the war, she could not talk with her neighbours of current events, she could not take up a newspaper, without reverting to her absent friend. She was haunted with the idea that he had not allowed himself time really to recover, and that a fortnight's exposure would send him back to the hospital. At last it occurred to her that common decency required that she should make a call upon Mrs Martin, the Captain's sister; and a vague impression that this lady might be the depositary of some farewell message— perhaps of a letter—which she was awaiting her convenience to present, led her at once to undertake this social duty. The carriage which had been ordered for her projected visit was at the door when, within a week after Severn's departure, Major Luttrel was announced. Gertrude received him in her bonnet. His first care was to present Captain Severn's message of good-bye, together with his regrets that he had not had a spare moment to come and see her. As Luttrel performed this office he watched his hostess narrowly, and was considerably re-assured by the unflinching composure with which she listened to it. The turn he had given to Severn's farewell had been the fruit of much mischievous cogitation. It had seemed to him that, for his purposes, to represent the absent officer as alluding hastily and mechanically to Miss Whittaker would be better than to represent him as not alluding at all, for that would have left a boundless void for the exercise of Gertrude's fancy. And he had reasoned well; for although he was tempted to infer from her calmness that his shot had fallen short of the mark, yet in spite of her silent and almost smiling assent to his words it had made but one bound to her heart. Before many minutes she felt that Captain Severn's excuse had done her a world of good. "He had not a spare moment!" Indeed, as she took to herself its full expression of indifference, she felt that her hard, forced smile was deepening into a sign of lively gratitude to the Major.

Major Luttrel had still another task to perform. He had spent half-an-hour on the preceding day at Richard's bedside, having ridden over to the farm, in ignorance of his illness, to see how matters stood with him. The reader will already have surmised that the Major was not a person of fastidious delicacy: he will therefore be the less surprised and shocked to hear that the sight of the poor young man—prostrate, fevered, delirious, and to all appearances rapidly growing worse—filled him with an emotion by no means akin to despair. In plain terms, he was very glad to find Richard a prisoner in bed. He had been racking his brains for a scheme to keep his young friend out of the way, and now, to his exceeding satisfaction, the doctors relieved him of this troublesome care. If Richard was booked for typhoid fever, which his symptoms seemed to indicate, he would not, even assuming that he should get well, be able to leave his room for many weeks. In a month much might be done; with energy everything might be done. The reader has been all but directly informed that the Major's present purpose was to possess himself of Miss Whittaker's confidence, hand and fortune. He had no money and he had many needs, and he was so well advanced in life—being thirty-six years of age—that he had no heart to think of building up by slow degrees a career which had not yet taken the luxurious shape he desired. A man of refined tastes, too, he had become sensible, as he approached middle age, of the many advantages of a well-appointed home. He had therefore decided that a wealthy marriage would spread the carpet of repose. A girl of rather a fainter outline than Gertrude would have been the woman— we cannot say of his heart; but, as he argued, beggars can't be choosers. Gertrude was a young lady with standards of her own; but, on the whole, he was not afraid of her—he was abundantly prepared to do his duty. He had, of course, as became a man of observation, duly weighed his drawbacks against his advantages; and after all his arithmetic there was a balance in his favour. The only serious difficulty in his path was the possibility that, on hearing of Richard's illness, Gertrude, with her confounded benevolence, would take a fancy to nurse him in person, and that in the course of her ministrations his delirious ramblings would force upon her mind the damning story of the deception practised upon Captain Severn. There was nothing for it but boldly to face this risk. As for that other fact, which many men of a feebler spirit would have deemed an invincible obstacle, Luttrel's masterly understanding had immediately converted it into the prime agent of success—the fact, namely, that Gertrude's affections were already engaged. Such knowledge as he possessed of the relations between Miss Whittaker and his comrade in the Volunteers he had gained by simply watching and taking little notes. These had been numerous and on the whole his knowledge was accurate. It was at least what he might have termed a good working knowledge. He had calculated on a passionate reactionary impulse on Gertrude's part, consequent on Severn's apparent delinquency. He knew that in a generous woman such an impulse, if left to itself, would not go very far; but on this point it was that his policy bore. He would not leave it to itself: he would take it gently into his hands, spin it out, play upon it, and mould it into a clue which should lead him to the point he wanted to reach. He thus counted much upon his skill and his tact; but he likewise placed a becoming degree of reliance upon his fine personal qualities—qualities a little too stiff and solid perhaps to be called charms, but thoroughly adapted to inspire confidence. The Major was not a handsome fellow; he left that to people who hadn't the beauty of cleverness: but his ugliness was of a masculine, aristocratic, intelligent stamp. His figure, moreover, was good enough to compensate for the absence of a straight nose and a fine mouth; and he looked like a man of action who was at the same time a man of culture and of society.

In her sudden anxiety on Richard's behalf Gertrude soon forgot her selfish heart-ache. The carriage which was to have conveyed her to Mrs Martin's was used for a more disinterested purpose. The Major, prompted by a strong faith in the salutary force of his own presence, having obtained her permission to accompany her, they set out for the farm and soon found themselves in Richard's darkened room. The young man was immersed in a sleep from which it was judged imprudent to arouse him. Gertrude, sighing as she compared his bare bedroom with her own upholstered quarters, drew up a mental list of objects indispensable which she would immediately send him. Not that he had not received, however, a sufficiency of homely care. The doctor was assiduous, and old Mrs Catching full of rough good-sense.

"He asks very often after you, Miss," she said, addressing Gertrude, but with a sly glance at the Major. "But I think you had better not come too often. I am afraid you would work him up more than you would quiet him."

"I am afraid you would, Miss Whittaker," remarked the Major, who could have hugged Mrs Catching.

"Why should I work him up?" asked Gertrude. "I am used to sick-rooms. I nursed my father for a year and a half."

"Oh, it's very well for an old woman like me, but it's no place for a fine young lady with a tail to her gown," said the goodwife, looking at Gertrude's muslins and laces.

"I am not so fine as to desert a friend in distress," said Gertrude. "I shall come again, and if it makes the poor fellow worse to see me, I shall stay away. I am ready to do anything that will help him to get well."

It had already occurred to her that in his unnatural state Richard might find her presence a source of irritation, and she was prepared to remain in the background. As she returned to her carriage she caught herself reflecting with so much pleasure upon Major Luttrel's kindness in expending a couple of hours of his valuable time on so unprofitable an object that, by way of expressing her satisfaction, she invited him to come home and dine with her.

After a short interval she paid Richard a second visit, in company with Miss Pendexter. He was a great deal worse; he lay there emaciated, exhausted, stupid; the issue seemed very doubtful. Gertrude immediately pushed on to the county-town, which was larger than her own, sought out a professional nurse, and arranged with her to relieve Mrs Catching, who was worn out with sitting-up. For a fortnight, moreover, she received constant tidings from the young man's physician. During this fortnight Major Luttrel carried on his siege.

It may be said to his credit, that he had by no means conducted his suit upon that narrow programme which he had drawn up at the outset. He very soon discovered that Gertrude's rancour—if rancour there was—was a substance impalpable to any tactile process that he was master of, and he had accordingly set to work to woo her like an honest man, from day to day, from hour to hour, trusting so devoutly for success to momentary inspiration that he felt his suit dignified by a certain flattering *faux air* of genuine passion. He occasionally reminded himself, however, that he might really be more indebted to the favour of accidental contrast than Gertrude's life-long reserve—for it was certain she would not depart from it—would ever allow him to measure.

It was as an honest man, then—a man of impulse and of action—that Gertrude had begun to like him. She was not slow to perceive what he was "after," as they said in that part of the world; and she was almost tempted at times to tell him frankly that she would spare him the intermediate steps and meet him at the goal without further delay. She knew very well that she should never fall in love with him, but it was conceivable she might live with him happily. An immense weariness had somehow come upon her, and a sickening sense of loneliness. A vague suspicion that her money had done her an incurable wrong inspired her with a profound disgust for the care of it. She felt cruelly hedged out from human sympathy by her bristling possessions. "If I had had five hundred dollars a year," she said, in a frequent parenthesis, "I might have pleased him." Hating her wealth, accordingly, and chilled by her isolation, the temptation was strong upon her to give herself up to this wise, brave gentleman who seemed to have adopted such a happy medium betwixt loving her for her fortune and fearing her for it. Would she not always stand between men who would represent the two extremes? She should make herself decently secure by an alliance with Major Luttrel.

One evening, on presenting himself, Luttrel read these thoughts so clearly in her eyes that he made up his mind to speak. But his mind was burdened with a couple of facts of which it was necessary that he should disembarrass it before it could enjoy the freedom of action the occasion required. In the first place, then, he had been over to see Richard Maule, and had found him suddenly and unexpectedly better. It was unbecoming, however—it was impossible—that he should allow Gertrude to dwell long on this pleasant announcement.

"I tell the good news first," he said, gravely. "I have some very bad news, too, Miss Whittaker."

Gertrude sent him a rapid glance. "Someone has been killed?"

"Captain Severn has been shot," said the Major—"shot by a beastly guerilla."

Gertrude was silent—no answer seemed possible to that immitigable fact. She sat with her head on her hand and her elbow on the table beside her, looking at the figures in the carpet. She uttered no words of commonplace regret, but she felt as little capable of giving way to serious grief. She had lost nothing, and, to the best of her knowledge, *he* had lost nothing. She had an old loss to mourn—a loss a month old, which she had mourned as she might. To surrender herself to passion now would have been but to impugn the sincerity of what had already taken place in her mind. When she looked up at her companion she was outwardly calm, though I must add that a single glance of her eye directed him not to presume upon it.

She was aware that this glance betrayed her secret; but in view both of Severn's death and of the Major's position such revelations were of little moment. Luttrel had prepared to act upon her hint, and to avert himself gently from the topic, when Gertrude, who had dropped her eyes again, raised them with a slight shudder. "I am very cold," she murmured. "Will you shut that window beside you, Major? Or stay, suppose you give me my shawl from the sofa."

Luttrel brought the shawl, placed it on her shoulders, and sat down beside her. "These are cruel times," he said, with studied simplicity. "It is always the best that are taken."

"Yes, they are cruel times," Gertrude answered. "They make one feel cruel. They make one doubt of all one has learnt from one's pastors and masters."

"Yes, but they teach us something new also."

"I am sure I don't know," said Gertrude, whose heart was so full of bitterness that she felt almost malignant. "They teach us how mean we are. War is an infamy, Major, though it *is* your trade. It's very well for you, who look at it professionally, and for those who go and fight; but it's a miserable business for those who stay at home, and do the thinking and the —the *missing!* It's a miserable business for women; it makes us more spiteful than ever."

"Well, a little spite isn't a bad thing, in practice," said the Major. "War is certainly an abomination, both at home and in the field. But as wars go, Miss Whittaker, our own is a very satisfactory one. It involves important issues. It won't leave us as it found us. We are in the midst of a revolution, and what is a revolution but a turning upside down? It makes sad work with our habits and theories—our traditions and convictions. But, on the other hand," Luttrel pursued, warming to his task, "it leaves something untouched which is better than these—I mean our capacity to *feel*, Miss Whittaker." And the Major paused until he had caught Gertrude's eyes, when, having engaged them with his own, he proceeded. "I think that is the stronger for the downfall of so much else, and, upon my soul, I think it's in that we ought to take refuge. Don't you think so?"

"To feel what?" Gertrude inquired.

"Affection, admiration, hope!" said the Major. "I don't advocate fiddling while Rome is burning, you know. In fact, it's only poor unsatisfied devils that are tempted to fiddle. There is one sentiment which is respectable and honourable, and even sacred, at all times and in all places, whatever they may be. It doesn't depend upon circumstances, but they upon it; and with its help, I think, we are a match for any circumstances. I don't mean religion, Miss Whittaker," added the Major, with a significant smile.

"If you don't mean religion," said Gertrude, "I suppose you mean love. That's a very different thing."

"Yes, a very different thing; so I have always thought, and so I am glad to hear you say. Some people, you know, mix them up in the most extraordinary fashion. I don't regard myself as an especially religious man; in fact I believe I am rather remiss in that way. It's my nature. Half mankind are born so, or I suppose the affairs of this world wouldn't move. But I believe I am a good lover, Miss Whittaker."

"I hope for your own sake you are, Major Luttrel."

"Thank you. Do you think now you could entertain the idea for the sake of any one else?"

Gertrude neither dropped her eyes, nor shrugged her shoulders, nor blushed, nor whimpered. If anything, indeed, she turned somewhat paler than before, as she sustained her companion's gaze and prepared to answer him as directly as she might.

"If I loved you, Major Luttrel, I should value the idea for my own sake."

The Major, too, blanched a little. "I put my question conditionally," he answered, "and I have got, as I deserved, a conditional reply. I will speak plainly, then, Miss Whittaker.

Do you value the fact for your own sake? It would be plainer still to say, Do you love me? but I confess I am not brave enough for that. I will say, Can you? or I will even content myself with putting it in the conditional again, and asking you if you could; although, after all, I hardly know what the *if* understood can reasonably refer to. I am not such a fool as to ask of any woman—least of all of you—to love me contingently. You can only answer for the present, and say yes or no. I shouldn't trouble you to say either if I didn't conceive that I had given you time to make up your mind. It doesn't take for ever to know Robert Luttrel. I am not one of the great unfathomable ones. We have seen each other more or less intimately for a good many weeks; and as I am conscious, Miss Whittaker, of having shown you my best, I take for granted that if you don't fancy me now you won't a month hence, when you shall have seen my faults. Yes, Miss Whittaker, I can solemnly say," continued the Major, with genuine feeling, "I have shown you my best, as every man is in honour bound to do who approaches a woman with those predispositions with which I have approached you. I have striven hard to please you"—and he paused. "I can only say, I hope I have succeeded."

"I should be very insensible if all your kindness and your politeness had been lost upon me," Gertrude said.

"In heaven's name don't talk about politeness!" cried the Major.

"I am deeply conscious of your devotion, and I am very much obliged to you for urging your claims so respectfully and considerately. I speak seriously, Major Luttrel," pursued Gertrude. "There is a happy medium of expression, and you have taken it. Now it seems to me that there is a happy medium of affection, with which you might be content. I don't love you—no, not at all. I question my heart, and it gives me that answer. The feeling that I have is not a feeling to work prodigies."

"May it at least work the prodigy of allowing you to be my wife?"

Gertrude was silent a moment. "If you can respect a woman who gives you her hand in cold blood, you are welcome to mine."

Luttrel moved his chair and took her hand. "Beggars can't be choosers," said he, raising it to his moustache.

"Oh, Major Luttrel, don't say that," she answered. "I give you a great deal; but I keep a little—a little," said Gertrude, hesitating, "which I suppose I shall give to God."

"Well, I shall not be jealous," said Luttrel.

"The rest I give to you, and in return I ask a great deal."

"I shall give you all."

"No, I don't want more than I give," said Gertrude.

"But, pray," asked Luttrel, with an insinuating smile, "what am I to do with the difference?"

"You had better keep it for yourself. What I want is your protection, sir, your advice, your support. I want you to take me away from this place, even if you have to take me down to the army. I want to see the world under the shelter of your name. I shall give you a great deal of trouble. I am a mere mass of possessions: what I am is nothing to what I have. But ever since I began to grow up, what I am has been the slave of what I have. I am weary of my chains, and you must help me to carry them." And Gertrude rose to her feet, as if to inform the Major that his audience was at an end.

He still held her right hand; she gave him the other. He stood looking down at her, an image of manly humility, while from his silent breast went up a thanksgiving to favouring fortune.

At the pressure of his hands Gertrude felt her bosom heave. She burst into tears. "Oh, you must be very kind to me!" she cried, as he put his arm about her, and she dropped her head upon his shoulder.

VII

WHEN once Richard's health had taken a turn for the better, it began very rapidly to improve. "Until he is quite well," Gertrude said one day to her accepted suitor, "I should like him to hear nothing about our engagement. He was once in love with me himself," she added, very frankly. "Did you ever suspect it? But I hope he will have got better of that sad malady, too. Nevertheless, I shall expect nothing reasonable from him until he is quite strong; and as he may hear of my new intentions from other people, I propose that, for the present, we confide them to one one."

"But if he asks me point-blank," said the Major, "what shall I answer?"

"It's not likely he will ask you. How should he suspect anything?"

"Oh," said Luttrel, "that gentleman is one of your suspicious kind."

"Tell him we are not engaged then. A woman in my position may say what she pleases."

It was agreed, however, that certain preparations for the marriage should meanwhile go forward in secret, and that the ceremony itself should take place in August, as Luttrel expected to be ordered back into service in the autumn. At about this moment Gertrude was surprised to receive a short note from Richard, so feebly scrawled in pencil as to be barely legible. "Dear Gertrude," it ran, "don't come to see me just yet. I'm not fit to be seen. You would hurt me, and I should shock you. God bless you! R. MAULE." Miss Whittaker explained his request to herself by the supposition that a report had come to him of Major Luttrel's late assiduities (which it was impossible should go unobserved); that, leaping at the worst, he had taken her engagement for granted; and that, under this impression, he could not trust himself to see her. She despatched him an answer, telling him that she would await his pleasure, and that, if the doctor would consent to his having letters, she would meanwhile occasionally write to him. "She will give me good advice," thought Richard impatiently; and on this point, accordingly, she received no account of his wishes. Expecting to leave her house and close it on her marriage, she spent many hours in wandering sadly over the meadow-paths and through the woodlands which she had known from her childhood. She had thrown aside the last ensigns of filial regret, and now walked, sad and splendid, in bright colours which those who knew her well must have regarded as a kind of self-defiance. It would have seemed to a stranger that, for a woman who had freely chosen a companion for life, she was curiously spiritless and sombre. As she looked at her pale cheeks and dull eyes in the mirror she felt ashamed that she had no fairer countenance to offer to her destined lord. She had lost her single beauty, her smile, and she would make but a ghastly figure at the altar. "I ought to wear a calico dress and an apron," she said to herself, "and not this glaring finery." But she continued to wear her finery, and to lay out her money, and to perform all her old duties to the letter. After the lapse of what she deemed a sufficient interval she went to see Mrs Martin, and to listen dumbly to her narration of her brother's death and to her simple eulogies.

Major Luttrel performed his part quite as bravely, and much more successfully. He observed neither too many things nor too few; he neither presumed upon his success nor hung back from the next steps. Having, on his side, received no prohibition from Richard, he made his way back to the farm, trusting that with the return of reason his young friend might be disposed to renew that anomalous alliance in which, on the hapless evening of Captain Severn's farewell, he had taken refuge against his despair. In the long, languid hours of his

early convalescence Richard had found time to survey his position, to summon back piece by piece the immediate past, and
to frame a general scheme for the future. But more vividly
than anything else there had finally disengaged itself from his
meditations a kind of horror of Robert Luttrel.

It was in this humour that the Major found him; and as he
looked at the young man's gaunt shoulders, supported by pillows, at his face, so livid and aquiline, at his great dark eyes,
which seemed to shine with the idea of their possessor's taking
a fresh start, it struck him than an invincible spirit had been
sent from a better world to breathe confusion upon his hopes.
If Richard hated the Major, the reader may guess whether
the Major loved Richard. Luttrel was amazed at his first
remark.

"I suppose you have got her by this time," Richard said,
calmly enough.

"Not quite," answered the Major. "There's a chance for
you yet."

To this Richard made no rejoinder. Then, suddenly, "Have
you had any news of Captain Severn?" he asked.

For a moment the Major was perplexed at his question. He
had supposed that the news of Severn's death would have
come to Richard's ears, and he had been half curious, half
apprehensive as to its effect. But an instant's reflection now
assured him that the young man's estrangement from his neighbours had kept him hitherto, and might still keep him, in ignorance of the truth. Hastily, therefore, and inconsiderately, the
Major determined to make this ignorance last a little longer;
it was always so much gained. "No," said he, "I have had no
news. Severn and I are not on writing terms."

The next time Luttrel came to the farm he found the master
sitting up in a chintz-covered arm-chair, which Gertrude had
sent him the day before out of her own dressing-room.

"Have you got her yet?" asked Richard.

The note of provocation in his tone was so strong that the

Major ceased to temporise. "Yes, I have 'got' her, as you elegantly express it. We are engaged to be married."

The young man's face betrayed no emotion.

"Are you reconciled to it?" asked Luttrel.

"Yes—so far as doing anything goes."

"What in the name of all that's conceited could you do? Explain yourself."

"A man in my state can't explain himself. I mean that, however much I hate you, I shall accept Gertrude's marriage."

"It will be very kind of you. And you will be a wise man," the Major added.

"I am growing wise. I feel like Solomon on his throne, in this chair. But I confess, sir, I don't see how she could have you."

"Well, there's no accounting for tastes," said the Major, good-humouredly.

"Yes, but I thought hers was better."

They came to no more express understanding than this with regard to the future. Richard continued to grow stronger, and to put off, in the same measure, the renewal of his intercourse with Gertrude. A month before he would have resented as an insult the intimation that he should ever be so resigned to lose her as he found himself now. He would not see her for two reasons: first, because he felt that it would be—or that at least, in reason, it ought to be—a painful experience to look upon his old mistress with a coldly critical eye; and secondly, because, justify to himself as he would his new-born indifference, he could not entirely cast away the suspicion that it was a last remnant of disease, and that, when he stood on his legs again under the sky and among those natural things with which he had long since established a sort of sensuous communion, he would feel, as with a tumultuous rush, the return of his impetuous manhood and of his old capacity. When he had smoked a pipe in the outer sunshine, when he had settled himself once more to the long elastic bound of his mare, then he would see Gertrude. The reason of the change which had come upon him was that she had disappointed him—she who had used to seem to him above his measure altogether. She had accepted Major Luttrel, a man whom he despised; she had so mutilated her magnificent nature as to match it with his. The validity of his dislike to the Major, Richard did not trouble himself to examine. He accepted it as an unerring instinct; and, indeed, he might have asked himself, had he not sufficient proof? Moreover he laboured under the sense of a gratituous wrong. He had suffered a great torment of remorse to drive him into brutishness, and thence to the very gates of death, for an offence which he had deemed mortal, and which was, after all, but a phantasm of his excited conscience. What a fool he had been—a fool for his passionate fears, and a fool for his penitence! Marriage with Major Luttrel—such was the end of Gertrude's imagined anguish. Such, too, we hardly need add, was the end of that idea of reparation which had been so formidable to Luttrel. Richard had been generous; he would now be just.

Far from impeding his recovery, these reflections hastened it. One morning in the beginning of August Gertrude received notice that he was in her house. It was still, a sultry day, and Miss Whittaker, her habitual pallor deepened by the oppressive heat, was sitting alone, in a white morning-dress, languidly fanning aside at once the droning flies and her equally importunate thoughts. She found the young man standing in the middle of the drawing-room, booted and spurred.

"Well, Richard," she exclaimed, with some feeling, "at last you are willing to see me!"

As his eyes fell upon her he stared and stood almost paralysed, heeding neither her words nor her extended hand. It was not Gertrude he saw, but her ghost.

"In heaven's name, what has happened to you?" he cried. "Have *you* been sick too?"

Gertrude tried to smile, in feigned surprise at his surprise;

but her muscles relaxed. Richard's words and looks reflected more vividly than any mirror the blighted state of her person, the extreme misery of her soul. She felt herself growing faint. She moved backward to a sofa, and sank down.

Then Richard felt as if the room were revolving about him and his throat were choked with imprecations—as if his old extravagant passion had again taken possession of him, like a mingled legion of devils and angels. It was through the most unexpected pity that his love returned. He went forward and dropped on his knees at Gertrude's feet. "Speak to me!" he cried, seizing her hands. "Are you unhappy? Is your heart broken? Oh Gertrude! what have you come to?"

Gertrude drew her hands from his grasp and rose to her feet. "Get up, Richard," she said. "Don't talk so wildly. I am not well. I am very glad to see you. *You* look well."

"I have got my strength again—and meanwhile you have been failing. You are unhappy, you are wretched! Don't say you are not, Gertrude: it's as plain as day. You are breaking your heart."

"The same old Richard!" said Gertrude, trying to smile again.

"Would that you were the same old Gertrude! Don't try to smile; you can't!"

"I *shall!*" said Gertrude, desperately. "I am going to be married, you know."

"Yes, I know. I don't congratulate you."

"I have not counted upon that honour, Richard. I shall have to do without it."

"You will have to do without a great many things!" cried Richard, horrified by what seemed to him her blind self-immolation.

"I have all I ask," said Gertrude.

"You haven't all *I* ask, then! You haven't all your friends ask."

"My friends are very kind, but I marry to suit myself."

"You have not suited yourself!" retorted the young man.
"You have suited—God knows what!—your pride, your despair, your desolation!" As he looked at her the secret history
of her weakness seemed to become plain to him, and he felt a
desire to throttle the man who had taken a base advantage of
it. "Gertrude!" he cried, "I entreat you to go back. It's not
for my sake—I'll give you up—I'll go a thousand miles away,
and never look at you again. It's for your own. In the name of
your happiness, break with that man! Don't fling yourself
away. Buy him off, if you consider yourself bound. Give him
your money. That's all he wants."

As Gertrude listened the blood came back to her face and
two flames into her eyes. She looked at Richard from head to
foot. "You are not weak," she said, "you are in your senses,
you are well and strong; you shall tell me what you mean. You
insult the best friend I have. Explain yourself! you insinuate
odious things—speak them out!" Her eyes glanced toward
the door, and Richard's followed them. Major Luttrel stood on
the threshold.

"Come in, sir!" cried Richard. "Gertrude swears she will
believe no harm of you. Come and tell her that she's wrong!
How can you keep on persecuting a woman whom you have
brought to this state? Think of what she was three months ago,
and look at her now!"

Luttrel received this broadside without flinching; he had
overheard Richard's voice from the hall, and he had steeled his
heart for the encounter. He assumed the air of having been so
amazed by the young man's first words as only to have heard
his last; and he glanced at Gertrude mechanically, as if to
comply with them. "What's the matter?" he asked, going
over to her and taking her hand; "are you ill?" Gertrude let
him have her hand, but she forbore to meet his eyes.

"Ill! of course she's ill!" cried Richard, passionately. "She's
dying—she's consuming herself! I know I seem to be playing
an odious part here, Gertrude, but, upon my soul, I can't help

it. I look like a betrayer, an informer, a sneak, but I don't feel like one! Still, I will leave you, if you say so."

"Shall he go, Gertrude?" asked Luttrel, without looking at Richard.

"No. Let him stay and explain himself. He has accused you —let him prove his case."

"I know what he is going to say," said Luttrel. "It will place me in a bad light. Do you still wish to hear it?"

Gertrude drew her hand hastily out of Luttrel's. "Speak, Richard!" she cried, with a passionate gesture.

"Ah, you won't enjoy it," said Richard. "Gertrude, I have done you a vile wrong. How great a wrong I never knew until I saw you to-day so miserably altered. When I heard that you were to be married I fancied that it didn't matter much, and that my remorse had been wasted. But I understand it now, and *he* understands it too. You once told me that you had ceased to love Captain Severn. It wasn't true—you never ceased to love him—you love him at this moment. If he were to get another wound in the next battle, how would you feel —how would you bear that?" And Richard paused for an instant, with the force of his interrogation.

"For God's sake," said Gertrude, "respect the dead!"

"The dead! Is he dead?"

Gertrude covered her face with her hands.

"You beast!" cried Luttrel.

Richard turned upon him savagely. "You're a precious one to talk!" he roared. "You told me he was alive and well!"

Gertrude made a movement of speechless distress.

"You would have it, my dear," said Luttrel, in a superior tone.

Richard had turned pale, he began to tremble. "Excuse me, Gertrude," he said, hoarsely, "I have been deceived. Poor, unhappy woman! Gertrude," he continued, going near to her and speaking in a whisper, "*I* killed him."

Gertrude fell back from him, as he approached her, with a look of unutterable horror. "I and *he*," Richard went on, pointing at Luttrel.

Gertrude's eyes followed the direction of his gesture, and transferred their scorching disgust to her suitor. This was too much for Luttrel's courage. "You eternal tormentor," she moaned at Richard, "speak out!"

"He loved you, though you believed he didn't," said Richard. "I saw it the first time I looked at him. To every one but you it was as plain as day. Major Luttrel saw it too. But he was too modest, and he never believed you cared for him. The night before he went back to the army he came to bid you good-bye. If he had seen you it would have been better for every one. You remember that evening, of course. We met him, Luttrel and I. He was all on fire—he meant to speak. I knew it; you knew it, Luttrel: it was in his fingers' ends. I intercepted him. I turned him off—I lied to him and told him you were absent from home. I was a coward, and I did neither more nor less than that. I knew you were waiting for him. It was stronger than my will—I believe I should do it again. Fate was against him, and he went off. I came back to tell you, but my damnable jealousy strangled me. I went home and drank myself into a fever. I have done you a wrong that I can never repair. I would go hang myself if I thought it would help you." Richard spoke slowly, softly, explicitly, as if irresistible Justice in person had her hand upon his neck and were forcing him down upon his knees. In the presence of Gertrude's dismay nothing seemed possible but perfect self-conviction. In Luttrel's attitude, as he stood with his head erect, his arms folded, and his cold gray eye fixed upon the distance, it struck him that there was something atrociously insolent; not insolent to him—for that he cared little enough—but insolent to Gertrude and to the dreadful solemnity of the hour. Richard sent the Major a look of the most aggressive contempt. "As for Major Luttrel," he said, "*he* was but a passive spectator. No, Gertrude, by heaven!"

he burst out; "he was worse than I! I loved you, and he didn't!"

"Our friend is correct in his facts, Gertrude," said Luttrel, quietly. "He is incorrect in his inferences. I *was* a passive spectator of his deception. He appeared to enjoy a certain authority with regard to your wishes—the source of which I respected both of you sufficiently never to question—and I accepted the act which he has described as an exercise of it. You will remember that you had sent us away on the ground that you were in no humour for company. To represent you, therefore, to another visitor as absent seemed to me rather officious, but still pardonable. You will consider that I was wholly ignorant of your relations to that visitor; that whatever you may have done for others, Gertrude, to me you never vouchsafed a word of information on the subject, and that Mr Maule's words are a revelation to me. But I am bound to believe nothing that he says. I am bound to believe that I have injured you only when I hear it from your own lips."

Richard made a movement as if to break out upon the Major; but Gertrude, who had been standing motionless, with her eyes upon the ground, quickly raised them, and gave him a look of imperious prohibition. She had listened, and she had chosen. She turned to Luttrel. "Major Luttrel," she said, "you *have* been accessory to something that has been for me a very serious pain. It is my duty to tell you so. I mean, of course, a perfectly unwilling accessory. I pity you more than I can tell you. I think your position more pitiable than mine. It is true that I never made a confidant of you. I never made one of Richard. I had a secret, and he surprised it. You were less fortunate." It might have seemed to a dispassionate observer that in these last four words there was an infinitesimal touch of tragic irony. Gertrude paused a moment while Luttrel eyed her intently, and Richard, from a somewhat tardy instinct of delicacy, walked over to the bow-window. "This is the most distressing moment of my life," she resumed. "I hardly know where my duty lies. The only thing that is plain to me is that I must ask you to release me from my engagement. I ask it most humbly, Major Luttrel," Gertrude continued, with warmth in her words and a chilling coldness in her voice—a coldness which it sickened her to feel there, but which she was unable to dispel. "I can't expect that you should give me up easily; I know that it's a great deal to ask, and"—she forced the chosen words out of her mouth—"I should thank you more than I can say if you would put some condition upon my release. You have done honourably by me, and I repay you with ingratitude. But I can't marry you." Her voice began to melt. "I have been false from the beginning. I have no heart to give you. I should make you a despicable wife."

The Major, too, had listened and chosen, and in this trying conjuncture he set the seal to his character as an accomplished man. He saw that Gertrude's movement was final, and he determined not to protest against the inscrutable. He read in the glance of her eye and the tone of her voice that the perfect dignity had fallen from his character—that his integrity had lost its bloom; but he also read her firm resolve never to admit this fact to her own mind nor to declare it to the world, and he was gratified by her forbearance. His hopes, his ambitions, his visions, lay before him like a heap of broken glass; but he would be as graceful as she was. She had divined him, but she had spared him. The Major was inspired.

"You have at least spoken to the point," he said. "You leave no room for doubt or for hope. With the little light I have I can't say I understand your feelings, but I yield to them religiously. I believe so thoroughly that you suffer from the thought of what you ask of me that I will not increase your suffering by assuring you of my own. I care for nothing but your happiness. You have lost it, and I give you mine to replace it. And although it's a simple thing to say," he added, "I must remark that I thank you for your implicit faith in my integrity." And he held out his hand. As she gave him hers

Gertrude felt horribly in the wrong; and she looked into his eyes with an expression, so humble, so appealing, so grateful, that, after all, his exit may be called triumphant.

When he had gone Richard turned from the window with a tremendous sense of relief. He had heard Gertrude's speech, and he knew that perfect justice had not been done; but still there was enough to be thankful for. Yet now that his duty was accomplished, he was conscious of a sudden lassitude. Mechanically he looked at Gertrude, and almost mechanically he came towards her. She, on her side, looking at him as he walked slowly down the long room, his face indistinct against the deadened light of the white-draped windows behind him, marked the expression of his figure with another pang. "He has rescued me," she said to herself; "but his passion has perished in the tumult." "Richard," she said aloud, uttering the first words of vague kindness that came into her mind, "I forgive you."

Richard stopped. The idea had lost its charm. "You are very kind," he said, wearily. "You are far too kind. How do you know you forgive me? Wait and see."

Gertrude looked at him as she had never looked before; but he saw nothing of it. He saw a sad, plain girl, in a white dress, nervously handling her fan. He was thinking of himself. If he had been thinking of her he would have read in her lingering, upward gaze that he had won her; and if, so reading, he had opened his arms Gertrude would have come to them. We trust the reader is not shocked at this piece of information. She neither hated him nor despised him, as she ought doubtless in consistency to have done. She felt that there was a gallantry in him, after all, and in this new phase he pleased her. Richard, on his side, felt humbly the same truth, and he began to respect himself. The past had closed abruptly behind him, and poor tardy Gertrude had been shut in. The future was dimly shaping itself without her image. So did he not open his arms.

"Good-bye," he said, holding out his hand. "I may not see you again for a long time."

Gertrude felt as if the world were deserting her. "Are you going away?" she asked, tremulously.

"I mean to sell out and pay my debts, and go to the war."

She gave him her hand, and he silently shook it. There was no contending against the war, and she gave him up.

With their separation my story properly ends, and to say more would be to begin a new story. It is perhaps my duty, however, expressly to add that Major Luttrel, in obedience to a logic of his own, abstained from revenge; and that, if time has not avenged him, it has at least rewarded him. General Luttrel, who lost an arm before the war was over, recently married Miss Van Winkel, of Philadelphia, and seventy thousand a year. Richard engaged in the defence of his country, with a commission in the Volunteers, obtained with much difficulty. He saw a great deal of fighting, but he has no scars to show. The return of peace found him in his native place, without a home and without resources. One of his first acts was to call dutifully and respectfully upon Miss Whittaker, whose circle of acquaintance was now much enlarged, and included even people who came from Boston to stay with her. Gertrude's manner was kindness itself, but a more studied kindness than before. She had lost much of her youth and her simplicity. Richard wondered whether she had pledged herself to spinsterhood, but of course he didn't ask her. She inquired very particularly into his material prospects and intentions, and offered urgently to lend him money, which he declined to borrow. When he left her he took a long walk through her place and beside the river, and, wandering back to the old days when he had yearned for her love, assured himself that no woman would ever again be to him what she had been. During his stay in this neighbourhood he became reconciled to one of the old agricultural magnates whom he had insulted in his unregenerate days, and through whom he was glad to obtain some momentary employment. But his present position is very distasteful to him, and he is eager to try his fortunes in the West. As yet, however, he has lacked the means to emigrate with advantage. He drinks no more than is good for him. To speak of Gertrude's impressions of Richard would lead us quite too far. Shortly after his return she broke up her household, and came to the bold resolution (bold, that is, for a woman young, unmarried, and ignorant of manners in her own country) to spend some time in Europe. At our last accounts she was living in the ancient city of Florence. Her great wealth, of which she was wont to complain that it excluded her from human sympathy, now affords her a most efficient protection. She passes among her fellow-countrymen abroad for a very independent, but a very contented woman; although, as she is by this time nearly thirty years of age, some little romantic episode in the past is vaguely alluded to as accounting for her continued celibacy.

THE STORY OF A MASTERPIECE

I

No longer ago than last summer, during a six weeks' stay at Newport, John Lennox became engaged to Miss Marian Everett of New York. Mr Lennox was a widower, of large estate, and without children. He was thirty-five years old, of a sufficiently distinguished appearance, of excellent manners, of an unusual share of sound information, of irreproachable habits and of a temper which was understood to have suffered a trying and salutary probation during the short term of his wedded life. Miss Everett was, therefore, all things considered, believed to be making a very good match and to be having by no means the worst of the bargain.

And yet Miss Everett, too, was a very marriageable young lady—the pretty Miss Everett, as she was called, to distinguish her from certain plain cousins, with whom, owing to her having no mother and no sisters, she was constrained, for decency's sake, to spend a great deal of her time—rather to her own satisfaction, it may be conjectured, than to that of these excellent young women.

Marian Everett was penniless, indeed; but she was richly endowed with all the gifts which make a woman charming. She was, without dispute, the most charming girl in the circle in which she lived and moved. Even certain of her elders, women of a larger experience, of a heavier calibre, as it were, and, thanks to their being married ladies, of greater freedom of action, were practically not so charming as she. And yet, in her emulation of the social graces of these, her more fully licensed sisters, Miss Everett was quite guiltless of any aberration from the strict line of maidenly dignity. She professed an almost religious devotion to good taste, and she looked with horror upon the boisterous graces of many of her companions. Beside being the most entertaining girl in New York, she was, therefore, also the most irreproachable. Her beauty was, perhaps, contestable, but it was certainly uncontested. She was the least bit below middle height, and her person was marked by a great fulness and roundness of outline; and yet, in spite of this comely ponderosity, her movements were perfectly light and elastic. In complexion, she was a genuine blonde—a warm blonde; with a midsummer bloom upon her cheek, and the light of a midsummer sun wrought into her auburn hair. Her features were not cast upon a classical model, but their expression was in the highest degree pleasing. Her forehead was low and broad, her nose small, and her mouth—well, by the envious her mouth was called *enormous*. It is certain that it had an immense capacity for smiles, and that when she opened it to sing (which she did with infinite sweetness) it emitted a copious flood of sound. Her face was, perhaps, a trifle too circular, and her shoulders a trifle too high; but, as I say, the general effect left nothing to be desired. I might point out a dozen discords in the character of her face and figure, and yet utterly fail to invalidate the impression they produced. There is something essentially uncivil, and, indeed, unphilosophical, in the attempt to verify or to disprove a woman's beauty in detail, and a man gets no more than he deserves when he finds that, in strictness, the aggregation of the different features fails to make up the total. Stand off, gentlemen, and let *her* make the addition. Beside her beauty, Miss Everett shone by her good nature and her lively perceptions. She neither made harsh speeches nor resented them; and, on the other hand, she keenly enjoyed intellectual cleverness, and even cultivated it. Her great merit was that she made no claims or pretensions. Just as there was nothing artificial in her beauty, so there was nothing pedantic in her acuteness and nothing sentimental in her amiability. The one was all freshness and the others all *bonhomie*.

John Lennox saw her, then loved her and offered her his hand. In accepting it Miss Everett acquired, in the world's eye, the one advantage which she lacked—a complete stability and regularity of position. Her friends took no small satisfaction in contrasting her brilliant and comfortable future with her somewhat precarious past. Lennox, nevertheless, was congratulated on the right hand and on the left; but none too often for his faith. That of Miss Everett was not put to so severe a test, although she was frequently reminded by acquaintances of a moralizing turn that she had reason to be very thankful for Mr Lennox's choice. To these assurances Marian listened with a look of patient humility, which was extremely becoming. It was as if for *his* sake she could consent even to be bored.

Within a fortnight after their engagement had been made known, both parties returned to New York. Lennox lived in a house of his own, which he now busied himself with repairing and refurnishing; for the wedding had been fixed for the end of October. Miss Everett lived in lodgings with her father, a decayed old gentleman, who rubbed his idle hands from morning till night over the prospect of his daughter's marriage.

John Lennox, habitually a man of numerous resources, fond of reading, fond of music, fond of society and not averse to politics, passed the first weeks of the Autumn in a restless, fidgety manner. When a man approaches middle age he finds it difficult to wear gracefully the distinction of being engaged. He finds it difficult to discharge with becoming alacrity the various *petits soins* incidental to the position. There was a certain pathetic gravity, to those who knew him well, in Lennox's attentions. One-third of his time he spent in foraging in Broadway, whence he returned half-a-dozen times a week, laden with trinkets and gimcracks, which he always finished by thinking it puerile and brutal to offer his mistress. Another third he passed in Mrs Everett's drawing-room, during which period Marian was denied to visitors. The rest of the time he spent, as he told a friend, God knows how. This was stronger language than his friend expected to hear, for Lennox was neither a man of precipitate utterance, nor, in his friend's belief, of a strongly passionate nature. But it was evident that he was very much in love; or at least very much off his balance.

"When I'm with her it's all very well," he pursued, "but when I'm away from her I feel as if I were thrust out of the ranks of the living."

"Well, you must be patient," said his friend; "you're destined to live hard, yet."

Lennox was silent, and his face remained rather more sombre than the other liked to see it.

"I hope there's no particular difficulty," the latter resumed; hoping to induce him to relieve himself of whatever weighed upon his consciousness.

"I'm afraid sometimes I—afraid sometimes she doesn't really love me."

"Well, a little doubt does no harm. It's better than to be too sure of it, and to sink into fatuity. Only be sure you love her."

"Yes," said Lennox, solemnly, "that's the great point."

One morning, unable to fix his attention on books and papers, he bethought himself of an expedient for passing an hour.

He had made, at Newport, the acquaintance of a young artist named Gilbert, for whose talent and conversation he had conceived a strong relish. The painter, on leaving Newport, was to go to the Adirondacks, and to be back in New York on the first of October, after which time he begged his friend to come and see him.

It occurred to Lennox on the morning I speak of that Gilbert must already have returned to town, and would be looking for his visit. So he forthwith repaired to his studio.

Gilbert's card was on the door, but, on entering the room, Lennox found it occupied by a stranger—a young man in painter's garb, at work before a large panel. He learned from this gentleman that he was a temporary sharer of Mr Gilbert's studio, and that the latter had stepped out for a few moments. Lennox accordingly prepared to await his return. He entered into conversation with the young man, and, finding him very intelligent, as well as, apparently, a great friend of Gilbert, he looked at him with some interest. He was of something less than thirty, tall and robust, with a strong, joyous, sensitive face, and a thick auburn beard. Lennox was struck with his face, which seemed both to express a great deal of human sagacity and to indicate the essential temperament of a painter.

"A man with that face," he said to himself, "does work at least worth looking at."

He accordingly asked his companion if he might come and look at his picture. The latter readily assented, and Lennox placed himself before the canvas.

It bore a representation of a half-length female figure, in a costume and with an expression so ambiguous that Lennox remained uncertain whether it was a portrait or a work of fancy: a fair-haired young woman, clad in a rich mediæval dress, and looking like a countess of the Renaissance. Her figure was relieved against a sombre tapestry, her arms loosely folded, her head erect and her eyes on the spectator, toward whom she seemed to move—"*Dans un flot de velours traînant ses petits pieds.*"

As Lennox inspected her face it seemed to reveal a hidden likeness to a face he well knew—the face of Marian Everett. He was of course anxious to know whether the likeness was accidental or designed.

"I take this to be a portrait," he said to the artist, "a portrait 'in character'."

"No," said the latter, "it's a mere composition: a little from here and a little from there. The picture has been hanging about me for the last two or three years, as a sort of receptacle of waste ideas. It has been the victim of innumerable theories and experiments. But it seems to have survived them all. I suppose it possesses a certain amount of vitality."

"Do you call it anything?"

"I called it originally after something I'd read—Browning's poem, 'My Last Duchess'. Do you know it?"

"Perfectly."

"I am ignorant of whether it's an attempt to embody the poet's impression of a portrait actually existing. But why should I care? This is simply an attempt to embody my own private impression of the poem, which has always had a strong hold on my fancy. I don't know whether it agrees with your own impression and that of most readers. But I don't insist upon the name. The possessor of the picture is free to baptize it afresh."

The longer Lennox looked at the picture the more he liked it, and the deeper seemed to be the correspondence between the lady's expression and that with which he had invested the heroine of Browning's lines. The less accidental, too, seemed that element which Marian's face and the face on the canvas possessed in common. He thought of the great poet's noble lyric and of its exquisite significance, and of the physiognomy of the woman he loved having been chosen as the fittest exponent of that significance.

He turned away his head; his eyes filled with tears. "If I were possessor of the picture," he said, finally, answering the artist's last words, "I should feel tempted to call it by the name of a person of whom it very much reminds me."

"Ah?" said Baxter; and then, after a pause—"a person in New York?"

It had happened, a week before, that, at her lover's request, Miss Everett had gone in his company to a photographer's and had been photographed in a dozen different attitudes. The proofs of these photographs had been sent home for Marian to choose from. She had made a choice of half a dozen—or rather Lennox had made it—and the latter had put them in his pocket, with the intention of stopping at the establishment and giving his orders. He now took out of his pocket-book and showed the painter one of the cards.

"I find a great resemblance," said he, "between your Duchess and that young lady."

The artist looked at the photograph. "If I am not mistaken," he said, after a pause, "the young lady is Miss Everett."

Lennox nodded assent.

His companion remained silent a few moments, examining the photograph with considerable interest; but, as Lennox observed, without comparing it with his picture.

"My Duchess very probably bears a certain resemblance to Miss Everett, but a not exactly intentional one," he said, at last. "The picture was begun before I ever saw Miss Everett. Miss Everett, as you see—or as you know—has a very charming face, and, during the few weeks in which I saw her, I continued to work upon it. You know how a painter works—how artists of all kinds work: they claim their property wherever they find it. What I found to my purpose in Miss Everett's appearance I didn't hesitate to adopt; especially as I had been feeling about in the dark for a type of countenance which her face effectually realized. The Duchess was an Italian, I take it; and I had made up my mind that she was to be a blonde. Now, there is a decidedly southern depth and warmth of tone in Miss Everett's complexion, as well as that breadth and thickness of feature which is common in Italian women. You see the resemblance is much more a matter of type than of expression. Nevertheless, I'm sorry if the copy betrays the original."

"I doubt," said Lennox, "whether it would betray it to any other perception than mine. I have the honor," he added, after a pause, "to be engaged to Miss Everett. You will, therefore, excuse me if I ask whether you mean to sell your picture?"

"It's already sold—to a lady," rejoined the artist, with a smile; "a maiden lady, who is a great admirer of Browning."

At this moment Gilbert returned. The two friends exchanged greetings, and their companion withdrew to a neighboring studio. After they had talked a while of what had happened to each since they parted, Lennox spoke of the painter of the Duchess and of his remarkable talent, expressing surprise that he shouldn't have heard of him before, and that Gilbert should never have spoken of him.

"His name is Baxter—Stephen Baxter," said Gilbert, "and until his return from Europe, a fortnight ago, I knew little more about him than you. He's a case of improvement. I met him in Paris in '62; at that time he was doing absolutely nothing. He has learned what you see in the interval. On arriving in New York he found it impossible to get a studio big enough to hold him. As, with my little sketches, I need only occupy one corner of mine, I offered him the use of the other three, until he should be able to bestow himself to his satisfaction. When he began to unpack his canvases I found I had been entertaining an angel unawares."

Gilbert then proceeded to uncover, for Lennox's inspection, several of Baxter's portraits, both of men and women. Each of these works confirmed Lennox's impression of the painter's power. He returned to the picture on the easel. Marian Everett reappeared at his silent call, and looked out of the eyes with a most penetrating tenderness and melancholy.

"He may say what he pleases," thought Lennox, "the resemblance *is*, in some degree, also a matter of expression. Gilbert," he added, wishing to measure the force of the likeness, "whom does it remind you of?"

"I know," said Gilbert, "of whom it reminds *you*."

"And do you see it yourself?"

"They are both handsome, and both have auburn hair. That's all I can see."

Lennox was somewhat relieved. It was not without a feeling of discomfort—a feeling by no means inconsistent with his first moment of pride and satisfaction—that he thought of Marian's peculiar and individual charms having been subjected to the keen appreciation of another than himself. He was glad to be able to conclude that the painter had merely been struck with what was most superficial in her appearance, and that his own imagination supplied the rest. It occurred to him, as he walked home, that it would be a not unbecoming tribute to the young girl's loveliness on his own part, to cause her portrait to be painted by this clever young man. Their engagement had as yet been an affair of pure sentiment, and he had taken an almost fastidious care not to give himself the vulgar appearance of a mere purveyor of luxuries and pleasures. Practically, he had been as yet for his future wife a poor man—or rather a man, pure and simple, and not a millionaire. He had ridden with her, he had sent her flowers, and he had gone with her to the opera. But he had neither sent her sugar-plums, nor made bets with her, nor made her presents of jewelry. Miss Everett's female friends had remarked that he hadn't as yet given her the least little betrothal ring, either of pearls or of diamonds. Marian, however, was quite content. She was, by nature, a great artist in the *mise en scène* of emotions, and she felt instinctively that this classical moderation was but the converse presentment of an immense matrimonial abundance. In his attempt to make it impossible that his relations with Miss Everett should be tinged in any degree with the accidental condition of the fortunes of either party, Lennox had thoroughly understood his own instinct. He knew that he should some day feel a strong and irresistible impulse to offer his mistress some visible and artistic token of his affection, and that his gift would convey a greater satisfaction from being sole of its kind. It seemed to him now that his chance had come. What gift could be more delicate than the gift of an opportunity to contribute by her patience and good-will to her husband's possession of a perfect likeness of her face?

On that same evening Lennox dined with his future father-in-law, as it was his habit to do once a week.

"Marian," he said, in the course of the dinner, "I saw, this morning, an old friend of yours."

"Ah," said Marian, "who was that?"

"Mr Baxter, the painter."

Marian changed color—ever so little; no more, indeed, than was natural to an honest surprise.

Her surprise, however, could not have been great, inasmuch as she now said that she had seen his return to America mentioned in a newspaper, and as she knew that Lennox frequented the society of artists. "He was well, I hope," she added, "and prosperous."

"Where did you know this gentleman, my dear?" asked Mr Everett.

"I knew him in Europe two years ago—first in the Summer in Switzerland, and afterwards in Paris. He is a sort of cousin of Mrs Denbigh." Mrs Denbigh was a lady in whose company Marian had recently spent a year in Europe—a widow, rich, childless, an invalid, and an old friend of her mother. "Is he always painting?"

"Apparently, and extremely well. He has two or three as good portraits there as one may reasonably expect to see. And he has, moreover, a certain picture which reminded me of you."

"His 'Last Duchess'?" asked Marian with some curiosity. "I should like to see it. If you think it's like me, John, you ought to buy it up."

"I wanted to buy it, but it's sold. You know it then?"

"Yes, through Mr Baxter himself. I saw it in its rudimentary state, when it looked like nothing that I should care to look like. I shocked Mrs Denbigh very much by telling him I was glad it was his 'last.' The picture, indeed, led to our acquaintance."

"And not *vice versa*," said Mr Everett, facetiously.

"How *vice versa?*" asked Marian, innocently. "I met Mr Baxter for the first time at a party in Rome."

"I thought you said you met him in Switzerland," said Lennox.

"No, in Rome. It was only two days before we left. He was introduced to me without knowing I was with Mrs Denbigh, and indeed without knowing that she had been in the city. He was very shy of Americans. The first thing he said to me was that I looked very much like a picture he had been painting."

"That you realized his ideal, etc."

"Exactly, but not at all in that sentimental tone. I took him to Mrs Denbigh; they found they were sixth cousins by marriage; he came to see us the next day, and insisted upon our going to his studio. It was a miserable place. I believe he was very poor. At least Mrs Denbigh offered him some money, and he frankly accepted it. She attempted to spare his sensibilities by telling him that, if he liked, he could paint her a picture in return. He said he would if he had time. Later, he came up into Switzerland, and the following Winter we met him in Paris."

If Lennox had had any mistrust of Miss Everett's relations with the painter, the manner in which she told her little story would have effectually blighted it. He forthwith proposed that, in consideration not only of the young man's great talent, but of his actual knowledge of her face, he should be invited to paint her portrait.

Marian assented without reluctance and without alacrity, and Lennox laid his proposition before the artist. The latter requested a day or two to consider, and then replied (by note) that he would be happy to undertake the task.

Miss Everett expected that, in view of the projected renewal of their old acquaintance, Stephen Baxter would call upon her, under the auspices of her lover. He called in effect, alone, but Marian was not at home, and he failed to repeat the visit. The day for the first sitting was therefore appointed through Lennox. The artist had not as yet obtained a studio of his own, and the latter cordially offered him the momentary use of a spacious and well-lighted apartment in his house, which had been intended as a billiard room, but was not yet fitted up. Lennox expressed no wishes with regard to the portrait, being content to leave the choice of position and costume to the parties immediately interested. He found the painter perfectly well acquainted with Marian's "points," and he had an implicit confidence in her own good taste.

Miss Everett arrived on the morning appointed, under her father's escort, Mr Everett, who prided himself largely upon doing things in proper form, having caused himself to be introduced beforehand to the painter. Between the latter and Marian there was a brief exchange of civilities, after which they addressed themselves to business. Miss Everett professed the most cheerful deference to Baxter's wishes and fancies, at the same time that she made no secret of possessing a number of strong convictions as to what should be attempted and what should be avoided.

It was no surprise to the young man to find her convictions sound and her wishes thoroughly sympathetic. He found himself called upon to make no compromise with stubborn and unnatural prejudices, nor to sacrifice his best intentions to a short-sighted vanity.

Whether Miss Everett was vain or not need not here be declared. She had at least the wit to perceive that the interests of an enlightened sagacity would best be served by a painting which should be good from the painter's point of view, inasmuch as these are the painting's chief end. I may add, moreover, to her very great credit, that she thoroughly understood how great an artistic merit should properly attach to a picture executed at the behest of a passion, in order that it should be anything more than a mockery—a parody—of the duration of that passion; and that she knew instinctively that there is nothing so chilling to an artist's heat as the interference of illogical self-interest, either on his own behalf or that of another.

Baxter worked firmly and rapidly, and at the end of a couple of hours he felt that he had begun his picture. Mr Everett, as he sat by, threatened to be a bore; laboring apparently under the impression that it was his duty to beguile the session with cheap aesthetic small talk. But Marian good-humoredly took the painter's share of the dialogue, and he was not diverted from his work.

The next sitting was fixed for the morrow. Marian wore the dress which she had agreed upon with the painter, and in which, as in her position, the "picturesque" element had been religiously suppressed. She read in Baxter's eyes that she looked supremely beautiful, and she saw that his fingers tingled to attack his subject. But she caused Lennox to be sent for, under the pretense of obtaining his adhesion to her dress. It was black, and he might object to black. He came, and she read in his kindly eyes an augmented edition of the assurance conveyed in Baxter's. He was enthusiastic for the black dress, which, in truth, seemed only to confirm and enrich, like a grave maternal protest, the young girl's look of undiminished youth.

"I expect you," he said to Baxter, "to make a masterpiece."

"Never fear," said the painter, tapping his forehead. "It's made."

On this second occasion, Mr Everett, exhausted by the intellectual strain of the preceding day, and encouraged by his luxurious chair, sank into a tranquil sleep. His companions remained for some time, listening to his regular breathing; Marian with her eyes patiently fixed on the opposite wall, and the young man with his glance mechanically travelling between his figure and the canvas. At last he fell back several paces to survey his work. Marian moved her eyes, and they met his own.

"Well, Miss Everett," said the painter, in accents which might have been tremulous if he had not exerted a strong effort to make them firm.

"Well, Mr Baxter," said the young girl.

And the two exchanged a long, firm glance, which at last ended in a smile—a smile which belonged decidedly to the family of the famous laugh of the two angels behind the altar in the temple.

"Well, Miss Everett," said Baxter, going back to his work; "such is life!"

"So it appears," rejoined Marian. And then, after a pause of some moments: "Why didn't you come and see me?" she added.

"I came and you weren't at home."

"Why didn't you come again?"

"What was the use, Miss Everett?"

"It would simply have been more decent. We might have become reconciled."

"We seem to have done that as it is."

"I mean 'in form.'"

"That would have been absurd. Don't you see how true an instinct I had? What could have been easier than our meeting? I assure you that I should have found any talk about the past, and mutual assurances or apologies extremely disagreeable."

Miss Everett raised her eyes from the floor and fixed them on her companion with a deep, half-reproachful glance, "Is the past, then," she asked, "so utterly disagreeable?"

Baxter stared, half amazed. "Good heavens!" he cried, "of course it is."

Miss Everett dropped her eyes and remained silent.

I may as well take advantage of the moment, rapidly to make plain to the reader the events to which the above conversation refers.

Miss Everett had found it expedient, all things considered, not to tell her intended husband the whole story of her acquaintance with Stephen Baxter; and when I have repaired her omissions, the reader will probably justify her discretion.

She had, as she said, met this young man for the first time at Rome, and there in the course of two interviews had made a deep impression upon his heart. He had felt that he would give a great deal to meet Miss Everett again. Their reunion in Switzerland was therefore not entirely fortuitous; and it had been the more easy for Baxter to make it possible, for the reason that he was able to claim a kind of roundabout relationship with Mrs Denbigh, Marian's companion. With this lady's

permission he had attached himself to their party. He had made
their route of travel his own, he had stopped when they stopped and been prodigal of attentions and civilities. Before a
week was over, Mrs Denbigh, who was the soul of confiding
good nature, exulted in the discovery of an invaluable kinsman.
Thanks not only to her naturally unexacting disposition, but
to the apathetic and inactive habits induced by constant physical suffering, she proved a very insignificant third in her companions' spending of the hours. How delightfully these hours
were spent, it requires no great effort to imagine. A suit conducted in the midst of the most romantic scenery in Europe is
already half won. Marian's social graces were largely enhanced
by the satisfaction which her innate intelligence of natural
beauty enabled her to take in the magnificent scenery of the
Alps. She had never appeared to such advantage; she had never
known such perfect freedom and frankness and gayety. For the
first time in her life she had made a captive without suspecting
it. She had surrendered her heart to the mountains and the
lakes, the eternal snows and the pastoral valleys, and Baxter,
standing by, had intercepted it. He felt his long-projected Swiss
tour vastly magnified and beautified by Miss Everett's part in
it—by the constant feminine sympathy which gushed within
earshot, with the coolness and clearness of a mountain spring.
Oh! if only it too had not been fed by the eternal snows! And
then her beauty—her indefatigable beauty—was a continual
enchantment. Miss Everett looked so thoroughly in her place
in a drawing-room that it was almost logical to suppose that
she looked well nowhere else. But in fact, as Baxter learned,
she looked quite well enough in the character of what ladies
call a "fright"—that is, sunburnt, travel-stained, overheated,
exhilarated and hungry—to elude all invidious comparisons.

At the end of three weeks, one morning as they stood
together on the edge of a falling torrent, high above the green
concavities of the hills, Baxter felt himself irresistibly urged to
make a declaration. The thunderous noise of the cataract

covered all vocal utterance; so, taking out his sketch-book, he wrote three short words on a blank leaf. He handed her the book. She read the message with a beautiful change of color and a single rapid glance at his face. She then tore out the leaf.

"Don't tear it up!" cried the young man.

She understood him by the movement of his lips and shook her head with a smile. But she stooped, picked up a little stone, and wrapping it in the bit of paper, prepared to toss it into the torrent.

Baxter, uncertain, put out his hand to take it from her. She passed it into the other hand and gave him the one he had attempted to take.

She threw away the paper, but she let him keep her hand.

Baxter still had a week at his disposal, and Marian made it a very happy one. Mrs Denbigh was tired; they had come to a halt, and there was no interruption to their being together. They talked a great deal of the long future, which, on getting beyond the sound of the cataract, they had expeditiously agreed to pursue in common.

It was their misfortune both to be poor. They determined, in view of this circumstance, to say nothing of their engagement until Baxter, by dint of hard work, should have at least quadrupled his income. This was cruel, but it was imperative, and Marian made no complaint. Her residence in Europe had enlarged her conception of the material needs of a pretty woman, and it was quite natural that she should not, close upon the heels of this experience, desire to rush into marriage with a poor artist. At the end of some days Baxter started for Germany and Holland, portions of which he wished to visit for purposes of study. Mrs Denbigh and her young friend repaired to Paris for the Winter. Here, in the middle of February, they were rejoined by Baxter, who had achieved his German tour. He had received, while absent, five little letters from Marian, full of affection. The number was small, but the young man detected in the very temperance of his mistress a certain delicious flavor of implicit constancy. She received him with all the frankness and sweetness that he had a right to expect, and listened with great interest of his account of the improvement in his prospects. He had sold three of his Italian pictures and had made an invaluable collection of sketches. He was on the high road to wealth and fame, and there was no reason their engagement should not be announced. But to this latter proposition Marian demurred—demurred so strongly, and yet on grounds so arbitrary, that a somewhat painful scene ensued. Stephen left her, irritated and perplexed. The next day, when he called, she was unwell and unable to see him; and the next —and the next. On the evening of the day that he had made his third fruitless call at Mrs Denbigh's, he overheard Marian's name mentioned at a large party. The interlocutors were two elderly women. On giving his attention to their talk, which they were taking no pains to keep private, he found that his mistress was under accusal of having trifled with the affections of an unhappy young man, the only son of one of the ladies. There was apparently no lack of evidence or of facts which might be construed as evidence. Baxter went home, *la mort dans l'âme*, and on the following day called again on Mrs Denbigh. Marian was still in her room, but the former lady received him. Stephen was in great trouble, but his mind was lucid, and he addressed himself to the task of interrogating his hostess. Mrs Denbigh, with her habitual indolence, had remained unsuspicious of the terms on which the young people stood.

"I'm sorry to say," Baxter began, "that I heard Miss Everett accused last evening of very sad conduct."

"Ah, for heaven's sake, Stephen," returned his kinswoman, "don't go back to that. I've done nothing all Winter but defend and palliate her conduct. It's hard work. Don't make me do it for you. You know her as well as I do. She was indiscreet, but I know she is penitent, and for that matter she's well out of it. He was by no means a desirable young man."

"The lady whom I heard talking about the matter," said Stephen, "spoke of him in the highest terms. To be sure, as it turned out, she was his mother."

"His mother? You're mistaken. His mother died ten years ago."

Baxter folded his arms with a feeling that he needed to sit firm. "*Allons,*" said he, "of whom do you speak?"

"Of young Mr King."

"Good heavens," cried Stephen. "So there are two of them?"

"Pray, of whom do *you* speak?"

"Of a certain Mr Young. The mother is a handsome old woman with white curls."

"You don't mean to say there has been anything between Marian and Frederic Young?"

"*Voilà!* I only repeat what I hear. It seems to me, my dear Mrs Denbigh, that you ought to know."

Mrs Denbigh shook her head with a melancholy movement. "I'm sure I don't," she said, "I give it up. I don't pretend to judge. The manners of young people to each other are very different from what they were in my day. One doesn't know whether they mean nothing or everything."

"You know, at least, whether Mr Young has been in your drawing-room?"

"Oh, yes, frequently. I'm very sorry that Marian is talked about. It's very unpleasant for me. But what can a sick woman do?"

"Well," said Stephen, "so much for Mr Young. And now for Mr King."

"Mr King is gone home. It's a pity he ever came away."

"In what sense?"

"Oh, he's a silly fellow. He doesn't understand young girls."

"Upon my word," said Stephen, 'with expression', as the music sheets say, "he might be very wise and not do that."

"Not but that Marian was injudicious. She meant only to be amiable, but she went too far. She became adorable. The first thing she knew he was holding her to an account."

"Is he good-looking?"

"Well enough."

"And rich?"

"Very rich, I believe."

"And the other?"

"What other—Marian?"

"No, no; your friend Young."

"Yes, he's quite handsome."

"And rich, too?"

"Yes, I believe he's also rich."

Baxter was silent a moment. "And there's no doubt," he resumed, "that they were both far gone?"

"I can only answer for Mr King."

"Well, I'll answer for Mr Young. His mother wouldn't have talked as she did unless she'd seen her son suffer. After all, then, it's perhaps not so much to Marian's discredit. Here are two handsome young millionaires, madly smitten. She refuses them both. She doesn't care for good looks and money."

"I don't say that," said Mrs Denbigh, sagaciously. "She doesn't care for those things alone. She wants talent, and all the rest of it. Now, if you were only rich, Stephen—" added the good lady, innocently.

Baxter took up his hat. "When you wish to marry Miss Everett," he said, "you must take good care not to say too much about Mr King and Mr Young."

Two days after this interview, he had a conversation with the young girl in person. The reader may like him less for his easily-shaken confidence, but it is a fact that he had been unable to make light of these lightly-made revelations. For him his love had been a passion; for *her*, he was compelled to believe, it had been a vulgar pastime. He was a man of a violent temper; he went straight to the point.

"Marian," he said, "you've been deceiving me."

Marian knew very well what he meant; she knew very well that she had grown weary of her engagement and that, however little of a fault her conduct had been to Messrs Young and King, it had been an act of grave disloyalty to Baxter. She felt that the blow was struck and that their engagement was clean broken. She knew that Stephen would be satisfied with no half-excuses or half-denials; and she had none others to give. A hundred such would not make a perfect confession. Making no attempt, therefore, to save her "prospects," for which she had ceased to care, she merely attempted to save her dignity. Her dignity for the moment was well enough secured by her natural half-cynical coolness of temper. But this same vulgar placidity left in Stephen's memory an impression of heartlessness and shallowness, which in that particular quarter, at least, was destined to be forever fatal to her claims to real weight and worth. She denied the young man's right to call her to account and to interfere with her conduct; and she almost anticipated his proposal that they should consider their engagement at an end. She even declined the use of the simple logic of tears. Under these circumstances, of course, the interview was not of long duration.

"I regard you," said Baxter, as he stood on the threshold, "as the most superficial, most heartless of women."

He immediately left Paris and went down into Spain, where he remained till the opening of the Summer. In the month of May Mrs Denbigh and her *protégée* went to England, where the former, through her husband, possessed a number of connections, and where Marian's thoroughly un-English beauty was vastly admired. In September they sailed for America. About a year and a half, therefore, had elapsed between Baxter's separation from Miss Everett and their meeting in New York.

During this interval the young man's wounds had had time to heal. His sorrow, although violent, had been short-lived, and when he finally recovered his habitual equanimity, he was very glad to have purchased exemption at the price of a simple heart-ache. Reviewing his impressions of Miss Everett in a calmer mood, he made up his mind that she was very far from being the woman of his desire, and that she had not really been the woman of his choice. "Thank God," he said to himself, "it's over. She's irreclaimably light. She's hollow, trivial, vulgar." There had been in his addresses something hasty and feverish, something factitious and unreal in his fancied passion. Half of it had been the work of the scenery, of the weather, of mere juxtaposition, and, above all, of the young girl's picturesque beauty; to say nothing of the almost suggestive tolerance and indolence of poor Mrs Denbigh. And finding himself very much interested in Velasquez, at Madrid, he dismissed Miss Everett from his thoughts. I do not mean to offer his judgment of Miss Everett as final; but it was at least conscientious. The ample justice, moreover, which, under the illusion of sentiment, he had rendered to her charms and graces, gave him a right, when free from that illusion, to register his estimate of the arid spaces of her nature. Miss Everett might easily have accused him of injustice and brutality; but this fact would still stand to plead in his favor, that he cared with all his strength for truth. Marian, on the contrary, was quite indifferent to it. Stephen's angry sentence on her conduct had awakened no echo in her contracted soul.

The reader has now an adequate conception of the feelings with which these two old friends found themselves face to face. It is needful to add, however, that the lapse of time had very much diminished the force of those feelings. A woman, it seems to me, ought to desire no easier company, none less embarrassed or embarrassing, than a disenchanted lover; premising, of course, that the process of disenchantment is thoroughly complete, and that some time has elapsed since its completion.

Marian herself was perfectly at her ease. She had not retained her equanimity—her philosophy, one might almost call it—during that painful last interview, to go and lose it now. She had no ill feeling toward her old lover. His last words had been —like all words in Marian's estimation— a mere *façon de parler*. Miss Everett was in so perfect a good humor during these last days of her maidenhood that there was nothing in the past that she could not have forgiven.

She blushed a little at the emphasis of her companion's remark; but she was not discountenanced. She summoned up her good humor. "The truth is, Mr Baxter," she said, "I feel at the present moment on perfect good terms with the world; I see everything *en rose;* the past as well as the future."

"I, too, am on very good terms with the world," said Mr Baxter, "and my heart is quite reconciled to what you call the past. But, nevertheless, it's very disagreeable to me to think about it."

"Ah then," said Miss Everett, with great sweetness, "I'm afraid you're not reconciled."

Baxter laughed—so loud that Miss Everett looked about at her father. But Mr Everett still slept the sleep of gentility. "I've no doubt," said the painter, "that I'm far from being so good a Christian as you. But I assure you I'm very glad to see you again."

"You've but to say the word and we're friends," said Marian.

"We were very foolish to have attempted to be anything else."

"'Foolish', yes. But it was pretty folly."

"Ah no, Miss Everett. I'm an artist, and I claim a right of property in the word 'pretty'. You musn't stick it in there. Nothing could be pretty which had such an ugly termination. It was all false."

"Well—as you will. What have you been doing since we parted?"

"Travelling and working. I've made great progress in my trade. Shortly before I came home I became engaged."

"Engaged?—*à la bonne heure*. Is she good?—is she pretty?"

"She's not nearly so pretty as you."

"In other words, she's infinitely more good. I'm sure I hope she is. But why did you leave her behind you?"

"She's with a sister, a sad invalid, who is drinking mineral waters on the Rhine. They wished to remain there to the cold weather. They're to be home in a couple of weeks, and we are straightway to be married."

"I congratulate you, with all my heart," said Marian.

"Allow me to do as much, sir," said Mr Everett, waking up; which he did by instinct whenever the conversation took a ceremonious turn.

Miss Everett gave her companion but three more sittings, a large part of his work being executed with the assistance of photographs. At these interviews also, Mr Everett was present, and still delicately sensitive to the soporific influences of his position. But both parties had the good taste to abstain from further reference to their old relations, and to confine their talk to less personal themes.

II

ONE afternoon, when the picture was nearly finished, John Lennox went into the empty painting-room to ascertain the degree of its progress. Both Baxter and Marian had expressed a wish that he should not see it in its early stages, and this, accordingly, was his first view. Half an hour after he had entered the room, Baxter came in, unannounced, and found him sitting before the canvas, deep in thought. Baxter had been furnished with a house-key, so that he might have immediate and easy access to his work whenever the humor came upon him.

"I was passing," he said, "and I couldn't resist the impulse to come in and correct an error which I made this morning, now that a sense of its enormity is fresh in my mind." He sat down to work, and the other stood watching him.

"Well," said the painter, finally, "how does it satisfy you?"

"Not altogether."

"Pray develop your objections. It's in your power materially to assist me."

"I hardly know how to formulate my objections. Let me, at all events, in the first place, say that I admire your work immensely. I'm sure it's the best picture you've painted."

"I honestly believe it is. Some parts of it," said Baxter, frankly, "are excellent."

"It's obvious. But either those very parts or others are singularly disagreeable. That word isn't criticism, I know; but I pay you for the right to be arbitrary. They are too hard, too strong, of too frank a reality. In a word, your picture frightens me, and if I were Marian I should feel as if you'd done me a certain violence."

"I'm sorry for what's disagreeable; but I meant it all to be real. I go in for reality; you must have seen that."

"I approve you; I can't too much admire the broad and firm methods you've taken for reaching this same reality. But you can be real without being brutal—without attempting, as one may say, to be *actual*."

"I deny that I'm brutal. I'm afraid, Mr Lennox, I haven't taken quite the right road to please you. I've taken the picture too much *au sérieux*. I've striven too much for completeness. But if it doesn't please you it will please others."

"I've no doubt of it. But that isn't the question. The picture is good enough to be a thousand times better."

"That the picture leaves room for infinite improvement, I,

of course, don't deny; and, in several particulars, I see my way
to make it better. But, substantially, the portrait is there. I'll
tell you what you miss. My work isn't 'classical'; in fine, I'm
not a man of genius."

"No; I rather suspect you are. But, as you say, your work
isn't classical. I adhere to my term *brutal*. Shall I tell you? It's
too much of a study. You've given poor Miss Everett the look
of a professional model."

"If that's the case, I've done very wrong. There never was
an easier, a less conscious sitter. It's delightful to look at her."

"Confound it, you've given all her ease, too. Well, I don't
know what's the matter. I give up."

"I think," said Baxter, "you had better hold your verdict
in abeyance until the picture is finished. The classical element
is there, I'm sure; but I've not brought it out. Wait a few days,
and it will rise to the surface."

Lennox left the artist alone; and the latter took up his
brushes and painted hard till nightfall. He laid them down only
when it was too dark to see. As he was going out, Lennox met
him in the hall.

"*Exegi monumentum*," said Baxter; "it's finished. Go and
look at your ease. I'll come to-morrow and hear your impressions."

The master of the house, when the other had gone, lit half-
a-dozen lights and returned to the study of the picture. It had
grown prodigiously under the painter's recent handling, and
whether it was that, as Baxter had said, the classical element
had disengaged itself, or that Lennox was in a more sympathetic mood, it now impressed him as an original and powerful work, a genuine portrait, the deliberate image of a human
face and figure. It was Marian, in very truth, and Marian most
patiently measured and observed. Her beauty was there, her
sweetness, and her young loveliness and her aerial grace, imprisoned forever, made inviolable and perpetual. Nothing
could be more simple than the conception and composition of

the picture. The figure sat peacefully, looking slightly to the right, with the head erect and the hands—the virginal hands, without rings or bracelets—lying idle on its knees. The blonde hair was gathered into a little knot of braids on the top of the head (in the fashion of the moment), and left free the almost childish contour of the ears and cheeks. The eyes were full of color, contentment and light; the lips were faintly parted. Of color in the picture, there was, in strictness, very little; but the dark draperies told of reflected sunshine, and the flesh-spaces of human blushes and pallors, of throbbing life and health. The work was strong and simple, the figure was thoroughly void of affectation and stiffness, and yet supremely elegant.

"That's what it is to be an artist," thought Lennox. "All this has been done in the past two hours."

It was his Marian, assuredly, with all that had charmed him —with all that still charmed him when he saw her: her appealing confidence, her exquisite lightness, her feminine enchantments. And yet, as he looked, an expression of pain came into his eyes, and lingered there, and grew into a mortal heaviness.

Lennox had been as truly a lover as a man may be; but he loved with the discretion of fifteen years' experience of human affairs. He had a penetrating glance, and he liked to use it. Many a time when Marian, with eloquent lips and eyes, had poured out the treasures of her nature into his bosom, and he had taken them in his hands and covered them with kisses and passionate vows, he had dropped them all with a sudden shudder and cried out in silence, "But ah! where is the heart?" One day he had said to her (irrelevantly enough, doubtless), "Marian, where *is* your heart?"

"*Where*—what do you mean?" Miss Everett had said.

"I think of you from morning till night. I put you together and take you apart, as people do in that game where they make words out of a parcel of given letters. But there's always one letter wanting. I can't put my hand on your heart."

"My heart, John," said Marian, ingeniously, "is the whole word. My heart's everywhere."

This may have been true enough. Miss Everett had distributed her heart impartially throughout her whole organism, so that, as a natural consequence, its native seat was somewhat scantily occupied. As Lennox sat and looked at Baxter's consummate handiwork, the same question rose again to his lips; and if Marian's portrait suggested it, Marian's portrait failed to answer it. It took Marian to do that. It seemed to Lennox that some strangely potent agency had won from his mistress the confession of her inmost soul, and had written it there upon the canvas in firm yet passionate lines. Marian's person was lightness—her charm was lightness; could it be that her soul was levity too? Was she a creature without faith and without conscience? What else was the meaning of that horrible blankness and deadness that quenched the light in her eyes and stole away the smile from her lips? These things were the less to be eluded because in so many respects the painter had been profoundly just. He had been as loyal and sympathetic as he had been intelligent. Not a point in the young girl's appearance had been slighted; not a feature but had been forcibly and delicately rendered. Had Baxter been a man of marvellous insight —an unparalleled observer; or had he been a mere patient and unflinching painter, building infinitely better than he knew? Would not a mere painter have been content to paint Miss Everett in the strong, rich, objective manner of which the work was so good an example, and to do nothing more? For it was evident that Baxter had done more. He had painted with something more than knowledge—with imagination, with feeling. He had almost *composed;* and his composition had embraced the truth. Lennox was unable to satisfy his doubts. He would have been glad to believe that there was no imagination in the picture but what his own mind supplied; and that the unsubstantial sweetness on the eyes and lips of the image was but the smile of youth and innocence. He was in a muddle—he was absurdly suspicious and capricious; he put out the lights and left the portrait in kindly darkness. Then, half as a reparation to his mistress, and half as a satisfaction to himself, he went up to spend an hour with Marian. She, at least, as he found, had no scruples. She thought the portrait altogether a success, and she was very willing to be handed down in that form to posterity. Nevertheless, when Lennox came in, he went back into the painting-room to take another glance. This time he lit but a single light. Faugh! it was worse than with a dozen. He hastily turned out the gas.

Baxter came the next day, as he had promised. Meanwhile poor Lennox had had twelve hours of uninterrupted reflection, and the expression of distress in his eyes had acquired an intensity which, the painter saw, proved it to be of far other import than a mere tribute to his power.

"Can the man be jealous?" thought Baxter. Stephen had been so innocent of any other design than that of painting a good portrait, that his conscience failed to reveal to him the source of his companion's trouble. Nevertheless he began to pity him. He had felt tempted, indeed, to pity him from the first. He had liked him and esteemed him; he had taken him for a man of sense and of feeling, and he had thought it a matter of regret that such a man—a creature of strong spiritual needs—should link his destiny with that of Marian Everett. But he had very soon made up his mind that Lennox knew very well what he was about, and that he needed no enlightenment. He was marrying with his eyes open, and had weighed the risks against the profits. Everyone had his particular taste, and at thirty-five years of age John Lennox had no need to be told that Miss Everett was not quite all that she might be. Baxter had thus taken for granted that his friend had designedly selected as his second wife a mere pretty woman—a woman with a genius for receiving company, and who would make a picturesque use of his money. He knew nothing of the serious character of the poor man's passion, nor of the extent to which his happiness was bound up in what the painter would have called his delusion. His only concern had been to do his work well; and he had done it the better because of his old interest in Marian's bewitching face. It is very certain that he had actually infused into his picture that force of characterization and that depth of reality which had arrested his friend's attention; but he had done so wholly without effort and without malice. The artistic half of Baxter's nature exerted a lusty dominion over the human half—fed upon its disappointments and grew fat upon its joys and tribulations. This, indeed, is simply saying that the young man was a true artist. Deep, then, in the unfathomed recesses of his strong and sensitive nature, his genius had held communion with his heart and had transferred to canvas the burden of its disenchantment and its resignation. Since his little affair with Marian, Baxter had made the acquaintance of a young girl whom he felt that he could love and trust forever; and, sobered and strengthened by this new emotion, he had been able to resume with more distinctness the shortcomings of his earlier love. He had, therefore, painted with feeling. Miss Everett could not have expected him to do otherwise. He had done his honest best, and conviction had come in unbidden and made it better.

Lennox had begun to feel very curious about the history of his companion's acquaintance with his destined bride; but he was far from feeling jealous. Somehow he felt that he could never again be jealous. But in ascertaining the terms of their former intercourse, it was of importance that he should not allow the young man to suspect that he discovered in the portrait any radical defect.

"Your old acquaintance with Miss Everett," he said, frankly, "has evidently been of great use to you."

"I suppose it has," said Baxter. "Indeed, as soon as I began to paint, I found her face coming back to me like a half-remembered tune. She was wonderfully pretty at that time."

"She was two years younger."

"Yes, and I was two years younger. Decidedly, you are right. I *have* made use of my old impressions."

Baxter was willing to confess to so much; but he was resolved not to betray anything that Marian had herself kept secret. He was not surprised that she had not told her lover of her former engagement; he expected as much. But he would have held it inexcusable to attempt to repair her omission.

Lennox's faculties were acutely sharpened by pain and suspicion, and he could not help detecting in his companion's eyes an intention of reticence. He resolved to baffle it.

"I am curious to know," he said, "whether you were ever in love with Miss Everett?"

"I have no hesitation in saying Yes," rejoined Baxter; fancying that a general confession would help him more than a particular denial. "I'm one of a thousand, I fancy. Or one, perhaps, of only a hundred. For you see I've got over it. I'm engaged to be married."

Lennox's countenance brightened. "That's it," said he. "Now I know what I didn't like in your picture—the point of view. I'm not jealous," he added. "I should like the picture better if I were. You evidently care nothing for the poor girl. You have got over your love rather too well. You loved her, she was indifferent to you, and now you take your revenge." Distracted with grief, Lennox was taking refuge in irrational anger.

Baxter was puzzled. "You'll admit," said he, with a smile, "that it's a very handsome revenge." And all his professional self-esteem rose to his assistance. "I've painted for Miss Everett the best portrait that has yet been painted in America. She herself is quite satisfied."

"Ah!" said Lennox, with magnificent dissimulation; "Marian is generous."

"Come, then," said Baxter; "what do you complain of? You accuse me of scandalous conduct, and I'm bound to hold you to an account." Baxter's own temper was rising, and with it his sense of his picture's merits. "How have I perverted Miss Everett's expression? How have I misrepresented her? What does the portrait lack? Is it ill-drawn? Is it vulgar? Is it ambiguous? Is it immodest?" Baxter's patience gave out as he recited these various charges. "Fiddlesticks!" he cried; "you know as well as I do that the picture is excellent."

"I don't pretend to deny it. Only I wonder that Marian was willing to come to you."

It is very much to Baxter's credit that he still adhered to his resolution not to betray the young girl, and that rather than do so he was willing to let Lennox suppose that he had been a rejected adorer.

"Ah, as you say," he exclaimed, "Miss Everett is so generous!"

Lennox was foolish enough to take this as an admission. "When I say, Mr Baxter," he said, "that you have taken your revenge, I don't mean that you've done so wantonly or consciously. My dear fellow, how could you help it? The disappointment was proportionate to the loss and the reaction to the disappointment."

"Yes, that's all very well; but, meanwhile, I wait in vain to learn wherein I've done wrong."

Lennox looked from Baxter to the picture, and from the picture back to Baxter.

"I defy you to tell me," said Baxter. "I've simply kept Miss Everett as charming as she is in life."

"Oh, damn her charms!" cried Lennox.

"If you were not the gentleman, Mr Lennox," continued the young man, "which, in spite of your high temper, I believe you to be, I should believe you—"

"Well, you should believe me?"

"I should believe you simply bent on cheapening the portrait."

Lennox made a gesture of vehement impatience. The other

burst out laughing and the discussion closed. Baxter instinctively took up his brushes and approached his canvas with a
vague desire to detect latent errors, while Lennox prepared to
take his departure.

"Stay!" said the painter, as he was leaving the room; "if
the picture really offends you, I'll rub it out. Say the word,"
and he took up a heavy brush, covered with black paint.

But Lennox shook his head with decision and went out.
The next moment, however, he reappeared. "You *may* rub it
out," he said. "The picture is, of course, already mine."

But now Baxter shook his head. "Ah! now it's too late," he
answered. "Your chance is gone."

Lennox repaired directly to Mr Everett's apartments. Marian
was in the drawing-room with some morning callers, and her
lover sat by until she had got rid of them. When they were
alone together, Marian began to laugh at her visitors and to
parody certain of their affectations, which she did with infinite
grace and spirit. But Lennox cut her short and returned to the
portrait. He had thought better of his objections of the preceding evening; he liked it.

"But I wonder, Marian," he said, "that you were willing to
go to Mr Baxter."

"Why so?" asked Marian, on her guard. She saw that her
lover knew something, and she intended not to commit herself
until she knew how much he knew.

"An old lover is always dangerous."

"An old lover?" and Marian blushed a good honest blush.
But she rapidly recovered herself. "Pray where did you get
that charming news?"

"Oh, it slipped out," said Lennox.

Marian hesitated a moment. Then with a smile: "Well, I
was brave," she said. "I went."

"How came it," pursued Lennox, "that you didn't tell me?"

"Tell you what, my dear John?"

"Why, about Baxter's little passion. Come, don't be modest."

Modest! Marian breathed freely. "What do you mean, my dear, by telling your wife not to be modest? Pray don't ask me about Mr Baxter's passions. What do I know about them?"

"Did you know nothing of this one?"

"Ah, my dear, I know a great deal too much for my comfort. But he's got bravely over it. He's engaged."

"Engaged, but not quite disengaged. He's an honest fellow, but he remembers his *penchant*. It was as much as he could do to keep his picture from turning to the sentimental. He saw you as he fancied you—as he wished you; and he has given you a little look of what he imagines moral loveliness, which comes within an ace of spoiling the picture. Baxter's imagination isn't very strong, and this same look expresses, in point of fact, nothing but inanity. Fortunately he's a man of extraordinary talent, and a real painter, and he has made a good portrait in spite of himself."

To such arguments as these was John Lennox reduced, to stifle the evidence of his senses. But when once a lover begins to doubt, he cannot cease at will. In spite of his earnest efforts to believe in Marian as before, to accept her without scruple and without second thought, he was quite unable to repress an impulse of constant mistrust and aversion. The charm was broken, and there is no mending a charm. Lennox stood half-aloof, watching the poor girl's countenance, weighing her words, analyzing her thoughts, guessing at her motives.

Marian's conduct under this trying ordeal was truly heroic. She felt that some subtle change had taken place in her future husband's feelings, a change which, although she was powerless to discover its cause, yet obviously imperilled her prospects. Something had snapped between them; she had lost half of her power. She was horribly distressed, and the more so because that superior depth of character which she had all along gladly conceded to Lennox, might now, as she conjectured, cover some bold and portentous design. Could he

meditate a direct rupture? Could it be his intention to dash
from her lips the sweet, the spiced and odorous cup of being
the wife of a good-natured millionaire? Marian turned a tremulous glance upon her past, and wondered if he had discovered
any dark spot. Indeed, for that matter, might she not defy him
to do so? She had done nothing really amiss. There was no
visible blot in her history. It was faintly discolored, indeed,
by a certain vague moral dinginess; but it compared well
enough with that of other girls. She had cared for nothing but
pleasure; but to what else were girls brought up? On the
whole, might she not feel at ease? She assured herself that she
might; but she nevertheless felt that if John wished to break
off his engagement, he would do it on high abstract grounds,
and not because she had committed a naughtiness the more or
the less. It would be simply because he had ceased to love her.
It would avail her but little to assure him that she would kindly
overlook this circumstance and remit the obligations of the
heart. But, in spite of her hideous apprehensions, she continued
to smile and smile.

The days passed by, and John consented to be still engaged.
Their marriage was only a week off—six days, five days, four.
Miss Everett's smile became less mechanical. John had apparently been passing through a crisis—a moral and intellectual crisis, inevitable in a man of his constitution, and with
which she had nothing to do. On the eve of marriage he had
questioned his heart; he had found that it was no longer young
and capable of the vagaries of passion, and he had made up his
mind to call things by their proper names, and to admit to himself that he was marrying not for love, but for friendship, and
a little, perhaps, for prudence. It was only out of regard for
what he supposed Marian's own more exalted theory of the
matter, that he abstained from revealing to her this common-
sense view of it. Such was Marian's hypothesis.

Lennox had fixed his wedding-day for the last Thursday in
October. On the preceding Friday, as he was passing up

Broadway, he stopped at Goupil's to see if his order for the framing of the portrait had been fulfilled. The picture had been transferred to the shop, and, when duly framed, had been, at Baxter's request and with Lennox's consent, placed for a few days in the exhibition room. Lennox went up to look at it.

The portrait stood on an easel at the end of the hall, with three spectators before it—a gentleman and two ladies. The room was otherwise empty. As Lennox went toward the picture, the gentleman turned out to be Baxter. He proceeded to introduce his friend to his two companions, the younger of whom Lennox recognized as the artist's betrothed. The other, her sister, was a plain, pale woman, with the look of ill health, who had been provided with a seat and made no attempt to talk. Baxter explained that these ladies had arrived from Europe but the day before, and that his first care had been to show them his masterpiece.

"Sarah," said he, "has been praising the model very much to the prejudice of the copy."

Sarah was a tall, black-haired girl of twenty, with irregular features, a pair of luminous dark eyes, and a smile radiant of white teeth—evidently an excellent person. She turned to Lennox with a look of frank sympathy, and said in a deep, rich voice:

"She must be very beautiful."

"Yes, she's very beautiful," said Lennox, with his eyes lingering on her own pleasant face. "You must know her— she must know you."

"I'm sure I should like very much to see her," said Sarah.

"This is very nearly as good," said Lennox. "Mr Baxter is a great genius."

"I know Mr Baxter is a genius. But what is a picture, at the best? I've seen nothing but pictures for the last two years, and I haven't seen a single pretty girl."

The young girl stood looking at the portrait in very evident admiration, and, while Baxter talked to the elder lady, Lennox bestowed a long, covert glance upon his *fiancée*. She had brought her head into almost immediate juxtaposition with that of Marian's image, and, for a moment, the freshness and the strong animation which bloomed upon her features seemed to obliterate the lines and colors on the canvas. But the next moment, as Lennox looked, the roseate circle of Marian's face blazed into remorseless distinctness, and her careless blue eyes looked with cynical familiarity into his own.

He bade an abrupt good morning to his companions, and went toward the door. But beside it he stopped. Suspended on the wall was Baxter's picture, *My Last Duchess*. He stood amazed. Was *this* the face and figure that, a month ago, had reminded him of his mistress? Where was the likeness now? It was as utterly absent as if it had never existed. The picture, moreover, was a very inferior work to the new portrait. He looked back at Baxter, half tempted to demand an explanation, or at least to express his perplexity. But Baxter and his sweetheart had stooped down to examine a minute sketch near the floor, with their heads in delicious contiguity.

How the week elapsed, it was hard to say. There were moments when Lennox felt as if death were preferable to the heartless union which now stared him in the face, and as if the only possible course was to transfer his property to Marian and to put an end to his existence. There were others, again, when he was fairly reconciled to his fate. He had but to gather his old dreams and fancies into a faggot and break them across his knee, and the thing were done. Could he not collect in their stead a comely cluster of moderate and rational expectations, and bind them about with a wedding favor? His love was dead, his youth was dead; that was all. There was no need of making a tragedy of it. His love's vitality had been but small, and since it was to be short-lived it was better that it should expire before marriage than after. As for marriage, that should stand, for that was not of necessity a matter of love. He lacked the brutal consistency necessary for taking away Marian's future. If he had mistaken her and overrated her, the fault was his own, and it was a hard thing that she should pay the penalty. Whatever were her failings, they were profoundly involuntary, and it was plain that with regard to himself her intentions were good. She would be no companion, but she would be at least a faithful wife.

With the help of this grim logic, Lennox reached the eve of his wedding day. His manner toward Miss Everett during the preceding week had been inveterately tender and kind. He felt that in losing his love she had lost a heavy treasure, and he offered her instead the most unfailing devotion. Marian had questioned him about his lassitude and his preoccupied air, and he had replied that he was not very well. On the Wednesday afternoon, he mounted his horse and took a long ride. He came home toward sunset, and was met in the hall by his old housekeeper.

"Miss Everett's portrait, sir," she said, "has just been sent home, in the most beautiful frame. You gave no directions, and I took the liberty of having it carried into the library. I thought," and the old woman smiled deferentially, "you'd like best to have it in your own room."

Lennox went into the library. The picture was standing on the floor, back to back with a high arm-chair, and catching, through the window, the last horizontal rays of the sun. He stood before it a moment, gazing at it with a haggard face.

"Come!" said he, at last, "Marian may be what God has made her; but *this* detestable creature I can neither love nor respect!"

He looked about him with an angry despair, and his eye fell on a long, keen poinard, given him by a friend who had bought it in the East, and which lay as an ornament on his mantelshelf. He seized it and thrust it, with barbarous glee, straight into the lovely face of the image. He dragged it downward, and made a long fissure in the living canvas. Then, with half a dozen strokes, he wantonly hacked it across. The act afforded him an immense relief.

I need hardly add that on the following day Lennox was married. He had locked the library door on coming out the evening before, and he had the key in his waistcoat pocket as he stood at the altar. As he left town, therefore, immediately after the ceremony, it was not until his return, a fortnight later, that the fate of the picture became known. It is not necessary to relate how he explained his exploit to Marian and how he disclosed it to Baxter. He at least put on a brave face. There is a rumor current of his having paid the painter an enormous sum of money. The amount is probably exaggerated, but there can be no doubt that the sum was very large. How he has fared —how he is destined to fare—in matrimony, it is rather too early to determine. He has been married scarcely three months.

THE ROMANCE OF
CERTAIN OLD CLOTHES

TOWARD the middle of the eighteenth century there lived in
the Province of Massachusetts a widowed gentlewoman, the
mother of three children. Her name is of little account: I shall
take the liberty of calling her Mrs Willoughby,—a name, like
her own, of a highly respectable sound. She had been left a
widow after some six years of marriage, and had devoted herself to the care of her progeny. These young persons grew up
in a manner to reward her zeal and to gratify her fondest hopes.
The first-born was a son, whom she had called Bernard, after
his father. The others were daughters,—born at an interval of
three years apart. Good looks were traditional in the family,
and this youthful trio were not likely to allow the tradition to
perish. The boy was of that fair and ruddy complexion and of
that athletic mould which in those days (as in these) were the
sign of genuine English blood,—a frank, affectionate young
fellow, a deferential son, a patronizing brother, and a steadfast
friend. Clever, however, he was not; the wit of the family had
been apportioned chiefly to his sisters. Mr Willoughby had
been a great reader of Shakespeare, at a time when this pursuit
implied more liberality of taste than at the present day, and in
a community where it required much courage to patronize the
drama even in the closet; and he had wished to record his
admiration of the great poet by calling his daughters out of his
favorite plays. Upon the elder he had bestowed the romantic
name of Viola; and upon the younger, the more serious one of
Perdita, in memory of a little girl born between them, who had
lived but a few weeks.

When Bernard Willoughby came to his sixteenth year, his mother put a brave face upon it, and prepared to execute her husband's last request. This had been an earnest entreaty that, at the proper age, his son should be sent out to England, to complete his education at the University of Oxford, which had been the seat of his own studies. Mrs Willoughby fancied that the lad's equal was not to be found in the two hemispheres, but she had the antique wifely submissiveness. She swallowed her sobs, and made up her boy's trunk and his simple provincial outfit, and sent him on his way across the seas. Bernard was entered at his father's college, and spent five years in England, without great honor, indeed, but with a vast deal of pleasure and no discredit. On leaving the University he made the journey to France. In his twenty-third year he took ship for home, prepared to find poor little New England (New England was very small in those days) an utterly intolerable place of abode. But there had been changes at home, as well as in Mr Bernard's opinions. He found his mother's house quite habitable, and his sisters grown into two very charming young ladies, with all the accomplishments and graces of the young women of Britain, and a certain native-grown gentle *brusquerie* and wildness, which, if it was not an accomplishment, was certainly a grace the more. Bernard privately assured his mother that his sisters were fully a match for the most genteel young women in England; whereupon poor Mrs Willoughby you may be sure, bade them hold up their heads. Such was Bernard's opinion, and such, in a tenfold higher degree, was the opinion of Mr Arthur Lloyd. This gentleman, I hasten to add, was a college-mate of Mr Bernard, a young man of reputable family, of a good person and a handsome inheritance, which latter appurtenance he proposed to invest in trade in this country. He and Bernard were warm friends; they had crossed the ocean together, and the young American had lost no time in presenting him at his mother's house, where he had made quite as good an impression as that which he had received, and of which I have just given a hint.

The two sisters were at this time in all the freshness of their youthful bloom; each wearing, of course, this natural brilliancy in the manner that became her best. They were equally dissimilar in appearance and character. Viola, the elder,—now in her twenty-second year,—was tall and fair, with calm gray eyes and auburn tresses; a very faint likeness to the Viola of Shakespeare's comedy, whom I imagine as a brunette (if you will), but a slender, airy creature, full of the softest and finest emotions. Miss Willoughby, with her candid complexion, her fine arms, her majestic height, and her slow utterance, was not cut out for adventures. She would never have put on a man's jacket and hose; and, indeed, being a very plump beauty, it is perhaps as well that she would not. Perdita, too, might very well have exchanged the sweet melancholy of her name against something more in consonance with her aspect and disposition. She was a positive brunette, short of stature, light of foot, with a vivid dark brown eye. She had been from her childhood a creature of smiles and gayety; and so far from making you wait for an answer to your speech, as her handsome sister was wont to do (while she gazed at you with her somewhat cold gray eyes), she had given you the choice of half a dozen, suggested by the successive clauses of your proposition, before you had got to the end of it.

The young girls were very glad to see their brother once more; but they found themselves quite able to maintain a reserve of good-will for their brother's friend. Among the young men their friends and neighbors, the *belle jeunesse* of the Colony, there were many excellent fellows, several devoted swains, and some two or three who enjoyed the reputation of universal charmers and conquerors. But the home-bred arts and the somewhat boisterous gallantry of those honest young colonists were completely eclipsed by the good looks, the fine clothes, the punctilious courtesy, the perfect elegance, the immense information, of Mr Arthur Lloyd. He was in reality no paragon; he was an honest, resolute, intelligent young man rich in pounds sterling, in his health and comfortable hopes, and his little capital of uninvested affections. But he was a gentleman; he had a handsome face; he had studied and travelled; he spoke French, he played on the flute, and he read verses aloud with very great taste. There were a dozen reasons why Miss Willoughby and her sister should forthwith have been rendered fastidious in the choice of their male acquaintance. The imagination of woman is especially adapted to the various small conventions and mysteries of polite society. Mr Lloyd's talk told our little New England maidens a vast deal more of the ways and means of people of fashion in European capitals than he had any idea of doing. It was delightful to sit by and hear him and Bernard discourse upon the fine people and fine things they had seen. They would all gather round the fire after tea, in the little wainscoted parlor,—quite innocent then of any intention of being picturesque or of being anything else, indeed, than economical, and saving an outlay in stamped papers and tapestries,—and the two young men would remind each other, across the rug, of this, that, and the other adventure. Viola and Perdita would often have given their ears to know exactly what adventure it was, and where it happened, and who was there, and what the ladies had on; but in those days a well-bred young woman was not expected to break into the conversation of her own movement or to ask too many questions; and the poor girls used therefore to sit fluttering behind the more languid—or more discreet—curiosity of their mother.

That they were both very fine girls Arthur Lloyd was not slow to discover; but it took him some time to satisfy himself as to the apportionment of their charms. He had a strong presentiment—an emotion of a nature entirely too cheerful to be called a foreboding—that he was destined to marry one of them; yet he was unable to arrive at a preference, and for such a consummation a preference was certainly indispensable, inasmuch as Lloyd was quite too gallant a fellow to make a choice by lot and be cheated of the heavenly delight of falling in love. He resolved to take things easily, and to let his heart speak. Meanwhile, he was on a very pleasant footing. Mrs Willoughby showed a dignified indifference to his "intentions," equally remote from a carelessness of her daughters' honor and from that odious alacrity to make him commit himself, which, in his quality of a young man of property, he had but too often encountered in the venerable dames of his native islands. As for Bernard, all that he asked was that his friend should take his sisters as his own; and as for the poor girls themselves, however each may have secretly longed for the monopoly of Mr Lloyd's attentions, they observed a very decent and modest and contented demeanor.

Towards each other, however, they were somewhat more on the offensive. They were good sisterly friends, betwixt whom it would take more than a day for the seeds of jealousy to sprout and bear fruit; but the young girls felt that the seeds had been sown on the day that Mr Lloyd came into the house. Each made up her mind that, if she should be slighted, she would bear her grief in silence, and that no one should be any the wiser; for if they had a great deal of love, they had also a great deal of pride. But each prayed in secret, nevertheless, that upon *her* the glory might fall. They had need of a vast deal of patience, of self-control, and of dissimulation. In those days a young girl of decent breeding could make no advances whatever, and barely respond, indeed, to those that were made. She was expected to sit still in her chair with her eyes on the carpet, watching the spot where the mystic handkerchief should fall. Poor Arthur Lloyd was obliged to undertake his wooing in the little wainscoted parlor, before the eyes of Mrs Willoughby, her son, and his prospective sister-in-law. But youth and love are so cunning that a hundred signs and tokens might travel to and fro, and not one of these three pair of eyes detect them in their passage. The young girls had but one chamber and one bed between them, and for long hours together they were under each other's direct inspection. That each knew that she was being watched, however, made not a grain of difference in those little offices which they mutually rendered, or in the various household tasks which they performed in common. Neither flinched nor fluttered beneath the silent batteries of her sister's eyes. The only apparent change in their habits was that they had less to say to each other. It was impossible to talk about Mr Lloyd, and it was ridiculous to talk about anything else. By tacit agreement they began to wear all their choice finery, and to devise such little implements of coquetry, in the way of ribbons and top-knots and furbelows as were sanctioned by indubitable modesty. They executed in the same inarticulate fashion an agreement of sincerity on these delicate matters. "Is it better so?" Viola would ask, tying a bunch of ribbons on her bosom, and turning about from her glass to her sister. Perdita would look up gravely from her work and examine the decoration. "I think you had better give it another loop," she would say, with great solemnity, looking hard at her sister with eyes that added, "upon my honor!" So they were forever stitching and trimming their petticoats, and pressing out their muslins, and contriving washes and ointments and cosmetics, like the ladies in the household of the Vicar of Wakefield. Some three or four months went by; it grew to be mid-winter, and as yet Viola knew that if Perdita had nothing more to boast of than she, there was not much to be feared from her rivalry. But Perdita by this time, the charming Perdita, felt that her secret had grown to be tenfold more precious than her sister's.

One afternoon Miss Willoughby sat alone before her toilet-glass combing out her long hair. It was getting too dark to see; she lit the two candles in their sockets on the frame of her mirror, and then went to the window to draw her curtains. It was a gray December evening; the landscape was bare and bleak, and the sky heavy with snow-clouds. At the end of the long garden into which her window looked was a wall with a little postern door, opening into a lane. The door stood ajar, as she could vaguely see in the gathering darkness, and moved slowly to and fro, as if someone were swaying it from the lane without. It was doubtless a servant-maid. But as she was about to drop her curtain, Viola saw her sister step within the garden and hurry along the path toward the house. She dropped the curtain, all save a little crevice for her eyes. As Perdita came up the path, she seemed to be examining something in her hand, holding it close to her eyes. When she reached the house she stopped a moment, looked intently at the object, and pressed it to her lips.

Poor Viola slowly came back to her chair, and sat down before her glass, where, if she had looked at it less abstractedly, she would have seen her handsome features sadly disfigured by jealousy. A moment afterwards the door opened behind her, and her sister came into the room, out of breath, and her cheeks aglow with the chilly air.

Perdita started. "Ah," said she, "I thought you were with our mother." The ladies were to go to a tea-party, and on such occasions it was the habit of one of the young girls to help their mother to dress. Instead of coming in Perdita lingered at the door.

"Come in, come in," said Viola. "We've more than an hour yet. I should like you very much to give a few strokes to my hair." She knew her sister wished to retreat, and that she could see in the glass all her movements in the room. "Nay, just help me with my hair," she said, "and I'll go to mamma."

Perdita came reluctantly, and took the brush. She saw her sister's eyes, in the glass, fastened hard upon her hands. She had not made three passes, when Viola clapped her own right hand upon her sister's left, and started out of her chair. "Whose ring is that?" she cried passionately, drawing her towards the light.

On the young girl's third finger glistened a little gold ring, adorned with a couple of small rubies. Perdita felt that she need no longer keep her secret, yet that she must put a bold face on her avowal. "It's mine," she said proudly.

"Who gave it to you?" cried the other.

Perdita hesitated a moment. "Mr Lloyd."

"Mr Lloyd is generous, all of a sudden."

"Ah no," cried Perdita, with spirit, "not all of a sudden. He offered it to me a month ago."

"And you needed a month's begging to take it?" said Viola, looking at the little trinket; which indeed was not especially elegant, although it was the best that the jeweller of the Province could furnish. "I shouldn't have taken it in less than two."

"It isn't the ring," said Perdita, "it's what it means!"

"It means that you're not a modest girl," cried Viola. "Pray does your mother know of your conduct? does Bernard?"

"My mother has approved my 'conduct,' as you call it. Mr Lloyd has asked my hand, and mamma has given it. Would you have had him apply to you, sister?"

Viola gave her sister a long look, full of passionate envy and sorrow. Then she dropped her lashes on her pale cheeks and turned away. Perdita felt that it had not been a pretty scene; but it was her sister's fault. But the elder girl rapidly called back her pride, and turned herself about again. "You have my very best wishes," she said, with a low curtsey. "I wish you every happiness, and a very long life."

Perdita gave a bitter laugh. "Don't speak in that tone," she cried. "I'd rather you cursed me outright. Come, sister," she added, "he couldn't marry both of us."

"I wish you very great joy," Viola repeated mechanically, sitting down to her glass again, "and a very long life, and plenty of children."

There was something in the sound of these words not at all

to Perdita's taste. "Will you give me a year, at least?" she said. "In a year I can have one little boy,—or one little girl at least. If you'll give me your brush again I'll do your hair."

"Thank you," said Viola. "You had better go to mamma. It isn't becoming that a young lady with a promised husband should wait on a girl with none."

"Nay," said Perdita, good-humoredly, "I have Arthur to wait upon me. You need my service more than I need yours."

But her sister motioned her away, and she left the room. When she had gone poor Viola fell on her knees before her dressing-table, buried her head in her arms, and poured out a flood of tears and sobs. She felt very much better for this effusion of sorrow. When her sister came back, she insisted upon helping her to dress, and upon her wearing her prettiest things. She forced upon her acceptance a bit of lace of her own, and declared that now that she was to be married she should do her best to appear worthy of her lover's choice. She discharged these offices in stern silence; but, such as they were, they had to do duty as an apology and an atonement; she never made any other.

Now that Lloyd was received by the family as an accepted suitor, nothing remained but to fix the wedding-day. It was appointed for the following April, and in the interval preparations were diligently made for the marriage. Lloyd, on his side, was busy with his commercial arrangements, and with establishing a correspondence with the great mercantile house to which he had attached himself in England. He was therefore not so frequent a visitor at Mrs Willoughby's as during the months of his diffidence and irresolution, and poor Viola had less to suffer than she had feared from the sight of the mutual endearments of the young lovers. Touching his future sister-in-law, Lloyd had a perfectly clear conscience. There had not been a particle of sentiment uttered between them, and he had not the slightest suspicion that she coveted anything more than his fraternal regard. He was quite at his ease; life promised so well, both domestically and financially. The lurid clouds of revolution were as yet twenty years beneath the horizon, and that his connubial felicity should take a tragic turn it was absurd, it was blasphemous, to apprehend. Meanwhile at Mrs Willoughby's there was a greater rustling of silks, a more rapid clicking of scissors and flying of needles, than ever. Mrs Willoughby had determined that her daughter should carry from home the most elegant outfit that her money could buy, or that the country could furnish. All the sage women in the county were convened, and their united taste was brought to bear on Perdita's wardrobe. Viola's situation, at this moment, was assuredly not to be envied. The poor girl had an inordinate love of dress, and the very best taste in the world, as her sister perfectly well knew. Viola was tall, she was stately and sweeping, she was made to carry stiff brocade and masses of heavy lace, such as belong to the toilet of a rich man's wife. But Viola sat aloof, with her beautiful arms folded and her head averted, while her mother and sister and the venerable women aforesaid worried and wondered over their materials, oppressed by the multitude of their resources. One day there came in a beautiful piece of white silk, brocaded with celestial blue and silver, sent by the bridegroom himself,—it not being thought amiss in those days that the husband-elect should contribute to the bride's trousseau. Perdita was quite at loss to imagine a fashion which should do sufficient honor to the splendor of the material.

"Blue's your color, sister, more than mine," she said, with appealing eyes. "It's a pity it's not for you. You'd know what to do with it."

Viola got up from her place and looked at the great shining fabric as it lay spread over the back of a chair. Then she took it up in her hands and felt it,—lovingly, as Perdita could see, —and turned about toward the mirror with it. She let it roll down to her feet, and flung the other end over her shoulder, gathering it in about her waist with her white arm bare to the elbow. She threw back her head, and looked at her image, and a hanging tress of her auburn hair fell upon the gorgeous surface of the silk. It made a dazzling picture. The women standing about uttered a little "Ah!" of admiration. "Yes, indeed," said Viola, quietly, "blue is my color." But Perdita could see that her fancy had been stirred, and that she would now fall to work and solve all their silken riddles. And indeed she behaved very well, as Perdita, knowing her insatiable love of millinery, was quite ready to declare. Innumerable yards of lustrous silk and satin, of muslin, velvet, and lace, passed through her cunning hands, without a word of envy coming from her lips. Thanks to her industry, when the wedding-day came Perdita was prepared to espouse more of the vanities of life than any fluttering young bride who had yet challenged the sacramental blessing of a New England divine.

It had been arranged that the young couple should go out and spend the first days of their wedded life at the country house of an English gentleman,—a man of rank and a very kind friend to Lloyd. He was an unmarried man; he professed himself delighted to withdraw and leave them for a week to their billing and cooing. After the ceremony at church,—it had been performed by an English parson,—young Mrs Lloyd hastened back to her mother's house to change her wedding gear for a riding-dress. Viola helped her to effect the change, in the little old room in which they had been fond sisters together. Perdita then hurried off to bid farewell to her mother, leaving Viola to follow. The parting was short; the horses were at the door and Arthur impatient to start. But Viola had not followed, and Perdita hastened back to her room, opening the door abruptly. Viola, as usual, was before the glass, but in a position which caused the other to stand still, amazed. She had dressed herself in Perdita's cast-off wedding veil and wreath, and on her neck she had hung the heavy string of pearls which the young girl had received from her husband as a wedding-gift. These things had been hastily laid aside, to await their possessor's disposal on her return from the country. Bedizened in this unnatural garb, Viola stood at the mirror, plunging a long look into its depths, and reading Heaven knows what audacious visions. Perdita was horrified. It was a hideous image of their old rivalry come to life again. She made a step toward her sister, as if to pull off the veil and the flowers. But catching her eyes in the glass, she stopped.

"Farewell, Viola," she said. "You might at least have waited till I had got out of the house." And she hurried away from the room.

Mr Lloyd had purchased in Boston a house which, in the taste of those days, was considered a marvel of elegance and comfort; and here he very soon established himself with his young wife. He was thus separated by a distance of twenty miles from the residence of his mother-in-law. Twenty miles, in that primitive era of roads and conveyances, were as serious a matter as a hundred at the present day, and Mrs Willoughby saw but little of her daughter during the first twelvemonth of her marriage. She suffered in no small degree from her absence; and her affliction was not diminished by the fact that Viola had fallen into terribly low spirits and was not to be roused or cheered but by change of air and circumstances. The real cause of the young girl's dejection the reader will not be slow to suspect. Mrs Willoughby and her gossips, however, deemed her complaint a purely physical one, and doubted not that she would obtain relief from the remedy just mentioned. Her mother accordingly proposed on her behalf a visit to certain relatives on the paternal side, established in New York, who had long complained that they were able to see so little of their New England cousins. Viola was despatched to these good people, under a suitable escort, and remained with them for several months. In the interval her brother Bernard, who had begun the practice of the law, made up his mind to take a wife.

Viola came home to the wedding, apparently cured of her heartache, with honest roses and lilies in her face, and a proud smile on her lips. Arthur Lloyd came over from Boston to see his brother-in-law married, but without his wife, who was expecting shortly to present him with an heir. It was nearly a year since Viola had seen him. She was glad—she hardly knew why—that Perdita had stayed at home. Arthur looked happy, but he was more grave and solemn than before his marriage. She thought he looked "interesting,"—for although the word in its modern sense was not then invented, we may be sure that the idea was. The truth is, he was simply preoccupied with his wife's condition. Nevertheless, he by no means failed to observe Viola's beauty and splendor, and how she quite effaced the poor little bride. The allowance that Perdita had enjoyed for her dress had now been transferred to her sister, who turned it to prodigious account. On the morning after the wedding, he had a lady's saddle put on the horse of the servant who had come with him from town, and went out with the young girl for a ride. It was a keen, clear morning in January; the ground was bare and hard, and the horses in good condition,—to say nothing of Viola, who was charming in her hat and plume, and her dark blue riding-coat, trimmed with fur. They rode all the morning, they lost their way, and were obliged to stop for dinner at a farm-house. The early winter dusk had fallen when they got home. Mrs Willoughby met them with a long face. A messenger had arrived at noon from Mrs Lloyd; she was beginning to be ill, and desired her husband's immediate return. The young man, at the thought that he had lost several hours, and that by hard riding he might already have been with his wife, uttered a passionate oath. He barely consented to stop for a mouthful of supper, but mounted the messenger's horse and started off at a gallop.

He reached home at midnight. His wife had been delivered of a little girl. "Ah, why weren't you with me?" she said, as he came to her bedside.

"I was out of the house when the man came. I was with Viola," said Lloyd, innocently.

Mrs Lloyd made a little moan, and turned about. But she continued to do very well, and for a week her improvement was uninterrupted. Finally, however, through some indiscretion in the way of diet or of exposure, it was checked, and the poor lady grew rapidly worse. Lloyd was in despair. It very soon became evident that she was breathing her last. Mrs Lloyd came to a sense of her approaching end, and declared that she was reconciled with death. On the third evening after the change took place she told her husband that she felt she would not outlast the night. She dismissed her servants, and also requested her mother to withdraw,—Mrs Willoughby having arrived on the preceding day. She had had her infant placed on the bed beside her, and she lay on her side, with the child against her breast, holding her husband's hands. The night-lamp was hidden behind the heavy curtains of the bed, but the room was illumined with a red glow from the immense fire of logs on the hearth.

"It seems strange to die by such a fire as that," the young woman said, feebly trying to smile. "If I had but a little of such fire in my veins! But I've given it all to this little spark of mortality." And she dropped her eyes on her child. Then raising them she looked at her husband with a long penetrating gaze. The last feeling which lingered in her heart was one of mistrust. She had not recovered from the shock which Arthur had given her by telling her that in the hour of her agony he had been with Viola. She trusted her husband very nearly as well as she loved him; but now that she was called away forever, she felt a cold horror of her sister. She felt in her soul that Viola had never ceased to envy her good fortune; and a year of happy security had not effaced the young girl's image, dressed in her wedding garments, and smiling with coveted triumph. Now that Arthur was to be alone, what might not Viola do?" She was beautiful, she was engaging; what arts might she not use, what impression might she not make upon the young man's melancholy heart? Mrs Lloyd looked at her husband in silence. It seemed hard, after all, to doubt of his constancy. His fine eyes were filled with tears; his face was convulsed with weeping; the clasp of his hands was warm and passionate. How noble he looked, how tender, how faithful and devoted! "Nay," thought Perdita, "he's not for such as Viola. He'll never forget me. Nor does Viola truly care for him; she cares only for vanities and finery and jewels." And she dropped her eyes on her white hands, which her husband's liberality had covered with rings, and on the lace ruffles which trimmed the edge of her nightdress. "She covets my rings and my laces more than she covets my husband."

At this moment the thought of her sister's rapacity seemed to cast a dark shadow between her and the helpless figure of her little girl. "Arthur," she said, "you must take off my rings. I shall not be buried in them. One of these days my daughter shall wear them,—my rings and my laces and silks. I had them all brought out and shown me to-day. It's a great wardrobe,—there's not such another in the Province; I can say it without vanity now that I've done with it. It will be a great inheritance for my daughter, when she grows into a young woman. There are things there that a man never buys twice, and if they're lost you'll never again see the like. So you'll watch them well. Some dozen things I've left to Viola; I've named them to my mother. I've given her that blue and silver; it was meant for her; I wore it only once, I looked ill in it. But the rest are to be sacredly kept for this little innocent. It's such a providence that she should be my color; she can wear my gowns; she has her mother's eyes. You know the same fashions come back every twenty years. She can wear my gowns as they are. They'll lie there quietly waiting till she grows into them,—wrapped in camphor and rose-leaves, and keeping their colors in the sweet-scented darkness. She shall have black hair, she shall wear my carnation satin. Do you promise me, Arthur?"

"Promise you what, dearest?"

"Promise me to keep your poor little wife's old gowns."

"Are you afraid I'll sell them?"

"No, but that they may get scattered. My mother will have them properly wrapped up, and you shall lay them away under a double-lock. Do you know the great chest in the attic, with the iron bands? There's no end to what it will hold. You can lay them all there. My mother and the housekeeper will do it, and give you the key. And you'll keep the key in your secretary, and never give it to any one but your child. Do you promise me?"

"Ah, yes, I promise you," said Lloyd, puzzled at the intensity with which his wife appeared to cling to this idea.

"Will you swear?" repeated Perdita.

"Yes, I swear."

"Well—I trust you—I trust you," said the poor lady, looking into his eyes with eyes in which, if he had suspected her vague apprehensions, he might have read an appeal quite as much as an assurance.

Lloyd bore his bereavement soberly and manfully. A month after his wife's death, in the course of commerce, circumstances arose which offered him an opportunity of going to England. He embraced it as a diversion from gloomy thoughts. He was absent nearly a year, during which his little girl was tenderly nursed and cherished by her grandmother. On his return he had his house again thrown open, and announced his intention of keeping the same state as during his wife's lifetime. It very soon came to be predicted that he would marry again, and there were at least a dozen young women of whom one may say that it was by no fault of theirs that, for six months after his return, the prediction did not come true. During this interval he still left his little daughter in Mrs Willoughby's hands, the latter assuring him that a change of residence at so tender an age was perilous to her health. Finally, however, he declared that his heart longed for his daughter's presence, and that she must be brought up to town. He sent his coach and his housekeeper to fetch her home. Mrs Willoughby was in terror lest something should befall her on the road; and, in accordance with this feeling, Viola offered to ride along with her. She could return the next day. So she went up to town with her little niece, and Mr Lloyd met her on the threshold of his house, overcome with her kindness and with gratitude. Instead of returning the next day, Viola stayed out the week; and when at last she re-appeared, she had only come for her clothes. Arthur would not hear of her coming home, nor would the baby. She cried and moaned if Viola left her; and at the sight of her grief Arthur lost his wits, and swore that she was going to die. In fine, nothing would suit them but that Viola should remain until the poor child had grown used to strange faces.

It took two months to bring this consummation about; for it was not until this period had elapsed that Viola took leave of her brother-in-law. Mrs Willoughby had shaken her head over her daughter's absence; she declared it was not becoming, and that it was the talk of the town. She had reconciled herself to it only because, during the young girl's visit, the household en-joyed an unwonted term of peace. Bernard Willoughby had brought his wife home to live, between whom and her sister-in-law there existed a bitter hostility. Viola was perhaps no angel; but in the daily practice of life she was a sufficiently good-natured girl, and if she quarrelled with Mrs Bernard, it was not without provocation. Quarrel, however, she did, to the great annoyance not only of her antagonist, but of the two spectators of these constant altercations. Her stay in the house-hold of her brother-in-law, therefore, would have been delight-ful, if only because it removed her from contact with the object of her antipathy at home. It was doubly—it was ten times—delightful, in that it kept her near the object of her old passion. Mrs Lloyd's poignant mistrust had fallen very far short of the truth. Viola's sentiment had been a passion at first, and a pas-sion it remained,—a passion of whose radiant heat, tempered to the delicate state of his feelings, Mr Lloyd very soon felt the influence. Lloyd, as I have hinted, was not a modern Petrarch; it was not in his nature to practise an ideal constancy. He had not been many days in the house with his sister-in-law before he began to assure himself that she was, in the language of that day, a devilish fine woman. Whether Viola really practised those insidious arts that her sister had been tempted to impute to her it is needless to inquire. It is enough to say that she found means to appear to the very best advantage. She used to seat herself every morning before the great fireplace in the dining-room, at work upon a piece of tapestry, with her little niece disporting herself on the carpet at her feet, or on the train of her dress, and playing with her woollens balls. Lloyd would have been a very stupid fellow if he had remained insensible to the rich suggestions of this charming picture. He was prodigiously fond of his little girl, and was never weary of taking her in his arms and tossing her up and down, and making her crow with delight. Very often, however, he would venture upon greater liberties than the young lady was yet prepared to allow, and she would suddenly vociferate her displeasure. Viola would then drop her tapestry, and put out her handsome hands with the serious smile of the young girl whose virgin fancy has revealed to her all a mother's healing arts. Lloyd would give up the child, their eyes would meet, their hands would touch, and Viola would extinguish the little girl's sobs upon the snowy folds of the kerchief that crossed her bosom. Her dignity was perfect, and nothing could be more discreet than the manner in which she accepted her brother-in-law's hospitality. It may be almost said, perhaps, that there was something harsh in her reserve. Lloyd had a provoking feeling that she was in the house, and yet that she was unapproachable. Half an hour after supper, at the very outset of the long winter evenings, she would light her candle, and make the young man a most respectful curtsey, and march off to bed. If these were arts, Viola was a great artist. But their effect was so gentle, so gradual, they were calculated to work upon the young widower's fancy with such a finely shaded *crescendo*, that, as the reader has seen, several weeks elapsed before Viola began to feel sure that her return would cover her outlay. When this became morally certain, she packed up her trunk, and returned to her mother's house. For three days she waited; on the fourth Mr Lloyd made his appearance,—a respectful but ardent suitor. Viola heard him out with great humility, and accepted him with infinite modesty. It is hard to imagine that Mrs Lloyd should have forgiven her husband; but if anything might have disarmed her resentment, it would have been the ceremonious continence of this interview. Viola imposed upon her lover but a short probation. They were married, as was becoming, with great privacy,—almost with secrecy,—in the hope perhaps, as was waggishly remarked at the time, that the late Mrs Lloyd wouldn't hear of it.

The marriage was to all appearance a happy one, and each party obtained what each had desired—Lloyd "a devilish fine woman," and Viola—but Viola's desires, as the reader will have observed, have remained a good deal of a mystery. There were, indeed, two blots upon their felicity; but time would, perhaps, efface them. During the first three years of her marriage Mrs Lloyd failed to become a mother, and her husband on his side suffered heavy losses of money. This latter circumstance compelled a material retrenchment in his expenditure, and Viola was perforce less of a great lady than her sister had been. She contrived, however, to sustain with unbroken consistency the part of an elegant woman, although it must be confessed that it required the exercise of more ingenuity than belongs to your real aristocratic repose. She had long since ascertained that her sister's immense wardrobe had been sequestrated for the benefit of her daughter, and that it lay languishing in thankless gloom in the dusty attic. It was a revolting thought that these exquisite fabrics should await the commands of a little girl who sat in a high chair and ate bread-

and-milk with a wooden spoon. Viola had the good taste, however, to say nothing about the matter until several months had expired. Then, at last, she timidly broached it to her husband. Was it not a pity that so much finery should be lost?—for lost it would be, what with colors fading, and moths eating it up, and the change of fashions. But Lloyd gave so abrupt and peremptory a negative to her inquiry, that she saw that for the present her attempt was vain. Six months went by, however, and brought with them new needs and new fancies. Viola's thoughts hovered lovingly about her sister's relics. She went up and looked at the chest in which they lay imprisoned. There was a sullen defiance in its three great padlocks and its iron bands, which only quickened her desires. There was something exasperating in its incorruptible immobility. It was like a grim and grizzled old household servant, who locks his jaws over a family secret. And then there was a look of capacity in its vast extent, and a sound as of dense fulness, when Viola knocked its side with the toe of her little slipper, which caused her to flush with baffled longing. "It's absurd," she cried; "it's improper, it's wicked"; and she forthwith resolved upon another attack upon her husband. On the following day, after dinner, when he had had his wine, she bravely began it. But he cut her short with great sternness.

"Once and for all, Viola," said he, "it's out of the question. I shall be gravely displeased if you return to the matter."

"Very good," said Viola. "I'm glad to learn the value at which I'm held. Great Heaven!" she cried, "I'm a happy woman. It's an agreeable thing to feel one's self sacrificed to a caprice!" And her eyes filled with tears of anger and disappointment.

Lloyd had a good-natured man's horror of a woman's sobs, and he attempted—I may say he condescended—to explain. "It's not a caprice, dear, it's a promise," he said,—"an oath."

"An oath? It's a pretty matter for oaths! and to whom, pray?"

"To Perdita," said the young man, raising his eyes for an instant, but immediately dropping them.

"Perdita,—ah, Perdita!" and Viola's tears broke forth. Her bosom heaved with stormy sobs,—sobs which were the long-deferred counterpart of the violent fit of weeping in which she had indulged herself on the night when she discovered her sister's betrothal. She had hoped, in her better moments, that she had done with her jealousy; but her temper, on that occasion, had taken an ineffaceable fold. "And pray, what right," she cried, "had Perdita to dispose of my future? What right had she to bind you to meanness and cruelty? Ah, I occupy a dignified place, and I make a very fine figure! I'm welcome to what Perdita has left! And what has she left? I never knew till now how little! Nothing, nothing, nothing."

This was very poor logic, but it was very good passion. Lloyd put his arm around his wife's waist and tried to kiss her, but she shook him off with magnificent scorn. Poor fellow! he had coveted a "devilish fine woman," and he had got one. Her scorn was intolerable. He walked away with his ears tingling, —irresolute, distracted. Before him was his secretary, and in it the sacred key which with his own hand he had turned in the triple lock. He marched up and opened it, and took the key from a secret drawer, wrapped in a little packet which he had sealed with his own honest bit of blazonry. *Teneo*, said the motto,—"I hold." But he was ashamed to put it back. He flung it upon the table beside his wife.

"Keep it!" she cried. "I want it not. I hate it!"

"I wash my hands of it," cried her husband. "God forgive me!"

Mrs Lloyd gave an indignant shrug of her shoulders, and swept out of the room, while the young man retreated by another door. Ten minutes later Mrs Lloyd returned, and found the room occupied by her little step-daughter and the nursery-maid. The key was not on the table. She glanced at the child. The child was perched on a chair with the packet in her hands. She had broken the seal with her own little fingers. Mrs Lloyd hastily took possession of the key.

At the habitual supper-hour Arthur Lloyd came back from his counting-room. It was the month of June, and supper was served by daylight. The meal was placed on the table, but Mrs Lloyd failed to make her appearance. The servant whom his master sent to call her came back with the assurance that her room was empty, and that the women informed him that she had not been seen since dinner. They had in truth observed her to have been in tears, and, supposing her to be shut up in her chamber, had not disturbed her. Her husband called her name in various parts of the house, but without response. At last it occurred to him that he might find her by taking the way to the attic. The thought gave him a strange feeling of discomfort, and he bade his servants remain behind, wishing no witness in his quest. He reached the foot of the staircase leading to the topmost flat, and stood with his hand on the banisters, pronouncing his wife's name. His voice trembled. He called again, louder and more firmly. The only sound which disturbed the absolute silence was a faint echo of his own tones, repeating his question under the great eaves. He nevertheless felt irresistibly moved to ascend the staircase. It opened upon a wide hall, lined with wooden closets, and terminating in a window which looked westward, and admitted the last rays of the sun. Before the window stood the great chest. Before the chest, on her knees, the young man saw with amazement and horror the figure of his wife. In an instant he crossed the interval between them, bereft of utterance. The lid of the chest stood open, exposing, amid their perfumed napkins, its treasure of stuffs and jewels. Viola had fallen backward from a kneeling posture, with one hand supporting her on the floor and the other pressed to her heart. On her limbs was the stiffness of death, and on her face, in the fading light of the sun, the terror of something more than death. Her lips were parted in entreaty, in dismay, in agony; and on her bloodless brow and cheeks there glowed the marks of ten hideous wounds from two vengeful ghostly hands.

A MOST EXTRAORDINARY CASE

I

LATE in the spring of the year 1865, just as the War had come to an end, a young invalid officer lay in bed in one of the uppermost chambers of one of the great New York hotels. His meditations were interrupted by the entrance of a waiter, who handed him a card superscribed *Mrs Augustus Mason*, and bearing on its reverse side the following words in pencil: "Dear Colonel Mason—I have only just heard of your being here, so ill and alone. It's too dreadful. Do you remember me? Will you see me? If you do, I think you *will* remember me. I insist on coming up.—M. M."

Mason was undressed, unshaven, weak, very feverish. His ugly little bedroom was in a state of confusion which had not even the merit of being picturesque. Mrs Mason's card was at once a puzzle and a heavenly intimation of comfort. But all that it represented was so dim to the young man's enfeebled perception that it took him some moments to collect his thoughts.

"It's a lady, sir," said the waiter, by way of assisting him.

"Is she young or old?" asked Mason.

"Well, sir, she's a little of both."

"I can't ask a lady to come up here," groaned the invalid.

"Upon my word, sir, you look beautiful," said the waiter. "They like a sick man. And I see she's of your own name," continued Michael, in whom constant service had bred great frankness of speech; "the more shame to her for not coming before!"

Colonel Mason made up his mind that, as the visit had been of Mrs Mason's own seeking, he would receive her without more ado. "If she doesn't mind it, I am sure I needn't," said the poor fellow, who hadn't the strength to be over-punctilious. So in a very few moments his visitor was ushered up to his bedside. He saw before him a handsome, middle-aged, fair stout woman, who displayed no other embarrassment than such was easily explained by the loss of breath consequent on the ascent of six flights of stairs.

"Do you remember me?" she asked, taking the young man's hand.

He lay back on his pillow and looked at her. "You used to be my aunt—my aunt Maria," he said.

"I am your Aunt Maria still. It's very good of you not to have forgotten me."

"It's very good of you not to have forgotten *me*," said Mason, in a tone which betrayed a deeper feeling than the simple wish to return a civil speech.

"Dear me, you have had the war and a hundred dreadful things. I have been living in Europe, you know. Since my return I have remained in the country, in your uncle's old house, on the river, of which the lease had just expired when I came home. I came to town yesterday on business, and accidentally heard of your condition and of your being in this hole. I knew you had gone into the army, and I had been wondering a dozen times what had become of you, and whether you wouldn't turn up now that the war is at last over. Of course I didn't lose a moment in coming to you. I'm *so* sorry for you." Mrs Mason looked about her for a seat. The chairs were encumbered with odds and ends belonging to her nephew's wardrobe, with strange military promiscuities, and with the remnants of his last repast. The good lady surveyed the scene with the mute irony of compassion.

The young man lay watching her comely face in contented submission to whatever form of utterance this feeling might take. "You are the first woman—to call a woman—I have seen in I don't know how many months," he said, contrasting her neat, rich appearance with that of his room, and reading her thoughts.

"I should suppose so. I propose to be very feminine." She disembarrassed one of the chairs, and brought it to the bed. Then, seating herself, she ungloved one of her hands, and laid it softly on the young man's wrist. "What a great full-grown young fellow you have become!" she pursued. "Now, tell me, are you very ill?"

"You must ask the doctor," said Mason. "I really don't know. I am extremely uncomfortable, but I suppose it's partly my circumstances."

"Lord, do you call these circumstances—all these queer things? I have seen the doctor. Mrs Middlemas is an old friend of mine; and when I come to town I always go to see her. It was from her I learned this morning that you were here in this state. We had begun by rejoicing over the new prospects of peace; and from that, of course, we had got to lamenting the numbers of young men who are to enter upon it with lost limbs and shattered health. It happened that Mrs Middlemas mentioned several of her husband's patients as examples, and yourself among the number. You were a remarkable young man, miserably sick, without family or friends, and with no asylum but a suffocating little closet in a noisy hotel. You may imagine that I pricked up my ears, and asked your baptismal name. Dr Middlemas came in and told me. Your name is luckily an uncommon one: it's absurd to suppose that there could be two Ferdinand Masons. In short, I felt that you were my husband's brother's child, and that at last I too might have my little turn at hero-nursing. The little that the Doctor knew of your history agreed with the little I knew, though I confess I was sorry to hear that you had never spoken of our relationship. But why should you? At all events you have got to acknowledge it now. I regret your not having said something about it before, only because the Doctor might have brought us together a month ago, and you would now have been well."

"It will take more than a month to make me well," said Mason, feeling that, if Mrs Mason intended to exert herself on his behalf, she should know the real state of the case. "I never spoke of you, because I had quite lost sight of you. I supposed you were still in Europe; and indeed," he added, after a moment's hesitation, "I heard that you had married again."

"Of course you did," said Mrs Mason, placidly. "I used to hear it once a month myself. But I had a much better right to suppose that you were married. Thank heaven, however, there's nothing of that sort between us. We can each do as we please. I promise to cure you in a month, in spite of yourself."

"What's your remedy?" asked the young man, with a smile very courteous, considering how sceptical it was.

"My first remedy is to take you out of this horrible *trou*. I talked it all over with Dr Middlemas. He says you must get into the country. Why, my dear boy, this is enough to kill you outright—one Broadway outside of your window and another outside of your door! Listen to me. My house is directly on the Hudson—only a matter of two hours by rail. You know I have no children. My only companion is my niece, Caroline Hofmann. You shall come and stay with us until you are as strong as you need be—if it takes twenty years. You shall have sweet, cool air, and proper food, and excellent attendance, and the devotion of a sensible woman. I shall not listen to a word of objection. You shall do as you please, get up when you please, dine when you please, go to bed when you please, and say what you please. I shall ask nothing of you but to let yourself be 'done for.' Do you remember how, when you were a boy at school, after your father's death, you were taken with measles, and your uncle had you brought to our own house? I helped to nurse you myself, and I remember what nice manners you had in the very midst of your measles. Your uncle was very fond of you; and if he had had any considerable property of his own I know he would have remembered you in his will. But of course he couldn't leave away his wife's money.

What I wish to do for you is a very small part of what he
would have done, if he had only lived and heard of your gallantry and your sufferings. So it's settled. I shall go home this
afternoon. To-morrow morning I shall despatch my servant
to you with instructions. He's a highly respectable Englishman,
he thoroughly knows his business, and he will put up your
things and save you every particle of trouble. You have only
to let yourself be dressed and driven to the train. I shall, of
course, meet you at your journey's end. Now don't tell me you
are not strong enough."

"I feel stronger at this moment than I have felt in a dozen
weeks," said Mason. "It's useless for me to attempt to thank
you."

"Quite useless. I shouldn't listen to you. And I suppose,"
added Mrs Mason, looking over the bare walls and scanty
furniture of the room, "you pay a fabulous price for this bower
of bliss. Do you need money?"

The young man shook his head.

"Very well, then," resumed Mrs Mason, conclusively,
"from this moment you are my property."

The young man lay speechless from the very fulness of his
heart; but he strove by the pressure of his fingers to give her
some assurance of his gratitude. His companion rose, and lingered beside him, drawing on her glove, and smiling quietly
with the look of a long-baffled philanthropist who has at last
discovered an infinite opportunity. Poor Ferdinand's weary
visage reflected her smile. Finally, after a lapse of years, he too
was being cared for. He let his head sink into the pillow, and
silently inhaled the fragrance of her good manners and good
nature. He was on the point of taking her dress in his hand and
asking her not to leave him—now that solitude would be so
much more dismal. His eyes, I suppose, betrayed this touching
apprehension—doubly touching in a war-wasted young officer. As she prepared to bid him farewell, Mrs Mason stooped
and kissed his forehead. He listened to the rustle of her dress

across the carpet, to the gentle closing of the door and to her retreating footsteps. And then, giving way to his weakness, he put his hands over his face and cried like a homesick schoolboy. He had been reminded of the exquisite side of life.

Matters went forward as Mrs Mason had arranged them. At six o'clock on the following evening Ferdinand found himself deposited at one of the small stations of the Hudson River railroad, exhausted by his journey and yet excited at the prospect of its drawing to a close. Mrs Mason was in waiting in a low basket-phaeton, with a magazine of cushions and coverlets. Ferdinand transferred himself to her side, and they drove rapidly homeward. Mrs Mason's house was a commodious villa, with a circular lawn, a sinuous avenue and a well-grown plantation of shrubbery. As the phaeton drew up before the porch a young lady appeared in the doorway. Mason will be forgiven if he regarded himself as presented *ex officio*, as I may say, to this young lady. Before he really knew it, and in the absence of the servant who, under Mrs Mason's directions, was busy in the background with his luggage, he had availed himself of her proffered arm, and had allowed her to assist him through the porch, across the hall, and into the parlour, where she graciously consigned him to a sofa which, for his especial use, she had caused to be wheeled up before a fire lighted for his especial comfort. He was unable, however, to take advantage of her good offices. Prudence dictated that without further delay he should betake himself to his room.

II

On the morning after his arrival he got up early, and made an attempt to be present at breakfast; but his strength failed him, and he was obliged to dress at his leisure and content himself with a simple transition from his bed to his arm-chair. The apartment assigned him was designedly on the ground-floor, so that he was spared all struggles with the staircase—a charming room, brightly carpeted and upholstered, and marked by a certain fastidious freshness which betrayed the uncontested dominion of women. It had a broad, high window, draped in chintz and crisp muslin and opening upon the greenery of the lawn. At this window, wrapped in his dressing-gown, and lost in the embrace of the most facile of arm-chairs, he slowly discussed his simple repast. Before long his hostess made her appearance on the lawn outside the window. As this quarter of the house was covered with warm sunshine Mason ventured to open the window and talk to her, while she stood on the grass beneath her parasol.

"It's time to think of your physician," she said. "You shall choose for yourself. The great man here is Dr Gregory, a practitioner of the old school. We have had him but once, for my niece and I have the health of dairy-maids. On that one occasion he—well, he made a fool of himself. His practice is among the 'old families,' and he only knows how to treat certain old-fashioned, obsolete complaints. Anything brought about by the war would be quite out of his range. And then he vacillates, and talks about his own maladies à lui. And, to tell the truth, we had a little repartee which makes our relations somewhat ambiguous."

"I see he would never do," said Mason, laughing. "But he's not your only physician?"

"No: there is a young man, a new-comer, a Dr Knight, whom I don't know, but of whom I have heard very good things. I confess that I have a prejudice in favour of the new generation. Dr Knight has a position to establish, and I suppose he's likely to be especially attentive and careful. I believe, moreover, that he has been a surgeon in the army."

"I knew a man of his name," said Mason. "I wonder if this is he. His name was Horace Knight—a fair-haired, near-sighted man."

"I don't know," Mrs Mason replied; "perhaps Caroline knows." She retreated a few steps, and called to an upper window. "Caroline, what is Dr Knight's first name?"

Mason listened to Miss Hofmann's answer—"I haven't the least idea."

"Is it Horace?"

"I don't know."

"Is he light or dark?"

"I have never seen him."

"Is he near-sighted?"

"How in the world should I know?"

"I suspect he's as good as anyone," said Ferdinand. "With you, my dear aunt, what does the doctor matter?"

Mrs Mason accordingly sent for Dr Knight, who, on arrival, turned out to be her nephew's old acquaintance. Although the young men had been united by no greater intimacy than the superficial comradeship resulting from a winter in neighbouring quarters, they were well pleased to come together again. Horace Knight was a young man of good birth, good looks, good faculties and good intentions, who, after a three years' practice of surgery in the army, had undertaken to seek his fortune—since evidently none was to come to him unsought—in Mrs Mason's neighbourhood. His mother, a widow with a small income, had recently removed to the country for economy, and her son had been unwilling to allow her to live alone. This long-settled, almost legendary region, moreover, offered a promising field for a man of energy—a field well stocked with large families of easy income and of those conservative habits which lead people to feel their pulse and look at each other's tongues. The local practitioner had survived the glory of his prime, and was not, perhaps, entirely guiltless of Mrs Mason's charge that he had not kept up with the progress of the new diseases. The world, in fact, was getting too new for him, as well as for his old patients. He had had money invested in the South—precious sources of revenue, which the war had swallowed up at a gulp; he had grown frightened and nervous and querulous; he had lost his presence of mind and his spectacles in several important conjuctures; he had been repeatedly and distinctly quite out of his reckoning; a vague dissatisfaction pervaded the breasts of his patrons; he was without competitors: in short, fortune was propitious to Dr Knight. Mason remembered the young surgeon only as an amusing and intelligent companion; but he soon had reason to believe that his medical skill would leave nothing to be desired. He arrived rapidly at a clear understanding of Ferdinand's condition; he asked intelligent questions, and gave simple and definite instructions. The disorder was obstinate and virulent, but there was no apparent reason why care and prudence should not subdue it.

"Your strength is very much reduced," he said, as he took his hat and gloves to go; "but you must have an excellent constitution. It seems to me, however—if you will pardon my saying so—to be partly your own fault that you have sunk so low. You have opposed no resistance; you haven't cared to get well."

"I confess I haven't—particularly. But I don't see how you should know it."

"Oh, I know everything."

"Well, it was natural enough. Until Mrs Mason discovered me, I hadn't a friend in the world. I had become demoralised by solitude. I had almost forgotten the difference between sickness and health. I had nothing before my eyes to remind me of what people are supposed to live for—of motives and interests for the sake of which a man continues in health and recovers from disease. I had forgotten that I ever cared for work or play, or anything but the preservation of my miserable carcass. My carcass had become quite too miserable to be an object worth living for. I was losing time and money at an appalling rate; I was getting worse rather than better; and I therefore gave up resistance. It seemed better to die easy than to die hard. I put this all in the past tense, because within these three days I have become quite another man."

"I wish very much I had known about you," said Knight. "I would have made you come home with me, if I could have done nothing else. It was certainly not a rose-coloured prospect. But what do you say now?" he continued, looking round the room. "I never have seen anything so pink."

Mason assented with an eloquent smile.

"I congratulate you cordially. Mrs Mason—if you don't mind my speaking of her—is so thoroughly (and, I should suppose, incorrigibly) philanthropic that it's quite a surprise to find her extremely sensible."

"Yes; and so practical and successful," said Ferdinand, "that it's quite a surprise to find her philanthropic. She's a dear woman."

"But I should say that your especial blessing was your servant. He looks as if he had come out of an English novel."

"My especial blessing! You haven't seen Miss Hofmann, then?"

"Yes: I met her in the hall. She looks as if she had come out of an American novel. I don't know that that's great praise; but, at all events, I make her come out of it."

"You are bound in honour then," said Mason, laughing, "to put her into another."

Mason's impression that he was now very happy needed no enforcement at the Doctor's hands. He felt that it would be his own fault if these quiet, irresponsible days were not among the most delightful of his life. He determined to give himself up without a stint to mere convalescence, utterly to vegetate. His illness alone would have been excuse enough for his simply floating with the tide; but Mason had other reasons for idleness. For three years he had been stretched without intermission on the rack of duty. Although constantly exposed to hard service, it had been his fortune never to receive a serious wound; and, until his health broke down, he had taken fewer holidays than

any officer of Volunteers. With an abundance of a certain kind
of equanimity and self-control—a faculty of ready self-
adaptation to the accomplished fact, in any direction—he was
yet in his secret soul a singularly nervous, over-scrupulous
being. On the few occasions when he had been absent from
the scene of his military duties, although duly authorised and
warranted in the act, he had suffered so acutely from the apprehension that something was happening, or was about to happen (some chance for distinction, some augmentation of
honour), which not to have witnessed or to have had a hand
in would be matter of eternal regret that he can be barely said
to have enjoyed his recreation. The sense of lost time was,
moreover, his perpetual bugbear—the feeling that precious
hours were now fleeting uncounted, which in more congenial
labours would suffice for making a lasting mark. This feeling
he strove to propitiate as much as possible by assiduous reading
and study, in the loathsome leisure of winter-quarters. I cite
the fact merely as an evidence of the uninterrupted austerity of
his life for a long time before he was laid up. I might triple this
period, indeed, by a glance at his college-years, and at certain
busy months which intervened between this close of his youth
and the opening of the war. Mason had always laboured. He
was fond of work, to begin with; and, in addition, the complete
absence of family-ties had allowed him to follow his tastes
without hindrance or criticism. This circumstance had been at
once a great gain to him and a serious loss. He reached his
twenty-seventh year a very accomplished scholar, as scholars
go, but a great dunce in certain social matters. He was quite
ignorant of all those lighter and more evanescent branches of
science attached to being somebody's son, brother or cousin.
At last, however, as he reminded himself, he was to discover
what it was to be the nephew of somebody's husband. Mrs
Mason was to teach him the meaning of the adjective *domestic*.
It would have been hard to learn it in a pleasanter way. Mason
felt that he should extract some instruction from his idleness

itself, and should probably leave the house a wiser as well as a better man. It became probable, thanks to that quickening of the faculties which accompanies the exercise of the domestic affections, that in this last respect he would not be disappointed. Very few days sufficed to reveal to him the many excellent qualities of his hostess—her warm capacious heart, her fairness of mind, her good temper, her good taste, her large fund of experience and reminiscence, and, indeed, more than all, a certain passionate devotedness, to which fortune, in leaving her a childless widow, had done but scant justice. The two accordingly established a friendship—a friendship that promised as well for the happiness of each as any that ever undertook to meddle with that province. If I were telling my story from Mrs Mason's point of view, I might make a very good thing of the statement that this lady had regularly determined to be very fond of my hero; but I am compelled to let it stand in this simple shape. Excellent, charming person that she was, she had every right to the satisfaction which belonged to a liberal yet not exaggerated estimate of her guest. She had divined him— so much the better for her. That it was very much the better for him is obviously one of the elementary facts of my narrative; a fact of which Mason became so rapidly and completely aware that he stopped thinking about it, as one ceases to think of an article of faith.

III

In the space of ten days, then, most of the nebulous impressions produced by change of scene had gathered into substantial form. Others, however, were still in the nebulous state— diffusing a gentle light upon Ferdinand's path. Chief among these was the mild radiance of which Miss Hofmann was the centre. For three days after his arrival Mason had been confined

to his room by the fatigue and fever which inevitably followed
his journey. It was not till the fourth day, therefore, that he
was able to renew the acquaintance so auspiciously com-
menced. When at last, at dinner-time, he reappeared in the
drawing-room, Miss Hofmann greeted him almost as an old
friend. Mason had already discovered that she was young and
conciliatory; he now rapidly advanced to the perception that
she was uncommonly pretty. Before dinner was over he had
made up his mind that she was a lovely being. Mrs Mason had
found time to give him a full account of her life. She had lost
her mother in infancy, and had been adopted by her aunt in the
early years of this lady's widowhood. Her father was a man of
evil habits—a drunkard, a gambler, a rake, outlawed from
decent society. His only dealings with his daughter were to
write her every month or two a begging letter, her mother's
property having been settled on the girl. Mrs Mason had taken
her niece to Europe, and given her every advantage. She had
had an expensive education; she had travelled; she had gone
into the world; she had been presented, like a good republican,
to sundry European sovereigns; she had been admired; she
had had half-a-dozen offers of marriage, to her aunt's knowledge, and others, perhaps, of which she was ignorant, and had
refused them all. She was now twenty-five years of age, beautiful, accomplished and conscious of good investments. She was
an excellent girl, with a will of her own. "I am very fond of
her," Mrs Mason remarked, "and I suppose she is equally fond
of me; but we long ago gave up all idea of playing at mother
and daughter. We have never had a disagreement since she was
fifteen years old; but we have never had an agreement either.
Caroline isn't clinging or dependent. She is honest, good-
tempered, and perfectly discriminating. She foresaw that we
were still to spend a number of years together, and she wisely
declined at the outset to affect a range of feelings that wouldn't
stand the wear and tear of time. She knew that she should make
a poor daughter, and she contented herself with being a good

niece. I never interfere with her life. She has it quite in her own hands. My position is little more than an affectionate curiosity as to what she will do with it. Of course she will marry, sooner or later; but I am curious to see the man of her choice. In Europe, you know, girls have no acquaintances but such as they share with their parents and guardians; and in that way I know most of the gentlemen who have tried to make themselves acceptable to my niece. There were some nice young men in that number; but there was not one—or, rather, there was but one—for whom Caroline cared a straw. That one she liked, I believe; but they had a quarrel, and she lost him. She has a very nice way of arranging such matters. I am sure no girl ever before got rid of so many admirers with so few scenes of violence. Ah, she's a dear, good girl!" Mrs Mason pursued. "She has saved me infinite trouble in my day. And when I think what she might have been, with her beauty and her little fortune! She has kept all her *prétendants* as friends. There are two of them who write to her still. She doesn't answer their letters; but once in a while she meets them, and thanks them for writing, and that contents them. The others are married, and Caroline remains single. I suppose it won't last for ever. Still, although she isn't one of the yearning sort, she won't marry a man she doesn't care for, merely because she's growing old. Indeed it's only the sentimental girls, to my belief, that do that. They covet a man for his money or his family, and then give the feeling some fine name. But there's one thing, Mr Ferdinand," added Mrs Mason, at the end of these remarks, "you will be so good as not to fall in love with my niece. I can assure you that she will not fall in love with you, and a hopeless passion will not hasten your recovery. Caroline is a civilised woman; you can live with her very well without that. She is good for common daylight, and you'll have no need of wax-candles and ecstasies."

"Be easy in your mind," said Ferdinand, laughing. "I'm quite too attentive to myself at present to think of any one else.

Miss Hofmann might be dying for a glance of my eye, and I shouldn't hesitate to sacrifice her. To fall in love a man must be all there, and you see I am not."

At the end of ten days summer had fairly set in; and Mason found it possible, and indeed profitable, to spend a large portion of his time in the open air. He was unable either to ride or to walk, and the only form of exercise which he found practicable was an occasional drive in Mrs Mason's phaeton. On these occasions Mrs Mason was his usual companion. The neighbourhood offered an interminable succession of beautiful drives; and poor Ferdinand took an immense satisfaction in reclining idly upon a pile of cushions, warmly clad, empty-handed, silent, with only his eyes in motion, and rolling rapidly between fragrant hedges and springing crops, and beside the outskirts of woods, and along the heights which overlooked the river. Detested war was over, and all nature had ratified the peace. Mason used to gaze up into the cloudless sky until his eyes began to water, and you would have actually supposed he was shedding sentimental tears. Besides these passive wanderings with his hostess, he had adopted another method of inhaling the sunshine. He used frequently to spend several hours at a time on the verandah beside the house, sheltered from the observation of visitors. Here, with an arm-chair and a footstool, a cigar and half-a-dozen volumes of novels, to say nothing of the society of either of the ladies, and sometimes of both, he suffered the mornings to pass unmeasured and uncounted. The chief incident of these mornings was the Doctor's visit, in which, of course, there was a strong element of prose—and very good prose, as I may add, for the Doctor was turning out an excellent fellow. But, for the rest, the summer unrolled itself like a gentle strain of music. Mason knew so little, from direct observation, of the *vie intime* of cultivated, intelligent women, that their habits, their manners, their household motions, possessed in his view all the charm of a spectacle—a spectacle which he watched with the indolence of an invalid, the sympathy of a man of taste, and a little of the awkwardness which women gladly allow, and indeed encourage, in a soldier, for the pleasure of forgiving it. It was a very simple matter to Miss Hofmann that she should be charmingly dressed, that her hands should be white and her attitudes felicitous: these things for her had long since become mechanical. But to Mason, who was familiar only with books and men, they were objects of constant, half-dreamy contemplation. He would sit for half-an-hour at once, with a book on his knees and the pages unturned, scrutinising with ingenious indirectness the agreeable combination of colour and outline which made up the physical personality of Miss Hofmann. There was no question as to her beauty, or as to its being a warm, sympathetic quality, and not a conventional, superficial perfection. She was the least bit taller than most women, and had an appearance of activity. Her hair was of a dark and lustrous brown, turning almost to black, and lending itself readily to those multitudinous ringlets which were then in fashion. Her forehead was rather high and very clear, and her eyes were of that pure sea-green which you may observe of a summer's afternoon when the declining sun shines through the crest of a wave. Her complexion was the hue of perfect health. These, with her full, mild lips, her generous and flexible figure, her magnificent hands, were items numerous enough to occupy Mason's attention, and it was but seldom that he allowed it to be diverted. Mrs Mason was frequently called away by her household cares, but Miss Hofmann's time was apparently quite her own. Nevertheless, it came into Ferdinand's head one day that she gave him her company only from a sense of duty, and when, according to his wont, he had allowed this impression to ripen in his mind, he ventured to assure her that, much as he delighted in her society, he should be sorry to believe that her gracious bestowal of it interfered with more profitable occupation. "I am no companion," he said. "I don't pretend to be one. I sit here deaf and dumb, and blind and halt, patiently waiting to be healed—waiting till vagabond Nature strolls my way and brushes me with the hem of her garment."

"You don't tire me at all," Miss Hofmann had been good enough to reply on this occasion. "What do you take me for? The hero of a hundred fights, a young man who has been reduced to a shadow in the service of his country—I should be very fastidious if I asked for anything better."

"Oh, if it's on theory!" said Mason. And, in spite of Miss Hofmann's protest, he continued to assume that it *was* on theory that she continued to look after him. But she stuck to her post, and with a sort of placid inveteracy which seemed to the young man to betray either a great deal of indifference or a great deal of self-command. "She thinks I am stupid," he said to himself. "Of course she thinks me stupid. How should she think otherwise? She and her aunt have talked me over; Mrs Mason has enumerated my virtues, and Miss Hofmann has added them up: total, a rather amiable bore. She has armed herself with patience. I must say it becomes her very well." Nothing was more natural, however, than that Mason should exaggerate the effect of his social incapacity. His remarks were desultory, but not infrequent; often trivial, but always good-humoured and easy to meet. The intervals of silence, indeed, which enlivened his conversation with Miss Hofmann, might have been taken for the natural, familiar pauses in the talk of old friends.

IV

ONCE in a while she would sit down at the piano and play to him. The verandah communicated with the little sitting-room by means of a long window, one side of which stood open. Mason would move his chair to this aperture, so that he might see the music as well as hear it. Seated at the instrument, at the farther end of the half-darkened room, with her figure in half-profile, and her features, her movements, the colour of her dress, but half defined in the cool obscurity, Miss Hofmann would wake up the echoes of Schubert and Mendelssohn. Mason's eyes rested awhile on the vague white folds of her dress, on the heavy convolutions of her hair, and the gentle movement of her head in sympathy with the music; then a glance in the other direction revealed another picture—the dazzling mid-day sky, the close-cropped lawn, lying almost black in its light, and the patient, round-backed gardener, in white shirt-sleeves, clipping the hedge or rolling the gravel. One morning, what with the music, the light, the heat, and the fragrance of the flowers—from the perfect equilibrium of his senses, as it were—Ferdinand fell into a doze. On waking he found that he had slept an hour, and that the sun had invaded the verandah. The music had ceased; but on looking into the parlour he saw Miss Hofmann still at the piano. A gentleman was leaning on the instrument, with his back toward the window, intercepting her face. Mason sat for some moments, hardly sensible, at first, of his transition to consciousness, languidly guessing at her companion's identity. In a short time his observation was quickened by the fact that the picture before him was animated by no sound of voices. The silence was odd—almost unnatural. Mason moved his chair, and the gentleman, looking round, showed the face of Horace Knight. The Doctor called out "Good morning!" from his place, and finished his conversation with Miss Hofmann before coming out to his patient. When he moved away from the piano Mason saw the reason of his friends' silence. Miss Hofmann had been trying to decipher a difficult piece of music, the Doctor had been trying to assist her, and they had both been brought to a stop.

"What a clever fellow he is!" thought Mason. "There he stands, rattling off musical terms as if he had never thought of anything else. And yet when he talks pathology, it's impossible to talk more to the point." Mason continued to be very well satisfied with Knight's handling of his ailments. He had been in the country now for three weeks, and he would hesitate indeed to say that he felt materially better; but he had a much higher standard. There were moments when he feared to inquire too closely, because he had a sickening apprehension that he should discover that in one or two important particulars he was not what he should be. In the course of time he imparted these fears to his physician. "But I may be mistaken," he added, "and for this reason. During the last fortnight I have become much more difficult. So long as I was in that beastly hotel I accepted each additional symptom as a matter of course. The more the better, I thought. But now I expect them to give an account of themselves. Now I have a positive wish to recover."

Dr Knight looked at his patient for a moment curiously. "You are right," he said; "a little impatience is a very good thing."

"Oh, I am not impatient. I am patient to a ridiculous extent. I allow myself six months, at the very least."

"That is certainly not unreasonable," said Knight. "And will you allow me a question? Do you think of spending those six months in this place?"

"How can I tell you? I suppose I shall finish the summer here, unless the summer finishes me. Mrs Mason will hear of nothing else. In September I hope to be well enough to go back to town, even if I am not well enough to think of work. What do you advise?"

"I advise you to put away the very name of work. That is imperative. Haven't you been at work all your life long? Can't you spare a pitiful little twelvemonth to recuperation and enjoyment?"

"Ah, enjoyment, enjoyment!" said Mason, ironically.

"Yes, enjoyment," returned the Doctor. "What has it done to you that you should speak of it in that manner?"

"Oh, it bothers me," said Mason.

"You are very fastidious. It's better to be bothered by pleasure than by pain."

"I don't deny it. But there is a way of being indifferent to pain. I don't mean to say that I have found it out, but in the course of my illness I have caught a glimpse of it. But it's beyond my strength to be indifferent to pleasure. In two words, I am afraid of dying of kindness."

"Ah, gammon!"

"Yes, it's gammon; and yet it's not. There would be nothing miraculous in my not getting well."

"It will be your fault if you don't. It will prove that you are fonder of being sick than of being sound, and that you're not fit company for reasonable mortals. Shall I tell you?" continued the Doctor, after a moment's hesitation. "When I knew you in the army I always found you a peg beyond my comprehension. You took things too hard. You had questions and considerations about everything. And on top of it all you were devoured with a mania for appearing to take things easily and not trouble your head. You played your part very well, but you must do me justice to confess that it *was* a part."

"I hardly know whether that's a compliment or an impertinence. I hope, at least, that you don't mean to accuse me of playing a part at the present moment."

"On the contrary. I am your medical adviser; you are frank."

"It's not because you're my medical adviser that I am frank," said Mason. "I shouldn't think of bothering you in that capacity with my miserable caprices and whims;" and Ferdinand paused a moment. "You're a man!" he pursued, laying his hand on his companion's arm. "There's nothing here but women—heaven reward them! I am saturated with whispers and perfumes and smiles, and the rustling of dresses. It takes a man to understand a man."

"It takes more than a man to understand you, my dear Mason," said Knight, with a kindly smile. "But I will try."

Mason remained silent, leaning back in his chair, with his eyes wandering slowly over the wide patch of sky disclosed by the window, and his hands languidly folded on his knees. The Doctor examined him with a look half amused, half perplexed. But at last his face grew more stern and a little fold appeared in his forehead. He placed his hand on Mason's arm and shook it gently, while Ferdinand met his gaze. The Doctor frowned, and, as he did so, his companion gave a vague, scarcely audible, rather foolish, laugh. "If you don't get well," said Knight,— "if you don't get well——" And he paused.

"What will be the consequence?" asked Ferdinand, still laughing.

"I shall hate you; I shall think you did it on purpose."

"What shall I care for your hating me?"

"I shall tell people that you were a poor spiritless creature —that you are no loss."

"I give you leave," said Ferdinand.

The Doctor got up. "I don't like patients who are so mysterious," he said.

Ferdinand began to laugh louder, and ended in a fit of coughing.

"I'm getting too amusing," Knight remarked; "I must go."

"Laugh and grow fat," exclaimed Ferdinand. "I promise to get well." But that evening, at least, he was no better, as it turned out, for his momentary exhilaration. Before turning in for the night he went into the drawing-room to spend half-an-hour with the ladies. The room was empty, but the lamp was lighted, and he sat down by the table and read a chapter in a novel. He felt excited, light-headed, light-hearted, half-intoxicated, as if he had been drinking strong coffee. He put down his book, and went over to the mantelpiece, above which hung a mirror, and looked at the reflection of his face. For almost the first time in his life he examined it, wondering considerably if there was anything in it. He was able to say to himself only that he looked very thin and pale, and utterly unfit for the business of life. At last he heard an opening of doors overhead, and a rustling of voluminous skirts on the stairs. Mrs Mason came in, fresh from the hands of her maid, and dressed for a party.

V

"AND is Miss Hofmann going?" asked Mason. He felt that his heart was beating and that he hoped Mrs Mason would say no. His momentary sense of strength, the mellow lamplight, the open piano, and the absence of the excellent woman before him, struck him as so many reasons for her remaining at home. But the sound of the young lady's step upon the stairs was not encouraging. She forthwith appeared upon the threshold, dressed in crape of a kind of violent blue, with desultory clusters of white roses. For some ten minutes Mason had the pleasure of watching that series of pretty movements and preparations with which women in full dress beguile the interval before their carriage is announced; their glances at the mirror, their slow assumption of their gloves, their mutual revisions and felicitations.

"Isn't she lovely?" said Miss Hofmann to the young man, nodding at her aunt, who looked precisely the handsome woman that she was.

"Lovely, lovely, lovely!" said Ferdinand, so emphatically, that Miss Hofmann transferred her glance to him; while Mrs Mason good-humouredly turned her back, and Caroline saw that Mason was engaged in a survey of her own person.

"I wish very much you might come," the girl said.

"I shall go to bed," answered Ferdinand, simply.

"Well, that's much better. We shall go to bed at two o'clock. Meanwhile I shall caper about the rooms to the sound of a piano and fiddle, and Aunt Maria will sit against the wall with her toes tucked under a chair. Such is life!"

"You will dance then," said Mason, not very brilliantly.

"I shall dance. Dr Knight has invited me."

"Does he dance well, Caroline?" asked Mrs Mason.

"That remains to be seen. I have a strong suspicion that he doesn't."

"Why?" Ferdinand inquired.

"He does so many other things well."

"That's no reason," said Mrs Mason. "Do you dance, Ferdinand?"

"The dance of death!" Mason murmured.

"I like a man to dance," said Caroline, "and yet I like him not to dance."

"That's a very womanish speech, my dear," Mrs Mason rejoined.

"I suppose it is. It's inspired by my white gloves, my low dress, my artificial roses. When once a woman gets on such things, Colonel Mason, expect nothing but nonsense.—Aunt Maria," the young lady continued, "will you button my glove?"

"Let me do it," said Ferdinand. "Your Aunt has her gloves on."

"Thank you." And Miss Hofmann extended a long white arm, and drew back with her other hand the bracelet from her wrist. Her glove had a succession of buttons, and Mason performed the operation with great deliberation and neatness.

"And now," said he gravely, "I hear the carriage. You want me to put on your shawl."

"If you please." Miss Hofmann passed her white cloak into his hands, and then turned about her fair shoulders. Mason solemnly covered them, while the waiting-maid, who had come in, performed the same service for the elder lady.

"Good-bye," said the latter, giving him her hand. "You are not to come out into the air." And Mrs Mason, attended by her maid, transferred herself to the carriage. Miss Hofmann gathered up her loveliness and prepared to follow. Ferdinand stood leaning against the parlour-door, watching her; and as she rustled past him she nodded farewell, with a silent smile. A characteristic smile, Mason thought it,—a smile in which there was no expectation of triumph and no affectation of reluctance, but just the faintest suggestion of perfectly good-humoured resignation. Mason went to the window and saw the carriage roll away with its lighted lamps, and then stood looking out into the darkness. The sky was cloudy. As he turned away the maid-servant came in, and took from the table a pair of rejected gloves. "I hope you are feeling better, sir," she said, politely.

"Thank you; I think I am."

"It's a pity you couldn't have gone with the ladies."

"I am not well enough yet to think of such things," said Mason, trying to smile. But as he walked across the floor he felt himself attacked by a sudden sensation which cannot be better described than as a general collapse. He felt dizzy, faint, and sick. His head swam and his knees trembled. "I am very ill," he said, sitting down on the sofa; "you must call William."

William speedily arrived, and conducted the young man to his room. "What on earth have you been doing, sir?" asked this most irreproachable of serving-men, as he helped him to undress.

Ferdinand was silent a moment. "I have been putting on Miss Hofmann's shawl," he said.

"Is that all, sir?"

"And I have been buttoning her glove."

"Well, sir, you must be very prudent."

"So it appears," said Ferdinand.

He slept soundly, however, and the next morning was the better for it. "I certainly am better," he said to himself, as he slowly proceeded to his toilet. "A month ago such an attack as that of last evening would have given me a fever. Courage, then! The devil isn't dead, but he's dying."

In the afternoon he received a visit from Horace Knight. "So you danced last evening at Mrs Bradshaw's," he said to his friend.

"Yes, I jumped about a little. It's a great piece of frivolity for a man in my position; but I thought there would be no harm in doing it just once, to show them I know how. My abstinence in future will tell the better. Your ladies were there. I danced with Miss Hofmann. She was dressed in blue, and she was the most beautiful woman in the room. Every one was crowding round her."

"I saw her before she went off," Mason said.

"You should have seen her there," Knight went on. "The music, the excitement, the spectators, and all that, bring out a woman's beauty."

"So I suppose."

"What strikes me," pursued the Doctor, "is her—what shall I call it?—her vitality, her quiet buoyancy. Of course, you didn't see her when she came home. If you had you would have noticed, unless I am very much mistaken, that she was as fresh and elastic at two o'clock as she had been at ten. While all the other women looked tired and jaded and used up, she alone showed no signs of exhaustion. She was neither pale nor flushed, but still light-footed, rosy, erect. She's a capital one to go. You see I can't help looking at such things rather professionally. She has a magnificent organisation. Among all those other poor girls she seemed to have something of the inviolable strength of a goddess;" and Knight smiled, himself, at this unexpected flight. "She wears her artificial roses and dew-drops as if she had gathered them on the mountain-tops instead of buying them in Broadway. She moves with long steps, her dress rustles, and to a man of fancy it's the sound of Diana on the forest-leaves."

Ferdinand nodded assent. "So you are a man of fancy."

"In my private capacity," said the Doctor.

VI

FERDINAND was not inclined to question his friend's estimate of Miss Hofmann or to weigh his words. They only served to confirm an impression which was already strong in his own mind. Day by day he had felt the growth of this impression. "He must be a strong man who would approach her," he said to himself. "He must be as swift and sure as she herself, or in the progress of courtship she will leave him far behind. He must be able to forget his lungs and his liver and his digestion. To have broken down in his country's defence, even, will avail him nothing. What is that to her? She needs a man who has defended his country without breaking down—a being complete, intact, well-seasoned, invulnerable. Then—then," thought Ferdinand, "perhaps she will consider him. Perhaps it will be to refuse him. Perhaps, like Diana, to whom Knight compares her, she is meant to live without us fellows. It's certain, at least, that she is able to wait. She will be young at fifty-five. Women who are young at fifty-five are perhaps not the most sympathetic. They are likely to have felt for nobody and for nothing. But it's often less their own fault than that of the men and women around them. This one at least *can* feel; the thing is to move her. Her soul is an instrument of a hundred strings, only it will take a strong hand to draw sound. Once really touched, they will reverberate for ever and ever."

In a word, Mason began to romance to himself exactly as if he had been in love, and there is no manner of doubt that he was. It will be seen that his passion was not arrogant nor uncompromising, but, on the contrary, considerate, discreet, modest—almost timid. For ten long days, the most memorable days of his life—days which, if he had kept a journal, would have been left blank—he held his tongue. He would have suffered everything rather than reveal his emotions, or allow them to come accidentally to Miss Hofmann's knowledge. He would cherish them in silence until he should feel in all his sinews that he was himself again, and then he would open his heart. Meanwhile he would be patient; he would be the most irreproachable, the most austere, the most insignificant of convalescents. He was as yet unfit to touch her, to look at her, to speak to her. A man was not to go a-wooing in his dressing-gown and slippers.

There came a day, however, when, in spite of his vigilance, Ferdinand came near losing his balance. Mrs Mason had arranged with him to drive in the phaeton after dinner. But it befell that, an hour before the appointed time, she was sent for by a neighbour who had been taken ill.

"But it's out of the question that you should lose your drive," said Miss Hofmann, who brought him her aunt's apologies. "If you are still disposed to go I shall be happy to take the reins. I shall not be as good company as Aunt Maria, but perhaps I shall be as good company as Thomas." It was settled, accordingly, that Miss Hofmann should act as her aunt's substitute, and at five o'clock the phaeton left the door. The first half of their drive was passed in silence; and almost the first words they exchanged fell from their lips as they finally drew near a tract of enclosed land, beyond which, through the trees at its further extremity, they caught a glimpse of a turn in the river. Miss Hofmann involuntarily pulled up. The sun had sunk low, and the cloudless western sky glowed with an exquisite tone. The trees which concealed the view flung over the grass a great screen of shadow, which reached out into the road. Between their scattered stems gleamed the broad white current of the Hudson. Our friends both knew the spot. Mason had seen it from a boat, when one morning a gentleman in the neighbourhood, thinking to do him a kindness, had invited him to take a short sail; and with Miss Hofmann it had long been a frequent resort.

"How beautiful!" she exclaimed, as the phaeton stopped.

"Yes, if it wasn't for those trees," said Ferdinand. "They conceal the best part of the view."

"I should rather say they indicate it," answered his companion. "From here they conceal it; but they suggest to you to make your way in, and lose yourself behind them, and enjoy the prospect in privacy."

"But you can't take a vehicle in."

"No: there is only a footpath, although I have ridden in. One of these days, when you are stronger, you must drive to this point, and get out, and walk over to the bank."

Mason was silent a moment—a moment during which he felt in his limbs the tremor of a bold resolution. "I noticed the place the day I went out on the water with Mr Masters. I immediately marked it as my own. The bank is quite high, and the trees make a little amphitheatre on its summit. I think there is a bench."

"Yes, there are two benches," said Caroline.

"Suppose, then, we try it now, "said Mason, with an effort.

"But you can never walk over that meadow. You see it's broken ground. And, at all events, I can't consent to your going alone."

"That, madam," said Ferdinand, rising to his feet in the phaeton, "is a piece of folly I should never think of proposing. Yonder is a house, and in it there are people. Can't we drive there, and place the horse in their custody?"

"Nothing is more easy, if you insist upon it. The house is occupied by a poor German family, and there are a couple of children, who are old friends of mine. When I come here on horseback they always clamour for 'coppers.' From their little garden the walk is shorter."

So Miss Hofmann turned the horse toward the cottage, which stood at the head of a lane, a few yards from the road. A little boy and girl, with bare heads and bare feet—the former

extremities very white, and the latter very black—came out to
meet her. Caroline greeted them good-humouredly in German.
The girl, who was the elder, consented to watch the horse,
while the boy volunteered to show the visitors the shortest
way to the Hudson. Mason reached the point in question without extreme fatigue, and found a prospect which would have
repaid even greater trouble. To the right and to the left, a hundred feet below them, stretched the broad channel of the noble
river. In the distance rose the gentle masses of the Catskills,
with all the intervening region vague and neutral in the gathering twilight. A faint odour of coolness came up to their faces
from the stream below.

"You can sit down," said the little boy, doing the honours.

"Yes, Colonel, sit down," said Caroline. "You have already
been on your feet too much."

Ferdinand obediently seated himself, unable to deny that he
was glad to do so. Miss Hofmann released from her grasp the
skirts which she had gathered up in her passage from the
phaeton, and strolled to the edge of the cliff, where she stood
for some moments talking with her little guide. Mason could
only hear that she was speaking German. Presently Miss Hofmann turned back, still talking—or rather listening—to the
child.

"He is very pretty," she said in French, as she stopped before
Ferdinand.

Mason broke into a laugh. "To think that that dirty little
youngster should forbid us the use of two languages! Do you
speak French, my child?"

"No," said the boy sturdily, "I speak German."

"Ah, there I can't follow you!"

The child stared a moment, and then replied, with pardonable irrelevancy, "I will show the way down to the water."

"There I can't follow you either. I hope *you* will not go,
Miss Hofmann," added the young man, observing a movement on Caroline's part.

"Is it hard?" she asked of the child.

"No, it's easy."

"Shall I tear my dress?"

The child shook his head; and Caroline descended the bank under his guidance.

As a certain time elapsed before she reappeared, Ferdinand ventured to the edge of the cliff, and looked down. She was sitting on a rock, on the narrow margin of sand, with her hat in her lap, twisting the feather in her fingers. In a few moments it seemed to Ferdinand that he caught the tones of her voice, wafted upward as if she were gently singing. He listened intently, and at last succeeded in distinguishing several words, they were German. "Confound her German!" thought the young man. Suddenly Miss Hofmann rose from her seat, and, after a short interval, reappeared on the platform. "What did you find down there?" asked Ferdinand, almost savagely.

"Nothing—a little strip of a beach and a pile of stones."

"You *have* torn your dress," said Mason.

Miss Hofmann surveyed her drapery. "Where, if you please?"

"There, in front." And Mason poked out his walking-stick, and inserted it into the injured fold of muslin. There was a certain unexpected violence in the movement which attracted Miss Hofmann's attention. She looked at her companion, and, seeing that his face was discomposed, supposed that he was annoyed at having been compelled to wait.

"Thank you," she said; "it's easily mended. And now suppose we go back."

"No, not yet," said Ferdinand. "We have plenty of time."

"Plenty of time to catch cold," said Miss Hofmann, kindly.

Mason had planted his stick where he had let it fall on withdrawing it from contact with his companion's skirts, and stood leaning against it, with his eyes on the girl's face. "What if I do catch cold?" he asked, abruptly.

"Come, don't talk nonsense," said Miss Hofmann.

"I never was more serious in my life." And, pausing a moment, he drew a couple of steps nearer. She had gathered her mantilla closely about her, and stood with her arms lost in it, holding her elbows. "I don't mean that quite literally," Mason continued. "I wish to get well, on the whole. But there are moments when this perpetual self-coddling seems beneath the dignity of man, and I am tempted to purchase one short hour of enjoyment, of happiness, at the cost—well, at the cost of my life, if necessary!"

This was a richer speech than Ferdinand had yet made; the reader may estimate his habitual reserve. Miss Hofmann must have been somewhat surprised, and even a good deal puzzled. But it was plain that he expected a rejoinder.

"I don't know what temptations you may have had," she answered, smiling; "but I confess that I can think of none in your present circumstances likely to involve the great sacrifice you speak of. What you say, Colonel Mason, is rather——"

"Rather what?"

"Rather ungrateful. Aunt Maria flatters herself that she has made existence as easy and as peaceful for you—as stupid, if you like—as it can possibly be for a—a clever man. And now, after all, to accuse her of introducing temptations!"

"Your Aunt Maria is the best of women, Miss Hofmann," said Mason. "But I am very far from being a clever man. I am deplorably weak-minded. Very little things excite me. Very small pleasures are gigantic temptations. I would give a great deal, for instance, to stay here with you for half-an-hour."

It is a delicate question whether Miss Hofmann now ceased to be perplexed; whether she perceived in the young man's accents—it was his tone, his attitude, his eyes, that were fully significant, rather than his words—an intimation of that sublime and simple truth in the presence of which a wise woman puts off coquetry and prudery, and tries to be human and charitable. But charity is nothing if not discreet; and Miss

Hofmann may very well have effected the little transaction I speak of, and yet have remained, as she did remain, gracefully wrapped in her mantle, with the same serious smile on her face. Ferdinand's heart was thumping under his waistcoat; the words in which he sought to tell her that he loved her were fluttering there like frightened birds in a storm-shaken cage. Whether his lips would form them or not depended on the next words she uttered. On the faintest sign of defiance or of impatience he would really give her something to coquet withal. I repeat that I do not undertake to follow Miss Hofmann's feelings; I only know that her words were those of a woman of superior instincts. "My dear Colonel Mason," she said, "I wish we might remain here the whole evening. Such moments as these are quite too pleasant to be wantonly sacrificed. I simply put you on your conscience. If you believe that you can safely do so—that you will not have some dreadful chill, or fit, or spasm, in consequence—let us by all means stay awhile. If you do not so believe, let us go back to the carriage. There is no good reason that I see for our behaving like very small children."

If Miss Hofmann apprehended a "scene"—I do not assert that she did—she was saved. Mason extracted from her words a refined assurance that he could afford to wait. "You are an angel, Miss Hofmann," he said, as a sign that he had understood her. "I think we had better go back."

Miss Hofmann accordingly led the way along the path, and Ferdinand slowly followed. A man who has submitted to a woman's wisdom generally feels bound to persuade himself that he has capitulated on his own terms. I suppose it was in this spirit that Mason said to himself as he walked along, "Well, I got what I wanted."

VII

THE next morning he was again an invalid. He woke up with
symptoms which as yet he had scarcely felt at all; and he was
obliged to acknowledge the bitter truth that, small as it was,
his effort the day before had exceeded his strength. The walk,
the evening air, the dampness of the spot, had combined to
produce a violent attack of fever. As soon as it became plain
that, in vulgar terms, he was "in for it," he took his heart in
his hands and let himself go. As his condition grew worse, he
was fortunately relieved from the custody of this valuable
organ, with all it contained of hopes deferred and shattered
visions, by several intervals of prolonged unconsciousness.

For three weeks he was a very sick man; for a couple of
days his recovery was doubted of. Mrs Mason nursed him with
inexhaustible patience and with the solicitude of real affection.
She was resolved that greedy death should not possess himself,
through any fault of hers, of a career so full of bright possibilities and of that active gratitude which a good-natured
elderly woman would relish, as she felt that of her *protégé* to be.
Her vigils were finally rewarded. One fine morning poor long-
silent Ferdinand found words to tell her that he was better.
His recovery was very slow, however, and it failed to bring
him back to his old point: it stopped many degrees short of
that. He was thus doubly a convalescent—a sufficiently miserable fellow. He professed to be very much surprised to find
himself still among the living. He remained silent and grave,
with a fresh fold in his forehead, like a man honestly perplexed
at the vagaries of destiny. "It must be," he said to Mrs Mason
—"it must be that I am reserved for great things."

Ferdinand learned that, in order to make the house as quiet
as possible, Miss Hofmann had gone to stay with a friend, at a

distance of some five miles. On the first day that the young man was well enough to sit in his arm-chair Mrs Mason spoke of her niece's return, which was fixed for the morrow. "She will want very much to see you," she said. "When she comes may I bring her into your room?"

"Good heavens, no!" exclaimed Ferdinand, to whom the idea was very repugnant. He met her accordingly at dinner, three days later. He left his room just in time for this repast, in company with Dr Knight, who happened then to be taking his departure. In the hall they encountered Mrs Mason, who invited the Doctor to remain, in honour of his patient's reappearance in society. The Doctor hesitated a moment, and, as he did so, Ferdinand heard Miss Hofmann's step descending the stair. He turned towards her just in time to catch on her face the vanishing glance of intelligence. As Mrs Mason's back was against the staircase, her glance was evidently meant for Knight. He excused himself on the plea of an engagement, to Mason's regret, while the latter greeted the younger lady. Mrs Mason proposed another day—the following Sunday; the Doctor assented, and it was not till some time later that Ferdinand found himself wondering why Miss Hofmann should have told him—in that inaudible way—not to remain. He rapidly perceived that during the period of their separation this young lady had not become any less attractive. It seemed to Mason, moreover, that the ripe cluster of her charms was held together by a certain pensive gentleness, a tender, submissive look, which he had hitherto failed to observe; and some reflections to which Mrs Mason treated him in a day or two persuaded him that he was not the victim of an illusion.

"I wonder what is the matter with Caroline," she said. "If it were not that she tells me that she never was better, I should believe she was going to be ill. Pray, is your sickness catching? I have never seen her so mild and vague. She looks like a person who has a great fright—but a fright not altogether unpleasant."

"She has been staying in a house full of people," said Mason.

"She has been excited, and amused, and preoccupied; she returns to you and me (excuse the juxtaposition—it exists); a kind of reaction asserts itself." Ferdinand's explanation was ingenious rather than plausible.

Mrs Mason had a better one. "I have an impression that George Stapleton, the second of the sons, is an old admirer of Caroline's. It's hard to believe that he could have been in the house with her for a fortnight without renewing his suit in some form or other."

Ferdinand was not made uneasy, for he had seen and talked with Mr George Stapleton—a young man, very good-looking, very good-natured, very clever, very rich, and very unlikely, as he conceived, to be cared for by Miss Hofmann. "You don't mean to say that your niece has listened to him," he answered, calmly enough.

"Listened! yes. He has made himself agreeable, and he has succeeded in making an impression—a temporary impression," added Mrs Mason, with a businesslike air.

"I can't believe it," said Ferdinand

"Why not? He's a very nice fellow."

"Yes—yes," said Mason, "very nice indeed. He is very rich too." And here the talk was interrupted by Caroline's entrance.

On Sunday the two ladies went to church. It was not till after they had gone that Ferdinand left his room. He came into the little parlour, took up a book, felt something of the stir of his old intellectual life. Should he ever again know what it was to measure his mind with something? In the course of an hour the ladies came home with that air of relief and reaction which people wear on emerging from their devotions. Mrs Mason soon went out again, leaving the others together. Miss Hofmann asked Ferdinand what he had been reading; and he was thus led on to declare that he really believed he should, after all, get the use of his head again. She listened with the respect which an intelligent woman who leads an idle life necessarily feels for a clever man when he consents to make her in some degree the confidant of his intellectual purposes. Mason talked with her for half-an-hour and told himself afterwards that he had "swaggered" a good deal. But she appeared to take his swagger very seriously; she drew him out so!

VIII

KNIGHT duly made his appearance at dinner, and proved himself once more the entertaining gentleman whom our friends had long since learned to appreciate. But Mason, fresh from his contest with morals and metaphysics, was forcibly struck with the fact that he was one of those men from whom these sturdy beggars receive more kicks than halfpence. He was nevertheless obliged to admit that, if he was not a man of meditation, he was a highly civilised being. After dinner the company adjourned to the piazza, where, in the course of half-an-hour, the Doctor proposed to Miss Hofmann to take a turn in the grounds. All around the lawn there wound a narrow footpath, concealed from view, in spots, by clusters of shrubbery. Ferdinand and his hostess sat watching their retreating figures as they slowly measured the sinuous strip of gravel; Miss Hofmann's light dress and the Doctor's white waistcoat gleaming at intervals through the dark verdure. At the end of twenty minutes they returned to the house. The Doctor came back only to make his bow and to take his departure; and, when he had gone, Miss Hofmann retired to her own room. The next morning she mounted her horse and rode over to see the friend with whom she had stayed at the time of Mason's relapse. Ferdinand saw her pass his window, erect in the saddle, with her horse scattering the gravel with his nervous steps. Shortly afterwards Mrs Mason came into the room, sat down by the young man, made her habitual inquiries as to his condition, and then paused in such a way that he instantly felt she had something to tell him. "You have something to tell me," he said; "what is it?"

Mrs Mason blushed a little, and laughed. "I was first made to promise to keep it a secret. If I am so transparent now that I have leave to tell it, what should I be if I hadn't? Guess."

Ferdinand shook his head with the least bit of irritation. "I can't guess."

"Caroline is engaged."

"To whom?"

"Not to Mr Stapleton—to Dr Knight."

Ferdinand was silent a moment, but he neither changed colour nor dropped his eyes. Then, at last, "Did she wish you not to tell me?" he inquired.

"She wished me to tell no one. But I prevailed upon her to let me tell *you*."

"Thank you," said Ferdinand, trying to smile.

"It's a great surprise," continued Mrs Mason. "I never suspected it. And there I was talking about Mr Stapleton! I don't see how they have managed it. Well, I suppose it's for the best. But it seems odd that Caroline should have refused so many superior offers to cast her lot at last with a country doctor!"

Ferdinand felt for an instant as if the power of speech was deserting him; but he made a successful effort to recover it.

"She might do worse," he said, mechanically.

Mrs Mason glanced at him as if she had been struck by the sound of his voice. "You are not surprised, then?"

"I hardly know. I never supposed there was anything between them, and yet, now that I look back, there has been nothing against it. They have talked of each other neither too much nor too little. Upon my word, they're an accomplished couple!" Glancing back at the manner in which his friends had kept their secret, Ferdinand—strange as it may seem—could not repress a certain impulse of sympathetic admiration. He had had no vulgar rival. "Yes," he repeated gravely, "she might do worse."

"I suppose she might. He's poor, but he's clever; and I am sure I do hope to goodness he loves her!"

"May I ask whether they became engaged yesterday on that walk around the lawn?"

"No; it would be fine if they had, under our very noses! It was all done while Caroline was at the Stapletons'. It was agreed between them yesterday that she should tell me at once."

"And when are they to be married?"

"In October, if possible. Caroline told me to tell you that she counts upon your staying for the wedding."

"Staying where?" asked Mason, with a little nervous laugh.

"Staying here, of course—in the house."

Ferdinand looked his hostess full in the face, taking her hand as he did so. "'The funeral baked meats did coldly furnish forth the marriage tables.'"

"Ah, hold your tongue!" cried Mrs Mason, pressing his hand. "How can you be so horrible? When Caroline leaves me, Ferdinand, I shall be quite alone. The tie which binds us together will be very much loosened by her marriage. I can't help thinking that it was never very close when I consider that I have had no part in the most important step of her life. I don't complain. I suppose it's natural enough. Perhaps it's the fashion —come in with striped petticoats and pea-jackets. Only it makes me feel like an old woman. It removes me twenty years at a bound from my own engagement, and the day I burst out crying on my mother's neck because your uncle had told a young girl I knew that he thought I had a lovely figure. I had then! Nowadays I suppose they tell the young ladies themselves, and have them cry on their own necks. It's a great saving of time. But I shall miss Caroline all the same; and then, Ferdinand, I shall make a great deal of you."

"The more the better," said Ferdinand; and at this moment Mrs Mason was called away.

Ferdinand had not been in the army for nothing; he had received a blow as sharp as a sabre-cut, and he resolved to bear it like a soldier. He refused to allow himself a single moment of self-compassion. On the contrary, he spared himself none of the hard names that occur to a man who finds he has been living in a fool's paradise. For not guessing Caroline's secret he was perhaps excusable. Women were all inscrutable, and this one especially so. But Knight was a man like himself—a man whom he esteemed and liked, but whom he was reluctant to credit with a deeper and more noiseless current of feeling than his own, for his own was no babbling brook, betraying its course through green leaves. Knight had loved modestly and decently, but frankly and heartily, like a man who was not ashamed of what he was doing, and if he had not found it out it was his own fault. What else had he to do? He had been a besotted day-dreamer, while his friend had simply come to the point. He deserved his injury, and he would bear it in silence. He had been unable to get well on an illusion; he would now try getting well on a truth. This was very tonic treatment, the reader will admit, likely to kill if it didn't cure.

Miss Hofmann was absent for several hours. At dinner-time she had not returned, and Mrs Mason and the young man accordingly sat down without her. After dinner Ferdinand went into the little parlour, quite indifferent as to how soon he should meet her. Seeing or not seeing her, time hung equally heavy. Shortly after her companions had risen from table she rode up to the door, dismounted, tired and hungry, passed directly into the dining-room, and sat down to eat in her habit. In half-an-hour she came out, and, crossing the hall on her way upstairs, saw Mason in the parlour. She turned round, and, gathering up her long skirt, stopped at the door to bid him good-day. He left his chair, and went towards her. Her face wore a somewhat tired smile.

"So you are going to be married," he began, abruptly.

"So they say."

"I congratulate you. Excuse me if I don't do it with the last grace. I feel all I dare to feel."

"Don't be afraid," said Caroline, patting her skirt softly with her whip.

"I am not sure that it's not more unexpected than even such things have a right to be. There's no doubt about it?"

"None whatever."

"Well, Knight is a very good fellow. I haven't seen him yet," he went on, as Caroline was silent. "I don't know that I am in any hurry to see him. But I mean to talk to him. I mean to tell him that if he doesn't do his duty by you I shall——"

"Well?"

"I shall remind him of it."

"Oh, I shall do that," said Miss Hofmann.

Ferdinand looked at her gravely. "By heaven, you know," he cried with intensity, "it must be either one thing or the other!"

"I don't understand you."

"Oh, I understand myself. You are not a woman to be wasted, sacrificed."

Caroline made a gesture of impatience. "I don't understand you," she repeated. "You must excuse me. I am very tired." And she went rapidly up stairs.

On the following day Ferdinand had an opportunity to offer his felicitations to the Doctor. "I don't congratulate you on doing it," he said, "so much as on the way you have done it."

"What do you know about the way?" asked Knight.

"Nothing whatever. That's just my point. You took good care of that. And you are to be married in October?"

"I hope so. Very quietly, I suppose. The parson to do it, and Mrs Mason and my mother and you to see it's done properly." And the Doctor put his hand on Ferdinand's shoulder.

"Oh, I am the last person to choose," said Mason. "If he were to omit anything I should take good care not to call attention to it." It is often said that, next to great joy, no state of mind is so frolicsome as great distress. It was in virtue of this truth, I suppose, that Ferdinand was able to be facetious.

He kept his spirits—he talked and smiled and lounged about with the same look of reluctant incapacity as before. During the interval before the time appointed for the wedding it was agreed between the parties interested that Miss Hofmann should go over and spend a few days with her future mother-in-law, where she might partake more freely and privately than at home of the pleasure of her lover's company. She was absent a week; a week during which Ferdinand was thrown entirely upon his hostess for entertainment and diversion—things he had a very keen sense of needing. There were moments when it seemed to him that he was living by mere force of will, and that if he loosened the screws for a single instant he should sink back upon his bed again and never leave it. He had forbidden himself to think of Caroline, and had prescribed a course of meditation upon that other mistress, his first love, with whom he had long since exchanged pledges— her of a hundred names—work, letters, philosophy, fame. But, after Caroline had gone, it was exceedingly difficult not to think of her. Even in absence she was supremely conspicuous. The most that Ferdinand could do was to take refuge in books —an immense number of which he now read, fiercely, passionately, voraciously—in conversation with Mrs Mason, and in such society as he found in his path. Mrs Mason was a great gossip—a gossip on a scale so liberal as to transform the foible into a virtue—a gossip, moreover, of imagination and sympathy, dealing with the future as well as the present and the past—with all the things people might do, as well as those they had already done or not done. With her, then, Ferdinand talked of his own future, into which she entered with enthusiasm, almost with violence. Mrs Mason planned out a residence in Europe for her nephew, in the manner of one who knew her ground. Caroline once married, she herself would go abroad and fix herself in one of the several capitals in which an American widow with an easy income may contrive to support existence. She would make her dwelling a base of supplies—a *pied-à-terre*—for Ferdinand, who, taking his time to it, should visit every object of interest in the ancient and modern world. She would leave him free to go and come as he pleased, and to live as he listed; and I may say that, thanks to Mrs Mason's observation of foreign manners, this allowance covered in her view quite as much as it did in poor Ferdinand's, who had never been out of his own country. All that she would ask of him would be to show himself two or three times a year in her drawing-room, and tell her stories of what he had seen; that drawing-room which she already saw in her mind's eye—a compact little *entresol*, with tapestry hangings in the doorways and a coach-house in the court. Mrs Mason was not a severe moralist; but she was too enlightened a woman to wish to demoralise her nephew—to persuade him to trifle with his future—that future of which the war had already made light in its own impudent fashion. She loved him; she thought him the most brilliant, the most promising, of the new generation. She looked to the day when his name would be on men's lips, and it would be a great piece of good fortune to have inadvertently married his uncle. Herself a great observer of men and manners, she wished to give him advantages which had been sterile in her own case.

IX

IN the way of society Ferdinand made calls with his hostess, went out twice to dine, and caused Mrs Mason herself to entertain company at dinner. He presided on these occasions with distinguished urbanity. It happened, moreover, that invitations had been out some days for a party at the Stapletons'—Miss Hofmann's friends—and that, as there was to be no dancing, Ferdinand boldly announced his intention of being present. "Who knows?" he said; "it may do me more good than harm.

We can go late, and come away early." Mrs Mason doubted of the wisdom of the act; but she finally assented, and prepared herself. It was late when they left home, and when they arrived the rooms—rooms of exceptional vastness—were at their fullest. Mason received on this his first appearance in society a flattering welcome, and in a very few moments found himself in exclusive possession of Miss Edith Stapleton, Caroline's particular friend. This young lady has had no part in our story, because our story is perforce short, and condemned to confine itself to the essential. If I had had more room to turn round I should long since have whispered to the reader that Miss Stapleton—who was a charming girl—had conceived a decided preference for our Ferdinand over all other men whomsoever. That Ferdinand was utterly ignorant of the circumstance is our excuse for passing it by; and we linger upon it, therefore, only long enough to suggest that the young girl must have been very happy at this particular moment.

"Is Miss Hofmann here?" Mason asked, as he accompanied her into an adjoining room.

"Do you call that being here?" said Miss Stapleton, looking across the apartment.

There he beheld Miss Hofmann, shining like a queen and fronted by a semi-circle of half-a-dozen men. Her head and shoulders rose serene from the vaporous surge of her white dress, and she looked and listened with that half-abstracted air which is pardonable in a woman beset by admirers. When Caroline's eye fell upon her friend she stared a moment, surprised, and then made him the friendliest bow in the world—a bow so friendly that her little circle divided to let it pass and looked round to see where the deuce it was going. Taking advantage of this circumstance, Miss Hofmann advanced several steps. Ferdinand went towards her, and there, in sight of all the company, she gave him her hand and smiled at him with extraordinary sweetness. They went back together to Miss Stapleton, and Caroline made him sit down, she and her friend placing themselves on either side. For half-an-hour Ferdinand had the honour of engrossing the attention of the two most charming persons present—and, thanks to this distinction, indeed the attention of the whole company. After which the two young ladies conducted him from room to room and presented to him the people of importance as if he had been a prince. Ferdinand rose to the level of the occasion, and conducted himself with unprecedented gallantry. Upon others, doubtless, he made a sufficiently good impression, but to himself he was an object almost of awe. He was obliged, however, to fortify himself with repeated draughts of wine; and even with the aid of this artificial stimulant he was unable to conceal from Mrs Mason and his physician that he was looking far too much like an invalid to be properly where he was.

"Was there ever anything like the avidity of these dreadful girls?" said Mrs Mason to the Doctor. "They will let a man swoon at their feet sooner than abridge a *tête-à-tête* that amuses them. Then they'll have up another. Look at little Miss Masters, yonder, with Ferdinand and George Stapleton before her. She has got them contradicting each other, and she looks like a Roman fast lady at the circus. What does she care, so long as she makes her evening? They like a man to look as if he were going to die—it's interesting."

Knight went over to his friend, and told him with much decision that it was high time he should be at home and in bed. "You're looking fearfully," he added, candidly, as Ferdinand resisted.

"You are looking as fresh as a rose, Colonel Mason," said Miss Masters, a very audacious little person, overhearing this speech.

"It isn't a matter of taste," said the Doctor, angrily; "it's a fact." And he led away his patient.

Ferdinand insisted that he had not hurt himself; that, on the contrary, he was feeling uncommonly well; but his face contradicted him. He continued for two or three days more to go through the forms of returning vitality with a courage worthy of a better cause. Then at last he broke down altogether. He settled himself on his pillows, and fingered his watch, and began to wonder how many revolutions he should still witness of those exquisite little needles. The Doctor came, and gave him a sound rating for his imprudence. Ferdinand listened to him patiently, and then assured him that prudence or imprudence had nothing to do with it, that death had taken fast hold of him, and that now his only concern was to make easy terms with his captor. In the course of the same day he sent for a lawyer and made certain alterations in his will. He had no known relatives, and his modest patrimony stood bequeathed to a gentleman of his acquaintance who had no real need of it. He now divided it into two unequal portions, the smaller of which he devised to William Bowles, Mrs Mason's man-servant and his personal attendant; and the larger—which represented a considerable sum—to Horace Knight. He informed Mrs Mason of these arrangements, and was pleased to have her approval.

From this moment his strength began rapidly to ebb, and the shattered fragments of his long-resisting will floated down its shallow current into dissolution. It was useless to attempt to talk, to beguile the interval, to watch the signs, or to count the hours. A constant attendant was established at his side, and Mrs Mason appeared only at infrequent moments. It seemed to the poor woman that her heart was broken, and she spent a great deal of time in weeping. Miss Hofmann remained, naturally, at Mrs Knight's. "As far as I can judge," Horace had said to her, "it will be a matter of a week. But it's the most extraordinary case I ever heard of. The man was steadily getting well. Everything was going on as it ought—up to that Sunday I dined at your aunt's. Then, suddenly, he went straight back. It's very puzzling." On the fifth day he had driven Miss Hofmann home, at her suggestion that it was no more than decent that she should give the young man some sign of sympathy.

Horace went up to Ferdinand's bedside, and found the poor fellow in the languid middle condition between sleeping and waking in which he had passed the last forty-eight hours. "Colonel," he asked gently, "do you think you could see Caroline?"

For all answer Ferdinand opened his eyes. Horace went out, and led his companion back into the darkened room. She came softly up to the bedside, stood looking down for a moment at the sick man, and then stooped over him.

"I thought I would come and make you a little visit," she said. "Does it disturb you?"

"Not in the least," Mason answered, looking at her steadily. "Not half as much as it would have done a week ago. Please sit down."

"Thank you. Horace won't let me. I will come again."

"You will not have another chance," said Ferdinand. "I am not good for more than two days yet. Tell them to go out. I wish to see you alone. I wouldn't have sent for you, but, now that you are here, I might as well take advantage of it."

"Have you anything particular to say?" asked Knight, kindly.

"Oh come," said Mason, with a smile which he meant to be good-natured, but which was only ghastly; "you are not going to be jealous of me at this time of day."

Knight looked at Miss Hofmann for permission, and then left the room with the nurse. But a minute had hardly elapsed before Miss Hofmann hurried into the adjoining apartment, with her face pale and discomposed.

"Go to him!" she exclaimed. "He is dying!"

When they reached him he was dead.

In the course of a few days his will was opened, and Knight came to the knowledge of his legacy. "He was a good, generous fellow," he said to Mrs Mason and Miss Hofmann, "and I shall never be satisfied that he might not have recovered. It was a most extraordinary case." He was considerate enough to his audience of abstain from adding that he would have given a great deal to be able to make an autopsy. Miss Hofmann's nuptials were of course not deferred; they took place in October, "very quietly." It seemed to her lover in the interval that she was very silent and thoughtful; but this certainly was natural under the circumstances.

A PROBLEM

September was drawing to an end, and with it the honey-moon of two young persons in whom I shall be glad to interest the reader. They had stretched it out in sovereign contempt of the balance of the calendar. That September hath thirty days is a truth known to the simplest child; but our young lovers had given it at least forty. Nevertheless, they were on the whole not sorry to have the overture play itself out, and to see the curtain rise on the drama in which they had undertaken the leading parts. Emma thought very often of the charming little house which was awaiting her in town, and of the servants whom her dear mother had promised to engage; and, indeed, for that matter, the young wife let her imagination hover about the choice of groceries with which she expected to find her cupboards stocked through the same kind agency. Moreover, she had left her wedding-gown at home—thinking it silly to carry her finery into the country—and she felt a great longing to refresh her memory as to the particular shade of a certain lavender silk, and the exact length of a certain train. The reader will see that Emma was a simple, unsophisticated person, and that her married life was likely to be made up of small joys and vexations. She was simple and gentle and pretty and young; she adored her husband. He, too, had begun to feel that it was time they were married in earnest. His thoughts wandered back to his counting-room and his vacant desk, and to the possible contents of the letters which he had requested his fellow-clerk to open in his absence. For David, too, was a simple, natural fellow, and although he thought his wife the sweetest of human creatures—or, indeed, for that very reason

369

—he was unable to forget that life is full of bitter inhuman necessities and perils which muster in force about you when you stand idle. He was happy, in short, and he felt it unfair that he should any longer have his happiness for nothing.

The two, therefore, had made up their trunks again, and ordered the vehicle in time for the morrow's train. Twilight had come on, and Emma sat at the window empty-handed, taking a silent farewell of the landscape, which she felt that they had let into the secret of their young love. They had sat in the shade of every tree, and watched the sunset from the top of every rock.

David had gone to settle his account with the landlord, and to bid good-bye to the doctor, who had been of such service when Emma had caught cold by sitting for three hours on the grass after a day's rain.

Sitting alone was dull work. Emma crossed the threshold of the long window, and went to the garden gate to look for her husband. The doctor's house was a mile away, close to the village. Seeing nothing of David, she strolled along the road, bareheaded, in her shawl. It was a lovely evening. As there was no one to say so to, Emma said so, with some fervor, to herself; and to this she added a dozen more remarks, equally original and eloquent—and equally sincere. That David was, ah! so good, and that she ought to be so happy. That she would have a great many cares, but that she would be orderly, and saving, and vigilant, and that her house should be a sanctuary of modest elegance and good taste; and, then, that she might be a mother.

When Emma reached this point, she ceased to meditate and to whisper virtuous nothings to her conscience. She rejoiced; she walked more slowly, and looked about at the dark hills, rising in soft undulations against the luminous west, and listened to the long pulsations of sound mounting from woods and hedges and the margins of pools. Her ears rang, and her eyes filled with tears.

Meanwhile she had walked a half-mile, and as yet David was not in sight. Her attention, however, was at this moment diverted from her quest. To her right, on a level with the road, stretched a broad, circular space, half meadow, half common, enclosed in the rear by a wood. At some distance, close to the wood, stood a couple of tents, such as are used by the vagrant Indians who sell baskets and articles of bark. In front, close to the road, on a fallen log, sat a young Indian woman, weaving a basket, with two children beside her. Emma looked at her curiously as she drew near.

"Good evening," said the woman, returning her glance with hard, bright black eyes. "Don't you want to buy something?"

"What have you got to sell?" asked Emma, stopping.

"All sorts of things. Baskets, and pincushions, and fans."

"I should like a basket well enough—a little one—if they're pretty."

"Oh, yes, they're pretty, you'll see." And she said something to one of the children, in her own dialect. He went off, in compliance, to the tents.

While he was gone, Emma looked at the other child, and pronounced it very handsome; but without touching it, for the little savage was in the last degree unclean. The woman doggedly continued her work, examining Emma's person from head to foot, and staring at her dress, her hands, and her rings.

In a few moments the child came back with a number of baskets strung together, followed by an old woman, apparently the mother of the first. Emma looked over the baskets, selected a pretty one, and took out her purse to pay for it. The price was a dollar, but Emma had nothing smaller than a two-dollar note, and the woman professed herself unable to give change.

"Give her the money," said the old woman, "and for, the difference, I'll tell your fortune."

Emma looked at her, hesitating. She was a repulsive old

squaw, with sullen, black eyes, and her swarthy face hatched across with a myriad of wrinkles.

The younger woman saw that Emma looked a little frightened, and said something in her barbarous native gutturals to her companion. The latter retorted, and the other burst out into a laugh.

"Give me your hand," said the old woman, "and I'll tell your fortune." And, before Emma found time to resist, she came and took hold of her left hand. She held it awhile, with the back upwards, looking at its fair surface, and at the diamonds on her third finger. Then, turning up the palm, she began to mutter and grumble. Just as she was about to speak, Emma saw her look half-defiantly at someone apparently behind her. Turning about, she saw that her husband had come up unperceived. She felt relieved. The woman had a horribly vicious look, and she exhaled, moreover, a strong odor of whiskey. Of this David immediately became sensible.

"What is she doing?" he asked of his wife.

"Don't you see. She's telling my fortune."

"What has she told you."

"Nothing yet. She seems to be waiting for it to come to her."

The squaw looked at David cunningly, and David returned her gaze with ill-concealed disgust. "She'll have to wait a long time," he said to his wife. "She has been drinking."

He had lowered his voice, but the woman heard him. The other began to laugh, and said something in her own tongue to her mother. The latter still kept Emma's hand and remained silent.

"This is your husband?" she said, at last, nodding at David.

Emma nodded assent. The woman again examined her hand. "Within the year," she said, "you'll be a mother."

"That's wonderful news," said David. "Is it to be a boy or a girl?"

The woman looked hard at David. "A girl," she said. And then she transferred here eyes to Emma's palm.

"Well, is that all?" said Emma.

"She'll be sick."

"Very likely," said David. "And we'll send for the doctor."

"The doctor'll do no good."

"Then we shall send for another," said Emma, laughing—but not without an effort.

"He'll do no good. She'll die."

The young squaw began to laugh again. Emma drew her hand away, and looked at her husband. He was a little pale, and Emma put her hand into his arm.

"We're very much obliged to you for the information," said David. "At what age is our little girl to die?"

"Oh, very young."

"How young?"

"Oh, very young." The old woman seemed indisposed to commit herself further, and David led his wife away.

"Well," said Emma, "she gave us a good dollar's worth."

"I think," said David, "she had been giving herself a good dollar's worth. She was full of liquor."

From this assurance Emma drew for twenty-four hours to come a good deal of comfort. As for David, in the course of an hour he had quite forgotten the prophecy.

The next day they went back to town. Emma found her house all that she had desired, and her lavender silk not a shade too pale, nor her train an inch too short. The winter came and went, and she was still a very happy woman. The spring arrived, the summer drew near, and her happiness increased. She became the mother of a little girl.

For some time after the child was born Emma was confined to her room. She used to sit with the infant on her lap, nursing her, counting her breathings, wondering whether she would be pretty. David was at his place of business, with his head full of figures. A dozen times Emma recurred to the old woman's prophecy, sometimes with a tremor, sometimes with indifference, sometimes with almost defiance. Then, she declared that it was silly to remember it. A tipsy old squaw—a likely providence for her precious child. She was, perhaps, dead herself by this time. Nevertheless, her prophecy was odd; she seemed so positive. And the other woman laughed so disagreeably. Emma had not forgotten that laugh. She might well laugh, with her own lusty little savages beside her.

The first day that Emma left her room, one evening, at dinner, she couldn't help asking her husband whether he remembered the Indian woman's prediction. David was taking a glass of wine. He nodded.

"You see it's half come true," said Emma. "A little girl."

"My dear," said David, "one would think you believed it."

"Of course she'll be sick," said Emma. "We must expect that."

"Do you think, my dear," pursued David, "that it's a little girl because that venerable person said so?"

"Why no, of course not. It's only a coincidence."

"Well, then, if it's merely a coincidence, we may let it rest. If the old woman's *dictum* was a real prediction, we may also let it rest. That it has half come true lessens the chances for the other half."

The reader may detect a flaw in David's logic; but it was quite good enough for Emma. She lived upon it for a year, at the end of which it was in a manner put to the test.

It were certainly incorrect to say that Emma guarded and cherished her little girl any the more carefully by reason of the old woman's assurance; her natural affection was by itself a guarantee of perfect vigilance. But perfect vigilance is not infallible. When the child was a twelvemonth old it fell grievously sick, and for a week its little life hung by a thread. During this time I am inclined to think that Emma quite forgot the sad prediction suspended over the infant's head; it is certain, at least, that she never spoke of it to her husband, and that he made no attempt to remind her of it. Finally, after a hard struggle, the little girl came out of the cruel embrace of disease, panting and exhausted, but uninjured. Emma felt as if her child was immortal, and as if, henceforth, life would have no trials for her. It was not till then that she thought once more of the prophecy of the swarthy sybil.

She was sitting on the sofa in her chamber, with the child lying asleep in her lap, watching the faint glow of returning life in its poor little wasted cheeks. David came in from his day's labour and sat down beside her.

"I wonder," said Emma, "what our friend Magawisca—or whatever her name is—would say to that."

"She would feel desperately snubbed," said David. "Wouldn't she, little transcendent convalescent?" And he gently tickled the tip of his little girl's nose with the end of his moustache. The baby softly opened her eyes, and, vaguely conscious of her father, lifted her hand and languidly clutched his nose. "Upon my soul," said David, "she's positively boisterous. There's life in the old dog yet."

"Oh, David, how can you?" said Emma. But she sat watching her husband and child with a placid, gleeful smile. Gradually, her smile grew the least bit serious, and then vanished, though she still looked like the happy woman that she was. The nurse came up from supper, and took possession of the baby. Emma let it go, and remained sitting on the sofa. When the nurse had gone into the adjoining room, she laid a hand in one of her husband's.

"David," she said, "I have a little secret."

"I've no doubt," said David, "that you have a dozen. You're the most secretive, clandestine, shady sort of woman I ever came across."

It is needless to say that this was merely David's exuberant humor; for Emma was the most communicative, sympathetic soul in the world. She practised, in a quiet way, a passionate devotion to her husband, and it was a part of her religion to make him her confidant. She had, of course, in strictness, very little to confide to him. But she confided to him her little, in the hope that he would one day confide to her what she was pleased to believe his abundance.

"It's not exactly a secret," Emma pursued; "only I've kept it so long that it almost seems like one. You'll think me very silly, David. I couldn't bear to mention it so long as there was any chance of truth in the talk of that horrible old squaw. But now, that it's disproved, it seems absurd to keep it on my mind; not that I really ever felt it there, but if I said nothing about it, it was for your sake. I'm sure you'll not mind it; and if you don't, David, I'm sure I needn't."

"My dear girl, what on earth is coming?" said David. "'If you don't, I'm sure I needn't!'—you make a man's flesh crawl."

"Why, it's another prophecy," said Emma.

"Another prophecy? Let's have it then, by all means."

"But you don't mean, David, that you're going to believe it?"

"That depends. If it's to my advantage, of course I shall."

"To your advantage! Oh, David!"

"My dear Emma, prophecies are not to be sneered at. Look at this one about the baby."

"Look at the baby, I should say."

"Exactly. Isn't she a girl? hasn't she been at death's door?"

"Yes; but the old woman made her go through."

"Nay; you've no imagination. Of course, they pull off short of the catastrophe; but they give you a good deal by the way."

"Well, my dear, since you're so determined to believe in them, I should be sorry to prevent you. I make you a present of this one."

"Was it a squaw, this time?"

"No, it was an old Italian—a woman who used to come on Saturday mornings at school and sell us sugar-plums and trinkets. You see it was ten years ago. Our teachers used to dislike her; but we let her into the garden by a back-gate. She used to carry a little tray, like a pedlar. She had candy and cakes, and kid-gloves. One day, she offered to tell our fortunes with cards. She spread out her cards on the top of her tray, and half a dozen of us went through the ceremony. The rest were afraid. I believe I was second. She told me a long rigmarole that I have forgotten, but said nothing about lovers or husbands. That, of course, was all we wanted to hear; and, though I was disappointed, I was ashamed to ask any questions. To the girls who came after me, she promised successively the most splendid marriages. I wondered whether I was to be an old maid. The thought was horrible, and I determined to try and conjure such a fate. 'But I?' I said, as she was going to put up her cards; 'am I never to be married?' She looked at me, and then looked over her cards again. I suppose she wished to make up for her neglect. 'Ah, you, Miss,' she said—'you are better off than any of them. You are to marry twice!' Now, my dear," Emma added, "make the most of that." And she leaned her head on her husband's shoulder and looked in his face, smiling.

But David smiled not at all. On the contrary, he looked grave. Hereupon, Emma put by her smile, and looked grave, too. In fact, she looked pained. She thought it positively unkind of David to take her little story in such stiff fashion.

"It's very strange," said David.

"It's very silly," said Emma. "I'm sorry I told you, David."

"I'm very glad. It's extremely curious. Listen, and you'll see—I, too, have a secret, Emma."

"Nay, I don't want to hear it," said Emma.

"You shall hear it," said the young man. "I never mentioned it before, simply because I had forgotten it—utterly forgotten it. But your story calls it back to my memory. I, too, once had my fortune told. It was neither a squaw nor a gipsy. It was a young lady, in company. I forget her name. I was less than twenty. It was at a party, and she was telling people's fortunes. She had cards; she pretended to have a gift. I don't know what I had been saying. I suppose that, as boys of that age are fond of doing, I had been showing off my wit at the expense of married life. I remember a young lady introducing me to this person, and saying that here was a young man who declared he never would marry. Was it true? She looked at her cards, and said that it was completely false, and that I should marry twice. The company began to laugh. I was mortified. 'Why don't you say three times?' I said. 'Because,' answered the young lady, 'my cards say only twice.'" David had got up from the sofa, and stood before his wife. "Don't you think it's curious?" he said.

"Curious enough. One would say you thought it something more."

"You know," continued David, "we can't both marry twice."

"'You know'," cried Emma. "Bravo, my dear. 'You know' is delightful. Perhaps you would like me to withdraw and give you a chance."

David looked at his wife, half surprised at the bitterness of her words. He was apparently on the point of making some conciliatory speech; but he seemed forcibly struck, afresh, with the singular agreement of the two predictions. "Upon my soul!" he said, "it's preternaturally odd!" He burst into a fit of laughter.

Emma put her hands to her face and sat silent. Then, after a few moments: "For my part," she said, "I think it's extremely disagreeable!" Overcome by the effort to speak, she burst into tears.

Her husband again placed himself at her side. He still took the humorous view of the case—on the whole, perhaps, indiscreetly. "Come, Emma," he said, "dry your tears, and consult your memory. Are you sure you've never been married before?"

Emma shook off his caresses and got up. Then, suddenly turning around, she said, with vehemence, "And you, sir?"

For an answer David laughed afresh; and then, looking at his wife a moment, he rose and followed her. "*Où diable la jalousie va-t-elle se nicher?*" he cried. He put his arm about her, she yielded, and he kissed her. At this moment a little wail went

up from the baby in the neighboring room. Emma hastened
away.

Where, indeed, as David had asked, will jealousy stow herself away? In what odd, unlikely corners will she turn up? She
made herself a nest in poor Emma's innocent heart, and, at her
leisure, she lined and feathered it. The little scene I have just
described left neither party, indeed, as it found them. David
had kissed his wife and shown the folly of her tears, but he had
not taken back his story. For ten years he hadn't thought of it;
but, now that he had been reminded of it, he was quite unable
to dismiss it from his thoughts. It besieged him, and harassed
and distracted him; it thrust itself into his mind at the most in-
opportune moments; it buzzed in his ears and danced among
the columns of figures in his great folio account books. Sometimes the young lady's prediction conjoined itself with a prodigious array of numerals, and roamed away from its modest
place among the units into the hundreds of thousands. David
read himself a million times a husband. But, after all, as he
reflected, the oddity was not in his having been predestined,
according to the young lady, to marry twice; but in poor
Emma having drawn exactly the same lot. It was a conflict of
oracles. It would be an interesting inquiry, although now, of
course, quite impracticable, to ascertain which of the two was
more to be trusted. For how under the sun could both have
revealed the truth? The utmost ingenuity was powerless to
reconcile their mutual incompatibility. Could either of the
soothsayers have made her statement in a figurative sense? It
seemed to David that this was to fancy them a grain too wise.
The simplest solution—except not to think of the matter at all,
which he couldn't bring himself to accomplish—was to fancy
that each of the prophecies nullified the other, and that when
he became Emma's husband, their counterfeit destinies had
been put to confusion.

Emma found it quite impossible to take the matter so easily.
She pondered it night and day for a month. She admitted that

the prospect of a second marriage was, of necessity, unreal for one of them; but her heart ached to discover for which of them it was real. She had laughed at the folly of the Indian's threat; but she found it impossible to laugh at the extraordinary co-incidence of David's promised fate with her own. That it was absurd and illogical made it only the more painful. It filled her life with a horrible uncertainty. It seemed to indicate that whether or no the silly gossip of a couple of jugglers was, on either side, strictly fulfilled; yet there was some dark cloud hanging over their marriage. Why should an honest young couple have such strange things said of them? Why should they be called upon to reach such an illegible riddle? Emma repented bitterly of having told her secret. And yet, too, she rejoiced; for it was a dreadful thought that David, unprompted to reveal his own adventure should have kept such a dreadful occurrence locked up in his breast, shedding, Heaven knows what baleful influence, on her life and fortunes. Now she could live it down; she could combat it, laugh at it. And David, too, could do as much for the mysterious prognostic of his own extinction. Never had Emma's fancy been so active. She placed the two faces of her destiny in every conceivable light. At one moment, she imagined that David might succumb to the pressure of his fancied destiny, and leave her a widow, free to marry again; and at another that he would grow enamoured of the thought of obeying his own oracle, and crush her to death by the masculine vigor of his will. Then, again, she felt as if her own will were strong, and as if she bore on her head the protecting hand of fate. Love was much, assuredly, but fate was more. And here, indeed, what was fate but love? As she had loved David, so she would love another. She racked her poor little brain to conjure up this future master of her life. But, to do her justice, it was quite in vain. She could not forget David. Nevertheless, she felt guilty. And then she thought of David, and wondered whether he was guilty, too—whether he was dreaming of another woman.

In this way it was that Emma became jealous. That she was a very silly girl I don't pretend to deny. I have expressly said that she was a person of a very simple make; and in proportion to the force of her old straightforward confidence in her husband, was that of her present suspicion and vagaries.

From the moment that Emma became jealous, the household angel of peace shook its stainless wings and took a melancholy flight. Emma immediately betrayed herself. She accused her husband of indifference, and of preferring the society of other women. Once she told him that he might, if he pleased. It was *à propos* of an evening party, to which they had both been asked. During the afternoon, while David was still at his business, the baby had been taken sick, and Emma had written a note to say that they should not be able to come. When David returned, she told him of her note, and he laughed and said that he wondered whether their intended hostess would fancy that it was his practice to hold the baby. For his part, he declared that he meant to go; and at nine o'clock he appeared, dressed. Emma looked at him, pale and indignant.

"After all," she said, "you're right. Make the most of your time."

These were horrible words, and, as was natural, they made a vast breach between the husband and wife.

Once in a while Emma felt an impulse to take her revenge, and look for happiness in society, and in the sympathy and attention of agreeable men. But she never went very far. Such happiness seemed but a troubled repose, and the world at large had no reason to suspect that she was not on the best of terms with her husband.

David, on his side, went much further. He was gradually transformed from a quiet, home-keeping, affectionate fellow, into a nervous, restless, querulous man of pleasure, a diner-out and a haunter of clubs and theatres. From the moment that he detected their influence on his life, he had been unable to make light of the two prophecies. Then one, now the other, dominated his imagination, and, in either event, it was impossible to live as he would have lived in ignorance. Sometimes, at the thought of an early death, he was seized with a passionate attachment to the world, and an irresistible desire to plunge into worldly joys. At other moments, thinking of his wife's possible death, and of her place being taken by another woman, he felt a fierce and unnatural impatience of all further delay in the evolution of events. He wished to annihilate the present. To live in expectation so acute and so feverish was not to live. Poor David was occasionally tempted by desperate expedients to kill time. Gradually the perpetual oscillation from one phase of his destiny to the other, and the constant change from passionate exaltation to equally morbid depression, induced a state of chronic excitement, not far removed from insanity.

At about this moment he made the acquaintance of a young unmarried woman whom I may call Julia—a very charming, superior person, of a character to exert a healing, soothing influence upon his troubled spirit. In the course of time, he told her the story of his domestic revolution. At first, she was very much amused; she laughed at him, and called him superstitious, fantastic, and puerile. But he took her levity so ill, that she changed her tactics, and humored his delusion.

It seemed to her, however, that his case was serious, and that, if some attempt were not made to arrest his growing alienation from his wife, the happiness of both parties might depart forever. She believed that the flimsy ghost of their mysterious future could be effectually laid only by means of a reconciliation. She doubted that their love was dead and gone. It was only dormant. If she might once awaken it, she would retire with a light heart, and leave it lord of the house.

So, without informing David of her intention, Julia ventured to call upon Emma, with whom she had no personal acquaintance. She hardly knew what she should say; she would trust to the inspiration of the moment; she merely wished to kindle a ray of light in the young wife's darkened household. Emma, she fancied, was a simple, sensitive person; she would be quickly moved by proffered kindness.

But, although she was unacquainted with Emma, the young wife had considerable knowledge of Julia. She had had her pointed out to her in public. Julia was handsome. Emma hated her. She thought of her as her husband's temptress and evil genius. She assured herself that they were longing for her death, so that they might marry. Perhaps he was already her lover. Doubtless they would be glad to kill her. In this way it was that, instead of finding a gentle, saddened, sensitive person, Julia found a bitter, scornful woman, infuriated by a sense of insult and injury. Julia's visit seemed to Emma the climax of insolence. She refused to listen to her. Her courtesy, her gentleness, her attempt at conciliation, struck her as a mockery and a snare. Finally, losing all self-control, she called her a very hard name.

Then Julia, who had a high temper of her own, plucked up a spirit, and struck a blow for her dignity—a blow, however, which unfortunately rebounded on David. "I had steadily refused, Madam," she said, "to believe that you are a fool. But you quite persuade me."

With these words she withdrew. But it mattered little to Emma whether she remained or departed. She was conscious only of one thing, that David had called her a fool to another woman. "A fool?" she cried. "Truly I have been. But I shall be no longer."

She immediately made her preparations for leaving her husband's house, and when David came home he found her with her child and a servant on the point of departure. She told him in a few words that she was going to her mother's, that in his absence he had employed persons to insult her in her own house, it was necessary that she should seek protection in her family. David offered no resistance. He made no attempt to resent her accusation. He was prepared for anything. It was fate.

Emma accordingly went to her mother's. She was supported in this extraordinary step, and in the long months of seclusion which followed it, by an exalted sense of her own comparative integrity and virtue. She, at least, had been a faithful wife. She had endured, she had been patient. Whatever her destiny might be, she had made no indecent attempt to anticipate it. More than ever she devoted herself to her little girl. The comparative repose and freedom of her life gave her almost a feeling of happiness. She felt that deep satisfaction which comes upon the spirit when it has purchased contentment at the expense of reputation. There was now, at least, no falsehood in her life. She neither valued her marriage nor pretended to value it.

As for David, he saw little of anyone but Julia. Julia, I have said, was a woman of great merit and of perfect generosity. She very soon ceased to resent the check she had received from Emma, and not despairing, still, of seeing peace once more established in the young man's household, she made it a matter of conscience to keep David by her influence in as sane and unperverted a state of mind as circumstances would allow. "She may hate me," thought Julia, "but I'll keep him for her." Julia's, you see, in all this business was the only wise head.

David took his own view of their relations. "I shall certainly see you as often as I wish," he declared. "I shall take consolation where I find it. She has her child—her mother. Does she begrudge me a friend? She may thank her stars I don't take to drink or to play."

For six months David saw nothing of his wife. Finally, one evening, when he was at Julia's house, he received this note:

"Your daughter died this morning, after several hours' suffering. She will be buried to-morrow morning."   E."

David handed the note to Julia. "After all," he said, "she was right."

"Who was right, my poor friend?" asked Julia.

"The old squaw. We cried out too soon."

The next morning he went to the house of his mother-in-law. The servant, recognizing him, ushered him into the room in which the remains of his poor little girl lay, ready for burial. Near the darkened window stood his mother-in-law, in conversation with a gentleman—a certain Mr Clark—whom David recognized as a favorite clergyman of his wife, and whom he had never liked. The lady, on his entrance, made him a very grand curtsy—if, indeed, that curtsy may be said to come within the regulations which govern salutations of this sort, in which the head is tossed up in proportion as the body is depressed—and swept out of the room. David bowed to the clergyman, and went and looked at the little remnant of mortality which had once been his daughter. After a decent interval, Mr Clark ventured to approach him.

"You have met with a great trial, sir," said the clergyman.

David assented in silence.

"I suppose," continued Mr Clark, "it is sent, like all trials, to remind us of our feeble and dependent condition—to purge us of pride and stubbornness—to make us search our hearts and see whether we have not by chance allowed the noisome weeds of folly to overwhelm and suffocate the modest flower of wisdom."

That Mr Clark had deliberately prepared this speech, with a view to the occasion, I should hesitate to affirm. Gentlemen of his profession have these little parcels of sentiment ready to their hands. But he was, of course, acquainted with Emma's estrangement from her husband (although not with its original motives), and, like a man of genuine feeling, he imagined that under the softening action of a common sorrow, their two hardened hearts might be made to melt and again to flow into one. "The more we lose, my friend," he pursued, "the more we should cherish and value what is left."

"You speak to very good purpose, sir," said David; "but I, unfortunately, have nothing left."

At this moment the door opened, and Emma came in—pale, and clad in black. She stopped, apparently unprepared to see her husband. But, on David's turning toward her, she came forward.

David felt as if Heaven had sent an angel to give the lie to his last words. His face flushed—first with shame, and then with joy. He put out his arms. Emma halted an instant, struggling with her pride, and looked at the clergyman. He raised his hand, with a pious sacramental gesture, and she fell on her husband's neck.

The clergyman took hold of David's hand and pressed it; and, although, as I have said, the young man had never been particularly fond of Mr Clark, he devoutly returned the pressure.

"Well," said Julia, a fortnight later—for in the interval Emma had been brought to consent to her husband's maintaining his acquaintance with this lady, and even herself to think her a very good sort of person—"well, I don't see but that the terrible problem is at last solved, and that you have each been married twice."

DE GREY: A ROMANCE

IT was the year 1820, and Mrs De Grey, by the same token, as they say in Ireland (and, for that matter, out of it), had reached her sixty-seventh spring. She was, nevertheless, still a handsome woman, and, what is better yet, still an amiable woman. The untroubled, unruffled course of her life had left as few wrinkles on her temper as on her face. She was tall and full of person, with dark eyes and abundant white hair, which she rolled back from her forehead over a cushion, or some such artifice. The freshness of youth and health had by no means faded out of her cheeks, nor had the smile of her imperturbable courtesy expired on her lips. She dressed, as became a woman of her age and a widow, in black garments, but relieved with a great deal of white, with a number of handsome rings on her fair hands. Frequently, in the spring, she wore a little flower or a sprig of green leaves in the bosom of her gown. She had been accused of receiving these little floral ornaments from the hands of Mr Herbert (of whom I shall have more to say); but the charge is unfounded, inasmuch as they were very carefully selected from a handful cut in the garden by her maid.

That Mrs De Grey should have been just the placid and elegant old lady that she was, remained, in the eyes of the world at large, in spite of an abundance of a certain sort of evidence in favor of such a result, more or less of a puzzle and a problem. It is true, that everyone who knew anything about her knew that she had enjoyed great material prosperity, and had suffered no misfortunes. She was mistress in her own right of a handsome property and a handsome house; she had lost her husband, indeed, within a year after marriage; but, as the late George De Grey had been of a sullen and brooding humor,—to that degree, indeed, as to incur the suspicion of insanity,—her loss, leaving her well provided for, might in strictness have been accounted a gain. Her son, moreover, had never given her a moment's trouble; he had grown up a charming young man, handsome, witty, and wise; he was a model of filial devotion. The lady's health was good; she had half a dozen perfect servants; she had the perpetual company of the incomparable Mr Herbert; she was as fine a figure of an elderly woman as any in town; she might, therefore, very well have been happy and have looked so. On the other hand, a dozen sensible women had been known to declare with emphasis, that not for all her treasures and her felicity would they have consented to be Mrs De Grey. These ladies were, of course, unable to give a logical reason for so strong an aversion. But it is certain that there hung over Mrs De Grey's history and circumstances a film, as it were, a shadow of mystery, which struck a chill upon imaginations which might easily have been kindled into envy of her good fortune. "She lives in the dark," someone had said of her. Close observers did her the honor to believe that there was a secret in her life, but of a wholly undefined character. Was she the victim of some lurking sorrow, or the mistress of some clandestine joy? These imputations, we may easily believe, are partially explained by the circumstance that she was a Catholic, and kept a priest in her house. The unexplained portion might very well, moreover, have been discredited by Mrs De Grey's perfectly candid and complacent demeanor. It was certainly hard to conceive, in talking with her, to what part of her person one might pin a mystery,—whether on her clear, round eyes or her handsome, benevolent lips. Let us say, then, in defiance of the voice of society, that she was no tragedy queen. She was a fine woman, a dull woman, a perfect gentlewoman. She had taken life, as she liked a cup of tea,—weak, with an exquisite aroma and plenty of cream and sugar. She had never lost her temper, for the excellent reason that she had none to lose. She was troubled with no fears, no doubts, no scruples, and. blessed with no sacred certainties. She was fond of her son, of the church, of her garden, and of her toilet. She had the very best taste; but, morally, one may say that she had had no history.

Mrs De Grey had always lived in seclusion; for a couple of years previous to the time of which I speak she had lived in solitude. Her son, on reaching his twenty-third year, had gone to Europe for a long visit, in pursuance of a plan discussed at intervals between his mother and Mr Herbert during the whole course of his boyhood. They had made no attempt to forecast his future career, or to prepare him for a profession. Strictly, indeed, he was at liberty, like his late father, to dispense with a profession. Not that it was to be wished that he should take his father's life as an example. It was understood by the world at large, and, of course, by Mrs De Grey and her companion in particular, that this gentleman's existence had been blighted, at an early period, by an unhappy love-affair; and it was notorious that, in consequence, he had spent the few years of his maturity in gloomy idleness and dissipation. Mrs De Grey, whose own father was an Englishman, reduced to poverty, but with claims to high gentility, professed herself unable to understand why Paul should not live decently on his means. Mr Herbert declared that in America, in any walk of life, idleness was indecent; and that he hoped the young man would—nominally at least—select a career. It was agreed on both sides, however, that there was no need for haste; and that it was proper, in the first place, he should see the world. The world, to Mrs De Grey, was little more than a name; but to Mr Herbert, priest as he was, it was a vivid reality. Yet he felt that the generous and intelligent youth upon whose education he had lavished all the treasures of his tenderness and sagacity, was not unfitted, either by nature or culture, to measure his sinews against its trials and temptations; and that he should love him the better for coming home at twenty-five an accomplished gentleman and a good Catholic, sobered and seasoned by experience, sceptical in small matters, confident in great, and richly replete with good stories. When he came of age, Paul received his walking-ticket, as they say, in the shape of a letter of credit for a handsome sum on certain London bankers. But the young man pocketed the letter, and remained at home, poring over books, lounging in the garden, and scribbling heroic verses. At the end of a year, he plucked up a little ambition, and took a turn through the country, travelling much of the way on horseback. He came back an ardent American, and felt that he might go abroad without danger. During his absence in Europe he had written home innumerable long letters,—compositions so elaborate (in the taste of that day, recent as it is) and so delightful, that, between their pride in his epistolary talent and their longing to see his face, his mother and his ex-tutor would have been at a loss to determine whether he gave them more satisfaction at home or abroad.

With his departure the household was plunged in unbroken repose. Mrs De Grey neither went out nor entertained company. An occasional morning call was the only claim made upon her hospitality. Mr Herbert, who was a great scholar, spent all his hours in study; and his patroness sat for the most part alone, arrayed with a perfection of neatness which there was no one to admire (unless it be her waiting-maid, to whom it remained a constant matter of awe), reading a pious book or knitting under-garments for the orthodox needy. At times, indeed, she wrote long letters to her son,—the contents of which Mr Herbert found it hard to divine. This was accounted a dull life forty years ago; now, doubtless, it would be considered no life at all. It is no matter of wonder, therefore, that finally, one April morning, in her sixty-seventh year, as I have said, Mrs De Grey suddenly began to suspect that she was lonely. Another long year, at least, was to come and go before Paul's return. After meditating for a while in silence, Mrs De Grey resolved to take counsel with Father Herbert.

This gentleman, an Englishman by birth, had been an intimate friend of George De Grey, who had made his acquaintance during a visit to Europe, before his marriage. Mr Herbert was a younger son of an excellent Catholic family, and was at that time beginning, on small resources, the practice of the law. De Grey met him in London, and the two conceived a strong mutual sympathy. Herbert had neither taste for his profession nor apparent ambition of any sort. He was, moreover, in weak health; and his friend found no difficulty in persuading him to accept the place of travelling companion through France and Italy. De Grey carried a very long purse, and was a most liberal friend and patron; and the two young men accomplished their progress as far as Venice in the best spirits and on the best terms. But in Venice, for reasons best known to themselves, they bitterly and irretrievably quarrelled. Some persons said it was over a card-table, and some said it was about a woman. At all events, in consequence, De Grey returned to America, and Herbert repaired to Rome. He obtained admission into a monastery, studied theology, and finally was invested with priestly orders. In America, in his thirty-third year, De Grey married the lady whom I have described. A few weeks after his marriage he wrote to Herbert, expressing a vehement desire to be reconciled. Herbert felt that the letter was that of a most unhappy man; he had already forgiven him; he pitied him, and after a short delay succeeded in obtaining an ecclesiastical mission to the United States. He reached New York and presented himself at his friend's house, which from this moment became his home. Mrs De Grey had recently given birth to a son; her husband was confined to his room by illness, reduced to a shadow of his former self by repeated sensual excesses. He survived Herbert's arrival but a couple of months; and after his death the rumor went abroad that he had by his last will settled a handsome income upon the priest, on condition that he would continue to reside with his widow, and take the entire charge of his boy's education.

This rumor was confirmed by the event. For twenty-five years, at the time of which I write, Herbert had lived under Mrs De Grey's roof as her friend and companion and counsellor, and as her son's tutor. Once reconciled to his friend, he had gradually dropped his priestly character. He was of an essentially devout temperament, but he craved neither parish nor pulpit. On the other hand, he had become an indefatigable student. His late friend had bequeathed to him a valuable library, which he gradually enlarged. His passion for study, however, appeared singularly disinterested, inasmuch as, for many years, his little friend Paul was the sole witness and receptacle of his learning. It is true that he composed a large portion of a History of the Catholic Church in America, which, although the manuscript exists, has never seen, and, I suppose, is never destined to see, the light. It is in the very best keeping, for it contains an immense array of facts. The work is written, not from a sympathetic, but from a strictly respectful point of view; but it has a fatal defect,—it lacks unction.

The same complaint might have been made of Father Herbert's personal character. He was the soul of politeness, but it was a cold and formal courtesy. When he smiled, it was, as the French say, with the end of his lips, and when he took your hand, with the end of his fingers. He had had a charming face in his younger days, and when gentlemen dressed their hair with powder, his fine black eyes must have produced the very best effect. But he had lost his hair, and he wore on his naked crown a little black silk cap. Round his neck he had a black cravat of many folds, without any collar. He was short and slight, with a stoop in his shoulders, and a handsome pair of hands.

"If it were not for a sad sign to the contrary," said Mrs De Grey, in pursuance of her resolve to take counsel of her friend, "I should believe I am growing younger."

"What is the sign to the contrary?" asked Herbert.

"I'm losing my eyes. I can't see to read. Suppose I should become blind."

"And what makes you suspect that you are growing young again?"

"I feel lonely. I lack company. I miss Paul."

"You will have Paul back in a year."

"Yes; but in the mean while I shall be miserable. I wish I knew some nice person whom I might ask to stay with me."

"Why don't you take a companion,—some poor gentlewoman in search of a home? She would read to you, and talk to you."

"No; that would be dreadful. She would be sure to be old and ugly. I should like someone to take Paul's place,—someone young and fresh like him. We're all so terribly old, in the house. You're at least seventy; I'm sixty-five" (Mrs De Grey was pleased to say); "Deborah is sixty, the cook and coachman are fifty-five apiece."

"You want a young girl then?"

"Yes, some nice, fresh young girl, who would laugh once in a while, and make a little music,—a little sound in the house."

"Well," said Herbert, after reflecting a moment, "you had better suit yourself before Paul comes home. You have only a year."

"Dear me," said Mrs De Grey; "I shouldn't feel myself obliged to turn her out on Paul's account."

Father Herbert looked at his companion with a penetrating glance. "Nevertheless, my dear lady," he said, "you know what I mean."

"O yes, I know what you mean,—and you, Father Herbert, know what I think."

"Yes, madam, and, allow me to add, that I don't greatly care. Why should I? I hope with all my heart that you'll never find yourself compelled to think otherwise."

"It is certain," said Mrs De Grey, "that Paul has had time to play out his little tragedy a dozen times over."

"His father," rejoined Herbert, gravely, "was twenty-six years old."

At these words Mrs De Grey looked at the priest with a slight frown and a flushed cheek. But he took no pains to meet her eyes, and in a few moments she had recovered, in silence, her habitual calmness.

Within a week after this conversation Mrs De Grey observed at church two persons who appeared to be strangers in the congregation: an elderly woman, meanly clad, and evidently in ill health, but with a great refinement of person and manner; and a young girl whom Mrs De Grey took for her daughter. On the following Sunday she again found them at their devotions, and was forcibly struck by a look of sadness and trouble in their faces and attitude. On the third Sunday they were absent; but it happened that during the walk, going to confession, she met the young girl, pale, alone, and dressed in mourning, apparently just leaving the confessional. Something in her gait and aspect assured Mrs De Grey that she was alone in the world, friendless and helpless; and the good lady, who at times was acutely sensible of her own isolation in society, felt a strong and sympathetic prompting to speak to the stranger, and ask the secret of her sorrow. She stopped her before she left the church, and, addressing her with the utmost kindness, succeeded so speedily in winning her confidence that in half an hour she was in possession of the young girl's entire history. She had just lost her mother, and she found herself in the great city penniless, and all but houseless. They were from the South; her father had been an officer in the navy, and had perished at sea, two years before. Her mother's health had failed, and they had come to New York, ill-advisedly enough, to consult an eminent physician. He had been very kind, he had taken no fees, but his skill had been applied in vain. Their money had melted away in other directions,—for food and lodging and clothing. There had been enough left to give the poor lady a decent burial; but no means of support save her own exertions remained for the young girl. She had no relatives to look to, but she professed herself abundantly willing to

work. "I look weak," she said, "and pale, but I'm really strong.
It's only that I'm tired,—and sad. I'm ready to do anything.
But I don't know where to look." She had lost her color and
the roundness and elasticity of youth; she was thin and ill-
dressed; but Mrs De Grey saw that at her best she must be
properly a very pretty creature, and that she was evidently, by
rights, a charming girl. She looked at the elder lady with lustrous, appealing blue eyes from under the hideous black bonnet
in which her masses of soft light hair were tucked away. She
assured her that she had received a very good education, and
that she played on the piano-forte. Mrs De Grey fancied her
divested of her rusty weeds, and dressed in a white frock and a
blue ribbon, reading aloud at an open window, or touching
the keys of her old not unmelodious spinnet; for if she took her
(as she mentally phrased it) Mrs De Grey was resolved that she
would not be harassed with the sight of her black garments. It
was plain that, frightened and faint and nervous as she was, the
poor child would take any service unconditionally. She kissed
her then tenderly within the sacred precinct, and led her away
to her carriage, quite forgetting her business with her confessor. On the following day Margaret Aldis (such was the
young girl's name) was transferred in the same vehicle to Mrs
De Grey's own residence.

This edifice was demolished some years ago, and the place
where it stood forms at the present moment the very centre of
a turbulent thoroughfare. But at the period of which I speak
it stood on the outskirts of the town, with as vast a prospect of
open country in one direction as in the other of close-built
streets. It was an excellent old mansion, moreover, in the best
taste of the time, with large square rooms and broad halls and
deep windows, and, above all, a delightful great garden, hedged
off from the road by walls of dense verdure. Here, steeped in
repose and physical comfort, rescued from the turbid stream
of common life, and placed apart in the glow of tempered sunshine, valued, esteemed, caressed, and yet feeling that she was

not a mere passive object of charity, but that she was doing her simple utmost to requite her protectress, poor Miss Aldis bloomed and flowered afresh. With rest and luxury and leisure, her natural gaiety and beauty came back to her. Her beauty was not dazzling, indeed, nor her gayety obtrusive; but, united, they were the flower of girlish grace. She still retained a certain tenuity and fragility of aspect, a lightness of tread, a softness of voice, a faintness of coloring, which suggested an intimate acquaintance with suffering. But there seemed to burn, nevertheless, in her deep blue eyes the light of an almost passionate vitality; and there sat on her firm, pale lips the utterance of a determined, devoted will. It seemed at times as if she gave herself up with a senuous, reckless, half-thankless freedom to the mere consciousness of security. It was evident that she had an innate love of luxury. She would sometimes sit, motionless, for hours, with her head thrown back, and her eyes slowly wandering, in a silent ecstasy of content. At these times Father Herbert, who had observed her attentively from the moment of her arrival (for, scholar and recluse as he was, he had not lost the faculty of appreciating feminine grace),—at these times the old priest would watch her covertly and marvel at the fantastic, soulless creature whom Mrs De Grey had taken to her side. One evening, after a prolonged stupor of this sort, in which the young girl had neither moved nor spoken, sitting like one whose soul had detached itself and was wandering through space, she rose, on Mrs De Grey's at last giving her an order, and moved forward as if in compliance; and then, suddenly rushing forward toward the old woman, she fell on her knees, and buried her head in her lap and burst into a paroxysm of sobs. Herbert, who had been standing by, went and laid one hand on her head, and with the other made over it the sign of the cross, in the manner of a benediction,—a consecration of the passionate gratitude which had finally broken out into utterance. From this moment he loved her.

Margaret read aloud to Mrs De Grey, and on Sunday evenings

sang in a clear, sweet voice the chants of their Church, and occupied herself constantly with fine needle-work, in which she possessed great skill. They spent the long summer mornings together, in reading and work and talk. Margaret told her companion the simple, sad details of the history of which she had already given her the outline; and Mrs De Grey, who found it natural to look upon them as a kind of practical romance organized for her entertainment, made her repeat them over a dozen times. Mrs De Grey, too, honoured the young girl with a recital of her own biography, which, in its vast vacuity, produced upon Margaret's mind a vague impression of grandeur. The vacuity, indeed, was relieved by the figure of Paul, whom Mrs De Grey never grew weary of describing, and of whom, finally, Margaret grew very fond of thinking. She listened most attentively to Mrs De Grey's eulogies of her son, and thought it a great pity he was not at home. And then she began to long for his return, and then, suddenly, she began to fear it. Perhaps he would dislike her being in the house, and turn her out of doors. It was evident that his mother was not prepared to contradict him. Perhaps—worse still—he would marry some foreign woman, and bring her home, and she would turn wickedly jealous of Margaret (in the manner of foreign women). De Grey, roaming through Europe, took for granted, piously enough, that he was never absent from his good mother's thoughts; but he remained superbly unconscious of the dignity which he had usurped in the meditations of her humble companion. Truly, we know where our lives begin, but who shall say where they end? Here was a careless young gentleman whose existence enjoyed a perpetual echo in the soul of a poor girl utterly unknown to him. Mrs De Grey had two portraits of her son, which, of course, she lost no time in exhibiting to Margaret,—one taken in his boyhood, with brilliant red hair and cheeks, the lad's body encased in a bright blue jacket, and his neck encircled in a frill, open very low; the other, executed just before his departure, a handsome young

man in a buff waistcoat, clean shaven, with an animated countenance, dark, close-curling auburn hair, and very fine eyes.
The former of these designs Margaret thought a very pretty
child; but to the other the poor girl straightway lost her heart,
—the more easily that Mrs De Grey assured her, that, although
the picture was handsome enough, it conveyed but the faintest
idea of her boy's adorable flesh and blood. In a couple of
months arrived a long-expected letter from Paul, and with it
another portrait,—a miniature, painted in Paris by a famous
artist. Here Paul appeared a far more elegant figure than in the
work of the American painter. In what the change consisted it
was hard to tell; but his mother declared that it was easy to see
that he had spent two years in the best company in Europe.

"Oh, the best company!" said Father Herbert, who knew
the force of this term. And, smiling a moment with inoffensive
scorn, he relapsed into his wonted gravity.

"I think he looks very sad," said Margaret, timidly.

"Fiddlesticks!" cried Herbert, impatiently. "He looks like
a coxcomb. Of course, it's the Frenchman's fault," he added,
more gently. "Why on earth does he send us his picture at all?
It's a great piece of impertinence. Does he think we've forgotten him? When I want to remember my boy, I have something better to look to than that flaunting bit of ivory."

At these words the two ladies went off, carrying the portrait
with them, to read Paul's letter in private. It was in eight pages,
and Margaret read it aloud. Then, when she had finished, she
read it again; and in the evening she read it once more. The
next day, Mrs De Grey, taking the young girl quite into her
confidence, brought out a large packet containing his earlier
letters, and Margaret spent the whole morning in reading them
over aloud. That evening she took a stroll in the garden alone,
—the garden in which *he* had played as a boy, and lounged and
dreamed as a young man. She found his name—his beautiful
name crudely cut on a wooden bench. Introduced, as it seemed
to her that she had been by his letters, into the precincts of his

personality, the mystery of his being, the magic circle of his feelings and opinions and fancies; wandering by his side, unseen, over Europe, and treading, unheard, the sounding pavements of famous churches and palaces, she felt that she tasted for the first time of the substance and sweetness of life. Margaret walked about for an hour in the starlight, among the dusky, perfumed alleys. Mrs De Grey, feeling unwell, had gone to her room. The young girl heard the far-off hum of the city slowly decrease and expire, and then, when the stillness of the night was unbroken, she came back into the parlor across the long window, and lit one of the great silver candlesticks that decorated the ends of the mantel. She carried it to the wall where Mrs De Grey had suspended her son's miniature, having first inserted it in an immense gold frame, from which she had expelled a less valued picture. Margaret felt that she must see the portrait before she went to bed. There was a certain charm and ravishment in beholding it privately by candlelight. The wind had risen,—a warm west wind,—and the long white curtains of the open windows swayed and bulged in the gloom in a spectral fashion. Margaret guarded the flame of the candle with her hand, and gazed at the polished surface of the portrait, warm in the light, beneath its glittering plate of glass. What an immensity of life and passion was concentrated into those few square inches of artificial color! The young man's eyes seemed to gaze at her with a look of profound recognition. They held her fascinated; she lingered on the spot, unable to move. Suddenly the clock on the chimney-piece rang out a single clear stroke. Margaret started and turned about, at the thought that it was already half-past ten. She raised her candle aloft to look at the dial-plate; and perceived three things: that it was one o'clock in the morning, that her candle was half burnt out, and that someone was watching her from the other side of the room. Setting down her light, she recognized Father Herbert.

"Well, Miss Aldis," he said, coming into the light, "what do you think of it?"

Margaret was startled and confused, but not abashed. "How long have I been here?" she asked, simply.

"I have no idea. I myself have been here half an hour."

"It was very kind of you not to disturb me," said Margaret, less simply.

"It was a very pretty picture," said Herbert.

"Oh, it's beautiful!" cried the young girl, casting another glance at the portrait over her shoulder.

The old man smiled sadly, and turned away, and then, coming back, "How do you like our young man, Miss Aldis?" he asked, apparently with a painful effort.

"I think he's very handsome," said Margaret, frankly.

"He's not so handsome as that," said Herbert.

"His mother says he's handsomer."

"A mother's testimony in such cases is worth very little. Paul is well enough, but he's no miracle."

"I think he looks sad," said Margaret. "His mother says he's very gay."

"He may have changed vastly within two years. Do you think," the old man added, after a pause, "that he looks like a man in love?"

"I don't know," said Margaret, in a low voice. "I never saw one."

"Never?" said the priest, with an earnestness which surprised the young girl.

She blushed a little. "Never, Father Herbert."

The priest's dark eyes were fixed on her with a strange intensity of expression. "I hope, my child, you never may," he said, solemnly.

The tone of his voice was not unkind, but it seemed to Margaret as if there were something cruel and chilling in the wish. "Why not I as well as another?" she asked.

The old man shrugged his shoulders. "O, it's a long story," he said.

The summer passed away and flushed into autumn, and the

narticu-
fist, he
irgaret
in his

have
bed.
I'm
but
'us

ly
,
/

finally expired in the cold embrace
Grey had written to her son of her
into her service. At this time came a
ing man was pleased to express his satis-
are. "Present my compliments to Miss
and assure her of my gratitude for the com-
my dear mother,—of which, indeed, I hope
to inform her in person." In writing these
ords Paul De Grey little suspected the infinite
hey were to have in poor Margaret's heart. A
rived a letter, which was handed to Mrs De Grey
"You will have received my letter of December
gan (a letter which had miscarried and failed to
nd will have formed your respective opinions of its
As Mrs De Grey read these words, Father Herbert
at Margaret; she had turned pale. "Favorable or not,"
er continued, "I am sorry to be obliged to bid you undo
again. But my engagement to Miss L. is broken off. It had
me impossible. As I made no attempt to give you a history
t, or to set forth my motives, so I shall not now attempt to
into the logic of the rupture. But it's broken clean off, I
ssure you. Amen." And the letter passed to other matters,
leaving our friends sadly perplexed. They awaited the arrival
of the missing letter; but all in vain; it never came. Mrs De
Grey immediately wrote to her son, urgently requesting an
explanation of the events to which he had referred. His next
letter, however, contained none of the desired information.
Mrs De Grey repeated her request. Whereupon Paul wrote
that he would tell her the story when he had reached home. He
hated to talk about it. "Don't be uneasy, dear mother," he
added; "Heaven has insured me against a relapse. Miss L. died
three weeks ago at Naples." As Mrs De Grey read these words,
she laid down the letter and looked at Father Herbert, who had
been called to hear it. His pale face turned ghastly white, and
he returned the old woman's gaze with compressed lips and a

stony immobility in his eyes. Then, suddenly, a fierce,
late cry broke from his throat, and, doubling up his
brought it down with a terrible blow on the table. M
sat watching him, amazed. He rose to his feet, seized he
arms, and pressed her on his neck.

"My child! my child!" he cried, in a broken voice, "I
always loved you! I have been harsh and cold and crab
I was fearful. The thunder has fallen! Forgive me, child.
myself again." Margaret, frightened, disengaged herself,
he kept her hand. "Poor boy!" he cried, with a tremul
sigh.

Mrs De Grey sat smelling her vinaigrette, but not visib
discomposed. "Poor boy!" she repeated, but without a sig
—which gave the words an ironical sound.—"He had cease
to care for her," she said.

"Ah, madam!" cried the priest, "don't blaspheme. Go down
on your knees, and thank God that *we* have been spared that
hideous sight!"

Mystified and horrified, Margaret drew her hand from his
grasp, and looked with wondering eyes at Mrs De Grey. She
smiled faintly, touched her forefinger to her forehead, tapped
it, raised her eyebrows, and shook her head.

From counting the months that were to elapse before Paul's
return, our friends came to counting the weeks, and then the
days. The month of May arrived; Paul had sailed from England. At this time Mrs De Grey opened her son's room, and
caused it to be prepared for occupation. The contents were
just as he had left them; she bade Margaret come in and see it.
Margaret looked at her face in his mirror, and sat down a
moment on his sofa, and examined the books on his shelves.
They seemed a prodigious array; they were in several languages, and gave a deep impression of their owner's attainments.
Over the chimney hung a small sketch in pencil, which Margaret made haste to inspect,—a likeness of a young girl, skilfully enough drawn. The original had apparently been very

handsome, in the dark style; and in the corner of the sketch was written the artist's name,—*De Grey*. Margaret looked at the portrait in silence, with quickened heartbeats.

"Is this Mr Paul's?" she asked at last of her companion.

"It belongs to Paul," said Mrs De Grey. "He used to be very fond of it, and insisted upon hanging it there. His father sketched it before our marriage."

Margaret drew a breath of relief. "And who is the lady?" she asked.

"I hardly know. Some foreign person, I think, that Mr De Grey had been struck with. There's something about her in the other corner."

In effect, Margaret detected on the opposite side of the sketch, written in minute character, the word "*obiit*, 1786."

"You don't know Latin, I take it, my dear," said Mrs De Grey, as Margaret read the inscription. "It means that she died thirty-four good years ago."

"Poor girl!" said Margaret, softly. As they were leaving the room, she lingered on the threshold and looked about her, wishing that she might leave some little memento of her visit. "If we knew just when he would arrive," she said, "I would put some flowers on his table. But they might fade."

As Mrs De Grey assured her that the moment of his arrival was quite uncertain, she left her fancied nosegay uncut, and spent the rest of the day in a delightful tremor of anticipation, ready to see the dazzling figure of a young man, equipped with strange foreign splendour, start up before her and look at her in cold surprise, and hurry past her in search of his mother. At every sound of footsteps or of an opening door she laid down her work, and listened curiously. In the evening, as if by a common instinct of expectancy, Father Herbert met Mrs De Grey in the front drawing-room,—an apartment devoted exclusively to those festivities which never occurred in the annals of this tranquil household.

"A year ago to-day, madam," said Margaret, as they all sat

silent among the gathering shadows, "I came into your house. To-day ends a very happy year."

"Let us hope," said Father Herbert, sententiously, "that to-morrow will begin another."

"Ah, my dear lady!" cried Margaret, with emotion; "my good father,—my only friends,—what harm can come to me with you? It was you who rescued me from harm." Her heart was swollen with gratitude, and her eyes with rising tears. She gave a long shudder at the thought of the life that might have been her fate. But, feeling a natural indisposition to obtrude her peculiar sensations upon the attention of persons so devoutly absorbed in the thought of a coming joy, she left her place, and wandered away into the garden. Before many minutes, a little gate opened in the paling, not six yards from where she stood. A man came in, whom, in the dim light, she knew to be Paul De Grey. Approaching her rapidly, he made a movement as if to greet her, but stopped suddenly, and removed his hat.

"Ah, you're Miss—the young lady," he said.

He had forgotten her name. This was something other, something less felicitous, than the cold surprise of the figure in Margaret's vision. Nevertheless, she answered him, audibly enough: "They are in the drawing-room; they expect you."

He bounded along the path, and entered the house. She followed him slowly to the window, and stood without, listening. The silence of the young man's welcome told of its warmth.

Paul De Grey had made good use of his sojourn in Europe; he had lost none of his old merits, and had gained a number of new ones. He was by nature and culture an intelligent, amiable, accomplished fellow. It was his fortune to possess a peculiar, indefinable charm of person and manner. He was tall and slight of structure, but compact, firm, and active, with a clear, fair complexion, an open, prominent brow, crisp auburn hair, and eyes—a glance, a smile—radiant with youth and intellect. His address was frank, manly, and direct; and yet it seemed to Margaret that his bearing was marked by a certain dignity and elegance—at times even verging upon formalism—which distinguished it from that of other men. It was not, however, that she detected in his character any signs of that strange principle of melancholy which had exerted so powerful an action upon the other members of the household (and, from what she was able to gather, on his father). She fancied, on the contrary, that she had never known less levity associated with a more exquisite mirth. If Margaret had been of a more analytical turn of mind, she would have told herself that Paul De Grey's nature was eminently aristocratic. But the young girl contented herself with understanding it less, and secretly loving it more; and when she was in want of an epithet, she chose a simpler term. Paul was like a ray of splendid sunshine in the dull, colorless lives of the two women; he filled the house with light and heat and joy. He moved, to Margaret's fancy, in a circle of almost supernatural glory. His words, as they fell from his lips, seemed diamonds and pearls; and, in truth, his conversation, for a month after his return, was in the last degree delightful. Mrs De Grey's house was *par excellence* the abode of leisure,— a castle of indolence; and Paul in talking, and his companions in listening, were conscious of no jealous stress of sordid duties. The summer days were long, and Paul's daily fund of loquacity was inexhaustible. A week after his arrival, after breakfast, Father Herbert contracted the habit of carrying him off to his study, and Margaret, passing the half-open door, would hear the changeful music of his voice. She begrudged the old man, at these times, the exclusive enjoyment of so much eloquence. She felt that with his tutor, Paul's talk was far wiser and richer than it was possible it should be with two simple-minded women; and the young girl had a pious longing to hear him, to see him, at his best. A brilliant best it was to Father Herbert's mind; for Paul had surpassed his fondest hopes. He had amassed such a store of knowledge; he had learned all the good that the old man had enjoined upon him; and, although he had not wholly ignored the evil against which the priest had warned him, he judged it so wisely and wittily! Women and priests, as a general thing, like a man none the less for not being utterly innocent. Father Herbert took an unutterable satisfaction in the happy development of Paul's character. He was more than the son of his loins: he was the child of his intellect, his patience, and devotion.

The afternoons and evenings Paul was free to devote to his mother, who, out of her own room, never dispensed for an hour with Margaret's attendance. This, thanks to the young girl's delicate tact and sympathy, had now become an absolute necessity. Margaret sat by with her work, while Paul talked, and marvelled at his inexhaustible stock of gossip and anecdote and forcible, vivid description. He made cities and churches and galleries and playhouses swarm and shine before her enchanted senses, and reproduced the people he had met and the scenery through which he had travelled, until the young girl's head turned at the rapid succession of images and pictures. And then, at times, he would seem to grow weary; and would sink into silence; and Margaret, looking up askance from her work, would see his eyes absently fixed, and a faint smile on his face, or else a cold gravity, and she would wonder what far-off memory had called back his thoughts to that unknown European world. Sometimes, less frequently, when she raised her eyes, she found him watching her own figure, her bent head, and the busy movement of her hands. But (as yet, at least) he never turned away his glance in confusion; he let his eyes rest, and justified his scrutiny by some simple and natural remark.

But as the weeks passed by, and the summer grew to its fulness, Mrs De Grey contracted the habit of going after dinner to her own room, where, we may respectfully conjecture, she passed the afternoon in dishabille and slumber. But De Grey and Miss Aldis tacitly agreed together that, in the prime and springtime of life, it was stupid folly to waste in any such fashion the longest and brightest hours of the year; and so they, on their side, contracted the habit of sitting in the darkened drawing-room, and gossiping away the time until within an hour of tea. Sometimes, for a change, they went across the garden into a sort of summer-house, which occupied a central point in the enclosure, and stood with its face averted from the mansion, and looking to the north, and with its side covered with dense, clustering vines. Within, against the wall, was a deep garden bench, and in the middle a table, upon which Margaret placed her work-basket, and the young man the book, which, under the pretence of meaning to read, he usually carried in his hand. Within was coolness and deep shade and silence, and without the broad glare of the immense summer sky. When I say there was silence, I mean that there was nothing to interrupt the conversation of these happy idlers. Their talk speedily assumed that desultory, volatile character, which is the sign of great intimacy. Margaret found occasion to ask Paul a great many questions which she had not felt at liberty to ask in the presence of his mother, and to demand additional light upon a variety of little points which Mrs De Grey had been content to leave in obscurity. Paul was perfectly communicative. If Miss Aldis cared to hear, he was assuredly glad to talk. But suddenly it struck him that her attitude of mind was a singular provocation to egotism, and that for six weeks, in fact, he had done nothing but talk about himself,—his own adventures, sensations, and opinions.

"I declare, Miss Aldis," he cried, "you're making me a monstrous egotist. That's all you women are good for. I shall not say another word about Mr Paul De Grey. Now it's your turn."

"To talk about Mr Paul De Grey?" asked Margaret, with a smile.

"No, about Miss Margaret Aldis,—which, by the way, is a very pretty name."

"By the way, indeed!" said Margaret. "By the way for you, perhaps. But for me, my pretty name is all I have."

"If you mean, Miss Aldis," cried Paul, "that your beauty is all in your name——"

"I'm sadly mistaken. Well, then, I don't. The rest is in my imagination."

"Very likely. It's certainly not in mine."

Margaret was, in fact, at this time, extremely pretty; a little pale with the heat, but rounded and developed by rest and prosperity, and animated—half inspired, I may call it—with tender gratitude. Looking at her as he said these words, De Grey was forcibly struck with the interesting character of her face. Yes, most assuredly, her beauty was a potent reality. The charm of her face was forever refreshed and quickened by the deep loveliness of her soul.

"I mean literally, Miss Aldis," said the young man, "that I wish you to talk about yourself. I want to hear *your* adventures. I demand it,—— I need it."

"My adventures?" said Margaret. "I have never had any."

"Good!" cried Paul; "that in itself is an adventure."

In this way it was that Margaret came to relate to her companion the short story of her young life. The story was not all told, however, short as it was, in a single afternoon; that is, a whole week after she began, the young girl found herself setting Paul right with regard to a matter of which he had received a false impression.

"Nay, he is married," said Margaret; "I told you so."

"Oh, he is married?" said Paul.

"Yes; his wife's an immense fat woman."

"Oh, his wife's an immense fat woman?"

"Yes; and he thinks all the world of her."

"Oh, he thinks all the world of her!"

It was natural that, in this manner, with a running commentary supplied by Paul, the narrative should proceed slowly. But, in addition to the observations here quoted, the young man maintained another commentary, less audible and more profound. As he listened to this frank and fair-haired maiden, and reflected that in the wide world she might turn in confidence and sympathy to other minds than his,—as he found her resting her candid thoughts and memories on his judgment, as she might lay her white hand on his arm,—it seemed to him that the pure intentions with which she believed his soul to be peopled took in her glance a graver and higher cast. All the gorgeous color faded out of his recent European reminiscences and regrets, and he was sensible only of Margaret's presence, and of the tender rosy radiance in which she sat and moved, as in a sort of earthly halo. Could it be, he asked himself, that while he was roaming about Europe, in a vague, restless search for his future, his end, his aim, these things were quietly awaiting him at his own deserted hearth-stone, gathered together in the immaculate person of the sweetest and fairest of women? Finally, one day, this view of the case struck him so forcibly, that he cried out in an ecstasy of belief and joy.

"Margaret," he said, "my mother found you in church, and there, before the altar, she kissed you and took you into her arms. I have often thought of that scene. It makes it no common adoption."

"I'm sure I have often thought of it," said Margaret.

"It makes it sacred and everlasting," said Paul. "On that blessed day you came to us for ever and ever."

Margaret looked at him with a face tremulous between smiles and tears. "For as long as you will keep me," she said. "Ah, Paul!" For in an instant the young man had expressed all his longing and passion.

With the greatest affection and esteem for his mother, Paul had always found it natural to give precedence to Father Herbert in matters of appeal and confidence. The old man possessed a delicacy of intellectual tact which made his sympathy and his counsel alike delightful. Some days after the conversation upon a few of the salient points of which I have lightly touched,

Paul and Margaret renewed their mutual vows in the summer-house. They now possessed that deep faith in the sincerity of their own feelings, and that undoubting delight in each other's reiterated protests, which left them nothing to do but to take their elders into their confidence. They came through the garden together, and on reaching the threshold Margaret found that she had left her scissors in the garden hut; whereupon Paul went back in search of them. The young girl came into the house, reached the foot of the staircase, and waited for her lover. At this moment Father Herbert appeared in the open doorway of his study, and looked at Margaret with a melancholy smile. He stood, passing one hand slowly over another and gazing at her with kindly, darksome looks.

"It seems to me, Mistress Margaret," he said, "that you keep all this a marvellous secret from your poor old Doctor Herbert."

In the presence of this gentle and venerable scholar, Margaret felt that she had no need of vulgar blushing and simpering and negation. "Dear Father Herbert," she said, with heavenly simpleness, "I have just been begging Paul to tell you."

"Ah, my daughter,"—and the old man but half stifled a sigh,—"it's all a strange and terrible mystery."

Paul came in and crossed the hall with the light step of a lover.

"Paul," said Margaret, "Father Herbert knows."

"Father Herbert knows!" repeated the priest,—"Father Herbert knows everything. You're very innocent for lovers."

"You're very wise, sir, for a priest," said Paul, blushing.

"I knew it a week ago," said the old man, gravely.

"Well, sir," said Paul, "we love you none the less for loving each other so much more. I hope you'll not love us the less."

"Father Herbert thinks it's 'terrible,'" said Margaret, smiling.

"O Lord!" cried Herbert, raising his hand to his head as if in pain. He turned about, and went into his room.

Paul drew Margaret's hand through his arm and followed the priest. "You suffer, sir," he said, "at the thought of losing us,—of our leaving you. That certainly needn't trouble you. Where should we go? As long as you live, as long as my mother lives, we shall all make but a single household."

The old man appeared to have recovered his composure. "Ah!" he said; "be happy, no matter where, and I shall be happy. You're very young."

"Not so young," said Paul, laughing, but with a natural disinclination to be placed in too boyish a light. "I'm six-and-twenty. *J'ai vécu,*—I've lived."

"He's been through everything," said Margaret, leaning on his arm.

"Not quite everything." And Paul, bending his eyes, with a sober smile, met her upward glance.

"Oh, he's modest," murmured Father Herbert.

"Paul's been all but married already," said Margaret.

The young man made a gesture of impatience. Herbert stood with his eyes fixed on his face.

"Why do you speak of that poor girl?" said Paul. Whatever satisfaction he may have given Margaret on the subject of his projected marriage in Europe, he had since his return declined, on the plea that it was extremely painful, to discuss the matter either with his mother or with his old tutor.

"Miss Aldis is perhaps jealous," said Herbert, cunningly.

"O Father Herbert!" cried Margaret.

"There is little enough to be jealous of," said Paul.

"There's a fine young man!" cried Herbert. "One would think he had never cared for her."

"It's perfectly true."

"Oh!" said Herbert, in a tone of deep reproach, laying his hand on the young man's arm. "Don't say that."

"Nay, sir, I shall say it. I never said anything less to her.

She enchanted me, she entangled me, but, before Heaven, I never loved her!"

"Oh, God help you!" cried the priest. He sat down, and buried his face in his hands.

Margaret turned deadly pale, and recalled the scene which had occurred on the receipt of Paul's letter, announcing the rupture of his engagement. "Father Herbert," she cried, "what horrible, hideous mystery do you keep locked up in your bosom? If it concerns me,—if it concerns Paul,—I demand of you to tell us."

Moved apparently by the young girl's tone of agony to a sense of the needfulness of self-control, Herbert uncovered his face, and directed to Margaret a rapid glance of entreaty. She perceived that it meant that, at any cost, she should be silent. Then, with a sublime attempt at dissimulation, he put out his hands, and laid one on each of his companions' shoulders. "Excuse me, Paul," he said, "I'm a foolish old man. Old scholars are a sentimental, a superstitious race. We believe still that all women are angels, and that all men——"

"That all men are fools," said Paul, smiling.

"Exactly. Whereas, you see," whispered Father Herbert, "there are no fools but ourselves."

Margaret listened to this fantastic bit of dialogue with a beating heart, fully determined not to content herself with any such flimsy explanation of the old man's tragical allusions. Meanwhile, Herbert urgently besought Paul to defer for a few days making known his engagement to his mother.

The next day but one was Sunday, the last in August. The heat for a week had been oppressive, and the air was now sullen and brooding, as if with an approaching storm. As she left the breakfast-table, Margaret felt her arm touched by Father Herbert.

"Don't go to church," he said, in a low voice. "Make a pretext, and stay at home."

"A pretext?——"

"Say you've letters to write."

"Letters?" and Margaret smiled half bitterly. "To whom should I write letters?"

"Dear me, then say you're ill. I give you absolution. When they're gone, come to me."

At church-time, accordingly, Margaret feigned a slight indisposition; and Mrs De Grey, taking her son's arm, mounted into her ancient deep-seated coach, and rolled away from the door. Margaret immediately betook herself to Father Herbert's apartment. She saw in the old man's face the portent of some dreadful avowal. His whole figure betrayed the weight of an inexorable necessity.

"My daughter," said the priest, "you are a brave, pious girl——"

"Ah!" cried Margaret, "it's something horrible, or you wouldn't say that. Tell me at once.

"You need all your courage."

"Doesn't he love me?—Ah, in Heaven's name, speak!"

"If he didn't love you with a damning passion, I should have nothing to say."

"Oh, then, say what you please!" said Margaret.

"Well then,—you must leave this house."

"Why?—when?—where must I go?"

"This moment, if possible. You must go anywhere,—the further the better,—the further from *him*. Listen, my child," said the old man, his bosom wrung by the stunned, bewildered look of Margaret's face; "it's useless to protest, to weep, to resist. It's the voice of fate!"

"And pray, sir," said Margaret, "of what do you accuse me?"

"I accuse no one. I don't even accuse Heaven."

"But there's a reason,—there's a motive—"

Herbert laid his hand on his lips, pointed to a seat, and, turning to an ancient chest on the table, unlocked it, and drew from it a small volume, bound in vellum, apparently an old illuminated missal. "There's nothing for it," he said, "but to tell you the whole story."

He sat down before the young girl, who held herself rigid and expectant. The room grew dark with the gathering storm-clouds, and the distant thunder muttered.

"Let me read you ten words," said the priest, opening at a fly-leaf of the volume, on which a memorandum or register had been inscribed in a great variety of hands, all minute and some barely legible. "God be with you!" and the old man crossed himself. Involuntarily, Margaret did the same. "'George De Grey,'" he read, "'met and loved, September, 1786, Antonietta Gambini, of Milan. She died October 9th, same year. John De Grey married, April 4th, 1749, Henrietta Spencer. She died May 7th. George De Grey engaged himself October, 1710, to Mary Fortescue. She died October 31st. Paul De Grey, aged nineteen, betrothed June, 1672, at Bristol, England, to Lucretia Lefevre, aged thirty-one, of that place. She died July 27th. John De Grey, affianced January 10th, 1649, to Blanche Ferrars, of Castle Ferrars, Cumberland. She died, by her lover's hand, January 12th. Stephen De Grey offered his hand to Isabel Stirling, October, 1619. She died within the month. Paul De Grey exchanged pledges with Magdalen Scrope, August, 1586. She died in childbirth, September, 1587.'" Father Herbert paused. "Is it enough?" he asked, looking up with glowing eyes. "There are two pages more. The De Greys are an ancient line; they keep their records."

Margaret had listened with a look of deepening, fierce, passionate horror,—a look more of anger and of wounded pride than of terror. She sprang towards the priest with the lightness of a young cat, and dashed the hideous record from his hand.

"What abominable nonsense is this!" she cried. "What does it mean? I barely heard it; I despise it; I laugh at it!"

The old man seized her arm with a firm grasp. "Paul De Grey," he said, in an awful voice, "exchanged pledges with

Margaret Aldis, August, 1821. She died—with the falling
leaves."

Poor Margaret looked about her for help, inspiration, comfort of some kind. The room contained nothing but serried
lines of old parchment-covered books, each seeming a grim
repetition of the volume at her feet. A vast peal of thunder resounded through the noonday stillness. Suddenly her strength
deserted her; she felt her weakness and loneliness, the grasp of
the hand of fate. Father Herbert put out his arms, she flung
herself on his neck, and burst into tears.

"Do you still refuse to leave him?" asked the priest. "If you
leave him, you're saved."

"Saved?" cried Margaret, raising her head; "and Paul?"

"Ah, there it is.—He'll forget you."

The young girl pondered a moment. "To have him do
that," she said, "I should apparently have to die." Then
wringing her hands with a fresh burst of grief, "Is it certain,"
she cried, "that there are no exceptions?"

"None, my child"; and he picked up the volume. "You see
it's the first love, the first passion. After that, they're innocent.
Look at Mrs De Grey. The race is accursed. It's an awful, inscrutable mystery. I fancied that you were safe, my daughter,
and that that poor Miss L. had borne the brunt. But Paul was
at pains to undeceive me. I've searched his life, I've probed his
conscience: it's a virgin heart. Ah, my child, I dreaded it from
the first. I trembled when you came into the house. I wanted
Mrs De Grey to turn you off. But she laughs at it,—she calls
it an old-wife's tale. *She* was safe enough; her husband didn't
care two straws for her. But there's a little dark-eyed maiden
buried in Italian soil who could tell her another story. She
withered, my child. She was life itself,—an incarnate ray of her
own Southern sun. She died of De Grey's kisses. Don't ask me
how it began, it's always been so. It goes back to the night of
time. One of the race, they say, came home from the East,
from the crusades, infected with the germs of the plague. He

had pledged his love-faith to a young girl before his departure, and it had been arranged that the wedding should immediately succeed his return. Feeling unwell, he consulted an elder brother of the bride, a man versed in fantastic medical lore, and supposed to be gifted with magical skill. By him he was assured that he was plague-stricken, and that he was in duty bound to defer the marriage. The young knight refused to comply, and the physician, infuriated, pronounced a curse upon his race. The marriage took place; within a week the bride expired, in horrible agony; the young man, after a slight illness, recovered; the curse took effect."

Margaret took the quaint old missal into her hand, and turned to the grisly register of death. Her heart grew cold as she thought of her own sad sisterhood with all those miserable women of the past. Miserable women, but ah! tenfold more miserable men,—helpless victims of their own baleful hearts. She remained silent, with her eyes fixed on the book, abstractly; mechanically, as it were, she turned to another page, and read a familiar orison to the blessed Virgin. Then raising her head, with her deep-blue eyes shining with the cold light of an immense resolve,—a prodigious act of volition,—"Father Herbert," she said, in low, solemn accents, "I revoke this curse. I undo it. *I curse it!*"

From this moment, nothing would induce her to bestow a moment's thought on salvation by flight. It was too late, she declared. If she was destined to die, she had already imbibed the fatal contagion. But they should see. She cast no discredit on the existence or the potency of the dreadful charm; she simply assumed, with deep self-confidence which filled the old priest with mingled wonder and anguish, that it would vainly expend its mystic force once and forever upon her own devoted, impassioned life. Father Herbert folded his trembling hands resignedly. He had done his duty; the rest was with God. At times, living as he had done for years in dread of the moment which had now arrived, with his whole life darkened by its shadow, it seemed to him among the strange possibilities of nature that this frail and pure young girl might indeed have sprung, at the command of outraged love, to the rescue of the unhappy line to which he had dedicated his manhood. And then at other moments it seemed as if she were joyously casting herself into the dark gulf. At all events, the sense of peril had filled Margaret herself with fresh energy and charm. Paul, if he had not been too enchanted with her feverish gayety and grace to trouble himself about their motive and origin, would have been at a loss to explain their sudden morbid intensity. Forthwith, at her request, he announced his engagement to his mother, who put on a very gracious face, and honoured Margaret with a sort of official kiss.

"Ah me!" muttered Father Herbert, "and now she thinks she has bound them fast." And later, the next day, when Mrs De Grey, talking of the matter, avowed that it really did cost her a little to accept as a daughter a girl to whom she had paid a salary,—"A salary, madam!" cried the priest with a bitter laugh; "upon my word, I think it was the least you could do."

"*Nous verrons*," said Mrs De Grey, composedly.

A week passed by, without ill omens. Paul was in a manly ecstasy of bliss. At moments he was almost bewildered by the fulness with which his love and faith had been requited. Margaret was transfigured, glorified, by the passion which burned in her heart. "Give a plain girl, a common girl, a lover," thought Paul, "and she grows pretty, charming. Give a charming girl a lover——" and if Margaret was present, his eloquent eyes uttered the conclusion; if she was absent, his restless steps wandered in search of her. Her beauty within the past ten days seemed to have acquired an unprecedented warmth and richness. Paul went so far as to fancy that her voice had grown more deep and mellow. She looked older; she seemed in an instant to have overleaped a year of her development, and to have arrived at the perfect maturity of her youth. One might have imagined that, instead of the further, she stood just on the

hither verge of marriage. Meanwhile Paul grew conscious of
he hardly knew what delicate change in his own emotions. The
exquisite feeling of pity, the sense of her appealing weakness,
her heavenly dependence, which had lent its tender strain to
swell the concert of his affections, had died away, and given
place to a vague, profound instinct of respect. Margaret was,
after all, no such simple body; her nature, too, had its mysteries.
In truth, thought Paul, tenderness, gentleness, is its own reward. He had bent to pluck this pallid flower of sunless household growth; he had dipped its slender stem in the living
waters of his love, and lo! it had lifted its head, and spread its
petals, and brightened into splendid purple and green. This
glowing potency of loveliness filled him with a tremor which
was almost a foreboding. He longed to possess her; he watched
her with covetous eyes; he wished to call her utterly his own.

"Margaret," he said to her, "you fill me with a dreadful
delight. You grow more beautiful every day. We must be married immediately, or, at this rate, by our wedding-day, I shall
have grown mortally afraid of you. By the soul of my father, I
didn't bargain for this! Look at yourself in that glass." And he
turned her about to a long mirror; it was in his mother's
dressing-room; Mrs De Grey had gone into the adjoining
chamber.

Margaret saw herself reflected from head to foot in the glassy
depths, and perceived the change in her appearance. Her head
rose with a sort of proud serenity from the full curve of her
shoulders; her eyes were brilliant, her lips trembled, her bosom
rose and fell with all the insolence of her deep devotion.
"Blanche Ferrars, of Castle Ferrars," she silently repeated,
"Isabel Stirling, Magdalen Scrope,—poor foolish women!
You were not women, you were children. It's your fault, Paul,"
she cried, aloud, "if I look other than I should! Why is there
such a love between us?" And then, seeing the young man's
face beside her own, she fancied he looked pale. "My Paul,"
she said, taking his hands, "you're pale. What a face for a happy

lover! You're impatient. Well-a-day, sir! It shall be when you please."

The marriage was fixed for the last of September; and the two women immediately began to occupy themselves with the purchase of the bridal garments. Margaret, out of her salary, had saved a sufficient sum to buy a handsome wedding gown; but, for the other articles of her wardrobe, she was obliged to be indebted to the liberality of Mrs De Grey. She made no scruple, indeed, of expending large sums of money, and, when they were expended, of asking for more. She took an active, violent delight in procuring quantities of the richest stuffs. It seemed to her that, for the time, she had parted with all flimsy dignity and conventional reticence and coyness, as if she had flung away her conscience to be picked up by vulgar, happy, unimperilled women. She gathered her marriage finery together in a sort of fierce defiance of impending calamity. She felt excited to outstrip it, to confound it, to stare it out of countenance.

One day she was crossing the hall, with a piece of stuff just sent from the shop. It was a long morsel of vivid pink satin, and, as she held it, a portion of it fell over her arm to her feet. Father Herbert's door stood ajar; she stopped, and went in.

"Excuse me, reverend sir," said Margaret; "but I thought it a pity not to show you this beautiful bit of satin. Isn't it a lovely pink?—it's almost red,—it's carnation. It's the colour of our love,—of my death. Father Herbert," she cried, with a shrill, resounding laugh, "*it's my shroud!* Don't you think it would be a pretty shroud?—pink satin, and blond-lace, and pearls?"

The old man looked at her with a haggard face. "My daughter," he said, "Paul will have an incomparable wife."

"Most assuredly, if you compare me with those ladies in your prayer-book. Ah! Paul shall have a wife, at least. That's very certain."

"Well," said the old man, "you're braver than I. You frighten me."

"Dear Father Herbert, didn't you once frighten me?"

The old man looked at Margaret with mingled tenderness and horror. "Tell me, child," he said, "in the midst of all this, do you ever pray?"

"God forbid!" cried the poor creature. "I have no heart for prayer."

She had long talks with Paul about their future pleasures, and the happy life they should lead. He declared that he would set their habits to quite another tune, and that the family should no longer be buried in silence and gloom. It was an absurd state of things, and he marvelled that it should ever have come about. They should begin to live like other people, and occupy their proper place in society. They should entertain company, and travel, and go to the play of an evening. Margaret had never seen a play; after their marriage, if she wished, she should see one every week for a year. "Have no fears, my dear," cried Paul, "I don't mean to bury you alive; I'm not digging your grave. If I expected you to be content to live as my poor mother lives, we might as well be married by the funeral service."

When Paul talked with this buoyant energy, looking with a firm, undoubting gaze on the long, blissful future, Margaret drew from his words fortitude and joy, and scorn of all danger. Father Herbert's secret seemed a vision, a fantasy, a dream, until, after a while, she found herself again face to face with the old man, and read in his haggard features that to him, at least, it was a deep reality. Nevertheless, among all her feverish transitions from hope to fear, from exaltation to despair, she never, for a moment, ceased to keep a cunning watch upon her physical sensations, and to lie in wait for morbid symptoms. She wondered that, with this ghastly burden on her consciousness, she had not long since been goaded to insanity, or crushed into utter idiocy. She fancied that, sad as it would have been to rest in ignorance of the mystery in which her life had been involved, it was yet more terrible to know it. During the week after her interview with Father Herbert, she had not slept half an hour of the daily twenty-four; and yet, far from missing her sleep, she felt, as I have attempted to show, intoxicated, electrified, by the unbroken vigilance and tension of her will. But she well knew that this could not last forever. One afternoon, a couple of days after Paul had uttered those brilliant promises, he mounted his horse for a ride. Margaret stood at the gate, watching him regretfully, and, as he galloped away, he kissed her his hand. An hour before tea she came out of her room, and entered the parlor, where Mrs De Grey had established herself for the evening. A moment later, Father Herbert, who was in the act of lighting his study-lamp, heard a piercing shriek resound through the house.

His heart stood still. "The hour is come," he said. "It would be a pity to miss it." He hurried to the drawing-room together with the servants, also startled by the cry. Margaret lay stretched on the sofa, pale, motionless, panting, with her eyes closed and her hand pressed tó her side. Herbert exchanged a rapid glance with Mrs De Grey, who was bending over the young girl, holding her other hand.

"Let us at least have no scandal," she said, with dignity, and straightway dismissed the servants. Margaret gradually revived, declaring that it was nothing,—a mere sudden pain,— that she felt better, and begged her companions to make no commotion. Mrs De Grey went to her room, in search of a phial of smelling-salts, leaving Herbert alone with Margaret. He was on his knees on the floor, holding her other hand. She raised herself to a sitting posture.

"I know what you are going to say," she cried, "but it's false. Where's Paul?"

"Do you mean to tell him?" asked Herbert.

"Tell him?" and Margaret started to her feet. "If I were to die, I should wring his heart; if I were to tell him, I should break it."

She started up, I say; she had heard and recognized her

lover's rapid step in the passage. Paul opened the door and
came in precipitately, out of breath and deadly pale. Margaret
came towards him with her hand still pressed to her side, while
Father Herbert mechanically rose from his kneeling posture.
"What has happened?" cried the young man. "You've been
ill!"

"Who told you that anything has happened?" said Margaret.

"What is Herbert doing on his knees?"

"I was praying, sir," said Herbert.

"Margaret," repeated Paul, "in Heaven's name, what *is* the
matter?"

"What's the matter with you, Paul? It seems to me that I
should ask the question."

De Grey fixed a dark, searching look on the young girl, and
then closed his eyes, and grasped at the back of a chair, as if his
head were turning. "Ten minutes ago," he said, speaking
slowly, "I was riding along by the riverside; suddenly I heard
in the air the sound of a distant cry, which I knew to be yours.
I turned and galloped, I made three miles in eight minutes.

"A cry, dear Paul? what should I cry about? and to be heard
three miles! A pretty compliment to my lungs."

"Well," said the young man, "I suppose, then, it was my
fancy. But my horse heard it too; he lifted his ears, and plunged
and started."

"It must have been his fancy too! It proves you an excellent
rider,—you and your horse feeling as one man!"

"Ah, Margaret, don't trifle!"

"As one horse, then!"

"Well, whatever it may have been, I'm not ashamed to confess that I'm thoroughly shaken. I don't know what has become
of my nerves."

"For pity's sake, then, don't stand there shivering and stag-
gering like a man in an ague-fit. Come, sit down on the sofa."
She took hold of his arm, and led him to the couch. He, in turn,

clasped her arm in his own hand, and drew her down beside him. Father Herbert silently made his exit, unheeded. Outside of the door he met Mrs De Grey, with her smelling-salts.

"I don't think she needs them now," he said. "She has Paul." And the two adjourned together to the tea-table. When the meal was half finished, Margaret came in with Paul.

"How do you feel, dear?" said Mrs De Grey.

"He feels much better," said Margaret, hastily.

Mrs De Grey smiled complacently. "Assuredly," she thought, "my future daughter-in-law has a very pretty way of saying things."

The next day, going into Mrs De Grey's room, Margaret found Paul and his mother together. The latter's eyes were red, as if she had been weeping; and Paul's face wore an excited look, as if he had been making some painful confession. When Margaret came in, he walked to the window and looked out, without speaking to her. She feigned to have come in search of a piece of needlework, obtained it, and retired. Nevertheless, she felt deeply wounded. What had Paul been doing, saying? Why had he not spoken to her? Why had he turned his back upon her? It was only the evening before, when they were alone in the drawing-room, that he had been so unutterably tender. It was a cruel mystery; she would have no rest until she learned it,—although, in truth, she had little enough as it was. In the afternoon, Paul again ordered his horse, and dressed himself for a ride. She waylaid him as he came downstairs, booted and spurred; and, as his horse was not yet at the door, she made him go with her into the garden.

"Paul," she said, suddenly, "what were you telling your mother this morning? Yes," she continued, trying to smile, but without success, "I confess it,—I'm jealous."

"O my soul!" cried the young man, wearily, putting both his hands to his face.

"Dear Paul," said Margaret, taking his arm, "that's very beautiful, but it's not an answer."

Paul stopped in the path, took the young girl's hands and looked steadfastly into her face, with an expression that was in truth a look of weariness,—of worse than weariness, of despair. "Jealous, you say?"

"Ah, not now!" she cried, pressing his hands.

"It's the first foolish thing I have heard you say."

"Well, it was foolish to be jealous of your mother; but I'm still jealous of your solitude,—of these pleasures in which I have no share,—of your horse,—your long rides."

"You wish me to give up my ride?"

"Dear Paul, where are your wits? To wish it is—to wish it. To say I wish it is to make a fool of myself."

"My wits are with—with something that's forever gone!" And he closed his eyes and contracted his forehead as if in pain. "My youth, my hope,—what shall I call it?—my happiness."

"Ah!" said Margaret, reproachfully, "you have shut your eyes to say that."

"Nay, what is happiness without youth?"

"Upon my word, one would think I was forty," cried Margaret.

"Well, so long as I'm sixty!"

The young girl perceived that behind these light words there was something very grave. "Paul," she said, "the trouble simply is that you're unwell."

He nodded assent, and with his assent it seemed to her that an unseen hand had smitten the life out of her heart.

"That is what you told your mother?"

He nodded again.

"And what you were unwilling to tell me?"

He blushed deeply. "Naturally," he said.

She dropped his hands and sat down, for very faintness, on a garden bench. Then rising suddenly, "Go, and take your ride," she rejoined. "But, before you go, kiss me once."

And Paul kissed her, and mounted his horse. As she went

into the house, she met Father Herbert, who had been watching the young man ride away, from beneath the porch, and who was returning to his study.

"My dear child," said the priest, "Paul is very ill. God grant that, if you manage not to die, it may not be at his expense!"

For all answer, Margaret turned on him, in her passage, a face so cold, ghastly, and agonized, that it seemed a vivid response to his heart-shaking fears. When she reached her room, she sat down on her little bed, and strove to think clearly and deliberately. The old man's words had aroused a deep-sounding echo in the vast spiritual solitudes of her being. She was to find, then, after her long passion, that the curse was absolute, inevitable, eternal. It could be shifted, but not eluded; in spite of the utmost strivings of human agony, it insatiably claimed its victim. Her own strength was exhausted; what was she to do? All her borrowed splendor of brilliancy and bravery suddenly deserted her, and she sat alone, shivering in her weakness. Deluded fool that she was, for a day, for an hour, to have concealed her sorrow from her lover! The greater her burden, the greater should have been her confidence. What neither might endure alone, they might have surely endured together. But she blindly, senselessly, remorselessly drained the life from his being. As she bloomed and prospered, he drooped and languished. While she was living for him, he was dying for her. Execrable, infernal comedy! What would help her now? She thought of suicide, and she thought of flight;—they were about equivalent. If it were certain that by the sudden extinction of her own life she might liberate, exonerate Paul, it would cost her but an instant's delay to plunge a knife into her heart. But who should say that, enfeebled, undermined as he was, the shock of her death might not give him his own quietus? Worse than all was the suspicion that he had begun to dislike her, and that a dim perception of her noxious influence had already taken possession of his senses. He was cold and distant. Why else, when he had begun really to feel ill, had he not spoken first to her? She was distasteful, loathsome. Nevertheless, Margaret still grasped, with all the avidity of despair, at the idea that it was still not too late to take him into her counsels, and to reveal to him all the horrors of her secret. Then at least, whatever came, death or freedom, they should meet it together.

Now that the enchantment of her fancied triumph had been taken from her, she felt utterly exhausted and overwhelmed. Her whole organism ached with the desire for sleep and forgetfulness. She closed her eyes, and sank into the very stupor of repose. When she came to her senses, her room was dark. She rose, and went to her window, and saw the stars. Lighting a candle, she found that her little clock indicated nine. She had slept five hours. She hastily dressed herself, and went downstairs.

In the drawing-room, by an open window, wrapped in a shawl, with a lighted candle, sat Mrs De Grey.

"You're happy, my dear," she cried, "to be able to sleep so soundly, when we are all in such a state."

"What state, dear lady?"

"Paul has not come in."

Margaret made no reply; she was listening intently to the distant sound of a horse's steps. She hurried out of the room, to the front door, and across the court-yard to the gate. There, in the dark starlight, she saw a figure advancing, and the rapid ring of hoofs. The poor girl suffered but a moment's suspense. Paul's horse came dashing along the road—riderless. Margaret, with a cry, plunged forward, grasping at his bridle; but he swerved, with a loud neigh, and, scarcely slackening his pace, swept into the enclosure at a lower entrance, where Margaret heard him clattering over the stones on the road to the stable, greeted by shouts and ejaculations from the hostler.

Madly, precipitately, Margaret rushed out into the darkness, along the road, calling Paul's name. She had not gone a quarter of a mile, when she heard an answering voice. Repeating her cry, she recognized her lover's accents.

He was upright, leaning against a tree, and apparently un-injured, but with his face gleaming through the darkness like a mask of reproach, white with the phosphorescent dews of death. He had suddenly felt weak and dizzy, and in the effort to keep himself in the saddle had frightened his horse, who had fiercely plunged, and unseated him. He leaned on Margaret's shoulder for support, and spoke with a faltering voice.

"I have been riding," he said, "like a madman. I felt ill when I went out, but without the shadow of cause. I was determined to work it off by motion and the open air." And he stopped, gasping.

"And you feel better, dearest?" murmured Margaret.

"No, I feel worse. I'm a dead man."

Margaret clasped her lover in her arms with a long, piercing moan, which resounded through the night.

"I'm yours no longer, dear unhappy soul,—I belong, by I don't know what fatal, inexorable ties, to darkness and death and nothingness. They stifle me. Do you hear my voice?"

"Ah, senseless clod that I am, I have killed you!"

"I believe it's true. But it's strange. What is it, Margaret?— you're enchanted, baleful, fatal!" He spoke barely above a whisper, as if his voice were leaving him; his breath was cold on her cheek, and his arm heavy on her neck.

"Nay," she cried, "in Heaven's name, go on! Say something that will kill me."

"Farewell, farewell!" said Paul, collapsing.

Margaret's cry had been, for the startled household she had left behind her, an index to her halting-place. Father Herbert drew near hastily, with servants and lights. They found Margaret sitting by the roadside, with her feet in a ditch, clasping her lover's inanimate head in her arms, and covering it with kisses, wildly moaning. The sense had left her mind as completely as his body, and it was likely to come back to one as little as to the other.

*

A great many months naturally elapsed before Mrs De Grey found herself in the humor to allude directly to the immense calamity which had overwhelmed her house; and when she did so, Father Herbert was surprised to find that she still refused to accept the idea of a supernatural pressure upon her son's life, and that she quietly cherished the belief that he had died of the fall from his horse.

"And suppose Margaret had died? Would to Heaven she had!" said the priest.

"Ah, suppose!" said Mrs. De Grey. "Do you make that wish for the sake of your theory?"

"Suppose that Margaret had had a lover,—a passionate lover,—who had offered her his heart before Paul had ever seen her; and then that Paul had come, bearing love and death."

"Well, what then?"

"Which of the three, think you, would have had most cause for sadness?"

"It's always the survivors of a calamity who are to be pitied," said Mrs De Grey.

"Yes, madam, it's the survivors,—even after fifty years."

A NOTE ON THE TEXT

In preparing these tales for publication, the editor had to choose between James's original magazine texts, those published in book form soon afterwards and those revised and rewritten for the New York Edition. The obvious choice, it seemed to him, was the original book form of the story where there was one. In that form it had the benefit of revision from magazine to volume; and in that form it was best known to James's generation. It seemed to the editor that in a chronological edition of James's shorter fictions, the New York Edition texts had no relevance. They belong exclusively to the edition for which they were designed; particularly since the revisions were often made several decades after the original publication.

The original magazine publications of the tales in this volume were as follows:

"A Tragedy of Error," *Continental Monthly,* February 1864.

"The Story of a Year," *Atlantic Monthly*, March 1865.

"A Landscape-Painter," *Atlantic Monthly*, February 1866.

"A Day of Days," *Galaxy*, 15 June 1866.

"My Friend Bingham," *Atlantic Monthly*, March 1867.

"Poor Richard," *Atlantic Monthly*, June–August 1867.

"The Story of a Masterpiece," *Galaxy*, January–February 1868.

"The Romance of Certain Old Clothes," *Atlantic Monthly*, February 1868.

"A Most Extraordinary Case," *Atlantic Monthly*, April 1868.

"A Problem," *Galaxy*, June 1868.

"De Grey: A Romance," *Atlantic Monthly*, July 1868.

James included "The Romance of Certain Old Clothes" in his first book, *A Passionate Pilgrim*, 1875; he also printed "A

Landscape-Painter," "A Day of Days," "Poor Richard" and "A Most Extraordinary Case" in *Stories Revived*, 1885. These texts have been used here. The rest of the tales follow the original magazine texts and have never before appeared in England. Those taken from *Stories Revived* (which was not published in America) have not appeared in the United States in their revised form.

For the complete bibliography of the tales the reader is referred to *A Bibliography of the Writings of Henry James* by Leon Edel and Dan H. Laurence (revised edition, London, 1961) in the Soho Bibliographies published by Rupert Hart-Davis.